AF485573

THE
BARGAIN
WITH
FATE

Dedication

To anyone struggling with finding their purpose.

Author's Note

I would like to start off by saying a huge THANK YOU for picking up this book and giving a debut Indie author a chance to borrow your mind for a few hours. I really hope that you can find a home, not only in this story, but in the world and characters too.

I just want to briefly remind readers going forward that this story is based off of Norse Mythology but will not be one hundred percent accurate to Lore and Legend, as I have used the stories of the Old Gods to help form and create the lore and magic systems that you will learn about and experience throughout 'The Bargain with Fate' series. And for your read through, there is a glossary at the back of the book if you need to reference it.

'The Bargain with Fate' has been through the hands of eight different beta readers, four different sensitivity readers, as well as a copy editor and a line editor. My goal for this series is to harbor a safe space for all who enjoy reading, and although I feel as if I have put forth a hundred and ten percent of my effort and intentions on making that a reality, I understand that things can still be missed. If you do find something harmful, hurtful, or otherwise, throughout this journey, please respectfully reach out to me through my author website: beccaannebooks.com.

Content Warning

This book contains sensitive content and may not be suitable for minors and should be read and purchased with discretion. *The Bargain with Fate* series is intended for New Adult and Adult audiences and contains adult language, violence, and sexual situations and is intended to be sold to adults 18+. This book and others in the series may contain scenes triggering to readers and should be read, purchased, and gifted with caution. If you have any questions or concerns on specific triggers, please reach out to me on social media @beccaannebooks or through my author website. The trigger warnings are as follows:

Graphic Violence

Adult Language

Graphic Sexual Content (the last few pages of chapter 13)

Sexual Situations

Physical Violence & Abuse

Themes of Depression

Themes of Anxiety

Death

Mentions of Slavery

Blood and Gore

Mentions of Violence towards Children (off-page)

Child Neglect (on-page/non-violent)

My Books Are Not For You If...

If you are Racist, Homophobic, Transphobic, Xenophobic, Queerphobic, Fat-phobic, Evangelical Far-Right Conservative, or hold prejudice and discriminate against people who struggle with mental illness, the content in my books is not intended for you. The content in my books will be extremely triggering for you and unless you will be reading these stories to expose yourself to a diverse world where love is love and you are not judged or treated differently for the color of your skin, how big someone's body is, who someone loves, or who someone has sex with, TO LEARN, DO NOT invest your time and money here.

OSERA
SKADI MOUNTAINS
THE NOTCH OF SISTERS
SYLPH MOUNTAINS
KINGDOM OF SOL
MOUNT EIR
LAKE LAGOM
FRITH
WILLINGMAN WOOD
KRON CASTLE
NÓTT FOREST
LYKKE VILLAGE AND PORT
EXBIS
PORT SISU
STILLRIDGE
REALMING RIVER
LAKE KYNDA
RÁN SEA
PORT REISA
KINGDOM OF SKIRRA

Prologue

Asgard: Loki
1,000 years ago, preceding Ragnarök

The harsh light from the midday sun was so bright that my eyes watered, blurring my vision. The suddenness of the fresh outdoor air caught my lungs by surprise, making it hard to breathe past the burning sensation that took over. I stumbled down the rocky pathway, catching myself on a tree, emotions of every nature rushing through my mind, stoking the raging fire growing inside me. I could hear Sigyn calling after me from inside the cave.

"Loki, WAIT!"

That I could not do; I had to get as far away from her as possible out of fear that the seething power under my skin might explode and cause her fatal harm. The energy had been caged under the entrails of its own offspring for Gods only knows how long and was clawing at its master to let it sink its teeth into the very same Gods who did this to them. So, I ran, setting everything I touched on fire behind me, heading straight for the door to Yggdrasil.

~ᛚᚢᚠᛁ~

The millions of thoughts and impulses running circles in my head were overwhelming. I couldn't think straight. Between having the inconsolable urge to kill everyone I see once I leave here and the crucial need to secure Sigyn's safety and our future together, I wasn't a hundred percent sure I was taking the right path to finding The Norns.

The darkness beneath The World Tree was suffocating. I thought I would be used to it since I was bound underground for years in that damn cave. But here I was, unable to breathe because the walls felt as if they would collapse on me at any moment.

The tunnel soon opened to a wide-reaching underground pocket. The massive roots of Yggdrasil spread several miles in each direction above me, creating a shield that holds the entirety of the Nine Realms on the other side. The Nine Realms I am destined to destroy, and right now, I welcome my destiny with open arms.

"God of Mischief." A *statement*, not a question, by a female voice echoed through the chamber. A voice that sounded old but also young, wise but naïve, alluring yet lethal, mortal and immortal all at once. I recognized the voice the three Norns shared as it called from a few miles away underneath Yggdrasil. Urd's well was leading water, as brilliant as starlight, through the center of the vast trunk. The waterfall of stars emptying into a hole so dark it seemed to absorb all light back into non-existence. Off to the left of the well, The Norns sat next to their great golden spinning wheel and continued to thread the silver strand of fate.

Skuld announced without turning from her eternal undertaking, "Your destiny awaits you, Loki. We were not expecting to meet with you."

The Norn of the Present, Verdandi, turned from the spool to face me. Black holes in place of eyes, her skin fair, soft lines ornamenting her face, her orange curly hair more vivid than the ripest of oranges in Asgard. "However, we will always entertain unexpected company." she purred with a smile.

"I need to make a deal with you," I stated this as a fact because I refuse to take no for an answer.

"We have never bargained with fate." Skuld declared. She stopped spinning and stood. The Norn of the Future's body gave the illusion of a much older woman, her arms and hands amounting to mere skin and bone protruding from under her silken shawl. Her hair, long and braided in two, was the color of ash from her roots and gradually turned black at the ends. The Norn moved on a misty breeze to find her place before me. She had three tattooed lines from her bottom lip to her chin, with matching singular lines sweeping out from the corners of her eyes, bringing my full attention to them. Those two black holes, surrounded by her sandy-wrinkled skin, reached for the thoughts running through my head to foresee what I might say next.

Urd, the Norn of the Past, emerged behind me and countered, "Just because we have never made a bargain with fate doesn't mean it might not exist in our future." Her golden-brown skin illuminated darkened eye sockets, and her silk headscarf was wrapped loosely around her seemingly younger face. She studied me quizzically. A large golden hoop hung from one side of her nose with a chain, drawing my attention to her hungry smile while it secured under her scarf near the back of her head.

Without hesitation, I declared, "I want Sigyn and I to be together. Forever. Make it happen."

The Norns disappeared in a cloud of smoke. Then, a sheer film fell over my eyes. I looked down at my body, which had vanished as The Norns had. I solidified again in the next moment. I was now standing at the base of a raised dais, which held three thrones, each made from the roots of Yggdrasil. The Norns each took their place in time order: past, present, and future.

"You ask us to not only alter your fate, but also the fate of another?" Skuld questioned.

"I can't lose her…not after everything that has happened," I pleaded, holding my head high, keeping a choke hold on my emotions that were testing my ability to control them.

"It seems unlikely that such an alteration could even be made in such a short time. Combing out the particulars of a bargain as large as this would take time. Unfortunately, time is what we do not have." Urd shared in contemplation.

"I don't care about the specifics!" I pushed in irritation. The rein on my emotions slipped from my grasp. The women sat back in their chairs, letting time pass in silence. If they were conversing with each other with whatever power they held, they didn't let any sign of it show. Finally, Verdandi stood and calmly reiterated, "We have never bargained with fate." The other two women stood in unison as if to conclude the meeting.

I did the only thing I thought I could do. I dropped to my knees and begged, "Please!... Please make it through any terms you see fit...I don't need to know the terms. I just need to know that our fate together is secure." My voice trailed off as tears stung my eyes—tears of anger, heartache, and longing. To pick just one emotion that could represent how I was feeling would be a disservice. "I'm begging you, under any circumstance, I will do anything to make this happen...I will give anything...Please."

The three women froze and looked down at me. I'm sure I was a sight to behold. The God of Mischief, the trickster, groveling on his knees before them. They shared a look with each other, the black holes on their faces aiding my inability to read what thoughts they might be sharing.

Finally, the Norns took their seats once more, all three of them speaking simultaneously, as one voice, "Loki, God of Mischief, we agree to the terms of the bargain you have requested." In unison, they motioned to the far side of the underground cave as they continued, "You are required to stay here, shackled by your own free will, for one thousand years. These shackles will inhibit your ability to use any physical magic. Once all consecutive one thousand years have been serviced, your shackles will free you, solidifying the binding of yours and the Goddess Sigyn's fates forever." They paused, turning back to me, "Do you accept this bargain and all the encompassing terms? Including those that you will not be made aware of?"

My breath stilled in my lungs, and my brain went blank. Finally, my emotions settled long enough for me to respond earnestly, "I accept."

~ᛚᚢᚴᛁ~

Midgard: Loki

1,000 years later, post - Ragnarök

A violent tremor shook me from my deep slumber. I heard crashing sounds directly ahead as the sunlight peeked through the rocks piling on the ground. The shackles binding me clicked and fell to the floor, freeing my wrists and ankles. I took a second to rub my skin that had gone raw during my containment, then wiped the thousand years of sleep from my eyes in hopes of helping them adjust to the sudden exposure to light.

I slowly stood and stretched every inch of my body. I took a few steps toward the freshly formed exit and stretched again for good measure. That's when I noticed the faint silver string—just a wisp in the air. It disappeared as I tried to grab it, reappearing a moment later. It clicked then. The Norns kept to their end of the deal. This must be the bond of fate. Me, on one end, with Sigyn undoubtedly on the other. I couldn't suppress the smile that tugged at the corner of my mouth. "I'm coming home, Sigyn."

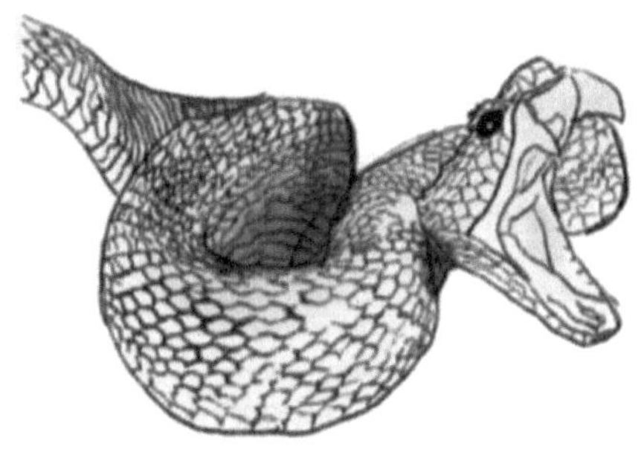

One

Midgard: Veronica

hy is it that the scales of justice always seem to weigh in favor of those in power? Why do so many people have to suffer while others exploit and prey on their suffering? Maybe this is the reason for our existence. To fight for those unable to fight for themselves and offer them a life of freedom and choice. Yes. That is why we are here.

Stars exploded behind my eyelids as a fist the size of a tree stump made contact with the right side of my face. I was airborne momentarily before crashing through one, no, two tables. The ache in my spine and left shoulder confirmed it was *definitely* two tables. I pried my eyes open, trying to gather my instincts. *I need to do something, fast.*

The fighting ring was about ten feet from me, with a cluster of tables blocking a clear path. The tavern was dimly lit with wall torches sporadically placed on the few smoother stones in the jagged cave. That said, the underground cave did not prove practical for such an event. Wooden rafters were added to brace the cave's ceiling, working around the root systems that hung from above. About fifty or so people were crammed in this obscure, stuffy cave with one entrance, and opposite from it, one tiny exit. If or *when* the patrol discovers it, there will be a brawl to get out of here.

The cheering of the patrons was deafening. *Paying* patrons, might I add, who will be lining my pockets tonight. Thank the Allfather.

"Stupid Bitch! That is why you need to stick to fighting women!" Some faceless voice mocked me. I would love to stick to fighting women. *If it would pay as much or more, I thought.* Those fights usually led to a more pleasurable celebration of victory. Since women's egos are much more difficult to offend, the fighters find more creative techniques to expel any lingering tension. *I remembered the last female fight night–*

"What are you laying on your ass for?! GET THE FUCK UP! I've put a lot of coin on you, girl!"

"That giant is going to have his way with her, and I would pay again to see it!"

"LET HIM TIE HER UP AND SEND HER ACROSS THE POND TO SKIRRA!"

Cheers erupted from the crowd. Horn mugs clanked together across the underground space.

I whipped my head around and caught a look at the patron who declared that last statement. *That one. That man will regret his words and won't see it coming.*

The ground began to shake even more violently with each step the giant made in my direction. Once my equilibrium returned, I rolled over the edge of the cracked table, spilling onto the floor. I spotted the giant's fur-lined boots a table away. *Patience. Breathe.*

He stopped moving on the other side of my cover. *One...Two...Three...NOW!* I dove and rolled to my right under the neighboring table just as the giant's fist finished splitting the table into two. The wood splintered in all directions, not just tiny slivers either. One of the patrons had a goat horn-sized piece protruding through his forearm. A look of disbelief and then rage flashed across his face as if he was about to try his luck with the giant towering before him. Luckily, someone who looked to be a relative sternly pulled him back as they made their way toward the back of the room.

This endearing interaction offered me enough time to gain an advantage over the giant. I snatched a beer horn from a patron and leaped into the makeshift fighting ring. Blood dripped from my eye. *Or is it my nose?* With the size of that man's hand across the room, it was undoubtedly my eye *and* nose, which bled into my onyx braids, reminding me of the constant stabs of pain that slowly began to encompass the entirety of my skull. Two big gulps and the beer was gone. My face twisted as the bubbles settled on top of my stomach. Gas rose in my throat, and the belch that exited my mouth was quite impressive, in my opinion. Sylve would have been impressed. Finally, I took aim at the back of the giant's head and hurled the horn at him. It made me wonder if I would ever control my impulsivity.

The giant named Trond, if I recall correctly, stood at least a foot taller and easily outweighed me by two hundred pounds. Even though he had the Giants' clan tattoos covering every inch of his body, you could see every battle scar. The jagged edges interrupted the once-straight lines that told not only this man's story but the story of the Giants as well. Anyone who glanced at this match-up would think it an easy bet. *That is what I need.* That is why these fights take priority over the construction of my face.

Trond craned his neck in my direction, one eyebrow arched and a look of *amusement* on his face? Alright, I might need to do something rash. He is too passive. I won't be able to take him down physically if I can't weaken him mentally.

"I thought you were fighting me tonight, my dear Trond. Do I not deserve the same attention as the bystander with the shard in their arm?" I plastered the most pleading look across my face as I waved my hands up and down the length of my body.

A deep, rumbling laugh emerged as he stalked back toward the fighting ring. "I'm honestly surprised you can still walk after that." His thunderous voice vibrated the walls as he pulled himself onto the wooden ring, the boards creaking under his weight. Once standing in front of me, he blocked out almost every torch lit on his side of the cavern, casting a menacing shadow over my five-foot-eight frame. Gods, he is the largest opponent I've ever fought.

"Have you not been heeding my advice? You need to exercise patience when connecting with a woman; let the tension build up." We started a slow dance around the center of the ring. I would usually say we were sizing each other up, but I'm sure he thinks he is playing with his next meal. Meanwhile, I just need to kill time and piss him off.

"I know plenty about *working* a woman." He retorted and threw his meaty left hand down toward my face. I slipped out of the way with ease, knowing now he was a 'ground and pound' kind of giant.

"Oh really? Is this the same technique you use? I get this overwhelming feeling that when you reach *your* climax, you *assume* your lady is satisfied as well. Am I right?" I threw my fist under his ribs. Trond moved back a fraction of a step, maybe to double-check I wasn't trying to tickle him. He pulled his fists above his head and slammed them down in my direction. I dropped onto the floor and rolled under his legs. As I stood upright, I noticed a *bright red* spider gleaming on its silk web string, floating hypnotically above the giant's head.

I watched as it climbed back up and perched itself in the rafters. It was then I knew what I was going to do. Working my way back around the ring, I seamlessly avoided the stream of full-powered punches Trond was throwing my way. "Trond, you *don't* have a wife, *right?*" The giant snarled in response. Ding! Ding! Ding! *Veronica, you've got him now.*

"You DO? Trond, please do me a favor and tell your wife I will meet her here next week so she can experience at least one night of pleasure in this life." I almost absorbed his next swing intended for my stomach. Then, my face. My ribs. He was angry. I had to seal the deal here, or we would be stuck in limbo for the next fortnight. The patrons were already growing tired of the lack of physical abuse.

"We didn't come here to watch a dance! Get on with it!" An eager voice sneered in the room of shadows.

"Is she beautiful? Oh, why am I even asking? Of course, she is!" I made sure my eyes lit up with excitement. I raised an eyebrow at him and made sure he held my gaze as I continued. "You know Trond, I've not only been with plenty of women, but I have pleasured those women in more ways than I'm sure you could even fathom." He staggered for a moment while his brain took its time to process what I'd said. I made a move, faked a strike at the right side of his face, and landed the real blow on the left side. I blocked his next swing with my bicep and forearm. Both of which immediately started throbbing in pain. *No more, Veronica, you're playing too many games.* "The way I would relish at the sight of your wife finding pleasure with just a single flick of my tongue-"

"COME HERE YOU CUNT!" The giant's voice thundered as the endgame commenced. Dodge the right hook, block the left, dodge the right hook again, and continue backing up. Slowly, one more step, then another. With us now situated within arm's length of the ring's corner, I dodged the right hook and lunged for his left arm, using it to catapult myself around and behind the giant's back. I dropped to the ground while the giant stumbled to catch his balance and intertwined my legs with his, twisting every inch of my body, with all of my strength, to get him to fall. And he did, like what I assumed could be comparable to the World Tree, Yggdrasil, collapsing. The ground shook, and Trond groaned, but not in pain. I didn't have time to be in awe at the fact the ground was still vibrating. I rolled backward, sprung onto my feet, leaped for the t-post in the corner, and climbed up to stand above the fighting ring. I jumped, grasped onto the rafters above, and began swinging to gain momentum.

As the giant stood and turned around to face me, I took all of my remaining strength and sent it straight into my boots, through his beard, and into his jaw. He staggered back one...two...three steps. His body went limp where he stood. The rafter I was still hanging from started to creak. *Oh shit.* The wood collapsed under my added weight and I fell to the floor, stumbling to catch myself. I stood straight, brushed off the dirt and rubble from my tights, wiped the smell of the earth from my nose, and stared up at the sleeping giant. I scanned him up and down, pressed my finger into his belly, and then gravity offered him a bed on the floor.

The judges and bet collector rushed over to the sleeping giant and examined him for themselves. They all turned to look at me with disbelief and...respect. *Dammit, now I will have to spend more time scoping out future audiences.* If a majority recognizes me, the betting stakes won't be as high in the next ring.

The judge walked over to me, grabbed my forearm, and raised it high above my head. I grunted in pain since he didn't spare me any sympathy from being tossed around by a pair of tree stumps. He rolled his eyes and, with a disgruntled attitude, announced to the tavern, "Valerian is victorious! Trond, the giant has fallen!"

A few sporadic cheers of expectant earnings sprinkled throughout the tavern, but the sound of moans and complaints filled most of the space. *That's music to my ears.* Complaints equate to significant winnings for the night.

Once the judge released my arm, I strutted over to the bet collector, trying to wipe the mixture of wet and dry blood from my face. Upon reaching the table, I extended an open palm and kept my innocent smile in place.

"You are more intelligent than any of these people will ever realize, ya know?"

"Don't you go telling everyone my secrets, brother," I quipped, offering a friendly wink. He handed me a satchel the size of a small melon. I sighed with disappointment. *How many families will this help? Is this even enough to acquire food for a boat full of people?*

"Is everything alright?" The collector looked at me, eyebrows knitting in confusion, questioning my reaction to the staggering earnings for a single person. *If only they knew, would they be willing to offer this money to the refugees instead of betting it away?*

"Yes, yes, everything is fine! Exhaustion is catching up to me right about now. I did take a few hits, ya know." I flung my bundle of braids behind my shoulder and emphasized my face with bloody hands. He nodded in acknowledgment.

Just as I secured the satchel to my belt, a man burst through the cave opening and yelled, "The patrol is coming!" At that exact moment, chaos erupted.

People of every size and stature ran for the same narrow opening we entered from. I pushed past the rush of the crowd to try and make my way toward the tavern bar. An irritated man shoved me out of his way with such force that my hip made friends with the bar's edge. I groaned in irritation, but at least I got to where I needed to be. As I slipped behind the counter, I looked back at the rushing crowd and noticed they all stopped moving. Instead, the mass of people began to back away slowly. My eyes worked their way up to the too-small door and took in the God-like man who ducked through the doorway, the first of the nightly patrol to feast his eyes on the room.

The man towered over that minuscule wooden door. He was way taller than me but not quite as tall as the giant I had just finished putting to sleep. Who, by the way, was beginning to stir in the center of the fighting ring. The man scanned the room, meticulously planning which poor soul he would apprehend first. His russet brown skin seemed to come alive and glow under the warm caress of the wall torches on either side of him. You could see his impressive physique from the back of the cave. Years of training to be a Kingdom Guard emanated from every inch of him. Even with his leather weapon belt secured over his sandy tunic and his grayish-brown patrol cape draped over his left shoulder, the whole ensemble emphasized his cut waist and massive arms almost too well. I'm sure all those looking at him were reconsidering if they would stand any chance of fighting their way out of there.

As more patrol guards piled inside behind him, I watched his bright brown eyes scan the room before making contact with my own. I noticed a concerned expression flash across his face before being quickly replaced with a facade of determination. Then he started towards me, knocking out the first patron in his path with his left elbow, catching them in his right arm. That had been the inaudible fighting bell to toll for the rest of the guards and patrons to start in on each other. The battle of 'get me the hel out of here' as I like to call it. Once the stunning patrol guard safely placed his unconscious arrestee against the wall, safe from flying fist traffic, he whipped his head back in my direction. His wide-set nostrils flared in annoyance at me, and his full lips hardened in a pressed line. *Whoops.*

I ducked down behind the bar and began rummaging through the cabinet where I had stashed my backup patrol cloak for this very moment, shoving bottles onto the floor. I searched the far back right corner where I knew for a FACT that I had stashed it well before the tavern had opened. So, where the fuck is it? I became overwhelmed with silent rage and slammed a bottle of wine into the stones behind me, hoping it would calm my irritation. Which it did. Just a smidgen.

A voice as smooth and calm as honey emerged from behind me. "Did you lose it already?"

I slowly crawled out from inside the furthest corner of the stupid cabinet. .As charmingly as one could, I lazily rested my head on my elbow on the exposed shelves. I turned to the man and, with an innocent grin, asked "Whatever do you mean, my friend?"

He hastily ducked down and whispered vehemently, "Veronica, I just gave you that cloak this morning! How, in Odin's name, have you already lost it?"

"I didn't lose it!" I snapped in an angry whisper. "Someone must have noticed it back here and taken it!"

"That is not any better, V. Now you've got a random villager able to play Kingdom Warrior at the next betting events!" He gestured his hand out at the crowd of fighting people. "That is not a good message to send our people or

The King. Especially with you already fighting in secret and risking getting recognized! We don't want anyone assuming the warriors are unfaithful to the Kingdom!"

"Sindre, I don't *need* a lecture. How could anyone recognize me when I've got this war paint ever-so-ridiculously painted across my face?" I patted him on the shoulder—his very hardened and massive shoulder. I squeezed it and wondered if it was at least the size of my head. We will have to compare sizes when we get back to town.

His intense eyebrows furrowed, and his head tilted to the side, studying the unmistakable faraway look on my face. In doing so, a small bundle of his black locs and braids fell over his shoulder. On the opposite side of his head, his locs were a bright hue of gold. A color so rare only the Goddess Sol herself could have harvested it from the sun and gifted it to the twins. The black and gold beautifully contrasted and met in the center. "Veronica, can you please stop thinking about whatever is going on in your head and go find the *fucking* cloak. Then get the hel out of here without one of the guards noticing you." Sindre stood and took half a second to scan the crowd. He looked down at me before giving me a look that immediately got me off my ass. He launched himself over the bar into the crowd, heading straight towards Trond, who was now standing in the fighting ring, eyes begging for one of the guards to test him. Once he noticed Sindre heading straight for him, his smile grew almost too wide, exposing his broken and bloody teeth. *Courtesy of yours truly.*

I guess if any of these guards would go for the big guy, Sindre was the obvious choice. Since we were young and in training, combat seemed to come naturally to him. Actually, both he and his sister are exceptional in all skill sets. However, Sindre picked up every fighting technique significantly easier than Sylve. Almost as if once he saw it, he could perform it flawlessly—photographic memory...but with...ya know, kicking someone's ass. I pulled my focus away from the lineup I so desperately wanted to watch and decided to keep myself low while I peeked around the side of the bar, scanning the mass of colliding bodies in the small space. I was looking for anything resembling the cape the guards had donned across their shoulders. *Where the hel could it be? Who in the world would have even noticed it?*

I groaned in annoyance and rolled my eyes along the rafters, finding that same bright red spider from before. *Unnaturally* red, especially for an arachnid. It was scarlet red. Honestly, the little thing could pass for a cherry with eight legs. As if in a trance, my eyes followed the spider, watching it crawl along the wood beams and come to a stop. It dropped itself down on its silver silky web. Down, down, down, until it stopped just above a man's head. I skimmed over to where it led me, and hanging through the man's belt strap was my cape. My eyes shot up to see who the thief was, and a wicked smile found its way across my lips. The cloak thief, coincidently, was the same dickhead who thought the idea of me being tied up and sent to Skirra was hilarious during the fight. *At least I will enjoy getting my shit back.*

I moved from behind the bar and crept along the rocky wall as I stalked toward my prey. A guard threw a larger woman directly before me, slamming into where I was along the wall. The woman, unfortunately, was knocked unconscious, and the guard turned his full attention to me. I hoped the mixture of dried blood and face paint was sufficient to disguise my identity. Although I didn't recognize the man in front of me, if he recognized me later when I was working on a patrol, that could cause me problems.

Don't talk, Veronica. Just keep your mouth shut and kick his ass. Well, kick his ass into somebody else. The guard eyed me as he headed my way, too confidently, might I add. I may not be as big as the woman he just knocked unconscious, but I'm not small by any definition of the word. I glanced around to find Sindre, who had made headway against Trond. *You're welcome for the head start.*

The guard's fist came at my face, and I blocked it with my forearm, responding with a swift jab to his ribs. He squared up, and I mirrored him for half a second but remembered that I needed to remain inconspicuous. So, instead, I dropped to the floor and attempted to swipe his legs out from underneath him. He was quick and stepped out of my range. As he did so, he spun and kicked me in my back, sending me forward onto my hands and knees. I followed the momentum and rolled, then turned to rush him, trying my best to not stay stagnant for too long. The guard braced himself to catch the brunt of my tackle, but I dropped to the floor and slid underneath his legs, latching onto the end of his cloak. I leveraged onto one knee and leaned back into the movement, swinging him around towards my outstretched leg. He twisted around in a semi-circle and stumbled over my little trippy trap into two other patrons. Perfect.

I turned away from the guard and scanned the room again for the dickhead with my cloak. I spotted him just as he slipped out of the small back exit with two other men. I ran straight to the door and paused. This exit opens to a short tunnel but spits out into Willingman Woods. The woods are easy enough to trek through during the day, but that could be an entirely different story at night. Between the Dark Elves that stalk the woods at the darkest hours of the night, the Nokken in the lake, and the Trolls, I hesitated to follow.

I scanned the room for Sindre, who looked to have settled things with Trond, meaning Trond was taking another nap in the middle of the cave. Sindre looked up in my direction and found me standing in the middle of the doorway. I nodded toward the tunnel, confirming I was insane and about to go find this guy in Willingman. He nodded in acknowledgment, a confirmation that he would come to find me if I didn't return. Of all possible scenarios, it would most likely be me being lured into the lake by a beautiful man, only to drown. Great.

I started a light jog through the pitch-black tunnel, keeping my footsteps light and my hand against the rock wall to guide me. Within the next minute, I was standing under the moonlight in a small clearing, staring at nothing but an army of trees in all forward directions. I took a second and quieted my breathing. I studied the environment around me, looking for any indication of which direction the men went. I closed my eyes and focused on my hearing. Nothing. No laughter or drunken conversation. They must also be aware of what lurks in these woods at night.

My thoughts quieted, and that was when I heard something—a hissing sound. I opened my eyes and followed the sound. Behind me, to my left, was a green snake slithering along the backside of the rock structure. A very lethal-looking snake. A viper? From just a few feet away from where I stood, I could see its thick venom glands on either side of its triangular head. The dark green scales, contrasting against the cool tones of the rock, constricted and released, moving it towards the tree line. As it passed the shadowy barrier where the moonlight stopped, its color changed to a bright, vibrant green. It became a beacon of green luminescence along the dark wooded floor. An overwhelming feeling took over my legs, and before I knew it, I was a few feet behind this glowing green snake, following it to wherever I felt it was trying to take me. The Nokken would have an easy time luring me to a watery death since I so willingly followed the first glowing snake I saw into an ominous forest. Odin, help me.

I'm not sure how long I followed this snake, weaving in and out of trees, keeping my guard up and eyes opened as wide as possible in hopes of seeing better. It's moments like these where I wish I had at least my knives on me, but "no weapons allowed in the tavern." I rolled my eyes at the situation. Eventually, the snake started to slow and dim in vibrancy as if it changed how and when it pleased. The whispers of conversation didn't take long to find my ears. I watched the snake turn a deep green and disappear into the ground. I'm convinced I will need to see a shaman once I return to Lykke because no one will believe what I just experienced.

"How did you even get that? I didn't see you near any guards long enough to nab it." A voice whispered through the trees. I turned in a few circles to make sure I continued toward the voices.

"That's a good question because I saw you were among the first to run away from them," pushed another in an inquiring, hushed tone.

I eyed them through a cluster of trees. They stood just outside of the forest's edge in a clearing. You could see Lykke in the distance with help from the handful of torches lit outside of peoples' homes. Getting back to the Inn should be easy enough, considering I must grab this cloak and cross the few acres of farmland.

"Well, actually, I ha–"

"Well, *actually*, I believe you stole it from the stash spot, which I had so thoroughly thought of," I cut in, stepping out from behind the trees and into the moonlight. The three men quickly turned to face me. "Now, I'm exhausted and would love to do nothing but head home and tend to my freshly acquired injuries." I stopped about four feet from the dickhead with my cloak and held out my hand. All remnants of amusement were gone from my face, my voice demanding. "Hand it over."

The men looked at each other and then made the unfortunate decision of sizing me up. The man with my cloak was bald with tattoos covering his scalp, his beard was pulled in a long braid, and his body seemed more on the retired side. He stepped toward me and pulled the cloak out of his belt. "Why should we believe this is yours? How would you have gotten your hands on this?" He inquired lazily.

The other two men moved to flank me on either side. Is this an attempt to intimidate me? I laughed audibly at the situation. Confusion and a flash of concern revealed itself on their faces.

"Remind me how any of that is your gods damn business?" I retorted.

I turned and landed a left hook into the guy's face on my right. I grabbed hold of his tunic and head-butted him, then used him as leverage to kick the guy on my left in the center of his chest, setting him off balance and falling on his ass. Dickhead grabbed a fistful of my braids and yanked my head back. I released his friend's tunic and grabbed the hand that held my hair, using that as another leverage point to send my legs flying through the air and across the right guy's face. Down one. Two to go.

He grabbed my left wrist, loosening my grip on his hand enough to tuck it behind me while taking a few steps backward, forcing me to keep my feet on the ground to stay somewhat standing. The guy on the left was now standing and heading straight for me, eyes shining with drunken annoyance. Dickhead took two surprise steps forward, forcing my legs to catch on the ground, leading me to fall onto my knees. His friend gave me a pretty good backhand across the mouth, good enough that I immediately tasted iron on my tongue. I eyed his hand and spotted the rings I had felt a second earlier. That will not look pretty tomorrow, or feel pretty, for that matter.

"I would've assumed you enjoyed talking after your performance, Valer ian...what happened between then and now?" Dickhead's friend was feeling bold right now, which was pissing me off. I could feel my anger gauge rising quickly under my skin. He stepped toward me and gripped my chin between his dirt-riddled fingers. "I wonder how long you would survive in Skirra." His head tilted in genuine curiosity. That gauge topped off, and I exploded.

I turned my head sharply and bit his fingers hard. I heard a crunch, and the man screamed, jerking his hand away from my face. I felt dickhead barely lean forward to readjust his grip on my hair, and I sent my head flying back into his face so hard I felt the world spin for half a second. It was worth it, though. I stood, my brain throbbing, and focused on his friend. I spit his dirty-ass hand residue back at his feet, and when he looked down at where I spat, I sent an uppercut into his nose. So now I'm standing above all three men. One was still asleep, and the other two were coddling their noses on the ground. I couldn't wait to rip their tongues out of their mouths.

I went to take a step towards them when the sound of hooves sprinting toward us stopped me. I turned around, and Sindre had stopped atop his white mare, Alsvid. He sent his honey-smoked voice out through the area when he questioned, "What is going on over here?" He eyed me up and down, then noticed the three men still trying to recover on the ground behind me.

Dickhead's friend quickly responded, "We saw she had tried stealing a Kingdom's patrol cloak from one of the guards at the tavern! We were trying to get it back to the patrol." He was still cupping his nose when I turned to face him. My mouth had dropped to the floor, an incredulous expression on my face. How dare he! That is the most pathetic bullshit lie I have ever heard.

"Yes, we were betting at the tavern, BUT we have children in the guard, sir. We are loyal to our Kingdom!" Dickhead added, blood running over his mouth.

Sindre dismounted Alsvid and walked toward the four of us. I bent down to pick up the cloak when suddenly, I felt a strong hand grasp the back of my neck and pull me upright, my eyes now aimed at the night sky. My hands flung to where I was being held out of instinct, but Sindre reached across me and caught my opposite wrist with lightning speed, cementing his arm around my waist and rendering both hands useless. At the same time, he had snuck his leg between mine and, when I was off balance, pushed my left leg out far enough for me to lean back onto him, relying on him to keep me upright. His heated breath danced along my neck as he whispered so only I could hear him. "Caught being bad again, have we?" A shiver tickled my spine, and my cheeks warmed instantly. I turned my head away from him. He can be such a dick when he knows he's got the upper hand.

He turned his head in the direction of the three men sitting there, gawking at the fact that he detained me in the blink of an eye without having to physically abuse me. "You can leave now. I've got her handled." They nodded in silent submission and began collecting themselves to head toward town.

Once they were out of earshot, I turned my head back to Sindre and explained, "You know I let you detain me, right?"

I could hear the eye roll in Sindre's voice when he responded with a mocking, drawn-out "Riiiiiight."

He released me from his interesting restraint technique, and I fell to the ground, barely catching myself on one knee. "You didn't even give me a chance to defend myself! After all I had to endure tonight, I couldn't plead my case before...That." I waved my hand through the air where we had just performed an amateur role play of 'guard flawlessly detains the unhinged criminal.' He stood there with his hands on his weapons belt, assessing the damage I received tonight.

"You look like shit."

"Gee, thank you. I'm swooning over here. Can we talk about your cheeky restraint technique? Some might consider it...cheating." I offered flatly.

"Oh, we are definitely going to talk more about it tonight, but we need to get you back to the Inn and cleaned up. Hopefully, Bryn will still have time to close your lip."

"What's wrong with my lip?" I wondered aloud, lifting my fingers to understand what he was referencing. "Ow, fuck!" My fingers found the split next to the left side of my cupid's bow. It felt significant enough to where I might need a stitch. Fresh blood was still dripping from the wound and now adorned my fingers.

"Come on." He bent down and grabbed my cloak, placing it over my shoulders and fastening it with a bronze patrol brooch. "And stop touching it; you'll get an infection."

He mounted Alsvid and offered me his hand. I hesitated, placing my palm on Alsvid's shoulder and looking off toward town. I couldn't help but worry about my grandfather's reaction to tonight's events. I've never taken on such a massive opponent before. I can only imagine what that giant's fists had done to my face. Per usual, I didn't tell him my plan either.

"Hey, he'll understand. You know he always does." Sindre offered knowingly. He was emphasizing that his hand was still outstretched in my direction. I took his offer, hoisted myself onto Alsvid, and settled behind him.

"I know. I just hate seeing him worried."

Sindre offered a warm laugh as he motioned Alsvid towards the Inn. "Maybe then, you should stick to doing things that won't worry him." I lightly punched him in his ribs, which earned me another laugh. I rested my forehead on the center of his back and kept it there while we rode in silence.

Two

I dismounted, waiting until Sindre landed beside me before offering to take Alsvid back to the stable. He shot me a look. The same look he gives me every time I offer to walk his horse back to the stable to avoid the scolding I've earned.

"If I were you," he paused to give me a thorough once-over, "I would at least attempt to wash off as much of that blood and paint before heading in." I silently nodded, and he placed the reins in my hand. I lead the large white mare to a makeshift wooden structure behind the Inn. Her black mane and tail caught my eye. The need for a good brushing was obvious. I may sneak in some grooming time before I head to the castle in the morning. I got the mare untacked and in her stall for the night. The neighboring enclosure had an unused water pail, so I filled it myself.

I sat on an overturned bucket near the barn's opening, preparing myself mentally for what I needed to do. Oh man, this is going to suck. I cupped my hands and reached into the frigid water, bringing it slowly up to my face. I hesitated, letting some water slip through my fingers before I pressed what remained onto my battered skin. The iciness bit at the open wounds on my lip and upper cheek. I lightly patted my face in hopes of lessening the pain, but to no avail. The stabbing continued to aggravate my exposed muscle and torn tissue relentlessly. Finally, I abandoned all reserves and scrubbed at the crust as unyielding as my tolerance would allow. When I finished, I grabbed the bottom of my tunic and lifted it to my face, stopping when I noticed the filth that riddled it. I dropped it and opted for a quick air-dry on my way to the house.

As I neared the back door, I watched through the window as Sindre wrapped his arms around the shoulders of an older couple, ushering them from the main room to the quaint sitting area in the library on the opposite side of the Inn. Their once ivory skin, now scarred by the sun, appeared significantly frailer in comparison to Sindre's glowing complexion. This sweet couple were just two of the ten people we rescued from Skirra in our latest raid. My grandfather always offers any available space at his estate for those we save during the interim between being freed until they travel to Frith. The estate was a retirement gift from the King when my grandfather resigned from being his Chieftain a few years ago. Since then, he has loathed how big and useless the building was, calling it "a waste of resources on just one person." So, in typical Brynjar fashion, he outfitted the inside to maximize its occupancy, so the Frithians had a temporary residence on their journey to a new life. If a room had a door, it was guaranteed to be used as a bedroom. Any used clothing items not needed throughout the town were secretly donated to my grandfather, and we washed and stored them all within every possible crevice of the house. It was his top priority that each person who stepped into the Inn not only felt, but *knew* they were safe, welcomed, and loved.

Once Sindre and the two elderly guests were out of sight, I quietly opened the back door and slipped inside. My covert mission to get to my room whilst avoiding my grandfather proved futile as soon as I heard the deep thuds of paws and nails scratching the wood floor. I didn't even have time to loosen my shoes before two thick paws met my chest as whimpers of excitement sounded throughout the house.

"Shhhh! Brax, buddy. Quiet down," I whispered. I hoped that if I kept him quiet enough, I still stood a chance to evade being seen. However, Brax had no intention of not celebrating my arrival tonight. His brown and black fur was all but a blur as he continued jumping up and down, running in circle after circle. I grabbed his shoulders in an attempt to keep him in one place, and thank the

Allfather, he stopped, turning his attention to the cuts on my face. He sniffed at them gently and followed through with soft kisses to my wounds. Unfortunately, it caused a sudden burning sensation to spread on the left side of my face again, making my eyes water and my nose scrunch up.

"Veronica? Are you trying to sneak past me again?" Brynjar called out from the front room. I was still just out of his sight. *If I don't answer, I could try sneaking around the back hall.* As if he read my mind, he said, "No, you can't. Come over and show me the damage. Let's get this over with." His gravelly voice guided me to accept the incoming consequences of my actions.

I grabbed Brax's' black muzzle and planted a big kiss on his snout. "I love you, but we will have to work on this if we are going to be a team." I stood and scratched his head before stepping into the common room.

I scooted around the corner, keeping my back to him with my eyes on the ceiling. Why am I so much more reluctant this time to show him?

"Really?" A hint of a smile teased itself in his question. That's it; butter him up. Maybe it will lessen the shock of seeing my face. I haven't even seen my reflection yet, but if the torture I endured from washing it was any indication. Holy hel.

I slowly turned and opened my eyes to meet his. Bryn was sitting on a bench near the hearth, rubbing the aging joints in his wrists. He wasn't much taller than me, but he outweighed me by a hundred pounds of muscle, most of which sat confidently in his torso. I knew he wasn't as muscular as he was in his prime, but the evidence of his previous physique was clear. His brown eyes widened as he assessed the damage. He went to say something but caught his breath and turned from me, stroking his braided, ashy beard as he began pacing the cozy space. He ran his hands over his battle-scarred face and through his shoulder-length peppered hair, the tribal tattoos on his forearms flexing.

"It can't be THAT bad. No need to be dramatic," I suggested, less than confidently.

"You haven't even seen yourself?" He asked, a look of complete surprise on his face.

"Well...no. I've been preoccupied. I had to put Sindre's horse up for the night, among other things." He strode over to me and paused momentarily before taking my chin with his fingers, lifting my face to the side to calculate the severity of my injuries. "This is bad, Veronica. What the hel did you do tonight?" He turned from me and headed towards the bathroom, pointing at the couch on his way out—a silent demand. I sat without protest and pulled my bundle of braided hair over my shoulder. "I did what I had to," I answered quietly, trying to be mindful of the guests throughout the Inn.

Bryn returned with a needle, medical thread, and a few different herbs. He placed them on the small table and got down on one knee, placing a hand on my shoulder. "We have talked about this time and time again, so I shouldn't need to keep repeating myself. However, I think this has been taken too far. It stops now." Anger blossomed in my chest.

"What?! How can you even say that?" My voice was raised, already forgetting about the guests I had just considered. I shrugged his hand off of my shoulder.

"You have no self-control. You obviously can't make rational decisions. You clearly have not mastered your fighting skill yet, considering the mess your face has become from just one fight." He spoke so calmly. So matter of fact. As if he knew he could influence me with just his words.

"Bryn, how can you say that!? You know more than all of us that the Frithians need all the help they can get! Anything helps, and busting the betting events has proven to be the easiest to exploit. We can't just stop!" I stood from where I was seated and walked to the bathing room. I found the mirror above the sink and stared back at my reflection. My hands gripped both edges of the counter as I took a small breath. It was THAT bad. My left eye was so swollen now that it was only open about halfway, no thanks to the cut along my cheekbone. Bruises with purple and blue hues were starting to replace the redness that seemed to have been painted along the left side of my face. The split in my upper lip looked like it had burst at its seam. Even I realized I was losing time to have it sewn back together before the swelling became too severe. Overall, I do, in fact, look like shit.

I found my way back to the couch and sat once again. Bryn handed me a small cup of the concoction created with the herbs he had brought earlier. I downed it in one go and made a face. Damn, these are always disgusting. I laid back as he set his arms sternly on either side of my head, squeezing inward to prevent me from moving. He held the needle and thread in his right hand, a bottle of vinegar in the other, with both over my face. "Please, try your best not to move. You know this will hurt," he said as reassuringly as he could.

I hissed in pain as Bryn poured vinegar over my lip and readjusted himself to press his chest onto my forehead. He then set the bottle on the table and grabbed my top lip with his free hand. "Breathe in," he encouraged. I took a deep breath, held it for two seconds while he touched the needle to my skin, and slowly pushed my breath out. At the same time, he plunged the needle into one side of my open wound, and my head jerked away involuntarily. He squeezed me harder with his elbows, keeping me from moving further. He quickly pinched it with his other hand and then pushed it through the other side, pulling the thread through. Tears fell past the inner corner of my eyes from the intense pain. He finished tying off the suture by the time I took my second breath.

Brynjar cut the excess thread from the new suture and whacked my arm, releasing me from my position. I sat up and wiped the tears that had stained my cheeks. He turned, grabbed his mortar and pestle, placed a few herbs and honey inside, and began concocting the healing paste for the other gashes on my skin. I noticed he paused for a moment while his eyes focused on the contents of the mortar.

"You know I understand how important it is for them. I lived their life," he began as a sigh followed his statement. "But I have been organizing raids for far longer than anyone currently involved with the Ravens. So, I need you to keep my advice in mind when you are faced with difficult decisions. Otherwise, you will force my hand into exercising my authority." He resumed grinding the herbs.

"I can't just stop. These people have nothing. I have to try to give them all we can. If there is a way to get even a few coins more, I'm going to try," I countered, attempting to avert his eyes from his working hands.

After a few moments of prolonged silence, he finished making the healing paste and offered me the bowl. I took it and gently dabbed the mixture on my facial injuries. Bryn stood and stared down at me, waiting for me to finish. Once I placed it on the table, he continued, "No more fighting. That's an order." The calm that had settled between us stirred with the wind of irritation.

"Are you kidding me?! Do you honestly expect me to know there is more I can do but do less?" I stood, waving my hands in the direction of my invisible task. "Do you even care how these people are supposed to create a new life after they leave the Inn? Have you accounted for their need to establish a new way of living?" I continued to press him.

"You are more than capable of busting the betting events and confiscating the money from the betting pots WITHOUT putting yourself at risk of fatal brain damage." He countered coolly, turning from me and tucking his hands behind his back. "You will be of no use to anyone if you can't remember your own name." He started to walk off. His ability to remain diplomatic is unmatched.

"Do you not care anymore? You're avoiding my questions. Is that because I'm right?" I demanded an answer. I refused to be expected to follow such a ridiculous order without an honest explanation.

He turned to me and crossed his arms across his puffed-out chest. "Veronica, please. Take a second to remember: I was a part of the original rebellion that started the war against Skirra fifty years ago. We formed the Kingdom of Sol from nothing. We didn't have the Ravens to help us get on our feet. Need I remind you THAT I myself formed Odin's Ravens and all of its rescue operations. So, I could be as bold to say that I understand their situation even more than they do."

"Just tell me your honest reasons why you think it's necessary to pull me from the fights?"

"I thought I made myself clear with my reasoning. You have no self-control, you can't make rational decisions, and your fighting skills are undisciplined. Is that not enough?"

"So, you have deemed me incapable of fighting because of a split lip and some bruises? Because I decided to take on a more difficult opponent? Whom I *won* against, by the way." I motioned to the coins on my waist.

"It isn't that simple. Can you honestly reflect on your affairs tonight and tell me that *that* small pouch of coins on your belt will be worth the trouble of explaining your appearance to the King tomorrow?" His head inclined towards the satchel still fastened to my waist. "Never mind the pain you will suffer over the next few days. Have you even thought about what excuse you are going to use for a busted lip and a bruise the size of my foot?"

I hesitated for a second; I hadn't thought that far ahead. I was so concerned about this unfolding conversation that I didn't consider how I would hide my injuries from the King. And Erikka was going to kill me. "If I'm being honest, my inconveniences caused solely by my appearance are incomparable to what the Frithians have endured." I set my hands on my waist, awaiting a response.

He stepped past me and sat on the couch, patting the open space next to him. I accepted his offer and sat, still annoyed over the conversation. Finally, he placed his arm over my shoulder and gave me a quick squeeze, instantly melting away any animosity I harbored toward his harsh decision. "I understand your devotion to saving the emigrants from Skirra. Anyone can see all of your actions are products of the heart."

I interjected, "Thrall, Bryn. They are thrall. You don't need to sugarcoat it." His eyes distanced; he seemed drawn off to relive some of the memories he refused to share. I gently nudged my elbow into his side, pulling him back to reality.

He sighed and let his shoulders sag with his exhale. "I see a lot of your mother in you." My heart felt heavy in my chest. "And, if I am being totally transparent...It scares the shit out of me." And, as if he could sense the heaviness blanketing the air, Brax walked into the room and made his way over to us. He placed his head in my grandfather's lap. While Bryn stroked Brax's head in a lazy rhythmic pattern, he continued. "Your mother drowned herself in her passion for the Ravens. She lived to rescue the remaining thralls and assist them in transitioning to their new life as freed people. She even invented the training program for the citizens of Frith so they could learn how to fight for themselves. I was so proud of everything she was accomplishing in such a short time that I didn't notice it had become a deadly obsession."

I looked up at him to find his eyes focused on the ceiling, the hint of tears starting to form. I leaned in and wrapped my arm over his stomach to hug him tightly. He returned my hug and kissed the top of my filthy head before taking a few calming breaths. "She sacrificed her life for this cause. She allowed herself to be captured by Skirra so the raid she led that night could escape with the thrall they freed."

I could feel his heart beating faster, as if it couldn't handle the reality of the memories he shared with me. I didn't dare let my mind wander. He has never shared what happened to my mother with me before. I've tried asking here and there, but he always answered, 'I'll tell you when it's time.'

Bryn cleared his throat. "I made sure I went on every raid since she disappeared. I asked as many Skirrians as I could for four years, and no one could tell me anything until one specific raid in the middle of winter. A storm had just begun to blow in from the south. We thought we would use that as cover to get us further up the river to the far side of Stillridge. Everything seemed to go according to plan until I noticed a shadow watching from across the bank. I figured our luck had run out. I would have to fight to keep the raid undisturbed." I looked up at him again. He was in a faraway place but held a soft smile that lifted the corners of his eyes. So much love waited there, longing to see his daughter again.

"As I got closer, I heard her voice. When she came close enough for me to see her..." A tear slipped and slid down his cheek, but he made no attempt to wipe it away. Bryn had always said tears were the only thing that allowed him to feel the presence of his loved ones. They reassure him. So, he let his tears fall—and exhaled another big sigh.

"You were so small and innocent, nestled in her arms. She handed you to me and only offered a brief introduction. I moved to lead her back to the longship, but she pulled away, insisting I return to Sol to give you the best shot at survival, as you were in grave danger in Skirra. Whoever owned her was too powerful and influential for her to return with us, and the raid's risk of exposure would increase tenfold. She had to stay in Skirra so that we could continue to save people." Tears stung my eyes now.

"She told me, 'One life is not worth the majority.' I tried everything possible to convince her to come home with me. I even tried to force her, but she was prepared for that. She kept her distance and soon ran back into the woods, disappearing before I could comprehend what she had done. She wasn't coming home." I sat up and turned towards him, unknowingly giving Brax enough space to claim the open six inches for himself. Once he got settled, laying over both mine and my grandfather's lap, Bryn locked his eyes onto mine, a somberness flowing through his words, "Your mother allowed her passion for Frith to consume her. She found every possibility that could aid the Frithians, no matter how insignificant it was, and she put her life on the line to make that small difference. I understand you only have good intentions when you make these impulsive decisions. I know. I used to be the same. But once your mother didn't come home…not just once but twice…I had to change the way I operated. Because no matter how much *good* you do for people, no matter how thin you stretch yourself, your sacrifices will never mean as much to them as they do to you. They won't mourn your loss. I *need* you to come home."

I peeled my eyes away from him and wiped the tears from my face. "I'm sorry, Bryn. I didn't understand, but I do now. I will try my best to control my impulses. Truly, I will try. I don't ever intend to make you worry." I placed my hand on his. "I'm sorry. I'll stop fighting."

His mood flipped instantly as he grunted to push Brax off us to stand and head towards the mead. "Hey, I'll make a deal with you. A compromise, if you will." He poured two mugs full and walked back to me, offering me one. "You go back to combat training with Sindre and Sylve in Frith, and with their recommendations, we can revisit the possibility of fighting." He held his mug out towards me, and I clanked mine with his in resolution. "I love you, kid."

I smiled at him. "Love you more, old man."

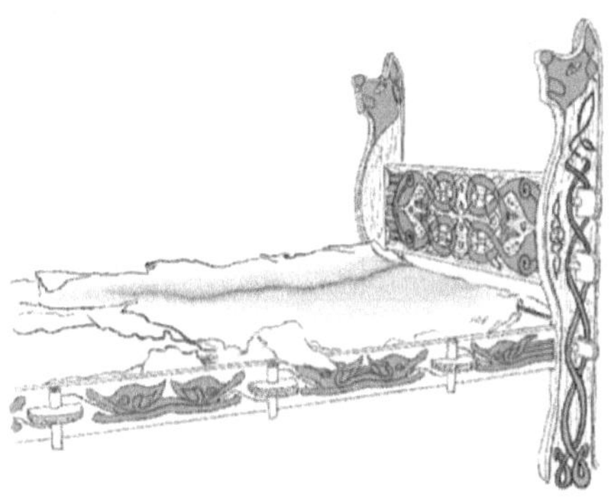

Three

A half-hour had passed when Sindre finished his rounds, checking on all of our temporary guests before finding his way back into the main room where Bryn and I were sitting. I was on the floor with Brax and in the middle of telling Bryn a very animated version of my fights tonight when he cleared his throat to get our attention. We both looked up at him at the same time to find a young woman standing shyly behind him. She had dark circles shadowing her sunken brown eyes and appeared to be swimming in the fabric of the clothes we had offered her. Her dark brown skin was as sun-scarred as the older couples, and her dull black hair pulled back to the nape of her neck was just as affected by the sun and malnourished as her complexion. She is stunning despite all of the obvious torture she has endured.

"I'm so sorry, but my children have taken most of the space in our given bed, and I don't have the heart to move them. They have never slept so comfortably before," her somber voice whispered apologetically. She stepped slightly out from behind Sindre's shadow and kept her head bowed and her eyes on her feet, hands clasped in front of her waist. Sindre slid in and explained, "When I went to check on them, she was going to sleep on the floor. So, I offered the couch in the main room. There was no need for her to be uncomfortable when there are soft places to rest."

Bryn stood, and his voice softened when he offered, "I will take the couch tonight. You can stay in my room on the first floor if you would prefer. It is no inconvenience to me, so please do not think otherwise." He reached out to her to offer the path to her new bedroom for the night when I stopped him. "No, please, Afi, keep your bed; she can use my room for the night. Besides, if I remember correctly, my room neighbors her current one. She might be more comfortable closer to her children." I looked towards her to receive her input on her sleeping arrangement, but she remained standing in the same manner. Hands folded in front of her, head bowed, eyes on the floor.

I quietly took a few steps towards her to close the space between us, leaving room to respect her personal space but offering my hand. She cautiously raised her eyes to stare at it, confusion adorning her exhausted face. "You are safe here. You are our equal here. *You* can decide what is best and most comfortable for you." I left my open hand outstretched towards her, and Bryn mirrored my offer to her as well.

She straightened her neck and dropped her hands by her side, taking a moment to look between Bryn, Sindre, and myself. Once the tension eased from her shoulders, she placed her delicate hand in mine and grinned, "Thank you. *All* of you."

"No need to thank us. I'll show you to your room. Please feel free to use it for the rest of the week. I will be out of the Inn, so it will be available for you." I smiled, placing my open hand tenderly on her shoulder, and leading her upstairs.

Once we reached the room, I started changing the linen for her. She jumped in to help me, and I protested, "Oh no, no, you don't have to help. Please relax. It will only take me a moment." She didn't even acknowledge what I had said and continued helping me. I smiled at her small act of rebellion and finished throwing the soft pelt blanket over the top of the hay-filled mattress.

"What is your name?" I inquired. She stopped fluffing a pillow and turned to face me, letting it fall onto the mattress. Her face brightened as if life itself had just breathed its magic back into her.

"Kalyani...My name is Kalyani." She placed the pillow at the top of the bed and sat on the edge, half-turned to me. "I'm sorry if my behavior seems...diffe rent. I had almost forgotten my own name. I haven't needed to say it. Nobody has asked to know it in years, it seems." Her eyebrows pinched in deep thought.

"You do not need to apologize for things like that. Ever. The people who will be helping you along your journey to Frith will be more than understanding of your situation. Some of us weren't around pre-war, so we can't fathom what horrors you've had to deal with. Please, don't apologize." I placed my hand over hers that rested on the bed and gave it a reassuring squeeze. I turned to the trunk that held my belongings and started to fill a travel bag with my clothes for the few days I would spend at Sol's castle. "Your name is beautiful, by the way."

"Oh, thank you." She tucked a loose strand of hair behind her ear. "What is your name?"

"Veronica Leif." I stood from the floor and slung my bag over my shoulder. I stuck my hand out, requesting hers in return. This time, she didn't hesitate as long and grasped my hand. I shook it and stated, "With your approval, I would like to consider us friends. If you need anything, you can come to me or Sindre if I'm unavailable, and we can help you the best we can. With anything. It would be an honor."

"I would like that," she answered shyly. "If I may ask, are you ever afraid to fight? Does it scare you to possibly get hurt badly or lose? Wouldn't it have then been a waste of time?" She glanced at the wounds on my face, not for long, but I noticed. She saw my reaction and blushed in embarrassment. "I'm sorry; I didn't mean to sound rude."

"No worries, Kalyani," I laughed. "You will have to get drastically more creative to offend me." I headed towards the door and stopped in the doorway to consider her question. "Yes."

"What?" Her eyes widened while I watched her thoughts spiral into whatever realization she might have come to.

"Everyone should be scared to fight...the possibility of not being victorious...of pain." I shrugged my shoulders and locked in on her inquisitive stare. "It's a normal human response. But if you have something worth fighting for, the fear won't outweigh the reward." My face twisted as if in pain while I rubbed the back of my neck and quickly followed up apologetically, "If that makes any sense anyway. My grandfather is much better at offering profound advice than I am." I giggled and whispered as I smoothly closed the door, "Or maybe I'm foolish and enjoy the challenge of taking on those with more power than me." I heard a soft laugh of acknowledgment from inside the room, lighting a fire of hope in me. If Kalyani can find it in her to laugh again, then everything we are doing is worth it. I smiled to myself as I headed down the stairs.

Brynjar and Sindre were sitting on the couch with Brax at their feet when I walked into the main room. "You can take my room tonight, and I will stay out here," Bryn offered.

"Thanks, but I can stay in Sylve's room at their house. There is no need to wake up with a crick in your neck." I turned to Sindre for reassurance. "She has been hunting in Exris with Jerrik the past two nights, right?"

"Yeah. I don't see a problem with it." He slapped his hands on his knees and groaned as he stood.

"Wow, you sound just as old as me." Bryn laughed and patted Sindre's back. I'm sure he was aiming for his shoulder, but Sindre towers over my grandfather, so the mid of his back would have to do. Sindre turned to him, and they grabbed each other's forearms in a warrior's embrace. "I'm grateful for you, son. I can't thank you enough for keeping her in check."

"Yeah, RIGHT! Okay, I'm leaving." I scoffed and turned on my heels toward the front door. "And I'm taking Brax!"

I motioned at Brax to follow me and heard both men exchange a hearty laugh. Sindre pet Brax's head as they walked out of the Inn.

Bryn called out as we were closing the door, "I love you guys!" and in unison, we both responded, "Love you too!" just before it clicked shut.

Four

B rax was stalking a few paces in front of us with his nose to the ground when we turned down the last dirt road to get to Sindre and Sylve's house. They lived on the outskirts of the village adjacent to the rolling farmlands that spread over several acres bordering the Willingman Woods. All of the homes along the outer part of Lykke were constructed in the same manner. Their walls and floors were built of stone and dirt, while the roofs were made of thatch and grass. From a distance, by land or sea, the clusters of homes could be mistaken as hills that blended into the natural landscape. Sylve loved their home, its coziness, and how it looked out at the expanse of beautiful valleys.

We were walking up to the front door when I spotted a bright streak of red in my periphery. I noticed Brax had taken an alert position, glued to the outside of my leg with his attention pointed in the same direction. Sindre had walked inside already when I called out, "Hey, Sindre! I'm going to make sure Brax pees outside quickly so he isn't tempted to give you a gift you didn't ask for."

"I appreciate that! I'll run a bath for you. And before he gets in here, let it be known that we, at the Nyhus residence, are not accepting any gifts at this time!"

I laughed to myself, and dropped my bag off my shoulder just outside the front door. I commanded Brax to heel, and we took off on a light jog up the hill, our eyes glued to our destination. As we approached the top, I whispered,

"Liggdu." Brax stopped walking, lowered himself to the ground, and remained on high alert. "Biddu," and he stayed, waiting for his next command.

I crept quietly to the crest of the hill and scanned the area on the other side. Nothing. There was nothing but open acreage and a few scattered trees. I was ready to return to the house when I took a second to study a tree about fifty yards from me. It looked out of place compared to the others in the vicinity, its leaves almost dark red. *That's weird.* I kept low and hurried over to inspect it.

Only when I was a few steps away from being underneath its shadow did I realize I was unarmed, far enough away from the house and Brax. Anything could happen to me, and no one would be close enough to help. I stood tall and extended my arms into a relaxed fighting stance. *You know, just in case.*

My breath quieted, and I softened my footsteps to listen for any signs of life around me. I didn't hear anything, so I placed a hand on the tree trunk and peered around it. Nothing.

I relaxed completely and spun in a circle to scan the area again for what I could have seen earlier. I looked up at the scarlet leaves, dimmed only by the darkness of the night. I could only imagine how stunningly bright they would be in the afternoon sun.

"Veronica!" I turned to look back toward Sindre's voice and barely noticed the top of his head break over the hill. "Veronica, what the *fuck* are you doing?"

"Come look at this! This tree is cra-" My words stopped halfway because when I turned back to the tree, it was gone. The hint of a light mist dissipating in its place. I turned back, and Sindre and Brax were standing on the hilltop waiting for me to return. I jogged back to them, frequently glancing back at the open space where the vibrant tree had just disappeared from existence.

"What were you doing? I thought Brax had to pee, and I came out here to find him held in position…not pissing."

"I thought I had seen something pass by over there earlier. Brax alerted to it too, so I was checking it out." Sindre didn't reply and we opted to walk back in silence.

Not two seconds after we walked through the front door, Sindre let me have it. "I was going to let tonight go, V. I figured your talk with Bryn was enough since it seemed heavy in there." He wiped his hands down his face before he took a deep breath. "But you're telling me that you thought you saw something pass by us, and you decided not to tell me and go out to investigate it on your own? Without Brax? And without even grabbing an axe?" His eyebrows were raised so high that they looked like they would pop off his head at any minute.

"Hey, rational decision-making starts tomorrow. The night is still young, so I've got to give it time to sink in." I winked and turned toward Sylve's room to change the blankets on the bed. However, Sindre hadn't finished with me yet.

"You can't keep dismissing these incidents with humor, Veronica. You have been extremely fortunate, and I honestly have no idea how you keep avoiding fatal outcomes, but that luck will run out one day. I need you to be more careful." He was leaning against the door frame with his arms crossed across his chest, one ankle crossed behind the other. A golden braid had fallen from his half-up bundle and swung across his eyes.

I finished making the bed and walked over to him, reaching up and tucking that loose braid back into his hair. "I will work on it. I promise." I punched him in the arm as I walked past him, heading to the bathroom.

"Bryn told me about your agreement. We'll start training the next time you come with us to Frith."

"When will that be?" I asked while pulling off a layer of blood-stained clothing, leaving on the dirty tunic that rested just above my knees. I attempted to work my braids out from my knotted mess but wasn't getting anywhere, so Sindre offered to help untangle my bird's nest, and I graciously accepted. I stepped into the wooden bathing tub and sat on the edge patiently while he started to navigate my hair.

"We have a raid planned on Stillridge the night you return from your shift at the castle. When we take that group of thrall to Frith the following day, we should have two or three days before you need to return for your next assignment with Calder."

"I'm looking forward to learning that fancy move you used on me tonight." I poked teasingly. He grabbed a handful of my hair and lightly pulled my hair back so I was looking up at him. In turn, my hands caught the edge of the basin, using one foot to catch myself on the other side.

"No." His voice was calm but contemplating. "I will only let you learn how to get out of it...Maybe." He gently lifted my head back upright and finished unbinding the last few braids. I could feel the tension release around my head.

"Well then," I laughed. I ran my fingers through my hair and rubbed out the tightness they had held in from the night. Sindre had already turned to leave the bathroom when I offered, "I'll clean out the tub and refill it for you when I'm finished."

"I would greatly appreciate that. Goodnight, Veronica." I was already submerged when he closed the door.

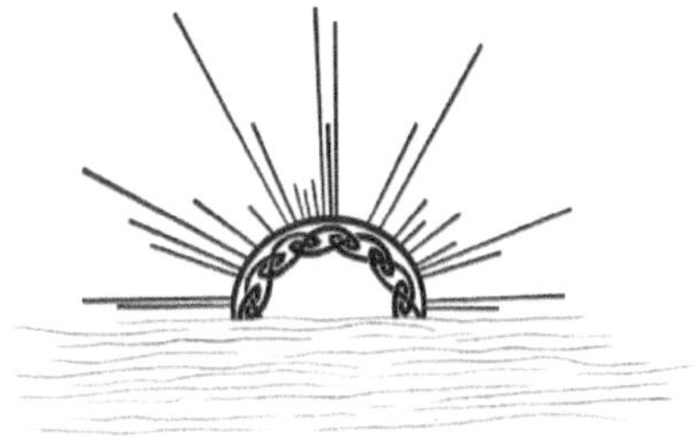

Five

I returned to the Inn right as the sun began to peak over the horizon. The morning light danced across the moisture, resting peacefully on the variety of ground cover. The hint of sea salt teased the breeze that came from the west. My head harbored a slow and steady pounding. I took a few minutes and found a drier spot on the ground to sit on to just breathe. Brax had a similar idea and scratched his back amidst the wet grass before reclining onto his side, taking in all the fresh day's smells.

The Inn was positioned directly across the road from the quaint Lykke port. A few merchants tended to their docked ships that idly rocked along with the waves. The two longships we use for fishing rested against the rocks that lined the shore. Everything was calm and at peace before Midgard woke. The front door squeaked behind me, and I turned to find Bryn making his way to join us.

"It's a beautiful morning, isn't it?" he suggested, his gravelly voice still raspy from the sleep taking refuge in his throat. I offered a quiet *hmm* in agreement. He sat down between Brax and me, mirroring the breathing I had done a few moments earlier. Once he had recentered himself, he opened his eyes and kept them on the brightening sky before us.

"I would be honored if you would give me a little insight on how you might explain your injuries to Calder. We need to try to keep the story straight across the board. The other guards and King's Warriors will be ordered to ask about it as well." I rubbed my forehead to minimize the growing headache caused by the physical and foreshadowed problems I'd acquired.

"I'm honestly not a hundred percent sold on one story or another." I leaned back on my hands and dropped my head, letting my gaze roll upwards. "Do you think people would believe me if I told them you had enough of my chaos and *disciplined* me?" I emphasized, letting out an amused scoff. Bryn showed a contemplative half-smile before shaking his head. "Well, that is probably the best I've got," I muttered. We both sat there running through any believable scenario that could stick before Bryn shared his thoughts again.

"Deceiving the King will be difficult, so whatever story we decide on has to be foolproof. I'm more worried than usual about his reaction."

"Why? We have known him forever. Look at Erikka and me. We have been inseparable for as long as I can remember," I suggested coolly. "I grew up in the castle with them when you were still Chieftain. Did you *not* trust him then?" I questioned a little *less* coolly while trying to conceal my inherent need to know the reasons behind his concern.

"I wouldn't knowingly have kept you in the care of someone I didn't trust. But I knew Calder wasn't involved with caring for the children, which is why I chose to keep you there. Thank the Gods for Petra."

"Wait, *excuse* me? You didn't trust him to be our caregiver?" My concern rose in the presence of Bryn's logic. I started braiding random strands of my onyx hair to hide the anticipation and frustration clawing at my mind.

"Not entirely. The King might be able to hold an aloof disposition, but he has a short fuse when it comes to his temper. I can't imagine he would have the patience to handle Erikka's tantrums. Add you on top of that, and I'm even less confident he wouldn't have put his hands on you." My hands froze, and my eyes lost focus as my thoughts ran beyond the reach of my control. Luckily, Sindre walked around the side of the Inn with Alsvid to take Bryn's attention off me.

"Okay, we've got your riding pack ready to go. You should have enough snacks for Alsvid and then Arvak when you meet with Sylve in Exris," he announced. He was wearing black baggy pants that cinched at the ankles, and his white tunic was half untucked and open at the chest, leaving the tribal tattoos that adorned it and his forearms on display. The sun ever so slightly illuminated the golden side of his hair while his skin seemed to come to life and shine like the sun. He was a remarkable sight.

"You know, you could save some beauty for those of us less fortunate," I interrupted, motioning at the butchered side of my face. Bryn coughed out a laugh, and Sindre shook his head, continuing to walk Alsvid over to me. I rejected his offer to help me, getting up on my own while he helped Bryn. "I need a reason for my face," I announced to no one in particular. "Like, right now." I threw half of my hair into a knot at the back of my head, securing the random braiding from earlier in my entangled mess. I fastened my travel bag onto Alsvid's back and ensured I had everything I needed.

"Why can't you just say you had a bad day in training?" Sindre offered.

"That would require the rest of the guards in Lykke to support the story," Bryn countered. "The same problem with using the excuse of her having helped the raid on the underground fighting. The other guards would know she wasn't involved in the raid that night." He stepped back inside the house and came out with a random assortment of raw meats in a wooden bowl, then offered it to Brax, who enthusiastically devoured it without hesitation.

"You can tell the story of you running into an invisible tree?" Sindre jabbed, peering at me from the corner of his eye. I elbowed him in his side, which earned us a puzzled look from Bryn.

"I can say I had an accident with the horses? Something like a snake in their stall; I tried to get it out, and the horse spooked, knocking me into the wagon…or a bucket of some sort," I suggested, taking advantage of the few moments I had to finger out the knots in Alsvid's tail. "It might not be the most honorable incident, but no one would have had to witness it. So, it really would be my word challenging his gullibility." Brynjar paused and began stroking his beard, considering the simplicity of the excuse I offered. He has a habit of doing that when he needs to focus and make a tough decision, specifically when planning raids for Odins' Ravens.

"It's a simple idea and an isolated incident. The King can't rely on other sources to confirm if he finds the injuries suspicious." He spoke aloud but to himself.

Sindre cut in, "Did I miss something? I know the King is a very *particular* person concerning his guards and warriors presenting themselves pristine and uniformed, but what reaction are you expecting, Bryn?"

His eyebrows pinched in annoyance before he cleared his throat and turned to explain, "Calder is not only brilliant but also cunning. The only reason he wasn't Chieftain before me was that his father and I were the ones to organize and mobilize the rebellion in Skirra. He brought forth many ideas and strategies that gave us an advantage towards the end of the war." Sindre and I exchanged a look, seemingly thinking the same thing.

"I don't think we are following where you are going with this," I suggested. Bryn put out his hand to signal us to find patience before continuing.

"Although he presented great strategy, war is brutal, and events rarely play out according to plan. It surprised many of us, his father included, the first time a strategy of his did not execute to his expectation." As Bryn began to welcome back these memories, his face grew increasingly disgusted. "He allows a minute margin of error in anything he oversees. His outbursts grew uncontrollable and even more shocking. He originally released his frustration on environmental objects. Break a chair, kick a bucket, things that seemed like reasonable targets for pent-up anger. But that changed quickly as the war continued. We learned too late that he had turned his anger on his comrades and the warriors who fought for freedom under his command."

"So, they all just let him beat up on everyone in the middle of a war? Nobody put him in his place?" I scoffed, my frustration rising. I dug my nails into the palms of my hands to displace the energy.

"Hand-to-hand combat has always been his specialty. He also never shied from using weapons on his own men. Calder hasn't *killed* his own people but has left more than a few warriors with deep scars. Since becoming King, I haven't seen or heard of any incidents. However, I'm sure it still happens. A man like that isn't capable of controlling his irrational anger. I keep my suspicions close." Bryn's words trailed off as he lost himself in his thoughts.

I kept my jaw clenched shut, resisting the urge to speak about the incidents I'd encountered at the castle. *It's not worth it. It's better this way*, I reminded myself.

"So, you think the King will *physically* 'reprimand' Veronica?" Sindre grumbled skeptically under his breath. I noticed his shoulders tensed at the same time my grandfather's did. "For getting shoved into the side of a wagon?"

"Even if we didn't know what happened, does the pattern of bruising *look* as if she got shoved into a wagon?" Bryn motioned his hand toward me, and they both stared, analyzing the aftermath of the fight. I gasped when I saw my reflection this morning, so I'm sure it isn't easy for them to look at me for long. Although not swollen shut, my eye is still bruised and a deep purple. The cuts on my cheek and lip are accompanied by a raised welt and lighter bruising. And then there is the random blue bruise in the center of my forehead from my headbutting everyone and their mothers last night. I need to find a new go-to move. They were both still watching me, waiting for my response. I could tell they were making an effort to neutralize their emotions.

Sindre broke the awkward silence that lingered in the air. "Is it really THAT hard of a story to believe?" He took a few steps toward me and threw his arm around my shoulder, gesturing down the length of my body, "I mean, it *is* Veronica we're talking about."

"What is *that* supposed to mean?" I challenged, pushing my elbow into his side to create space between us.

He raised his eyebrow curiously. "Really? I need to explain myself?" He gave me a genuine laugh accompanied by a smirk. "I don't think anyone needs to know you for longer than a few minutes to know you're nothing but trouble, and I say that most endearingly." He squeezed my shoulder, pulling me back into him, then kissed the top of my head. I forcefully shoved him away from me and flashed him my middle finger. Bryn's voice was solemn and stern when he cut in, bringing us back to the severity of the conversation.

"If Calder finds her ruse less than convincing, nothing would matter. Not how long he has known you, not how close his daughter is with you, not even that he and I fought in a war together. Since I have no way to confirm whether these occurrences still happen, I don't know how to prepare or avoid the possibility."

"Snake in a horse stall, I went in to remove it, the horse spooked and bumped into me, which sent me face first into the feed wagon." I nodded with confidence, walking towards Bryn and placing my hands on his shoulders. "That's the story. I will be fine." I hugged him and then started to walk back towards Alsvid when I felt him grab my arm, stopping me.

"If he puts his hands on you...promise me, you will tell me," he begged. His brown eyes were soft, urging me to honor his request. *However, I can't. No matter how bad it might be this time, I can't tell Bryn.*

"Should I tell you before or after I beat the shit out of him?" I laughed. His stare remained unchanged, and he wasn't the least bit amused. "Of course, Bryn. I promise I will tell you." I placed my hand over his that was still holding me back; his hold loosened, and then his arm fell to his side. "I love you," I emphasized, readying myself to mount up.

"I love you too," He responded. Sindre interlocked his fingers and offered his hands towards my feet as a lift. Since Alsvid's back stands as tall as Sindre's shoulders, I accepted.

I was wearing a deep olive-green dress that fell right above the ankles at the request of the King. Calder expects his guards to present themselves in a certain way. Usually, we are required to wear a tunic with a skirt, and depending on the weather, we would be permitted to include tights underneath. However, Calder came up with a reason why I had to wear an ankle-length *dress* when guarding Erikka that I didn't care to remember. I am sure it was a bullshit excuse. I pulled the bottom of the dress up above my knees to hike my leg up and over Alsvid. While getting situated on the saddle, I noticed Sindre eying the hilt of a small knife strapped to my ankle that peeked over the top of my boot. I pulled my skirt further up, around the middle of my thigh, to display the larger knife I had secured there, a sister blade still hidden on my opposite leg. He gave me a nod of approval and began double-checking the straps on the travel bags.

I pulled the tight sleeves of the dress to the end of my wrists and fastened my arm guards to my forearms over the fabric. A raven was stitched into the brown leather on both, thanks to Jerrik's craftsmanship, a nod to our secret organization. One we kept hidden from the King and every other citizen of Sol whose families were not already involved when it was established. Only the villagers living in Lykke knew rumors of our raids and what we strived to achieve. So, in good faith, they played along and went about their routines as if the freed thrall we brought home had lived in Lykke their whole lives. Some offered food and clothes until the Ravens could assist the future Frithians on their final journey through the Willingman Woods to Frith. The city was also established under the Kingdom's nose and remains a safe haven for all who have found the opportunity to live a free life.

Once I finished, I turned to both men and saw Sindre offering me a cloak. I whipped it over my shoulders, fastened the King's brooch in the center of my chest, and pulled the fur-lined hood up to rest on the middle of my head. I noticed Bryn was looking up at me with a tear rolling down his cheek. "Bryn! Don't tell me you are that worried? I will be fine," I reassured. He shook his head in response.

"No, it's not that. Although I *am* worried." He started to walk towards me. "You look just like your mother, and it caught me off guard. The only unique reminder sometimes is your eyes and birthmark...But I see so much of her in you." My hazel eyes were the only difference between my green-eyed mother and me...that and the birthmark on my left eye, a thick brown line that poured out of my pupil to the bottom of my iris, similar to a keyhole. Believed to be a hereditary trait, it was the only evidence of a father I hope to never know. "Your bravery, passion...how you hold yourself, even your quick tongue." He reached for me, and I leaned over to return his warrior's greeting. "I am so proud of you." He declared softly. I smiled warmly, nodded, and sat back straight. I pulled the reins to guide Alsvid in a tight circle and paused before the two men once more.

"I will see you both in four nights from now. Don't have any fun without me," I warned with a glaring look. They both responded with a laugh, and just as I was about to head off, the front door of the Inn opened again. All three of us turned our attention to the woman and two young boys standing in the doorway.

It was Kalyani, and I assumed her two sons. One looked to be around four and clung to his mom's skirt shyly. The other seemed older, maybe seven? He stood next to Kalyani with his hands behind his back, head slightly lowered, eyes peering up through his long eyelashes. Both boys' auburn hair was disheveled from sleeping. Kalyani leaned over and whispered something to them, and in turn, they offered small waves goodbye.

I couldn't help but smile and laugh at the sweet, innocent gesture. I decided to offer them a quick display with Alsvid. I adjusted myself in the saddle to sit close to her head, pulled back on the reins, and leaned forward to pat her neck. In turn, she reared, earning a bright and excited look from both boys. Brax began barking and turning excitedly, keeping a safe distance from us. We trotted in another tight circle, and once we were facing the Inn, I signaled Alsvid to lower her front end into a very poised 'bow.' I mirrored her and swept an arm across my stomach, holding the end of my cloak out with my opposite hand.

The boys both began pulling at Kalyani's skirt, ecstatically asking questions I couldn't quite hear. I waved a final goodbye to my small audience and ushered Alsvid into a steady trot down the path that led me toward Exris.

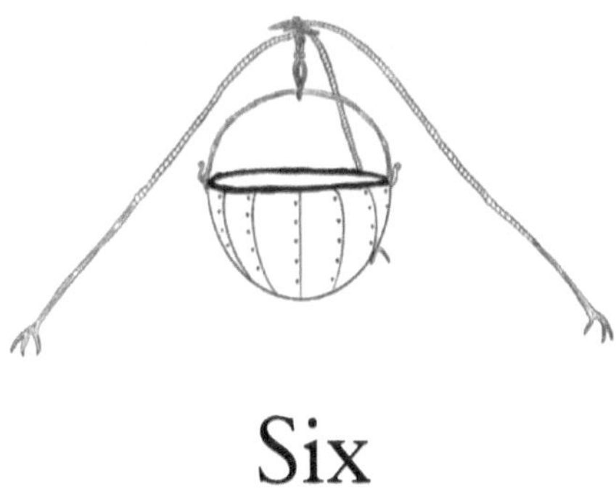

Six

Exris is the Kingdom's main trades town, the focal point of commerce and marketplace bargains. Most of the population resides there, so it is of considerable size, making Port Sisu the largest settlement of the three in the Kingdom. During the formation of Sol, the King and other noble leaders thought it was essential to keep all the hustle and bustle away from Sol's Town and the Royal Family. It's *safer* that way.

As I rode to the edge of Exris, I could see the homes of the villagers a mile or two northwest of the more populated area surrounding the port. Despite the time-consuming walk, the villagers are not deterred from spending the day in town to either work their trade, sell, barter, or simply enjoy some mead at The Dark Sun Tavern.

I arrived in Exris an hour or so past midday. I decided to dismount from Alsvid so she could have a partial break, opting to lead her through the crowded town to our rendezvous point. People were going every which way, fueling the constant murmur of conversation while the music from a few street musicians set the pace for the crowd.

I continued maneuvering through and around the townsfolk, passing rows upon rows of small wooden shop fronts with an array of merchants selling their craft—anyone from iron workers to armor repair, farmers to jewelry makers, carpenters to weavers. If you need it, someone here offers it. Not only could the materials be found to build you a ship by hand, but the vendors selling the food required for a long journey are scattered throughout the streets as well. The smell of freshly baked bread wafted past my nose just before I passed a small storefront with a delicious-looking stew simmering in a cauldron. My stomach growled in need, but I pushed onward, knowing I didn't have much time to waste before needing to rush to the castle.

We always meet Jerrik at his shop on the northeast side of town when I travel between shifts. He designs clothing items like cloaks, fur-lined trousers, and tunics, along with handmade leather belts, arm guards, and corsets, all for sale. He plans a big hunt every weekend to gather different pelts for his creations while donating the extra meat and forage to the orphanage in Frith. Sylve usually tags along, not only to take his donations back with her but also to practice mastering her tracking and bow and arrow skills. Since Jerrik could pass as the inventor of both crafts, he offers her pointers when she asks, even though we have all agreed she is masterfully skilled and doesn't need the practice.

I stretched my neck upward as we turned onto his shop's street to try and spot either of my friends. The only one I found was my horse, Arvak, tethered to a hitching rail halfway down the road. She must have gotten bathed recently because her tan coat shimmered in the sun, along with her blonde mane and tail. She noticed Alsvid and me as we neared her and got antsy, trotting in place against her reins.

Sylve came out of the shop and tried to calm the mare down. Her hair was down in twists that tickled the top of her waist, and a few scattered silver rings decorated the black half of her head. Although she and Sindre were twins, they had their differences. Her bright brown doe eyes and sculpted brows kept her demeanor cheerful, while her round face and full lips completed the ethereal-esque aura. She shares the same towering height along with the half-black and half-gold hair as Sindre, but that is about the only physical qualities they have in common. While Sindre presents a bulky stature, Sylve is lean, but both are extremely strong and talented in combat. Sylve has mastered every possible art of weaponry the Warrior's Guild could throw at her. Similar to Sindre's mastery of hand-to-hand combat styles. Even though they are only twenty-seven years old, they fight more efficiently than most seasoned veterans. Together, they are a force to be reckoned with.

She noticed Arvak kept her attention down the street, so she followed her gaze until she finally found us amongst the crowd. Her expression switched from confusion to excitement as she began jumping up and down along with Arvak. The sight of it made me laugh. Once we were close enough that I could drop the reins and not risk Alsvid wandering off from me, Sylve closed the distance and embraced me in one of her famous warm hugs.

"A week is too long! Too long!" she squealed into my ear, pushing me away from her and reaching for Alsvid, tethering her alongside her friend. The two horses greeted each other as if they had been reunited for the first time in years. *Oh, the dramatics!*

"Sorry, Sylve, but Calder requested my presence longer than my usual three days last week. Unfortunately, I couldn't make it back in time to go to Frith." I apologized while I dug through the travel pack for the snacks for both mares. She turned to me with the most genuine smile on her face. Everything about her emanated warmth and life.

"I understand. But it really is too long. I might have to request a trial to become a part-time Royal Warrior so we can work together more often," she offered playfully.

"You might have to! So much seems to happen when our schedules keep us apart." I joked, over-emphasizing a wink with my swollen and bruised eye. She paused. I knew what she was going to ask next, so I walked over and fed the horses their treats before leaning against the hitching rail, crossing my arms over my chest.

"Don't," I warned. She worries too much, and I knew she would make a bigger deal out of this than it needed to be.

"Fine." She replied. She started loosening my travel pack from Alsvid to transfer to Arvak, her dragon tattoo peeking out from her sleeve. "At least tell me how much."

"Fifty coins," I muttered under my breath.

"Excuse me?" She choked, halting what she was doing while slowly turning her hardened stare toward me. "Did you say *fifty coins?*" She took a step toward me. I suddenly noticed the short axe she had strapped against her hip, and I put my hands up in a show of innocence. She glanced down at it and rolled her eyes.

"Oh, don't be so ridiculous!" She chuckled as she walked over and leaned against the rail beside me. She continued whispering, "That is not nearly enough coin for an..." She glanced around to ensure no ears were listening. "*Event.*" She emphasized the word with her eyes. "Especially an event that leaves such a mess behind."

"What? You don't think I'm beautiful?" I teased, holding a hand to my chest in fake offense.

"Veronica, I don't think *any* person would call that beautiful." She countered with an apologetic look.

A booming voice interrupted us from just inside the storefront. "Is that THE Veronica Leif I hear outside of my shop?" Jerrik emerged from his shop and spotted me quickly, his expression instantly shifting to one of concern. His blue eyes softened as he made his way to us. His curly auburn hair was pulled back out of his face and rested on his shoulders, his precisely groomed beard was shaped neatly to his chin, and his chest hair peeked through the opened 'v' in his purple tunic. He pulled up the fur skirt he had wrapped around his waist that layered over his pants to lower himself onto a knee. He gently took my chin between his fingers and turned my head to take in the injuries on my face. He huffed, "I mean, if this is the look you are going for, it's beautiful," he offered, trying his best to stifle his laughter at his bald-faced lie while pushing off his knee to tower over me. I turned to look at Sylve with one raised eyebrow, motioning with my head at Jerrik's choice of descriptive words. She rolled her eyes and stood as well.

"Let's continue our talk inside," Jerrik offered. He extended his arm and as I interlaced mine with his, I followed his lead into the shop. Once inside, he turned back to close the door but a man who was a few steps from the entrance. Jerrik held out his hand to catch the man's attention and exclaimed, "We are closed for the next hour." He then tried closing the door, but the man stuck his foot in the door's pathway, leaning on it to keep it open. Jerrik looked back at us with a pitiful attempt at an unbothered smile before turning back to the man. "Excuse you."

"There are other people in there. Why can't I shop? I need to buy a few things for my wife." The man pleaded. Sylve and I exchanged a look and continued to the back of the shop, finding a seat until this was sorted.

"I don't give a flying fuck what you *think* you need. I said we are closed." He responded, pushing harder against the door, disregarding the man's foot still making a home in the doorway. I can tell he was withholding his true strength because there wasn't a broken foot yet. I'm shocked the man wasn't more intimidated by Jerrik because even if his definitive tone didn't send the man packing, his sheer size should have.

Jerrik is a burly man. He had to be around three hundred pounds or more, all stuffed into a six-foot body. The man outside the shop might be fooled by how the weight sits on him because he is one of the strongest men in the Kingdom. When we were returning from a hunting trip one weekend, he had carried a mature bull elk on his shoulders for our entire trek back. So, if he wanted this man's foot out of his way, I'm more than certain he would have no issue closing the door.

The man continued rambling on about how *'this is unfair, I am a paying patron too'* blah blah blah. I heaved a sigh, which was the last straw for Jerrik. He slammed his hand into the wall, making the shutters over the windows rattle. "Sorry, sir, but we seem to be completely sold out of everything you are looking for." He pushed through gritted teeth. The man attempted to protest, but Jerrik cut him off again, "And if you do not remove your foot from my door frame, it will be removed from your leg." I nodded my head triumphantly. *I knew it. I knew he was holding back.*

The man removed his foot, and Jerrik slammed the door closed. He turned to us and took a deep breath in and out while running his hands through his curls. "Okay, now that *that* is over with. What happened?" He asked as he headed behind the counter.

"There was a snake in Alsvid's stall back at the Inn. When I went in to get it out, she spooked and shoved me face-first into the feed wagon." I offered, shaking my head at my realization of how ridiculous this sounded out loud. Jerrik paused, contemplating me through his confused grin. He was trying everything in his power not to laugh but also read me. *Could he tell I was lying? There is no way. He is the most gullible person I've ever met.*

Once he took his time filling up three mugs of beer and offered them to Sylve and I. He responded. "You will need to come up with a better reason than that." My heart sank. *If not even Jerrik could believe my lie, then I am royally fucked.* "That is extremely embarrassing, Veronica." He shook his head and laughed from deep within his torso. My eyebrows pinched in the middle, and I looked at Sylve for some guidance. She shrugged in return, her eyebrows raised in confusion. Once Jerrik gathered himself, he placed his hands on the counter, looking at us expectantly.

"Come on. We need to come up with a more badass story. How many people have you told that to? We should change the story before it's too late. At least a fight or something." He snickered. "I speak too highly of you to my neighbors to tell them you fell into a feed wagon. It's a pride thing." He downed the rest of his beer.

"I'm so sorry to disappoint you, Jer." I forced out a laugh. "But that is what happened. The whole truth." I walked over to a rack with different pelts hanging on it and changed the subject, "What is in the works after this weekend? Anything new?"

"Oh, definitely!" He answered passionately. "We were lucky enough to find an older wolf, along with a couple of injured elk. So, besides a big haul of meat Sylve gets to take," he winked at her before he continued, "I plan on using the beautiful wolf's pelt to fashion a heavy winter cloak."

"That sounds like heaven! How many do you think you could make like that before winter?" I questioned.

"Well, I've got at least six months before fall starts turning. If I'm lucky with finding a few more sick wolves or bears, I hope to make six," he explained. "You have to feel this pelt. Let me go grab it from the storage room," he insisted before making his way around the counter and through a small door that led to the back of the store.

I returned to my seat, and Sylve jumped up, sliding herself along the top of the counter, forcing me to sit straight so she didn't run into me. She craned her neck back to check the door, then gravitated closer to me. "Is that what you plan on telling Calder?"

"Yes, that is the best I've got." I hushed under my breath, double-checking for Jerrik.

"Veronica, do you expect him to believe that?" She questioned, her face full of worry.

"No. But it is what it is." I answered with defeat. Two more people have heard this story, and none believed me, even for a second. She put her hands on my shoulders, ducking her head down so our eyes were level.

"Hey, don't say that. We can try to come up with another reason. Maybe we can duke it out in the square right now," she proposed.

"No. I have to stick to this plan. Bryn and Sindre both know what to expect from my story. I'm not changing it." I retorted, shaking her hands off my shoulders.

"That doesn't matter. I'll go back to Lykke once you leave for the castle. I can tell them about the change of plans. We need to think of something better," she continued, searching for anything in the air that could offer a new idea.

"Sylve..." I waited for her to stop thinking and focus back on me. "I will be okay. I always am." I smiled half-heartedly at her and stretched my arms to the side, referencing my existence. She is the only person besides Erikka who knows about the King's disciplinary habits. I had her swear on everything she has ever cared about to keep it a secret until death. She accidentally walked in on me bathing a couple of years ago and found me tending to the aftermath. Since then, she has been the only one I can go to for pain management and wound care if the punishments were too severe. She gave me a familiar look. *I hate that look.* "Don't pity me," I demanded through gritted teeth. We were interrupted by a loud crash from the back room Jerrik was in.

"Are you okay?" Sylve and I both yelled back in his direction. We both stood to go back and help him when he popped up in the back doorway with a box in his hands. "All good! My *extraordinary* ass just got in the way of some shit I left piled up back there." He teased. "I'll fix it later; look at this." He ushered me to follow him to a table, where he set the box down and pulled out a full body-length wolf pelt.

My mouth fell open in awe of the beautiful sable fur. I reached out to feel it, and it was just as soft as it looked. "Damn, Jerrik, it's beautiful. Stunning!" I remarked. I examined the pelt a little closer and noticed there wasn't a laceration anywhere on the body. "Is this yours? I don't see any damage from a weapon. It seems quite perfect." Jerrik handed me the pelt and I ran my hand over the fur. There was an aged texture to it that was oddly reassuring.

Jerrik threw his arm around Sylve's shoulder. She was taller than him by about four inches, so she leaned her head to rest atop his while he explained. "Killed quick and clean by the queen herself. A much kinder end than most likely struggling to capture food for itself and ultimately starving. I had been watching this wolf for some time. He was an older wolf that had been driven out of the pack. Alone, he had been struggling." He motioned at Sylve, who stood straight and bent over in a curtsy.

"Sylve, are you fucking joking?" I questioned in amazement. "You had to have gone in one ear and out the other to get a pelt so clean."

She continued smiling her beautiful wide smile as she skipped over to an ice box on the floor. My smile fell as I feared what might be waiting in there, and sure enough, she bent over and pulled out the entire decapitated wolf's head. A single arrow protruding out of the side, in one ear…out the other. She held up her trophy with glowing pride, a solid testament to her archery skills. "I know a woman back in Lykke who can use all of the left-over parts that Jerrik doesn't process. That way, there is minimal waste, and the animal's spirit knows we value its sacrifice," she added.

"That's great! And as wonderful as it is, having such…*convincing* proof of your ability," I gulped, feeling my stomach turn as I couldn't seem to avert my gaze from the soulless eyes that met mine. "I will vomit in the next five seconds if you don't put that thing back in the box."

Sylve laughed at my sorry attempt to be impressed by her trophy and put it away. "I was in a tree when I took this shot. I even impressed myself." She giggled. My mouth remained open in disbelief. I shook my head to bring myself back to the room.

"Is it a bad thing that you kind of scare me?" I admitted sheepishly. Jerrik moved out from behind me and headed towards the front door of his shop with a packed bag of dry meats.

"Anything with a heartbeat should tremble before her. It's the survival instinct doing its job." He added. Sylve rolled her eyes at us and followed him out. She didn't deny our comments because she knows *exactly* how lethal she is.

I followed them outside and helped switch my travel bags to Arvak and Sylve's to Alsvid. A man with free-flowing, long blonde hair approached Jerrik, who placed his hand between the man's shoulders and ushered him down the street to talk. The two men were all smiles and laughs as they spoke to one another. I turned slightly to Sylve, keeping my attention on the two smitten men, and questioned, "Who is that?"

"That's Elias." She smiled and continued fastening the straps. "Apparently, they have known each other for a while. He joins Jerrik on his hunting trips."

"Are-Are they together?" I turned to her excitedly, approaching her in hopes she would speak faster.

"I don't think they are officially a thing quite yet." She giggled. She ducked under Arvak's neck, and I followed closely behind, waiting for her to give me any scrap of information.

"Oh, Jerrik!" I hissed under my breath. "He is always playing hard to get." I peered around Arvak's behind to spot the two men still caught in an enthralling conversation. "He looks like he enjoys his company, at least," I mentioned.

"I think he has finally noticed how Elias lacks the necessary skills for our hunts. He isn't well versed in using *any* weapon to kill *anything* and can't tell the difference between water dropwort and parsley." She explained. "But he continues to go on his hunting trips. I told Jerrik that he seems more interested in him than the hunting, but he didn't believe me until last week."

"So, he puts on a brave face for these hunting trips just so he can spend time with Jerrik?" I pondered aloud. I walked back over to Alsvid to fasten his set of bags and stole another glance at the two of them. Elias bent over in a bow toward Jerrik before they made their way over to the small group of people dancing in front of the street musicians. "How romantic," I stated. I admired them from afar, how they could dance without worry, and that left a heaviness on my chest. To be able to live in the moment, enjoy those you cherish without a worry in the world, if even for just one dance. My thoughts drifted to my imminent encounter with the King. *I could possibly avoid seeing him tonight. However, my post will be with him in the morning with the Chieftains. Would it be easier to make sure he sees me before tomorrow? Would waiting make him angrier? It might soften the discipline since he would have to finish his meeting...or it could worsen.*

Sylve had snuck up behind me and noticed my faraway stare. She lightly grabbed my elbow and slid her hand down my arm to interlace it with mine. "Get out of that head of yours," she enticed softly with a smile. "Come on." She pulled my hand and tried leading me to the square of dancing people. I attempted to pull my hand away from her in protest, but she only tightened her grip.

"I really should get going," I suggested. "I have to get to the bridge before it's raised for the night."

"One dance won't kill you." She offered, her eyes pleading. "Please. It will only be a few moments." She smiled, pulling me along with her toward the crowd. I smiled at the spring in her step. Leave it to Sylve to find the light and run towards it, head-on and with open arms.

Once we reached the square's center, we started finding the beat while holding each other's hands. Swinging our arms and stepping side to side, we got on the beat, and the chorus changed, progressively growing faster and faster. Sylve pulled me in so we were chest to chest, and then we were off. One of our arms wrapped around the other's waist and the other out to our sides, stepping in a circle to make our way around the square. As the beat quickened, so did our pace. We changed direction along with half of the crowd, intertwining in and out of the others gracefully.

Sylve grabbed my hand and spun me into Jerrik, who caught me in step. I laughed in surprise and looked back for Sylve, who was now dancing her way around the circle with Elias. Both matched in height, but Elias was a little bulkier. Sylve and Elias were laughing with each other as the song sped up again. Jerrik pulled me in and whirled me outwards while our hands remained interlocked. We both were laughing about how silly we felt trying to keep the quickening pace. The music grew louder, and the bystanders' clapping intensified.

The climax of the song was nearing. As we danced around the square, I twirled Jerrik back towards Elias, and Sylve was spun back to me, and we continued spinning in step. Sylve was smiling and laughing so hard it was contagious. My head flung back with laughter. We turned faster and stepped faster as the song neared its end. And with a final note, the song ended abruptly, and all of us dancing had folded our arms behind our backs and stomped in time to finalize the dance with the last chord.

Jerrik and Elias walked back with us to the shop, and we all laughed at the ridiculous fun we had dancing together. I cleared my throat, "Okay, guys, I really must be going now," I announced.

"You're leaving me already?" Jerrik questioned. I rolled my eyes and hugged him before turning to Elias.

"I apologize we were not properly introduced before. My name is Veronica Leif." I offered my hand, and he took it. His grip was strong and sure.

"Elias Wigdahl." He beamed; his beautiful smile accentuated his almond gold eyes and strong jaw.

"A pleasure." I smiled back. "Jerrik, I hope to see you on my journey back in a few days." I reached out to him, and we embraced each other's forearms.

"I hope so, too. Until then, you know I love you." He proclaimed, yanking me in for a bear hug.

"Love you, too," I muffled into his shirt. Once he released me, Sylve offered me her hand, which I accepted quickly, and we left Jerrik and Elias to their conversation.

She walked me to Arvak and turned to me abruptly, her tone so low only I could hear her. "Not to bring the mood back down, but since I know you are going to do it to yourself as soon as you mount up, are you going to be okay?" She asked. I heaved a sigh and put on a brave face for her.

"I will be just fine."

"Because I can go with you. I can request a room for the few days you will be there as your guest. I don't know…Maybe it would *deter* him?" She offered, but the way her shoulders slumped as she watched me mount up told me she knew it was futile.

"We might all be worried over nothing." I offered with a forced laugh. "The King might keep himself so busy this week that he won't care enough to notice. It *has* happened before." I rubbed at my pounding forehead as Sylve untied Arvak's reins from the post and handed them to me. She stroked the mare's nose briefly before her eyes softened as she looked back at me.

"It has never been this bad before…You can't *honestly* believe that." She turned and rummaged through her travel pack, pulled out a small vial, a remedy for my headache, and handed it to me.

"It doesn't matter what I think. He can be unpredictable, so we won't know until we are in the moment." I downed the small dose, hoping for relief, and backed Arvak into the dirt road. "I love you! I'll see you in a few days." Her smile was weak and didn't reach her eyes. I knew she was worried.

"I love you, too. Safe travels. Maybe you can distract yourself and focus on finding out where the ships will be so we can avoid them this weekend," she reminded, waving goodbye. "Will do, my dear." I smiled and ushered Arvak forward, away from my friends. Once I was out of sight, my stomach twisted, and my throat tightened. The weight of not knowing what to expect might kill me even before I arrive at Sol's castle.

Seven

The sun barely kissed the horizon as I rode up to the wooden drawbridge that connected the surrounding village to the royalty and nobles who lived within the castle walls. Sol's town was the Kingdom's first settlement upon its establishment. The area was quaint and inviting. The homes and shops weren't disguised into the landscape like Lykke or overrun with crowds like Exris. Instead, the longhouses were all uniform and made of wood, with curved walls from floor to ceiling. From the outside, it could pass as an overturned ship. The roofs were wooden and slanted past the edge of the exterior walls, offering cover for the walkway in front of the homes.

Every couple of houses, there would be a gathering of quaint shops and stands that sold a variety of crops, fruits, vegetables, milk, and even firewood. It is a peaceful city where most residents live with the freedom they had earned fighting in the war with Skirra. With the natural landscape consisting of acres of rolling hills as far north as the eye could see until it met with Mount Eir, anyone would wish to retire here. Then, add the early spring season, kissing the flowers into bloom with a bright display of colors, from light lavender, royal blues, and deep reds to pale pinks. Anybody would fight for this to be their homestead.

As I drew closer to the bridge, the sun was blocked by the wall surrounding the entire castle. Although the King and Chieftains didn't expect an attack from

Skirra or other Kingdoms in the near future, they wanted to ensure the castle's security by including the curtain wall during the establishment of Sol. Once inside, Sol's Town consisted of a few larger homes that filled the space between the wall and the castle itself.

The castle was a decent size. Probably not the largest castle anyone has built, but when Erikka and I were younger, we had to steal a map of the grounds to figure out how to navigate the building. Four towers on each corner of the stone castle housed archers on a rotating patrol schedule. One tower in the center reached higher than the rest and donned the Kingdom of Sol's flag from the top. White triangular fabric with a golden sun outlined in the center, encircling the intricate line work of Yggdrasil.

I crossed the bridge and entered the heart of the Kingdom, waving a greeting at the guards on either end. We approached the royal barn where the King, Chieftains, and warriors housed their horses. Once at the barn's door, I dismounted from Arvak and led her inside to an open stall. I unfastened all the travel packs I had secured to her and laid them on the floor, removing her saddle and hanging it outside her stall. Next, after locking the gate, I loosened her bridle and swung it over her saddle. As I heaved the travel packs over my shoulders and headed towards a side entrance, I heard a deep voice call to me from behind.

"Where do you think you're going? Looking like that…" The voice was dark, almost as if death itself was taunting me. I turned to find the King's Chieftain leaning against a post outside the barn, with his solid scarred arms crossed over his broad chest. This man always emanated a negative aura. His green eyes permanently sported a cunning stare as if he constantly conspired against you. He kept his dirty blonde hair short in an attempt to draw attention away from his gray roots, but his goatee had already lost its color. A sneer was plastered on his face, and a gnarly scar reached across his broken nose.

"I'm going to my room for the night, Ulrik. What does it matter to you anyway?" I retorted, rolling my eyes and stepping into the back hallway. I was hoping the door would close before he could follow me. However, he was agile for his age and caught it just before it shut. I quickened my steps so I could get to my room before I lost control of my anger.

"The King will not be pleased with having to look at such a disfigured face, Veronica. If I need to remind you, you are only a member of the Royal Guard because of your relation to Brynjar. I don't think there is any special treatment left for you after using it all on such an honor." His hand latched onto my forearm, slowing my pace to fall in step with his leisurely stroll.

"Are you *jealous*?" I jested with a mocking smile. I yanked my arm out of his grip, shot him a nasty look, and then quickened to my previous pace. I turned the corner into the main entrance hall, eyeing the stairs leading to my sanctuary opposite where we had just entered. "Need I remind *you* that you are the King's Chieftain because Brynjar allowed it to happen."

"You little twit," he growled as he tried to pull me to him, but I rolled my shoulder back, avoiding his grip, and tried to maneuver ahead of him until I felt his heavy hand grab my cloak from between my shoulder blades. He threw me back behind him, and I stumbled, trying to maintain my balance. When it comes to Ulrik, my anger gauge is considerably smaller than its usual pitiful size. I clenched my jaw tight, hoping somehow *that* would keep my hands at my sides. I noticed maids and guards alike halted their duties to watch our confrontation.

"What the *fuck* do you want?" I hissed through gritted teeth.

"Are you avoiding being seen? *Trying*, anyway?" His whole attitude had changed once we entered the main hall. His question almost sounded honest and concerned. *Oh, so now that we've conjured up an audience, you want to play nice?* I couldn't care less. If I expect to be disciplined soon, what are a few more minutes? If I can get under his skin, it's worth it.

"I'm tired from traveling." I turned, stepping towards him, chest to chest. I stared up at him, challenging him to match my posture. I want him to break this pathetic character. "I would much rather be bathing in horse shit than be your source of entertainment right now." I held his stare, waiting for a response.

His wild eyebrows lifted in amusement. "King Calder would be appalled at the words leaving your mouth," he spat. His demeanor shifted as he moved his arms and held them behind his back, puffing his chest out and staring down at me as if I was the scum of the earth.

"Oh, are you going to tell on me?" I asked, feigning betrayal. I placed my hand on my heart, then rolled my eyes once more, brushing past him towards the stairs. Ulrik turned and watched as I headed towards my escape, a grimace twisting his face. I turned to face him as I reached the bottom step. "Is the only useful information you offer him about me?"

"Feeling confident today, are we?" He quipped, followed by a smug laugh. *His character's mask seemed to be cracking. Maybe I could set him off.* "I would suggest keeping your mouth shut so the right side of your face doesn't end up like the left." He threatened coolly.

"I would suggest keeping your mouth closed when the King's dick is around. But hey, you do what you got to do." I offered sincerely. His face turned red with rage. I eyed him with an evil grin as I watched him fight every muscle in his body to resist beating the shit out of me in front of everyone gathered around. Their faces were a mixture of horror, terror, and a few eager expressions that waited silently for the next sequence of words. I gestured my middle finger at him and turned to begin my ascent up the grand staircase I've climbed a thousand times since I was a child, now seeming a mile long. I kept my composure and climbed at a regular pace until I reached the top and turned the corner.

Once I was absolutely positive I was out of sight from anyone downstairs, I paused, placing a hand on the cold stone wall. I took a couple of breaths to help ease the tension in my chest before continuing toward my room. I will pay for that interaction later, but seeing that bastard itch in his own skin brings me *immeasurable* joy. The mere fact that people like him continue to exist and hold power in Sol proves the Skirrian regime had its influential claws sunken deeper than even Bryn could have imagined.

I continued down the hallway, passing by a few doors that belonged to other guards until I came to mine. I dug through my travel pack to grab the key to unlock it, then slipped inside quietly. All the warriors' rooms were the same. One hay-stuffed pad barely big enough for the average person to sleep on, a trunk or two for any clothes or belongings, and a tiny window with a wooden shutter to keep out the winter chill. If you take into consideration the few fur pelts along the walls and strewn across the makeshift bed, they've really made this storage closet a home. *Hmm, so homey.* I let out an audible sigh. I threw my bags on top of the trunk in the corner of the room and kicked off my boots. I'd only just unstrapped the small knife around my ankle and one around my thigh when I heard a light knock on the door. *Knock...Knock knock...*then a light *jiggle* of the doorknob. It was Erikka's and my secret code we established when we were about six and eight; she is two years older, but it never hindered our ability to get along. I walked over to the door and unlocked it. I hadn't even opened it all the way when Erikka forced her way in, locking the door behind her. I didn't have time to prepare her or explain myself when her angular ocean eyes narrowed in on me.

"What the hel happened to you?" She questioned calmly, as was expected of a serene and poised Princess. However, I expected her to loosen up soon. Instead, she kept her face collected as her delicate fingers brushed past the injuries on my cheek. Her silvery blonde hair was divided into two plaits and pulled over her shoulders, where they fell past her chest. "Do you need more healing paste? That's a dumb question. Let's put more on." She insisted, walking over to the bed, dropping to her knees, and lifting my sleeping pad to access the loose floorboard hidden underneath. We kept all our healing potions and herbs there since we would always find our way back into *my* room growing up. Erikka hated her room, as it was too close to her father's.

"Here, just hand it to me and get up. I'll put it back," I offered. Her hand popped above her head a few seconds later with a jar full of healing paste, which I took and layered on quickly, helping her stand before I returned it to its hiding spot. I slowly lowered the pad back to the ground and ushered my words out quickly. "I swear I just got the short end of the stick. It's a stupid thing that happened." She wiped the dirt from her knees, fixed her dress, and brushed a loose strand of hair out of her eyes.

"What happened?" She asked, taking a seat on the edge of a chest near the bed. I scooted back onto the pad, leaning onto my hands and crossing my ankles while I repeated the situation again. *At least I will have a lot of practice in telling this pathetic story.* She stood and leaned over me, placing one hand on my face, analyzing the pattern of bruising, and then lowered herself beside me until her nose was only a few inches away from mine. Her pale skin was unblemished. Since she had been forbidden to explore outside the castle walls, she had no reason to have any. The pendant she kept pinned to her chest made sure she wouldn't be allowed access to the world outside. This pendant featured a phoenix lying amongst a bed of peonies, inlaid with kingfisher feathers and blue-green precious stones. As the heir apparent to the throne, it is a requirement from the King. Her blue eyes searched mine, searching for a crack in my story. "I don't believe you. Maybe you should tell the truth because whatever *actually* happened might seem more realistic coming from you." Her silky voice stated.

"What do you mean?" I questioned honestly. I sat up on the bed, forcing her backward to give me space.

"You're asking what I mean?! With all the chaos that seems to willingly follow you around, I would never expect you to admit to something so ridiculous." She explained. I guess she was right. If this horse debacle had happened, I definitely would never have admitted to it. I flung myself back, letting my arms spread out beside me, gazing out the small window. Any hint of sunlight was gone now; the early hours of the night were emerging. My stomach knotted again while my thoughts drifted to the invisible countdown looming in the back of my mind.

Erikka hiked up her silky blush dress above her knees and climbed on me, straddling my waist. The knots in my stomach morphed into butterflies that tickled my lower abdomen. We've grown up together, but I've never looked at her as family. She's my best friend, the person I am closest to. We have gone through so much together, and I can't imagine my life without her. I love her dearly, but to what degree, I'm not entirely certain. I have been questioning it myself for months now, still unsure if she feels the same. She flicked my nose and offered a solemn, "I'm sorry."

"Don't apologize. It's not your fault. I should have been more careful." I assured her while twirling the end of her braid in my fingers.

"I don't expect you to tell me the truth. I have long accepted there are things I shouldn't know with my relation to the Crown. I wish this didn't have to be added to your list of concerns," she sighed. I could see the misplaced guilt weighing heavy on her shoulders, which was interlaced with her apologetic expression. I shifted to sit up, so she swung her leg off me and came to sit next to me on the mat. I nudged her shoulder with mine.

"Seriously, Erikka, don't beat yourself up over things we *both* know we can't control," I urged. "Besides, I'm twenty-two summers old. I should know by now how to make better decisions and consider the effects it may have on me later," I suggested, smiling slightly.

She raised her eyebrows and nodded in agreement but didn't speak. Erikka and Bryn are alike in that way. They both continuously tell me I need to control my impulses. She didn't need to say anything; her *'I told you so'* look said enough.

"You should probably get ready for bed." She stated, creating space between us. I heaved a sigh and got up to look through my bags for the shorter nightgown I wear to sleep in. I loosened my arm guards, slipping them off, and placed them atop the windowsill.

Erikka came over and helped undo the leather laces that fastened the back of my dress near the nape of my neck. She lightly lifted it off my shoulders and slowly guided it down my arms, her fingers sending electricity to my spine as they caressed my skin. My dress fell past my hips and pooled at my feet. I hurriedly pulled my black nightgown over my head and straightened it as it fell just above my knees. I was so distracted that I didn't think to unfasten the knife still strapped to my right leg. I just hoped she didn't notice the bumps she left along my skin in the wake of her touch. I undid the knot I had thrown my hair in earlier today and let the waves fall past my shoulders.

She started to take my braids out when she paused. "Go sit down. Let me brush through this." I did as she instructed since I was struggling to keep my thoughts and desires as far away from her as possible. I sat with one leg tucked under the other, facing the wall, and watched out the window, silently praying to whatever Gods may be listening to help cool my thoughts. She sat behind me a moment later with a comb in hand and began releasing my onyx braids, brushing through the knots that I struggled to avoid accumulating. *Not that I'm trying very hard.*

Once she finished, she passed me the comb, which I placed on the chest beside me. She continued to run her fingers through my hair, blessing me with a euphoric sensation at the base of my skull. I shuddered as the feeling moved down my spine. I turned around to face her, and she dropped her hands into her lap. Erikka Kron, Princess of Sol, the sole heir to the throne, stared back at me. I could tell when she put that mask on. The one she wore to hide her feelings or to suppress her genuine reaction in honor of her title, yet too proud to admit the sad reality of her life.

But what would she be hiding from me at this moment? I cocked my head and followed it with a questioning look.

"Wait...are you–is...What's happening?" I stuttered under my breath. Her mask melted away, and her expression became suggestive. Her blue eyes seemed to deepen in color, her posture loosening as she pulled her bottom lip between her teeth, seeming to contemplate her words.

"I think you know." She murmured in an inviting voice, slowly leaning towards me. I wondered if she was listening to my thoughts. I realized then that the confusion I'd been battling for months wasn't in vain. I moved to close the distance between us, and our mouths crashed together with haste. A ripple of pain shot through my still-healing lip, but I didn't care. My hands found her waist, and hers found the back of my head as we deepened our kiss, as if it was the only thing keeping us alive. Everything about this made sense; it felt right. The uncertainty fogging my emotions had cleared in seconds. I loved her; I am in love with her.

Erikka moved her hands from my head to my shoulders and pushed me back onto the bed. She loosened the laces of her dress that tightened over her chest and let it fall to her waist. I moved back to give her room to toss the silky material onto the floor. She left her white undergarments on, which matched mine in length, and placed one leg between mine, the other to my side, carefully avoiding my leg with the knife still strapped to it. Her hands explored my skin, over my cuts and bruises, down my neck, and over the top of my breast. Her fingers spread wide, sensually massaging around its aroused peak.

I loosened a quiet moan between our desperate breaths and parted her mouth with my tongue, beckoning for hers to find mine. I put my hand on her waist and guided her to face me. Erikka grabbed my leg and pulled it over her hip, pushing her leg up to fill any open space between my legs. My arms wrapped around her neck as she wrapped one around my back, and the other continued grasping at my waist, guiding my hips back and forth along her thigh.

I could feel the warmth emanating from her center, so I laced my arm under hers and pulled her into me, forcing my thigh up until her wetness graced my skin. My heart was pounding so hard that I thought the entire Kingdom could hear it. I knew her erratic pulse matched mine through the throbbing sensation radiating from between her legs.

She pulled her face away and ran her mouth along my jawline. She took a handful of hair and tugged my head back, exposing my neck, laying a trail of tender kisses down its side to the center of my chest, then down over my belly button. My core tightened as her nose tickled my belly button, her lips slowing and lingering at my waist. Her fingers danced along the outside of my legs and played with the hem of my gown, inching it up slower than I wanted her to. Her eyes locked on mine, and my back arched with eagerness. Then, as I felt the slip begin to reveal the bottom of my groin, someone pounded outside the door, causing us both to jump violently.

"Your Highness! It is time for you to return to your private chambers." A male voice informed from the hallway. Erikka and I looked at each other as disappointment at the sudden cutoff turned into concealed laughter.

"It's Mazen." She giggled, kissing my stomach before climbing off me and reaching for her dress strewn across the floor. My head took a few more seconds to come back to earth before realizing what she had said. Mazen is one of her personal guards. Part of my duties when working my shifts at the castle is to fill in for him so he can have a few days off. And since I technically don't start until tomorrow, he is still in charge of making sure she retires to her quarters at night. The other part of my *duties* is to gather intel for the Ravens, listen in on the meetings I'm patrolling, and overhear conversations people have as they pass by: all those sneaky things I definitely shouldn't be doing.

I sat on the bed and watched Erikka pick up her dress and slip it back on, tying her laces up with ease. She held her arms out to her side, an inaudible *'How do I look?'*. I snorted at the sight of her. With the redness still lingering under her cheeks, along her chest, and her hair half fallen out of the once pristine braid, there was no hiding what happened here. She flipped her middle finger, and we both laughed at the state of each other. I walked over to her and tucked one of the loose strands behind her ear.

"Your hair looks like mine," I smirked.

"Gods help me." She quipped. I laid my hand on her neck and pulled her into me once more, placing a light kiss on her lips. Something about it seemed so easy, natural. Why had we waited so long? She pushed her forehead against mine and moved her hand to hold my face close for a moment.

"I have been wanting to do that for a long time." She whispered onto my lips before kissing me again.

"I'm glad to learn I wasn't the only one." I joked.

"By the way, you look just as crazy as I probably do." She stated as she turned to open the door, giving me no time to fix myself. Mazen was off to the right of the opening, standing tall in an orderly position with his arms folded across his chest. Well, as tall as he could. He is the same height as Erikka, and she is at least two inches shorter than me.

Mazen turned to look at us and raised one of his brown eyebrows as he scanned us both from head to toe with his nearly black eyes. I realized I was standing before him in my nighttime attire, but it was too late to shy away now. He didn't say anything. Not that we expected him to. He is a man of very few words. In turn, making it hard to tell Mazen's emotions because if he was surprised, happy, or judging, we sure as hel couldn't tell.

"Good evening, Mazen." I offered politely. He turned and bowed his head slightly in greeting, which I pinched the end of my slip and tightly curtsied in response. Erikka nudged my arm and covered her mouth with her fingertips to muffle her laugh. She cleared her throat and brought her *Princess* mask front and center. She clasped her hands in front of her stomach and straightened her back as she left my room and strode down the hall.

"Good night, Veronica. I will see you in the morning." She teased as she turned back to send me a wink.

"Good night, Your *Highness*." I taunted. "Mazen, if you want to join next time, just say so. Maybe we can give you a code word." I added. Erikka whipped her head back towards me with an incredulous look. However, my attempt to fish a reaction from Mazen fell flat. He only responded with a wave of his hand. *I'll get him one day.*

I closed the door behind my back and locked it, finally removing the knife from my leg and extinguishing the oil lamp on the wall before jumping into bed. Butterflies took flight in my abdomen once again. Sleeping tonight will be difficult.

Eight

The next morning, I finished securing my leather corset around my waist with the Kingdom's insignia of Yggdrasil encircled in the sun embroidered at its center when I heard a knock on my door. I put my two short swords on either side of my hips before answering.

I opened the door to Mazen and Erikka. Mazen said nothing, only offered his forearm in greeting, which I accepted. He then bowed deeply towards Erikka, who tipped her head and waved him off. I stuck my head out the door and called down the hallway, "Enjoy your time off, Mazen!" He kept forward and waved his hand above his head again—a man of so few words. Ulrik should take some notes on how to keep his mouth shut.

I stepped to the side, letting Erikka into my room. She wore a blue dress that nearly matched her eyes, and her phoenix and peony pendant was pinned onto it. Her hair was braided in a halo around the top of her head before falling freely and laying neatly down her back with her crown atop her head. The crown consisted of intricate strands of intertwined gold, beautifully mimicking roots, and vines, with jade gemstones placed delicately throughout. She was stunning…but a sadness hid far beneath her composed and confident expression. Something I knew nobody else would notice but me.

"My apologies, Your Highness, for I am not fully prepared for today's shenanigans yet." I offered a sincere apology, curtsying deeply and bowing my head to hide the smirk forming at the corner of my mouth. Her face remained stoic as she watched me rise from the floor.

"Unacceptable," she stared blankly. I tilted my head in confusion as she took a few steps toward me. "You must make up for the inconveniences you will cause me," she reiterated. Erikka stopped a few inches from me and waited. I searched her face for any hint of what I was supposed to do and caught her eyes stealing a glance at my mouth. *I understand.* I wrapped my hands around either side of her neck and pulled her face to mine. She lifted her hands to hold the backs of my arms, and I felt her smile on my lips. I quickly pulled away and took a step back.

"That is all I can offer, Your Excellency. My hair needs fixing," I laughed. I walked over to the small glass mirror I had laid on top of a chest and attempted to work my hair into a braid. My bruising had lightened significantly, and the open wound on my lip had scabbed over despite the brief time frame. The cut on my cheek has closed completely by the grace of the Gods. The healing paste that Erikka creates with the herbs she has access to at the castle has always been superior to what we can scrounge up in Lykke. I finished my hair and secured it in a knot at the base of my head. When I walked back into the bedroom, Erikka was standing there waiting with the jar of paste in her hand. A few strands of her hair had fallen in front of her shoulders, and there was a light smudge of dust on her dress.

"Erikka! I could have gotten that, as my dress is black, at least." I pushed. I hurried over to her and attempted to wipe off the dirt that streaked across her knees. While I was rubbing the dirt further into the fabric instead of off it, she gently applied the concoction to my face again. I took the jar from her and shoved it under my pillow. "You have to change. You can't go down there like this," I began. I double-checked that I had everything I needed, then ushered her out the door. "If we run, we can make it to the King's meeting in time," I pushed.

"I'm sorry, I didn't even think about the dirt. I guess I was distracted," she offered. From the corner of my eye, I saw her personality shift from her best friend mode to...something else, someone apprehensive. Then she started to retract herself, somewhere very far away from here.

"*Hey*, don't worry about it. Just run with me," I coaxed softly, offering my hand with a reassuring smile. Once she placed her hand in mine, we hiked up the bottom of our dresses and took off. We ran down the hallway and up another flight of stairs, turning down two other hallways until we reached the one that led to her room. We couldn't stop laughing between our heavy breaths as we bolted through her door, heading straight for her armoire. I removed her crown before she pulled her dress off and slipped the fresh one on. It was a darker shade of blue, but hopefully, Calder would be more interested in my face and not notice. She ran her hands through her hair while I shuffled through her previous gown to find her peony pin. She turned to me and offered a smile that didn't reach her eyes. I walked over to her, placed her crown back on her head, and pinned the pendant securely to her chest.

"You're okay," I smiled. "Let's go." I offered my arm, she placed her perfectly manicured hand on it, and we made our way to face the King.

We were a few doors from the war room when Ulrik found us. He stepped into our path and bowed deeply to Erikka, who nodded at him with a hint of disgust playing around her eyes.

"Princess," his tone curious while eying me. I kept my eyes forward, awaiting Erikka's order to head into the meeting. When I am on duty as Erikka's guard, I am required to be barely seen and not heard. My job was to protect her with my life and take whatever abuse Ulrik was getting ready to spew at me without a hint of a reaction. He turned to me as if to speak, but Erikka raised her hand, stopping him.

"If you will, please excuse us," she said serenely.

He snapped his jaw shut as fast as he had opened it and watched us pass in disbelief. Once we were walking again, I kept my face impassive but nodded slightly at her as a thank you. I think I saw her smile but didn't turn my head to check as we made our entrance. *The moment of truth is upon me.* We stopped at the threshold once we were in the King's presence. Erikka lowered her head and curtsied deeply. I mirrored her.

"May you live ten thousand years." Erikka greeted her father.

"Daughter," was all his emotionless voice asserted across the room. When we both stood, I raised my eyes to see what I would be up against, and I wasn't surprised to find his stormy eyes churning as they swept over me. It was only a moment, but I swear I felt electricity travel through the air, from his eyes to mine, creating an invisible chain and keeping me at the forefront of his thoughts until he released me. *Well, until he unleashes himself on me later.* I took a deep breath. *Calm.*

Calder strode to the head of the long wooden table in the center of the room and cleared his throat. Everyone in attendance stood in front of their designated seats, awaiting the King's permission to sit, with their personal guards standing at attention directly behind them. With a wave of his hand, everyone took their seat, except for those of us who were expected to stand guard over the meeting. We all took a step back and remained stationed behind our assigned personnel. I folded my hands behind my back and tried to focus on my job and not the looming aura I felt radiating from the King.

He stood, lecturing about general things that affected the Kingdom, preparing to open the floor to those in the room. His crown sat firmly on his head and looked significantly rougher than Erikka's more delicate and feminine counterpart. The golden headdress had a thick band along the bottom with two intertwining dragons embellished around it. It consisted of nine peaks, each tall and sharp. The one in the center was the largest and made from a jade stone. This peak represented the spearhead of Gungnir and dropped below the band to rest on the top of his forehead. His brown hair was as pin-straight as Erikka's and fell an inch or two past his shoulders. He kept his fading beard short and clean, including his mustache that connected to it on the sides of his mouth. He finished prepping his delegates and swept his black cape out from behind him as he took his seat at his throne—a *ridiculously oversized chair, in my opinion.* The wooden throne was not only tall but wide. It had exquisitely carved dragon heads for the armrests, each adorned with jade stones in place of their eyes. A throne well suited for a self-absorbed man.

As each delegate took their turn either expressing concerns or updating Calder on their plans for the next week, I was stealing bits of information and locking it away in the back of my mind.

"We are stationing our patrol ships along the coast and will be moving them toward Exris by the end of the week."

"We will have the advanced warriors' final trials this week and formed for your upcoming trip to Lykke, per your request." *What the hel is he going to Lykke for?*

I noticed Ulrik grab a cup and pour tea into it from a pot that had been delivered to him by the head servant. He slid it across the table for Erikka, but before she took it, I slapped my hand on the table, stopping her. I kept my eyes on Ulrik as I took the cup of tea and sipped it, slowly placing it back down, holding my arm in front of Erikka as I began to count in my head. Ulrik scoffed loudly and then turned towards the King.

"Isn't this a bit ridiculous? Do you really believe I would try to poison the Princess, Veronica?" I didn't answer. Instead, I kept my eyes on him and continued counting. He waved his hand at my behavior and looked at Calder again. I'm sure he was expecting me to be reprimanded. Instead, the King's eyes burned into the bruised albeit healing side of my face. I could feel every glance he had thrown at me this morning. And with each look, he tugged on that mental chain he entrapped me in.

"She is doing her job, as is expected," Calder stated coolly, without taking his eyes off me.

"This seems more accusatory than just *taste testing*."

"She is doing what I require of her. Sacrificing her life without hesitation to ensure my daughter's safety," Calder boomed. He finally took his eyes off me and slowly turned his attention to Ulrik. "Is there a problem with my expectations?" Ulrik briefly held the King's stare before yielding and lowering his head begrudgingly.

"Of course not, Your Majesty."

My internal timer expired, and I gracefully picked up the tea and offered it to Erikka, who nodded and accepted it.

"Thank you," she whispered. Her fingers ran over the outside of my hands, a touch so subtle yet unusual in the presence of others that I dared to lift my eyes to find hers. There was something there...yearning? Calder's voice brought me back to the room then.

"Fall back in position," he commanded. I moved swiftly and corrected myself.

The rest of the meeting was tiresome. Nothing interesting was happening within the Farmers' Guilds or with the smaller groups of warriors sent into the Nott Forest on 'scouting' missions. No reports led them toward the Odin's Ravens' activity, meaning we have successfully remained under the radar.

Calder stood and made a final address to his small audience, dismissing everyone but Erikka and Ulrik. I noticed Erikka stiffen and barely turn her head in my direction. At the same time, I watched as the hint of a smirk appeared on Ulrik's lips. My anger started to rise, and I had to strangle that insatiable urge to chuck the remaining tea at his smug face.

"Ulrik, escort Erikka to her private quarters. Veronica needs to update me on how things are going in Lykke."

"Of course, Your Grace," he smiled and stood to head toward the door. Calder offered his hand to Erikka, who took it pensively. I stayed stationary at my post, watching Erikka walk by me, not sparing a glance, her hand placed in her father's. Once they got to the door, Calder passed her to Ulrik, who greedily took her hand and interlaced his arm with hers. The King closed the doors and turned the lock, commencing my anticipated discipline.

Nine

Calder turned and walked toward the large window behind his throne.

"Follow me," he ordered plainly. I fell in step behind him, and we stopped in front of the tall display of glass that opened to a small balcony. I positioned myself behind him while he contemplated the view of the castle's courtyard a few floors below. "I see great potential in you," he declared. I pinched my brows in confusion while his back was still to me. *I have no idea where he is taking this conversation.*

"You possess the capability to follow in Brynjar's footsteps and serve as Chieftain to the crown," he said. I was taken aback at the statement, considering the judgmental stares he always presents when I find myself near him. "You may even be a strong Queen one day if Erikka chooses." Now I was gawking. *How would he know about last night? There is no way he knows about that.* My mind started spinning, and the box that withheld my panic slowly creaked open. I snapped my jaw shut and forced my features to neutralize when Calder turned slightly to analyze my reaction. His eyes lazily digested every breath, muscle twitch, or shift in weight I offered. His eyebrows raised in slight amusement, and he turned to gaze out of the window once more. *What was that? What did he see?* The inner voice in my head quivered as the panic had now snaked out of its confinement and licked at the back of my neck. I could feel its effect tighten my throat. *Was the room getting warmer?*

"Either of those two positions are of great importance to the Kingdom and even more so to the Royal Family. It requires immense physical capabilities and high levels of intelligence. Which I know you possess." He paused, unclasping his hands from behind and moving them in front of him. "But so is loyalty," he elaborated; his voice had turned cold. *Breathe.* "So...I am offering you *one* opportunity to explain what might've happened to you. What scarred your face?"

He didn't turn around to watch me answer him. I knew what I had planned to say, but every cell of my body was buzzing in warning as if it sensed the dangerous ledge I found myself on. I swallowed hard and took a deep breath in an attempt to steady my voice before I answered.

"There was an incident at the stables in Lykke."

"At the estate?" he inquired.

"Yes, your Majesty." I raised my chin, trying to pull off the facade of objectiveness. Calder kept facing forward and seemed to be throwing scenarios around in his head for a few moments.

"Continue."

"One of the mares was showing signs of distress in her stall. I went in to see what it was and found a snake in the corner. As I tried to remove it, she spooked and threw me into a feed wagon." I declared with the only confidence I could muster in my situation. He didn't respond to my answer. Instead, he turned and walked past me, heading for the table. I listened to him pour himself tea, take a sip...and then another. Then, the cup clinked down onto the table. It felt as if an hour had passed before he cleared his throat to speak again.

"You know...Brynjar has never approved of my methods." As I began to turn around to face him, the left side of my face absorbed the brutal force of his hand, sending me to the floor. I felt my head kiss the ground, and I had to blink more than a few times before I could make out my surroundings beyond the black dots shrouding my vision. "But I think they are as effective as I need them to be," he snarled.

I felt along the left side of my face to check if he had reopened either of my cuts. No blood. I was taken aback. He has never struck visible parts of my body. He ensured any residual marks would be covered by clothing so that if anyone found these marks and questioned him, I would earn another disciplinary meeting due to my inability to keep them hidden.

I braced my upper body on one of my forearms, still in shock, but kept my eyes on the floor. His thick leather boots made their way into my peripheral vision and came to a halt beside my head, the end of his cape falling in line behind them. Then fire ripped through my scalp as Calder seized a fistful of my hair and jerked my head back to meet his gaze. I was met with '*that look*,' the bloodthirsty look of an animal that has been starved of food for too long. His pupils were dilated and hungry to see more, his facial expression eager. If Bryn is right and this is a suppressed version of him, I can't imagine what horrible things he had done to people before he was crowned. Calder's eyes bore into mine.

"Do you remember when I mentioned that being Queen takes immense *intelligence?*" He squeezed his fist tighter around the hair he had pulled out of place.

"Yes, Your Majesty," I hissed through gritted teeth. The pressure was so tight on my head that I lifted one of my hands to find his, which kept me suspended in the air. I would pay for that later, but my eyes were beginning to water, and I needed to find relief.

"Well...It's safe to say you aren't there yet." He threaded his free arm underneath the one holding my head in place, winding up another back-handed attack. I watched as he raised his hand and I closed my eyes to brace for impact. With nowhere for my head to go, the force of the blow was more intense the second time. I felt warm liquid run down my lips. *Dammit*. The taste of iron crept onto my tongue. He spared me no recovery time before standing and walking towards the windows, dragging me along by my hair.

"Do you remember when I mentioned that being Chieftain takes immense physical capabilities?" he questioned as he pulled me to my feet, finally releasing his death grip on my hair. I stumbled to find my footing while my head spun.

"Yes. Your Majesty." I answered in between deep breaths. He turned his back to me and rolled his neck around. His muscles contracted sharply, almost predatorily. Within a split second, I watched him grab the edge of his cape and swirl the end of it up and behind his back. Then, before my brain could register what he was doing, his foot made contact with my stomach and sent me flying back into the glass wall. The window screeched as it sent a massive crack toward the ceiling. The breath was ripped from my lungs as I fell to the floor and curled into a ball to protect myself, gasping to find an ounce of air.

"VERONICA!" His cold voice barked my name. His intensity increased with each word, along with the ferociousness behind each syllable, "Do you *remember* when I said that either of those two positions REQUIRE. IMMENSE. LOYALTY. TO THE CROWN?" I risked looking at him as he approached the fireplace on one side of the room. He pulled an iron pole from the hearth and made his way slowly back to me. I squinted to try to make out what he held. The end was glowing white. My eyes widened in terror as the realization ran cold over my skin. He had a brand of the Kingdom's insignia.

Calder watched my face morph from confusion into fear, his smile twisting with delight. *This is going too far. I have to stop this.* I pushed myself off the floor and somehow managed to get onto my knees, bracing myself with an elbow on the glass. However, my small display of strength only seemed to ignite the flame within him, quickening his pace to close the distance between us before I could fully stand to face him. His thick hand clamped onto my throat, pinning me against the wall. He turned his head at me in confusion.

"Are you rejecting my solution to prove your loyalty?" His voice had lost all aggression, and he seemed astonished as if anyone would be willing to be branded just to appease some sick control fetish. I grabbed his hand that was crushing my neck with both of mine and shoved my foot into his bicep in a feeble attempt to hold off his advancement, only to bring the brand closer to my face. The end of my dress had gathered at my hip, nearly exposing me. In times like these, I despise his delusional requests.

"Your *Grace*," I hissed, with no attempt to hide my annoyance, "This is...a bit extreme...I've done nothing wrong."

"Do you think I'm *fucking stupid*, girl?" Calder laughed and ran his tongue over his lips in anticipation of his actions. He released his grip only to shove my leg back down before ramming his elbow into my chest, knocking the wind out of me. His knee met my ribs repeatedly until I could no longer curl up to block them. "This will ensure your loyalty to the Kingdom. It will only take a moment," he offered sternly.

As he lowered the iron in my direction, I began thrashing against his weight. I tried kicking anywhere I could. I was clawing at his arm, which was slowly restricting my airflow. My stamina was failing me. I couldn't get enough air, and the room was beginning to spin. *I can't let him do this.* All I could do was scream, so I did. I screamed as loud as I could, startling him; a surprised look crossed his face. He removed his arm from my throat, and I could only get one breath in before he covered my mouth with his hand, silencing any future attempts to garner someone's attention.

"You *stupid child*," he sneered into the side of my face. "This is the same reason your mother disappeared. She didn't know when to keep her fucking mouth shut." My eyes widened in anger, but there was nothing I could do. He had pinned me against the wall, and no matter how hard I thought I was fighting him, I wasn't strong enough to free myself. While holding my mouth closed, he forced my face to the side, exposing my bruised skin to the red brand nearing its target. I felt the searing heat radiating from the iron on my flesh when the windows shattered completely.

Twisting branches burst through the glass wall behind me, growing uncontrollably throughout the space. Calder was knocked away from me, and I dropped to the floor, gathering any energy left to fight whatever force just breached the castle walls. I barely caught a glimpse of Calder sprawled out on the other side of the room before the limbs intertwined around me, forming a solid wall between me and the King.

"Calder!" I called out to him, my voice cracking. There was no response, and my view was obstructed completely. I turned to check for a way out, but I was fully enclosed in some type of cage. *Breathe. I need to get out of here and get to Calder.* My stamina was flickering in and out like the final embers of a dying fire. Whatever I decided to do had to be effective. Otherwise, I would fail at the only job that mattered now. Protect the Royal Family. Protect the King.

I got up on one knee and unsheathed my short swords, which felt slightly heavier than usual. As I stood, the enclosure grew, untangling itself as if making room for me to stand. As the branches untwisted, scarlet red leaves sprouted along them, just like the tree I saw by Sindre's house. I took a step and slashed at them with my weapon, but where I expected to make contact was open space. I swiped again, and the branches in the targeted area parted before I could inflict damage. *What the hel is this?*

I sheathed one sword and reached out to touch the wall of limbs as they continued to untangle and open for me. Released from my confinement, I headed straight to where I last saw the King. Sprawled out with the branches gradually growing towards his body, I unsheathed my second weapon again. I dropped mid-sprint, sliding to a stop in front of him, and hacked at the growing branches. They avoided my attack and began to retreat. I held my position, weapons drawn, and had a stare-down...with a...tree? *I might need to meet with that shaman now.*

"What did you do?" Calder hissed under his breath. I turned slightly to check on him out of the corner of my eye. He bled from a cut that began from his forehead all the way down to his chin, but other than that, I couldn't see any other injuries.

"Me?!" I responded, astounded that he thought I did any of this. He began to roll off his side to face the enemy, but I put my hand on his shoulder, stopping him. "Don't move," I ordered, my voice still hoarse from his earlier assault. I kept my eyes and body facing whatever this enemy might be. It had stopped moving and appeared to be observing me. Both of us were watching...waiting to see what would happen next.

Shouting came from down the hall, and soon, panicked pounding on the other side of the door. The branches began to retreat slowly, and I removed my hand from Calder, letting him prop himself up to watch. The tree was barely halfway out of the room when the Royal Warriors broke through the wooden doors and flooded in. A handful ran over to us, grabbing the King and helping him off the floor. I stayed. Watching. Entranced.

Above the overwhelming myriad of questions thrown at the King and me, I heard Calder speak over everyone in the room.

"I need half of you at the first level courtyard. *Find* the assailant." His order was filled with anger, but it was strong and clear. "The other half secure the castle, and everyone who lives or works here needs to be in their respective rooms within the hour." And just like that, the room cleared. Erikka came running in, pushing past the rushing crowd piling out the door, with Ulrik right behind her.

Her face paled at our state among the shattered glass that was quite literally everywhere. It blanketed the ground and furniture as if it had snowed. I was slow to get up, and Erikka hurried over to me, helping me off the floor.

"What happened?" she questioned the room, concerned. Her sad eyes examined me and then focused on my bleeding lip. Her parted lips pursed, and she straightened her back. She knew half of that answer.

"I honestly am not sure how to explain it..." I fumbled with my words as I remembered I was still in the presence of the King and not just Erikka. I put both my weapons away and weakly repositioned myself to attention, clasping my hands behind my back, waiting for instruction. She looked at her father for a response.

He contemplated the room and looked between the broken window panes, the slowly retreating branches, the fireplace, me, and Erikka for a few moments. Calder then took in an audible breath. "Something breached the castle walls and made an attempt on my life."

Ulrik snatched a wet towel from a handmaiden that had entered the room and offered it to the King, who took it and gently wiped away the blood coursing down his face. "Veronica fought off whatever had been sent to kill me after the shock of the initial attack. I sent guards to the courtyard to try and locate the attacker, and the rest of the guards are issuing a lockdown as we speak." After cleaning his face, he threw the bloodied towel at Ulrik, who grimaced after Calder turned his back to us. "Veronica, you are back on duty as Erikka's personal guard. Escort her to her room. *Now.* And *do not* leave until another member of the guard relieves you." He turned and left the room, Ulrik following in his shadow. Calder paused for a moment and spoke over his shoulder. "I will send a shaman to Erikka's quarters to treat the injuries you received from the attack. Wear a face covering for the remainder of your shift at the castle, and do not remove it until after you have left the grounds," he commanded calmly. He locked eyes with mine and gave me a threatening look that said, '*Open your mouth, and I'll finish what I started.*' before he continued down the hall.

For a few minutes, Erikka and I stood next to each other in shock. With her hand on my arm, she analyzed the room while I replayed everything that had happened. My thoughts were on a loop. Each exchange, every statement, question, response, everything was being repeated and stored away in the archives of my memory. Only the slow, methodical creaking and twisting of tree branches pulled me away from my thoughts as I felt Erikka's grip tighten.

I looked at her and saw her eyes had widened into a blank stare as if she had been frozen solid. It didn't look like she was even breathing. I whipped around, stepping in front of her and crossing both arms across my waist to pull out my swords. The tree branches had vanished, and at the edge of the room where the windows once were, stood a man.

My breath caught in my chest as I took in every detail of the person standing before us. He was tall, potentially as tall as Sindre, and slender but defined. I could see his muscular chest and sculpted abdomen through the loosened deep V in his beige tunic. He stood casually with his hands in the pockets of his pants, which were of a deep green silk. *I need to remember that since silk is only worn by the Royal Family in Sol.* He must be from outside the Kingdom. And he was *barefoot?* Who breaks into a castle barefoot?

I continued analyzing the man, working my eyes up his body. There was something on the right side of his neck, which could be a scar. He had no facial hair, but his hair was long, longer than mine. It stopped just above where his belly button would be and had a slight wave throughout. But what caught my attention was the color, scarlet red. It was barely a brighter hue than the leaves on the branches from earlier. All I could fixate on was the similarity between the two. My eyes met his, and I felt a shiver dance along the back of my head and down my neck. I could tell his eyes were bright green despite the distance between us as they were curiously gazing into mine. Then, with a slight tilt of his neck, he took one step forward. I moved Erikka back with one arm and pointed my weapon toward him as a warning.

A mischievous smile spread across his face, and he threw his hands up lazily, a sign of no ill intention. As the man was about to speak, we heard a guard call out from the courtyard below.

"Archers! Level three!" The man turned to look at the commotion below. I watched as the archers on the towers at either corner of the castle ran over to their ledges and scanned the building until they found him, taking aim.

"Why did you protect him?" the man asked, turning back to me. His voice was smooth and sensual, like a log fire's light dancing along the walls within a fleeting midnight romance. However, I sensed a hint of annoyance behind the curious and intrigued tone.

I'm not sure why I felt compelled to answer him. Maybe I was prolonging our interaction so the archers would have time to apprehend him. Or perhaps I wanted to explore this familiarity I felt with the man who was now stepping back onto the ledge of the small balcony, balancing on his toes with his heels hanging off.

"It's my job." I wiggled one of my swords into Erikka's hand and slowly walked toward him. "Come off the ledge," I ordered him as softly as possible. I didn't want him to jump. We needed to know who sent him first.

He eyed me, then looked down below him and back at me before flashing me a breathtaking crooked smile that stopped me where I stood. *Why does he seem so familiar?*

"Well...you sound like her," he contemplated aloud. My eyebrows met in the middle, confusion forming on every inch of my face. *What?* The man spread his arms out to his sides and threw his head back, sending him off the ledge toward the courtyard below. Erikka screamed, and I heard steel clang against the floor.

"No!" I yelled at him, throwing my weapon down and running towards the open window. I cautiously looked over the ledge, expecting to see the man splattered on the ground, but found nothing. Instead, only two arrows, about two feet below me, jutted from the wall. They looked like they crossed past each other when they should have hit a body. He disappeared. I wasted no time and turned back, grabbing both swords and sheathing them. I noticed the iron brand on the floor near the window, broken into two pieces. I took Erikka by the arm and rushed her out of the room and back to her private quarters before another beautiful, deranged man popped out of the floor.

Ten

After an hour of meticulously poking, prodding, and manipulating my body to find anything causing me discomfort, the shaman finished tending to my wounds. She had requested that I remove my clothing so she could treat me thoroughly, but we agreed I could keep my undergarments on. So, I sat on the light orange chaise in the quaint sitting area of Erikka's quarters, nearly naked, wrapped from head to toe in bandages and greased up with healing ointment.

The shaman bowed deeply to Erikka as she entered the room after spending an entire hour on the balcony while I was being treated. We had yet to speak, as the extra company kept our conversation on the back burner. Still, we usually took time to sit and decompress before exchanging experiences from our *meetings*.

"Your Highness, I have finished treating your guard. Is there any other way I may be of service to you, M'Lady?" she asked quietly. Her thin hands trembled slightly from age. Astrid has been serving the Royal Family since the founding of Sol. She spent her entire life learning her craft and knew how to treat any ailment. Erikka, in her spare time, learns how to make healing concoctions and brews from her as she finds it interesting.

"That will be all I need from you for now, Astrid." She bowed respectfully in return, and Astrid's cheeks reddened.

"Princess! Don't bow to me, darling." She pleaded with her frail voice, hobbling over to steer her upright. Erikka laughed lovingly and intertwined her arm with the elder shaman, assisting her to the door.

"You know I appreciate everything you do for us. Thank you dearly." She leaned over and kissed her cheek.

"You girls stay out of trouble now."

"Yes, ma'am." Erikka agreed as she closed and locked the door after her.

I got up, walked through her room toward her armoire, and fished around its contents for her hairbrush. She followed me, opened a drawer, and pulled it out, holding it for me to take. I couldn't help how flustered I felt. I couldn't continue with this facade. I couldn't pretend what just happened wasn't affecting me, and it didn't take Erikka long to notice after I snatched the brush out of her hand and stormed back to the sitting area. I heard her sigh as I sat down to pull my knotted bun apart.

"It's *okay* to feel emotions, Veronica," she offered solemnly.

"No, it's *not*. They hinder my ability to perform my duties."

"I don't believe that. I feel that they might help you."

"With all due respect, you have not trained, nor have you fought a physical fight in your life. So, please excuse my annoyance when I tell you that they, in fact, *do not* help." She rolled her eyes, shook her head at me, and walked toward the balcony's double doors. She stood in the opening and let the soft spring breeze blow through her hair. "I'm sorry. I don't mean to be rude...I just," my voice trailed off. I don't know what to say.

"Don't apologize." She half turned to face me. "I just mean it's okay to feel overwhelmed. I need you to tell me what happened." Her voice remained soft. She motioned me over to her as she pushed a chair onto the balcony. "Being able to talk through what we experience is important. Keeping our reactions and feelings to ourselves can be harmful. To you *and* to others."

"I need to work on controlling myself. My feelings cause me to be impulsive," I explained frankly and stood my ground, refusing her offer by remaining seated where I was. She threw her hands on her hips and frowned at me.

"You are *always* exceptional when you are here. Maybe not as perfect as Mazen," she paused to fish a laugh from me without success, "but you more than surpass Ulrik. He works under my father directly every day and is still alive." She grabbed her robe that was laid over the chair and threw it at me.

"It's not about that," I retorted sourly, pulling it on.

"Then what the *hel* are you talking about?" she demanded. Her voice rose for the first time in a long time. My thoughts were whirling inside my head, creating a cyclone of emotions and flashbacks with nowhere to go.

"EVERYONE!" I yelled back at her. I could hear Bryn's words, plain as day: *"You have no self-control. You obviously can't make rational decisions. And your fighting skills are clearly not mastered yet, considering the mess that your face has become from just one night."..."Your mother allowed her passion for Frith to consume her."*

Sindre's voice was converging with Bryn's. *"You are extremely fortunate, and I honestly have no idea how you keep avoiding such negative outcomes, but that luck will run out one day."..."You should try and stick to doing things that won't worry him."*

Jerrik: *"You're leaving me already?"*

Sylve: *"It has never been this bad before."*

Erikka: *"I just wish this didn't have to be added to your list of concerns."*

Then there was Calder's, twisting them together into a violent storm. *"Being Queen takes immense intelligence"..."It's safe to say you aren't there yet."..."This is the same reason your mother disappeared. She didn't know when to keep her fucking mouth shut."*

Two soft, warm hands cradled either side of my face, bringing me back to a reality I hadn't realized I had distanced from. My breathing had become frantic, and my nails dug into the edge of the couch. I looked up and met Erikka's compassionate gaze.

"Breathe," she beckoned sweetly. Her voice was barely above a whisper. She unlatched my grip from the couch and helped me stand, guiding me to the balcony. Once outside, she placed my hand on the banister and stood, kicking off her shoes and placing her hands on the railing to mirror me. "I do this when I feel overwhelmed." She took a deep breath through her nose and exhaled through her mouth. She kept her eyes closed.

"Astrid called it *'Grounding'*...It helps bring me back to Midgard when my thoughts and emotions seem as if they will get the best of me." She opened one eye to peak at me. I snapped my head forward and closed my eyes. I heard her laugh through her next breath.

"Focus on breathing. Slow and steady."

I took a few breaths, being mindful to prolong each inhale and exhale. Already, I felt my chest loosen and my shoulders relax.

"Bring your focus to your senses. What do you hear? What can you smell? What can you feel?"

I directed my attention to my senses as she instructed. I could feel the gentle breeze caressing my skin. I could smell the slight scent of pine, white dryas, and peonies carried into the air from the courtyard below. I heard the rustling of the tree leaves, the movement of guards below surveying the grounds…a knock on the door. I was slow to open my eyes, and when I turned to look at Erikka, she was already halfway across the room, heading to answer it. I sprinted to catch up and cut her off abruptly.

"What the hel?! Are you intentionally trying to get me reprimanded?" I asked through frustrated whispers. I bent over on my way to open the door, grabbed my belt with my swords attached to it, and secured it around my waist, over my robe...*shit*. I opened the door to find Ulrik standing there.

He scrutinized me, looking me up and down with greedy eyes, and wet his lips, making my stomach turn. I had to focus on not visibly gagging at him. He tried to peer into the room, so I closed the door, leaving a crack that was enough only for half of my body to be seen. He raised an eyebrow, "By order of the King, you may leave the Princess's private quarters and continue on with your day as scheduled," he declared with annoyance.

"Was the man found?" I asked shortly.

"No."

"Is there an explanation for the tree...thing?"

"No."

"So, it is true...You have nothing valuable to offer unless it has to do with me?" I taunted.

His eye twitched, making the corner of my mouth turn up.

"How *was* your meeting? Before the disturbance, that is?" He questioned smugly. *Fuck him.* I went to shut the door, but he put his hand out and stopped it. "Where is the Princess?"

"Indecent. Why?" I questioned him while trying my best to maintain neutrality. I knew he was trying to bait me, but I had to at least attempt to withhold my initial reaction. *Control yourself, Veronica.*

"Oh, actually, this might be a good time for us to pick up where we left off before your screaming interrupted us earlier." He made a move as if he was going to push open the door and walk past me, but I rammed my shoulder into the center of his chest, sending him stumbling back. His face reddened with anger, replacing the surprise. *Fuck control.*

He took a step towards me. "HOW DARE-"

My foot met his chest next, using a move I had recently learned from the King himself. Once he stumbled back into the wall, I was on him. I grabbed hold of one of his arms and turned my back to him, bringing his arm over my shoulder as I bent over, kicking one of his legs out and heaving his body weight over me onto the floor. Then, I jumped on top of him, straddling his stomach with each of my legs pressing down onto both of his arms, pinning them to the ground along his sides. I slipped the small knife I kept fastened to my ankle out of its hiding spot and held the tip of it to his throat, just under his jaw.

"Let me make this *crystal clear*. If you ever put your hands on her, you will lose them." I applied more pressure to his skin, and he stretched his neck out to try and relieve some of it. His eyes were murderous, and he tried to shift out from under me, but Erikka cleared her throat.

"That will be more than enough, Veronica," she announced graciously. "It's time to get prepared for dinner." From where I pinned Ulrik to the ground, I looked up to find her standing beside us, her hand outstretched towards me. I slipped my knife back into hiding and took her hand, purposely putting my full weight on my knees as I rose to stand over Ulrik. He rose onto his elbows, and I fought the urge to spit on him as he attempted to sneak a look up the opening of my robe.

As Ulrik stood and brushed the evidence of a scuffle from his uniform, Erikka turned and drawled, "I expect this incident not to be mentioned to my father.

Otherwise, he will be informed of the insinuation you made towards me this evening." She strode inside with her usual grace, but I glanced back at him before closing the door completely. His war-ridden face had paled, but he realigned his posture and set off down the hallway.

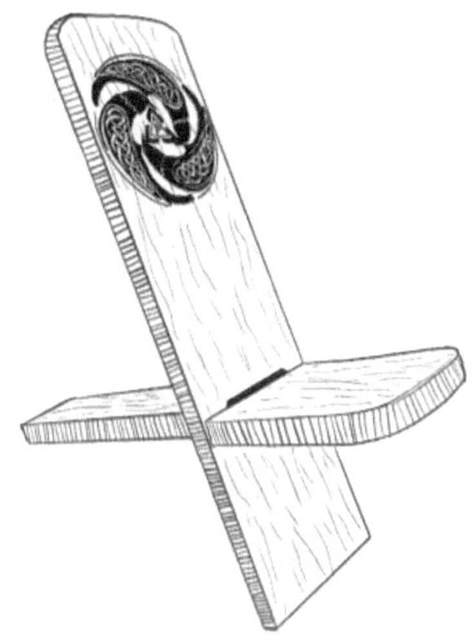

Eleven

The rest of the evening went smoothly. Dinner was oddly uneventful but finished with Calder requesting a debriefing. Erikka and I would have ours separately in the morning. We still hadn't discussed what happened between ourselves since we didn't trust the proximity to the King's room. With a shared glance, we both silently agreed to wait until we returned to my room before we got into the details.

As I closed and locked the door to my small room, Erikka sighed loudly and ripped her crown off her head before placing it on my nightstand.

"Finally," she sighed through another long breath.

"Long day for you?" I joked.

"I have been waiting all day to talk to you about what happened. Do you blame me?"

"Well, what do you want to know?" I questioned defensively. I knew what she wanted to know, but I hated telling her. Watching her expression change from horror to anger to guilt is heartbreaking. I hate making her feel as if she is somehow responsible for her father's actions. I walked over to my trunk and pulled out my outfit for tomorrow to lay over the wooden chair near the door.

"What did he do to you? Your lip wound reopened, and it had almost completely scabbed over this morning." It seems she had skipped over her usual flow of emotions and gone straight to guilt. Her shoulders sagged in defeat.

"Nothing worse than the usual." I lied with a straight face because there was no reason for her to take on the boldness of his actions.

"Why would Astrid take an entire HOUR?" She watched me intently as she brushed through her curls, pulling them straight. I lowered my voice to a whisper, knowing that sometimes the walls have ears.

"Look, I got a couple of *very* solid knees to the ribs, a quick backhand to the face, AND he yanked my hair out of place. That was all he could do before the attack." *Half-truths. Half-truths should be enough.* I slipped my dress off and pulled my night slip over my head. I left my favorite daggers strapped to each thigh, and my sweet little knife was attached to my ankle.

"Are those necessary?" Erikka questioned, eyeing the weapons I left on as I continued to get ready for the night.

"Of course. I'm on duty as your guard tonight." I struck a pose, holding one leg out and seductively teasing the bottom of my slip up my leg. "Or maybe I know how delicious I look with knives strapped to my legs." I raised my eyebrows a few times and earned a laugh from her.

"I mean, you're not wrong." She stood and walked over to me, placing both hands on either arm. "I'm sorry for what he does to you. I hate that I can't do anything about it."

"It's not like we are the only ones who experience this with him. So don't apologize. I could fight back to protect myself, but I don't." I pulled her in to hug her. The light scent of violet and lily of the valley was still present in her hair. I couldn't help but get lose myself in the small moment we shared. I felt relaxed here, and I knew she did as well when she rested her head on my shoulder. I kissed the top of her head and rested my chin there, enjoying the momentary peace. Then, there was a knock on the door.

"Gods, Fuck! What now?" I growled under my breath. I swung it open with such haste that I was frozen in surprise to find Mazen waiting at the doorway. "Oh. Mazen. Is everything okay?" I asked, looking up and down the hallway.

He nodded, completely ignoring the way I was dressed. "Yes, I was just checking on you two. I finally got someone to explain to me what happened today." I stood there in shock and felt Erikka peer over my shoulder. I turned to look at her, and we both held the same gaping expression of surprise. I don't think I've heard so many words come out of his mouth at one time.

He raised his chin towards the room, and we both moved back, allowing him to join us inside. I turned around after closing the door, and Mazen looked about as uncomfortable and out of place as one could be. This is twice in twenty-four hours that he has seen me in this slip. The thought of me yelling after him to 'ask next time' crossed my mind and made me laugh internally.

"You can sit, Mazen. We won't bite." I offered and watched him look between his two options. "Unless you want us to, of course."

His face flushed pink, and he shook his head at my suggestion. He carefully swept the end of my dress off to the side of the chair and sat down. Erikka mirrored him and sat on the bed. I remained standing, mindful that I was still *technically* on duty. Mazen cleared his throat, which made us wipe the dumbfounded look off our faces.

"I *do* speak, you know," he announced, slightly embarrassed by our reactions.

"Not to us." Erikka cut in. "I assumed it was because we annoyed you."

"I would have thought the same, but I don't think I've seen you speak to anyone," I added.

"No, it's nothing personal." We both eyed him up and down doubtfully. "I promise," he reiterated, creating an x motion over his heart.

"Fine then." I began to pace the room in front of him, my hands clasped behind my back as if in an interrogation. "What did you hear?" I questioned.

"The castle was breached, and an attempt was made on the King...on *your* watch."

I snapped my head at him, taking offense at his insinuation. "What is *that* supposed to mean?"

He shrugged his shoulders and forced back a smile. "Are you...is that an attempt to tease me?" He smiled shyly, and I snorted a laugh.

"Interesting. There is a lot I still need to learn about you, I see." I leaned against the windowsill. "What else?"

"Higher-ups believe the attack was conducted using a form of Seidr." Mazen said contemplatively.

"They banned the practicing of magic once Sol was formed. I thought most of Seidr was spellwork anyway." I cut in.

"Basic practice usually begins with spellwork. But advanced magic-wielders can use it for healing, cause psychic phenomena, or even use it as a form of weaponry." Mazen answered.

"What does psychic phenomena mean?" Erikka asked.

"Umm, like object manipulation," Mazen replied. He watched as Erikka and I exchanged a confused look between us. He sighed. "Moving things with your mind?" he offered, and we both shook our heads in understanding.

"How do you know so much about this? I figured they didn't teach it anymore." I questioned.

"I spend most of my time in the library when I'm not working," He said with a shrug. "They might not teach about it, but the information remains."

"Why do you want to know about it?" Erikka chimed in, her voice lowering to a whisper. "Do you practice?" Surprise adorned his face at the bluntness of her question.

"No." He chuckled under his breath. "I believe the greatest weapon in any battle is knowledge. If there is something the people in power don't want you to know, you should go out of your way to learn why."

I contemplated what he said for a moment. Why wouldn't they want people to practice magic? *Especially* if someone could develop their skills to grow trees as a form of attack. It seemed like an effective tool today. *Wait a minute...How did I never know Mazen was so rebellious?*

"Of course, the man was using Seidr. He disappeared in thin air," I offered.

"What?"

"Yeah, he fell back off the window ledge, and when I went to look for him, he was gone."

"No one told me that..." He rubbed his chin in thought. "That *'ability'* isn't mentioned in any of the text about Seidr. Well, ones I've read so far anyways."

"What *did* they tell you about him?" I asked cautiously.

"Nothing, really. Only a few people caught a glimpse of...*him*. I guess we know that now...and he had red hair. But no one has mentioned anything else.

Especially not that he jumped off the ledge and vanished." That was strange. Since the archers shot at him, they would have seen him jump. "What happened in the room with him?" He inquired, sitting back and pulling one leg over his knee. I glanced at Erikka, who avoided my eyes.

"We debrief with the King in the morning," I stated.

"I understand. They will let us know what's important after that," he stood and turned to open the door.

"Thank you for checking on us." Erikka voiced before he stepped through the doorway. He bowed his head at both of us and then closed the door behind him. I locked it in his wake and looked at Erikka, pleasantly surprised.

"Has he spoken to you that much before?" I questioned, taking a seat in the chair he kept warm.

She shook her head enthusiastically. "No! Not at all. I can't believe that."

"Why would the archers withhold that they saw him vanish? You saw what I saw, right?" I asked for reassurance, tilting my head to the side.

"Yes. But there is something I have been meaning to talk to you about."

"What is it?"

"Why did he say '*You sound like her*' to you? Why didn't he attack you? He looked as if he heeded your warning when he tried to move towards us." I turned to analyze her question…what was she *insinuating?*

"I don't know who he is," I stated flatly, a bit confused.

"I'm not saying that. It just seemed like the man knew *you*." I waited and said nothing. Either she would backtrack completely, or she would continue to imply that I knew the man who attacked her father and, in turn, attacked the Kingdom of Sol.

I began to feel uneasy at the thought. "Are you going to tell your father that tomorrow?"

She paused, contemplating her next words. "I'm going to tell him the truth. Someone attacked us."

"You are going to *tell him* it seemed like he *knew me*?!" The look on my face must have been a window to the anger and rising betrayal I felt; every muscle in my body tensed. "Are you *fucking* joking?"

"No! That was a thought I wanted to discuss with you!" She waved her hands as if she were swatting away the ill intent that had taken hold of the conversation.

"But I am telling him what he said. He needs to know if the man knows of you and might be targeting you."

I didn't know what to think. I felt nauseous, but that might be from the looming concern of how the King would react to that information. I didn't know how to respond, knowing the truth behind Erikka's words.

"We need to go to bed. The morning comes faster than we think," I stated.

Erikka grabbed the top pelted blanket from the bed and walked over to me, placing it over my shoulders. She waited until I looked up at her and kissed me, momentarily relieving the building anger. Then, she walked back over to the bed, removed her dress, and slipped under the covers.

"Oh, before I forget to bring it up. Calder told me I had great potential as a future Queen." She shot up with lightning speed and turned to me, holding the linen to her chest.

"What!?" I couldn't quite see her face since I had turned the oil lamp off, but she sounded embarrassed. "Why would he say that?" *Yeah, that was embarrassment.*

"I have no idea. I thought he had learned about two nights ago somehow. I almost shat myself."

"No. Gods, what the hel. He inquired about my getting married a few nights ago, and I had asked. I ONLY ASKED, 'What if I married a Queen instead'? That's all!" She laid back down and pulled the covers over her face.

"I'm flattered, really." I put my hand on my chest even though I knew she couldn't see me. "I'm guessing he wasn't opposed to the idea, considering he mentioned it to me." I laughed.

"No. He only said it would have to be someone worthy of such a task or something specific like that," she mumbled.

"I see. Well, on that note, goodnight, my Queen." I teased.

She rolled over and tucked herself as far away as possible. "Goodnight."

Twelve

Erikka walked right past me without a glance as she exited the meeting room, arm interlaced with Ulrik as he whisked her down the hallway with two additional guards in tow.

A Royal Guard wearing a mask stepped out of the room. "He will see you now."

As I followed this man, I silently ogled at his sheer size. He had to be part-giant because every inch of his body seemed inhumanly large. Yet, I didn't recognize him, and that planted a seed of doubt within me. Why I didn't know this man or even notice him before today was concerning. He peered back at me, and a blonde curl fell onto his forehead. I pretended not to notice and kept walking. Two guards stood watch outside the door, and as I was escorted in, there were four more, one on watch in front of each window. No, they were posted outside the windows, in the small yard. Calder had clearly increased security precautions, but seven guards for one room seemed excessive, even for him.

The Royal Guards and warriors were only differentiated by skills and abilities. They are both hand-picked by the Royal Family and their advisers after numerous grueling trials before being separated based on their levels of skill mastery.

Those who are quick and excel with restraint when unarming attackers are commissioned as guards. At the same time, those who can wield their weapons masterfully and effectively to kill during structured attacks are tasked as warriors. Those who do not meet the requirements for either position within the royal order or choose not participate in trials are stationed throughout Sol as regular patrol guards. As far as whatever they mentioned yesterday about advanced warriors, I have no clue what that is or why they would need an "advanced" warrior's sector in the first place.

Once I was fully in Calder's presence, I stopped and greeted him with a deep bow. "May you live ten thousand years." I was promptly ignored.

"Leave us. Ensure all guards are posted where they should be and report back." Calder ordered the man who led me into the room.

The masks must be new because I have never seen any royal hands at the castle sport such an odd decorum. The molded steel mask was carved into the face of a wolf covering mainly the eyes, leaving the nose and mouth exposed. He also wore steel armor over the usual Sol warrior attire. The man left without a word. No departing gestures. No verbal acknowledgment. We are always expected to acknowledge the King. Always.

"Take a seat, Veronica." He gestured to a small cluster of chairs in the center of the room stationed in front of his throne that must've been brought down to this room for his use. I could tell Erikka had sat in the center earlier while the guards sat around her. I bowed my head towards him and then took my seat, the surrounding chairs remaining empty.

"You may remove your covering," he stated coldly as he strode over and took his seat. I had worn a black cloth that covered the lower half of my face, starting at the bridge of my nose, and hung loosely below my chin to hide most of the injuries and bruising. Erikka had helped create a fastener with a small chain she twisted through my braid that came out of either side of my bun and clasped the ends of the mask together, securing it to my head. Therefore, I only had to unclip one side at the back, and the covering would fall to expose my face.

"I permit you to speak freely in this meeting." He leaned back in his seat, laying both hands on the armrests, turning still and stoic. Almost as if he turned to stone. "We both know that you acquired your injuries in a different way than what you explained yesterday. However, since there has been such a severe development of events, I will dismiss your dishonesty and insubordination."

"I'm not lying, and I've never been insubordinate." If he was allowing me to speak freely, I was going to take full advantage of it.

"Do you think I am stupid?" *Yes, yes, I do.*

"No, but I know you can't be wrong even if you are." My heart jumped in my throat, stopping more words from flowing. Maybe I should be cautious about this gift of free speech. He raised an eyebrow, a shadow of astonishment passed over his face, then it was gone.

"That is an interesting way to put it." He waved his hand to dismiss the conversation. "Tell me about your experience of the attack. Start with the breach."

Erikka had most likely told him everything. I must explain this without possibly incriminating myself. I took a deep breath in and shifted awkwardly in my chair. The damn dress code he required of me felt significantly more suffocating in situations like this.

"After the branches broke through the windows, I fell to the floor and tried catching my breath while immediately trying to assess the situation. My priority was to find you and analyze from across the room what state you might have been in." He didn't react to my hint at how he had been suffocating me prior to the break-in. No flinch. No eyebrow raises. No shift in position. No remorse.

"I called out to you, but I was quickly closed in by the branches." He kept to himself, waiting for me to continue. "I pulled out my weapons and found myself completely enclosed in some sort of cage? I had no idea what it was or what was happening, but I immediately started cutting away at it to escape and protect you." I paused; he kept waiting. "Once I got out, I ran over to where you laid on the floor and barely made it in time to try striking at the branches and vines growing towards your body."

"*Try* to strike?" he interjected, cocking his head. "Explain."

"I don't understand the confusion. What would you like me to expand on, Your Highness?"

"You *attempted* to strike at the attacker. That implies you missed." He lifted one leg and folded it over the opposite knee, now resting his chin on his hand. *How can someone seem so bored yet be equally as critical?*

"I, actually, didn't have to swing. It stopped attacking as soon as I got in front of you."

"Why?"

I didn't have any words for a moment. It's too early, and I've had too little sleep for this bullshit. *What does he want me to say? Maybe the magical tree branches became so stunned by my beaten and battered beauty that they froze in place.* I straightened my back, interlocked my hands, and delicately placed them on my crossed legs. "I have no idea how or why usually inanimate objects decide to destroy things and attack people."

"Let's skip to what happened after I left you and Erikka in the room." Calder motioned for me to skip ahead in my recounting with a wave of his hand.

"We stayed there for a few minutes while the last few guards left."

"Why did you stay in the room when I had given you clear instructions to initiate lockdown procedures with my daughter?" *Shit.* I could say Erikka wanted to check out the room, but that would be too risky.

"Shock. That was my error for not moving her immediately. Everything hit me at once, and I fumbled with the information or lack thereof."

"You put her life in danger because you were confused about the situation? I thought I had made myself clear with my instructions."

"They were clear. I had a lapse in judgment." He scoffed at my statement, but before he could expand on this error of mine, I tried to move the story along. "Had we not waited a few more minutes, we wouldn't have a description of the man or even known it was a man, for that matter."

His cold eyes narrowed in on mine. "Yes, risking my daughter's *life* to get a glimpse of a man that we still know nothing about is worth your lapse in judgment. Correct?"

"No! That is not what I meant!" I raised my voice at him. My hands gripped the arms of the chair as I became ready to launch myself forward to defend myself. I swear I could hear Bryn's words in the back of my head, straining to rein in that impulsiveness. The King clicked his tongue at me three times as if he were scolding a child. Finally, he stood slowly from his throne and walked over to me, circling like a vulture.

"Now Veronica, I permitted you to speak freely. NOT disrespect me." He stopped in front of me and placed a firm grip on my shoulder. "Remember *that* as we continue." He tightened his grip until I yielded and let him force my back to meet the chair. He did not return to sit on his throne. Instead, he remained standing before me, hands behind his back—a beckoning stance inviting me to play his game like a lure in the ocean.

"I apologize." I maintained eye contact and dipped my head slightly as a gesture of respect.

"Sure. Now, was there a conversation between you?" I'm sure he skipped to this question expecting a particular response. I'm getting annoyed at this 'tell me what I already know' type of questioning.

"Not necessarily. If I remember *correctly*, the attacker only said two things."

His hand shot up. "Remember *correctly*," he demanded sternly. He flashed a wicked grin like a wolf baring its teeth at cornered prey.

"One was a question; one was a statement." I crossed my legs before continuing. *A little pause for effect never hurt anyone.* "'Why did you protect him?' and 'You sound like her.'" Erikka must've held true to what she said because that seemed to have been what he was waiting to hear. Confirmation. Nothing alarmed or concerned him yet.

"How did you respond?"

"It's my job." I know he would only care to hear my answer to the man's question. He wants to know the bounds of my loyalty to the crown. So, I left it at that, hoping my answer would meet his standards.

"Did you say anything else to him during this time?"

"Yes, I responded to his question and then attempted to coax him off the window ledge." He took a breath to speak, but I interjected quickly, "I also shouted after him once he jumped from the ledge. Well, fell...well, not really. He sort of purposefully fell?" He held a hand up to silence me.

"I understand. What did you say to coax the man from the ledge?"

"Come off the ledge." Calder waited for me to add more, but his lips hardened into a thin line once he realized there was nothing more to come. He nodded as he turned to stand next to his throne and monitor the windows. Now that I said it out loud, I sounded like a fucking idiot.

"It seems you need to work on your apprehending ability. Since you are a guard, let it be known that I expect a drastically different approach to your situation." He spoke over his shoulder towards me but didn't make eye contact, probably because he was still suffering from secondhand embarrassment on my behalf.

"I did what I thought was best at the moment. I couldn't just go tackle the man." I swung my arm out toward the windows in the room as if I was showing him the memory from yesterday.

"I have other guards here that could have." His eyebrows raised as he turned to me, proud of his hot-headed meathead warriors.

"That would have exposed Erikka. I wouldn't stray too far from her with just us three in that room. Especially since he was possibly a magic wielder."

"Who told you that?" His question was sudden, and he turned to face me abruptly, walking in my direction. I paused, confused.

"Wha–I was in the room when the man appeared? I am only assuming because when he appeared, the branches completely disappeared. Wouldn't that indicate an ability?"

"DON'T question me!" He stormed over and braced his hands on the back of my chair, parallel to my head. My eyes widened, and I sank into the chair to avoid any potential physical repercussions. Someone suddenly entered the room unannounced, and Calder dropped his hands to his sides, switching to a calm demeanor effortlessly. The unannounced guest spoke without permission.

"Guards are where they are supposed to be." He stood there, waiting for Calder's response. I didn't dare look at the man whose presence I could now feel looming directly behind me—no need to encourage a group disciplinary session.

"Replace your covering." Calder returned to sit on his throne, and once my covering was secured, he waved the man forward, who then heavily dragged one of the chairs across the floor to set it directly in front of me. It was the masked man from earlier, and his oversized torso was partially blocking the King's view. *Wow, this guy is something else.* He must not give a shit about Calder in general. I don't understand why the King allows this man to act as if he were an equal?

The man turned curiously and took only a few seconds to look me over before he got caught in my eyes.

"What is your name?" he questioned. His voice was harsh, almost scratchy.

"*Do not* answer his questions." Calder boomed from behind him. The man turned partially to give a half-ass bow in Calder's direction before turning back to me and did not speak again.

"I need you to explain the description of the man you encountered yesterday in every detail to him. Once you are finished, he will escort you back to your quarters for your rest period. Do not speak to him unless instructed by me. Do you understand?"

"Yes, your Majesty."

Once I finished recounting every detail of the attacker from the day before, I motioned at the King to let him know I was done so he could dismiss me. Well...us, considering the masked man stayed no less than half a step behind me the whole time. A bit excessive, considering I am a guard myself, but I expect nothing less from Calder at this point. We finally made it to the last hall just before my room when he broke the uncomfortable silence.

"If I may, you have the most intriguing eyes."

"You may not." I didn't look at him and kept forward, even though I could feel his stare weighing heavily on me from behind his metal facade.

"Ah, not one for following orders, are you?" He pulled his eyes off me and nodded as if taking a mental note. *What is this guy's deal?* I sped up my pace, but he kept up with me easily.

"You're one to talk." I retorted, annoyed. Any attempt at controlling myself flew out the window. I stretched my neck to try and ease the growing tension.

"Touché." I didn't respond, and we continued the rest of the way in silence, the sound of our footsteps colliding against the stone walls. We reached my room, and I went to open my door, but the man's large hand grabbed the knob first and held it shut.

"My name is Vali," he offered, bowing his head slightly so he could look into my eyes from under his mask. His eyes were silver. Not the gray-blue like Calder's, but actually silver, matching the hue of the steel that covered his face. I'm not sure how I didn't notice them in the meeting room, but they are very bright now, almost illuminated.

"I didn't ask." I reminded him sweetly, giving him a slight curtsy. He laughed quietly, but the hushed sound came from deep in his chest.

"It has been quite a pleasure to make your acquaintance this morning." He stood straight again, now towering over me.

"Has it?" A vexed question. I motioned for him to remove his hand so I could enter my room, but he remained there, staring down at me and smiling gently.

My heart began to shrink as the moments passed, an eerie feeling overcoming me quickly. I went to slide my hand over my short sword when he abruptly stepped back from the door. His eyes seemed to dim as he stepped out of the shadow he had created between us.

"What should I call you? If you will give me no name." He placed a hand over his chest while tucking the other behind his back.

"Nothing. As the King has ordered me not to answer any of your questions, information about me must be inconsequential." I remained turned halfway so as to not turn my back to him while I unlocked my door lazily—an attempt to keep my façade of aloof annoyance.

"Well, I look forward to seeing you again, *nothing*." He bowed again, and I could feel those silver eyes calling mine. Instead, I entered my room without looking back.

"Likewise." I offered shortly before engaging the lock swiftly.

Thirteen

I was awoken by a persistent light knocking at my door. I pried my eyes open, threw the blankets to the side, and sat up, running my hands down my face. My room was still enveloped with general darkness from the curtain I had pulled over the window, but it seemed later in the afternoon, which meant no more sleep for Veronica.

Knock...Knock...Knock...Jiggle.

I shuffled over to the small chair next to the door and flung on Erikka's robe that she had left from the night before. When I opened the door, she stood there in a beautiful lilac evening gown, which emphasized her waist and flowed freely to the floor. The dress had thicker armbands that draped loosely off her shoulders with delicate golden vines and flowers precisely embroidered throughout, matching the crown on top of her head. The phoenix and peony pendant she is required to wear was secured to her chest. Her hair was pulled up into a loose, twisted bun secured at the nape of her neck. She was, once again, the perfect Princess. One I am currently drooling at.

She cleared her throat, "I'm sorry for intruding on your rest period." Her gaze scanned my body, and she stifled a laugh, clearing her throat again. I looked at myself, knowing I was completely naked under her robe, and hugged the fabric a little tighter around me.

"My hair is a mess, isn't it?" I whispered to her. She nodded and tried her best to keep her composure. I stepped out and glanced down the hall to find Ulrik waiting a few rooms away.

"You still have a few hours until your scheduled shift, and I had the rest of my evening cleared, so I wanted to ask if you could accompany me to the hot spring? It's wash day." I noticed her fiddling with her fingers. I looked up to find an eyebrow raised. I sucked my bottom lip in between my teeth.

"Of course, Your Highness. It would be my honor." I announced. "Let me get dressed, and I will walk with you. Is that okay?"

"That is all right with me."

When I opened the door again, I offered her my arm and led her down to the private bathing quarters reserved solely for the Royal Family's use. Ulrik followed silently behind us. As we approached the backside of the rock formation that protected the spring from prying eyes, she wet her lips and turned to Ulrik, who had stopped beside us.

"Ulrik, I will be spending the majority of your shift here. Do not interrupt my time unless there is a life-threatening emergency." She didn't wait for his response as she walked around the rocks, disappearing to the other side. Ulrik turned and stationed himself on the outside of the naturally formed wall. I flipped him my middle finger before stepping through it, following Erikka's lead.

"How has he been today?" I asked, turning to find her fumbling with the strings at the back of her dress.

"Nothing less than tiresome." I reached out to help her loosen her gown, but she turned to face me. "Don't. I can handle it myself." She continued to undress while I walked over to the edge of the hot spring. A small waterfall kept the pool filled, and I stuck my hand under the flowing water. It was the perfect degree of warmth, so much so that it sent chills up my arm.

"How was your debriefing?" I grabbed my comb from the small bathing bag I had taken with me and pulled it through my hair, waiting for her response. I paused mid-stroke when she didn't answer. I stepped towards her and gave her a confused look as she laid her dress across a rock bench near the outer wall. I cleared my throat to get her attention.

"I've been strictly bound by a vow of silence," she answered plainly, turning her back to me. She sat on the edge of a rock closer to the spring in her pale purple undergarments, saying nothing more.

"So, you are going to leave me in the dark on this one? Really?" I turned and threw the hairbrush onto my bag, facing her and crossing my arms across my chest. No response. Instead of explaining anything to me, she crossed her legs and neatly stacked her hands on her knees. *So, I'm speaking to Princess Kron, am I?* "Even after you insinuated I might have known the intruder and didn't even look at me when you passed by leaving your meeting this morning?" *Am I crazy? Or am I not owed an explanation?*

"Some orders need to be followed despite your personal beliefs."

"I follow orders." I retorted sourly, standing my ground.

"You follow orders when you know you can't keep the repercussions to a minimum. And that's just orders, Veronica. Need I get into laws?" She kept her voice level and low but held out her hand as if she were holding evidence of this in her empty palm.

"What the fuck does that mean?" I dropped my arms to my side, completely taken aback by what she said. My chest felt tight, with what emotion I couldn't decipher.

"Do you think I'm blissfully ignorant just because I don't beat you for hiding things from me?" She questioned in a way that made my stomach turn. I have never felt this way around her. Probably because she puts on this façade of ignorance and indifference when I brush off her questions. It turns out she has noted every time I do. Words couldn't form. *Why have I never questioned her on not pushing me on these things?* The bruises and cuts I never explain. I have never thought about her theories or whether she put any thought behind them in the first place. I wonder what laws she might think I'm breaking and why she keeps that to herself.

"Even now, I'm not going to question you about it. Because, like I've said before, I understand my title creates walls. I can only trust that I know you and your heart; whatever you aren't telling me is coming from a good place. For a worthy cause. Whatever that is, though, I have no fucking idea." She kept her voice lowered and glanced at the opening between the rocks, a reminder of possible ears on the other side.

I said nothing. To pick a question from the mass that has collected at the forefront of my mind was too difficult. So, I remained silent.

"So, I'm sorry, but I am not going into any details from my debriefing. It is for everyone's safety. Especially *yours*." Princess Kron spoke in finality and brought her hands back to her knee.

I nodded in silent acceptance and turned my back to her. I undressed myself and stepped into the hot spring. The scalding water calmed my frantic and confused emotions, eliminating clusters of rushing thoughts with each step further into the water. I waded over and stood underneath the waterfall until my mind was clear and my skin burned.

Time passed quickly while I remained stoic in my safe space of utter nothingness. Erikka slipped in the spring behind me, but I couldn't hear her over the roaring water that pounded against my head. Before I could pull myself out of my semi-conscious state, I felt her behind me, wrapping her arms to hug me, holding me so my back was against her chest while she rested her head between my shoulders.

"May I join you?" she asked, her voice breaking through the veil that kept me in a faraway place.

"Lose the Princess act, and I'll stay, considering you're already in here," I answered firmly, ready to step back into that veil of safety I was warily emerging from.

"I get submerged by it. I don't mea–"

"I don't want to talk about it anymore. It's been a stressful week for both of us. Let's leave it at that." I interrupted cautiously. I pulled her arms out from around me and turned to face her, shielding her from most of the falling water. In turn, she lowered her eyes to where my hands lay within hers. I reached up to cup her face to guide her eyes back to mine. "Do you trust me?" I questioned, wanting confirmation on what she mentioned earlier.

"Yes, fully," she answered in a whisper.

I pulled her face closer, leaving only an inch or two between our mouths. I looked deeply into her eyes, which resembled clear meltwater, freshly released from its icy entrapment in the spring, and saw only my closest friend at this moment. "Then I trust you fully," I said confidently, letting the weight of uncertainty fall off my shoulders.

She reached a hand behind my head and pulled in to kiss me, long and hard. A feeling of relief settled between us, and one of need took its place. Instantly, we were feeling, grabbing, and holding onto this moment. We needed this. We deserved it. *Didn't we?*

Erikka's mouth moved to my ear while she slid a hand between my legs. Her fingers started to slowly massage around my opening, which pulled my hips with her in anticipation of their entry. She found my lips with hers again, and as her tongue entered my mouth, she slipped a finger inside me. Warmth spread upwards through my torso, and as I sucked her tongue further into my mouth, she pushed further into me. The motion she created with her finger matched the dance of our tongues.

I pushed my forehead against her, separating our mouths in an attempt to catch my breath. She removed herself from me briefly before the pressure between my legs increased as she pushed two fingers back inside, using her thumb to play with the sensitive spot near the top of my groin. I moaned breathlessly and let my head roll back. The water from the outer edge of the fall slipped past my face, spraying my neck and trickling down my chest. Her soft lips trailed kisses towards my breast and enclosed on its hardened tip, sucking it, my nipple meeting the wet roughness of her tongue.

She kept a steady rhythm as she pumped her fingers in and out, up and down, rubbing my bundle of nerves with the right amount of pressure to allow for a proper buildup of anticipation. Finally, my breathing started to quicken, and I brought my forehead down to press against hers, anchoring myself by holding onto the back of her neck with both hands. I flexed the muscles surrounding her fingers, and she caressed them in return, sending me over the edge.

She grabbed my mouth with hers as an intense heat spread across my entire being. I felt every inch of my body release the stress it had clenched onto all week, all at once, spinning my head in ecstasy. I could feel my muscles contracting and relaxing around the fingers she let linger inside me. A sweet embrace of gratitude for their service. She slowly pulled her fingers from me, forcing my legs to tremble slightly in response.

I pulled our mouths apart and watched as she lifted the hand that had just pleasured me towards her face before she put one finger in her mouth and slowly removed it, sucking the remnants of me from it. I grabbed her hand to stop her from continuing to the second finger and brought her hand towards me, coaxing it into my mouth with my tongue. Erikka's eyes lowered, and she ran her tongue over her bottom lip, dragging it between her teeth. I guided her to the edge of the spring and lifted her to sit on top of it, exposing her torso to the chilled air while her legs lingered in the hot water.

I watched as the tips of her breasts hardened, and I ran my hands up the inside of her legs, spreading them apart in one swift motion. I leaned in to kiss one thigh, then the other. I wrapped my hands around her ass and scooted her to the edge before slowly caressing the silky skin of her torso, massaging her breasts. I applied a little pressure to push her back against the rocky floor, and she gasped at the quick introduction to the coldness. I crept my kisses up her leg, switching from the inside of one to the other. Spending time teasing her like this has made my arousal spike even more.

I laid a final kiss just above her apex before completely imprisoning her with my mouth. She pushed into me with surprise at the suddenness of my decision. I want her to experience the euphoria I felt, better than my own.

I guided her legs from being spread open to lay over the top of my shoulders, swirling my tongue around her more sensitive area. I spelled my name at least a couple of times before moving lower. I reached up, palmed her breast as I opened my mouth, and licked up her center. Her hips rolled in time with my movement as if my taste buds were latching onto her skin, dragging her with me on my way up. I repeated this once more before going even lower and ran my hands down her legs before anchoring my grip around her thighs and pulling her into me.

I felt her opening with my tongue and tasted the change in consistency of the liquid that gathered there. I swirled my tongue along its edges, holding off on making my entrance until she shoved a hand into my hair and used her legs to pull me towards her, nearly begging me to make my way past the barrier.

I did as she requested and slipped my tongue inside, reaching as far as possible. She released a moan that made me catch fire, sending me into a frenzy. I made sure my tongue would remember every curve of hers, moving my tongue in and out, studying the walls that encompassed it before I reintroduced my fingers. Her breath caught again, and her fingers tightened their grip on my hair.

I grabbed her knee and pushed one leg to the side, and Erikka mirrored the desired position with her other one. I stood above her and pushed and pulled my fingers inside her. I watched her face twist in utter pleasure as she looked up at me, completely open and bare, asking for more as she squeezed her own breast. *Yes, Your Majesty.* I removed my fingers and lowered my mouth back to the bundle of nerves, pushing her legs out to the side. Erikka was writhing against me in full force while I sucked and licked her folds, grinding against me confidently, moaning shamelessly toward the sky above us. She looked stunning, empowered even. If this is what it took for her to find this type of energy, I will offer my services daily.

Her moaning grew louder and more frequent. I returned my fingers inside, curving them to rub against her walls. I kept my pace fixed and opened my mouth to run the middle of my tongue flat over her apex, over and over, until she collapsed into herself and tightened against my fingers. The quick pulsing of her release around me was a feeling I wanted to recreate immediately.

I guided her as she slid lifelessly back into the hot spring, keeping my fingers inside as she finished riding her orgasm. She wrapped her arms around my neck and legs around my waist before I removed myself. I made sure to move just as painfully slow as she had done to me. I followed up with a cheeky smile and stuck a finger in my mouth to taste her a final time. She leaned forward, and I placed my other one on her awaiting tongue, and she sucked on it, taking with her the lingering evidence of our pleasure. She leaned into me as I lowered us both into the water.

"I love you," she whispered.

"I love you too." I smiled, and we finished bathing ourselves. We both dressed and let Ulrik accompany us back to my room. His face was red, and I noted the bulge in his pants. I let out a small laugh as we passed him, and he cleared his throat, visibly uncomfortable.

"It is almost time to retire for the night, Princess," Ulrik announced.

"I will be spending the night at Veronica's quarters, per usual." She responded, and he nodded, falling silently behind us. When we got to my room, Erikka continued to ready herself for bed while I got ready for my night shift. When it was time for me to send Ulrik on his way, I creaked open the door and waited for him to turn toward me before speaking.

"I've got it from here." I offered the best sarcastic smile I could conjure up.

"I hope you aren't easily distracted," he spat at me. *Jealous, are we?* I snorted a laugh.

"Don't worry. I make moves when I'm off-duty," I offered sincerely. "It seems to carry a higher success rate than being a prick while you're working." He shot a nasty look at me and then turned to head down the hallway. I locked the door and turned the light off just as Erikka crawled onto my pathetic sleeping pad.

"Why do you instigate?" she asked quietly with a light laugh.

"It brings me joy," I answered in a mischievous tone as I took a seat in my trusty wooden chair. "Sleep well."

Fourteen

I still wore my face covering as Mazen, Erikka, and I walked through the cramped servant hallways. We were nearing the door that leads to the barn when Erikka spoke.

"I bet you can't wait to be rid of that."

I glanced over, but her eyes kept forward as a Princess is expected. There is no need to address who you speak to when everyone is to be attentive toward your every breath in the first place. I emphasized my eye roll with a gentle elbow to her arm, making her turn her head to look at me incredulously.

"Excuse me, Princess, but I would have to disagree with you. I have enjoyed wearing whatever face I want without anyone seeing it."

Both she and Mazen shook their heads at my statement as we approached the door. I reached for Erikka's hand and stopped walking. She looked down, confused at my action, while Mazen peered at me from behind her.

"I'll go get Arvak ready," he offered plainly. I nodded at him, and he stepped through the door, leaving it open slightly to allow bright morning light to shine across the wall of the darkened hallway. Erikka reached up and unclipped one side of the covering, letting it fall.

"Everything has healed. I don't know why you still need to wear it." She ran her fingers lightly around where my eye had previously homed a bruise. Her eyes glanced over my mouth, and the corner of her lips turned down. "Except that one...I couldn't stop that from scarring."

"It gives me character." I laughed as I reached up to rest my hand on top of hers that was now cupping my face. "Don't apologize. Or. Stop apologizing for anything I bring onto myself."

"I can't help it. I'm s-"

"Ah, Ah!" I held my hand up, stopping her from speaking. "Going forward, if you choose to apologize for this," I motioned at my face, "I will hit you in public, earning a rightful beat down from the man himself. Then, only then, would that be an appropriate time to apologize. Because that would *definitely* be your fault." Her mouth dropped open, and I snorted at her look of utter bewilderment. "Hey, drastic times call for drastic measures."

"Oh my," she said with a smile. "Despite the harshness of your deal, I'll allow it." She eyed my mouth again, and a needy smile cracked at the corner of her mouth. "It's not the worst-looking scar."

I held her face in both hands and pulled her in to kiss her. When I pulled away, I offered a quiet "Thank you, Your Highness," but Erikka grabbed my waist and pulled me back for another one. A knock on the door signaled it was time for me to exit.

"Try not to come back with more injuries, okay? Be safe." She pleaded quietly.

"I'll be safe. I'll see you next week." I offered in return. I stepped away from her, and our hands tore apart. I opened the door, and Mazen was waiting on the other side, with Arvak ready to go. I took the reins from him, and he stepped back into the hallway next to Erikka, holding the door open until she informed him she was finished speaking with me.

"Give Brynjar a hug for me."

"As always, of course." I bowed halfway at the waist, then mounted up onto Arvak. She nodded at Mazen, and he gave me a slight nod before closing the door. I clipped my face covering back in place and headed to the gate at the outskirts of the inner city. As I rode up, I saw Ulrik waiting with a small group of guards—my payment for the week in his hand.

"Ulrik! My favorite person in the Kingdom! I am beyond honored that you are delivering my payment this week." I announced in an over-friendly manner. I clasped my hands together at my chest to sell my role-playing.

"Miss Leif, the honor is mine." He played with me in return. I have a love-hate relationship with having an audience when Ulrik and I get the chance to speak. Right now is one of the instances I thoroughly enjoy it.

"Don't make me blush." I offered my hand out for him to put the satchel in. I noticed the rest of the guards sharing a look with each other, confused at the sudden friendliness between the two of us. "I look forward to this day the most. When you give me coin for making your acquaintance, I get to experience for a moment what it's like to be a woman in your life." He couldn't see my smile, but it was as wicked as they come.

He lowered his head and forced a laugh under his breath. He handed my payment to me and attempted to speak, but I would not allow him. Instead, I signaled Arvak to move forward, forcing Ulrik to take a few steps back before we sprinted across the bridge. I saluted him with my middle finger and yelled, "THANK YOU!"

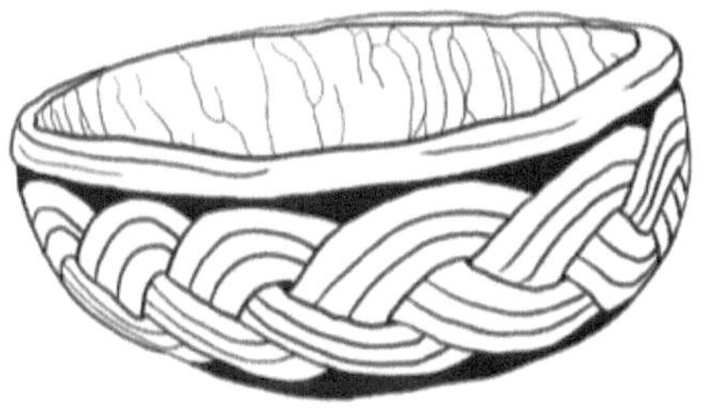

Fifteen

I dismounted from Arvak while outside Jerrik's shop and fastened the reins to the hitching rail before I set her up with her midday snack. I opened the heavy wooden door and stepped inside to find Jerrik with his back turned to me, entertaining a customer with his selection of leather corsets. I took the opportunity to slip in between some of the racks of cloaks and blend in with the environment, hoping to surprise him once he finished.

"Come back anytime," he called out to his visiting patrons. I could hear his smile in his voice. "Now, how can I help you today?" He had turned to question me, as his voice sounded significantly clearer and more direct, but I couldn't see him past the racks I stood between.

I watched as his large frame projected a shadow that grew when he drew closer to me. He placed his thick hands on the top of the rack I stood behind and peered over the top.

"Hey, Jerrik!" I greeted him abruptly, which caused him to jump. Then, I pushed my way through the center of the cloak rack and came out the other side to wrap my arms around his waist for a hug.

"Ver-Veronica? Wait, Veronica!" He gasped aloud. He put his hands on my shoulders and pushed me away from him, looking me over with worry.

"What are you doing, Jer?" I questioned, annoyed that he didn't reciprocate my enthusiasm.

"Are you okay? Are you hurt?" He fired off his questions while lifting my arms and checking my face. I flailed my arms around and took a few steps back to get him to stop.

"I'm fine! What the hel are you doing?" I demanded.

"Are you sure? We heard about the breach at the castle! You and the King were at the center of it. Are you okay?" he exclaimed, a concerned look on his face.

"Oh. Um, how do you know about that?" I asked, scanning the store for signs of any patrons who might be lingering. I pulled him lightly by the arm towards the back of the store, away from the shuttered windows neighboring us.

"The entire Kingdom should know by now. The King issued an announcement about the incident and told everyone to be on the lookout for a suspect. What happened?"

"I can't talk about it here," I clarified under my breath. "But I'm okay. All good!" I offered sincerely. He nodded in understanding but kept an interrogating eye on me as he headed behind the counter.

"Elias, I'm taking Veronica to the tavern!" He yelled toward the back rooms of the shop.

"Wait, Elias is here?" I marveled at Jerrik with wide eyes as if it was the morning of the winter solstice. "We can snack here! I haven't spent time with him yet." I suggested eagerly.

"You haven't spent time with ME. So, we are going to the tavern." he reiterated, crossing his arms over the broadest part of his chest. Elias appeared and raised an eyebrow at our stand-off.

"You guys go ahead, and I'll keep an eye on things here. We can all go out next time," he urged shyly. He had his long hair tied up in a high ponytail today and had some dust and dirt smudged across his face.

"Thank you, Elias. Since Veronica promised me last time, I want to make sure she keeps her word. Otherwise, I would have you come along." Jerrik assured him as he stepped to the side to grab a towel to hand him.

"I understand completely." He smiled in response as he wiped the towel down his face. Jerrik smiled at him lovingly, and I turned my eyes away. I am so far behind in the development of this relationship that I have no idea how to act around them. They seem as if they have known each other for years. *Where have I been?*

"Thank you, Elias. I'm sorry he is being a stickler on my verbiage, but I hope next time Jerrik will share you with me." I laughed and shot Jerrik a dirty look before waving and heading toward the front door.

"I'll be here! If I don't see you, Veronica, it's been a pleasure." Elias called from inside as Jerrik shoved me through the front door.

"Geez, Jerrik! What's the deal?" I questioned while I untied Arvak.

"I have limited time with you as it is. If you two were to start talking...Gods. I know it wouldn't stop." He laughed to himself and offered to hold the reins while we walked to The Dark Sun, which made me smile. We walked the rest of the way in a comfortable silence, both of us running off with whatever thoughts had grabbed our attention at the moment.

The tavern sat toward the center of Exris, surrounded by shops, small inns, and smaller taverns that all seemed stacked on top of one another. However, The Dark Sun Tavern is Sol's largest building outside the inner walls. The first floor was built out of stone, with a solid base for the second level that hung over every side, almost as if the building had been turned upside down. The weathered wood used to build the second level brings a welcoming look during the day but a terrifying one under the cover of the night.

We tied Arvak to the side of the building and walked around to enter through the large double front doors. Once we stepped inside, the mid-morning light immediately choked out and dissipated from the lack of windows. Instead, the large chandeliers hanging from the center of the room offered a warm light, with a balcony running along the upper floor overlooking them.

"Check your weapons at the door," ordered a man who stepped into our path. He was no taller than me but was twice as large and grungy. He wore an eye patch over one eye and offered no friendliness in his stare.

"You got it, Ragnar," Jerrik answered and saluted him as he turned around and put his fists on his hips.

"Right." I huffed. I walked over to an empty hook in the crowded entryway and unfastened every knife and sword I had worn coming from the castle. All save the small knife on my ankle, which I pushed further down into my boot in hopes Ragnar wouldn't notice it while I removed the knives around my thighs. Ragnar raised an eyebrow at me when I turned around.

"What?" I demanded. I threw my arms out to my sides and spun in a circle to show I held no more weapons. He held out his hand to stop another patron from coming in and waved us in before turning his full attention to them. Jerrik led me past the couple dozen wooden tables sprinkled with villagers toward the long bar opposite the entrance. He waved at the woman who stood against the wall, cleaning a mug out with a rag.

I last visited the tavern a few months ago, but the tavern keeper is a woman you couldn't forget even if you tried. Her smooth ebony skin shone, complementing her deep maroon dress that donned a slit from the hem up to her hip, showcasing her toned leg. Her thigh-length apron was pulled off to the side and tucked under a white corset that almost matched her hair and accentuated her bust. Her coiled hair framed her face and was pulled back slightly with a matching maroon scarf that cascaded down her bare back. When the woman's frosty blue eyes met mine and Jerrik's, she blessed us with a smile as bright as the full moon as she made her way toward us.

"Gods! Veronica Leif, it's been ages!" Her usual raucous voice had gone hoarse. I'm sure it was from keeping these brutes in constant check.

"Rune!" I smiled and reached over the top of the counter for her, and she met me in the middle for a giant hug.

"I see you have a new facial adornment," she nodded at the scar on my lip. "Staying busy, are we?"

"As busy as I need to be. How have things been?"

"Typical. I just put that poor bastard in his place just before you walked in, actually." She nodded towards a guy sitting at one of the booths in the back corner of the tavern. He held a rag to his busted eye, and blood stained his teeth red. I looked back at Rune and scanned her over, but there was no sign she had just forced blood from someone. I shook my head in awe.

"Rune, I love you dearly. However, my time with Veronica is fleeting. Do you mind giving us some time?" Jerrik suggested with pleading eyes and an outstretched hand with a coin offering in his palm. Rune eyed the offering in his hand, then looked at me, embarrassed.

"I hope you find comfort in knowing that I must be bribed to leave you alone, hun." She leaned over the counter for another hug, and I met her halfway. She kissed my cheek before assuring me, "Come back SOON. We can catch up then. I'll get you two something to eat."

"I'll make it a priority next time I'm in town." I smiled and turned back to Jerrik, my face falling flat with annoyance. "*Really*, Jerrik?"

"Do you blame me? You have been telling me we would do this for months," he argued. Rune put two mugs of mead on the counter before us and a plate of cheeses and meats. Jerrik picked up a small block of cheese and tossed it into his mouth, raising his eyebrows at me in anticipation of a retort.

"No...but you don't need to come off so rude towards everyone." I took a sip of my drink and gave him a sideways glance.

"I've not been rude!" He clamored.

"We can agree to disagree. Moving on." I declared, waving my hand in the air. "You, catch me up to speed with Elias."

"Tell me about the castle." He pushed, setting his mug down on the counter.

"I can't. But I might give you some details on the way to the edge of town if you tell me about Elias." I counter-offered. He shot me a skeptical glare, then raised his mug at me in agreeance.

"Fine. Ask me what you want to know," he grumbled, taking a drink.

"Are you guys an official thing?"

"Not as of right now."

"What's the hold-up?" I questioned through narrowed eyes.

"What's the rush?" He retorted with a mirrored look.

"Touché..." I paused, contemplating what I wanted to know next. "How long have you guys known each other exactly? Sylve mentioned he has been going on your hunting trips for a while. Is that how you guys met?" I asked while stuffing blocks of cheese into my cheeks.

"A few months now. I first met Elias when he came into my shop looking for a gift for his mother. Since then, he has volunteered to help with our hunting excursions since before the winter solstice."

"Wow, where have I been?" I pondered aloud, trying to access my shitty memory for any idea of what I might've been doing to miss this series of events.

"Ha ha! I hadn't noticed his intention until Sylve brought it up a few weeks ago. So, we have only been exploring a more meaningful relationship since then."

"Well, things must be going well enough. You left him to run your shop?"

"He had offered a few times to help me out when I needed to be in multiple places at once. I let him watch over it once before, and it went smoothly." He shrugged off how huge a deal that actually was. Jerrik hadn't even let Sylve and I run his store so he could run a quick errand. *Elias must be important to him.*

"Do you...*trust* him?" I asked while taking a sip from my mug. He hesitated to answer, letting his eyes wander to the wooden counter. I waved my hand in front of him to get his attention.

"I'm not sure. I'll need more time."

I nodded my head in understanding. "Well, I think it's time for me to head home." We finished the rest of the food and chugged the final ounces of our drinks before heading out. I scanned the tavern to find Rune and waved goodbye. Once I had finally reattached my weapons, I flipped a coin to the weapons keeper and sent him a wink. "Thank you for your service, brother." He looked at me with his one good eye as if he wished someone would come and punch me in the face. *Tough crowd.*

While we walked to the edge of Exris, I tried my best to explain what had happened during the attack without speaking openly at face value. We've long since established a code word system for my job elements, so he can stay up-to-date for the most part. There are so many curious ears in town that it's never safe to assume your conversations are your own.

"Thank you for making my day and sticking to your word." Jerrik praised me with an honest smile.

"There is nothing I enjoy more than being held prisoner to my word." I teased and offered a curtsy. "Next time, maybe Elias can join us," I emphasized with a raised eyebrow.

"Of course. As she requests." He bowed in response before pulling me in for a hug. I was lost instantly between his bulging arms and chest. I attempted to move my face so I could breathe, but he only squeezed me tighter. So, I reciprocated his action in exchange for my release. "I love you, girl," he added with a strong squeeze of my shoulder.

"I love you too. I'll see you soon," I responded with a light punch to his stomach before climbing onto Arvak's back and waving back at him as I headed home to Lykke.

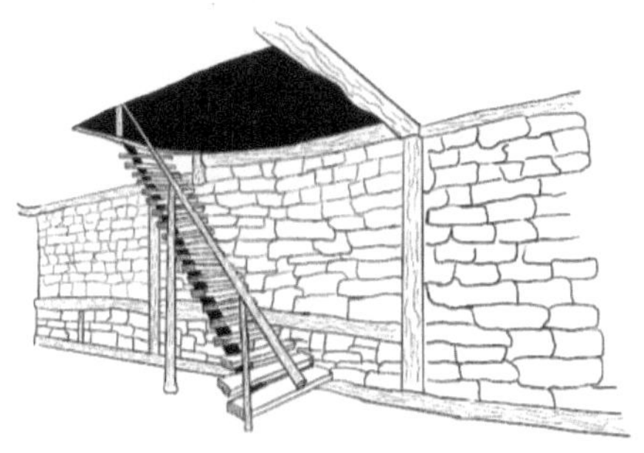

Sixteen

A few houses down from the Inn, I heard Brax barking excitedly. He ran towards us at full speed, his tongue hanging out the side of his mouth like a maniac. Arvak reared nervously, and I didn't blame her. If I saw that thing running at me, I would probably turn and run, too. I dismounted and gave her neck a reassuring stroke before telling her to wait while I walked a few paces ahead to greet the threat at hand...One that was not showing any signs of slowing down. I braced myself lower to the ground, but it didn't help. Brax barreled into one of my legs, which sent me sprawling backwards to the ground.

"Gods dammit, Brax," I muttered under my breath as I pushed myself back onto my feet. Brax jumped on my back, pushing me to my hands and knees, and slapped me in the face with his slobbery tongue. "Hey, buddy," I laughed between his attack of kisses.

"Veronica!?" I heard Bryn's distinctive voice bellow from down the street. When I turned my head to look for him, I saw him running towards me at a speed I didn't know he could achieve at his age. I pushed Brax off from on top of me, lucky that he seemed to have gotten his craziness out because as soon as I stood, Bryn slammed into me, folding me into his arms. I lost my breath from the impact.

"Bryn." I squeaked between breaths. "Wha-I'm okay." I tapped on his back a few times with my fingers before he released me, but only to arm's length. His face was murderous, but even through his anger, tears glistened on his cheeks.

"What did he do to you?" He croaked, placing his warm palm on my cheek and running his thumb over where my injuries had been when I last saw him.

"Nothing. Calder didn't touch me."

"Don't *lie* to me, girl!" he warned.

"I'm not! He didn't touch me." I offered softly, hoping he would accept my word as truth.

"Was there actually an attack on the castle?"

"Yes." I answered quickly.

His eyebrows raised with concern and confusion. I noticed movement coming from behind him, and when I peered over his shoulder, Sylve and Sindre were quickly closing the distance between us. Bryn pulled his hands away and turned to open the conversation to them.

"Gods...she's okay," Sylve commented breathlessly. Her arms were wrapped around my neck within the next moment.

"I told you she could hold her own," Sindre reassured as he clapped a hand onto Bryn's shoulder. "We almost had to tie him to a post. He was adamant about going to the castle to make sure you were alive." I looked at Bryn, who didn't shy away from the eye contact, confident that he thought that was the right thing to do.

"Why would you think I wasn't alive?"

"The official announcement didn't state whether you or the King survived the attack," Sylve answered, stepping around me to gather Arvak. "All it said was, 'There has been a breach at Kron Castle. King Calder, along with personal Royal Guard Veronica Leif, were at the center of the attack. Keep a look out for the culprit.' Then they described what the attacker supposedly looked like."

"Wha-Why would they word an announcement like that?" I questioned, looking back at Bryn, who had grabbed Arvak from Sylve and started towards the Inn.

"It's getting dark. We can talk about it inside," Bryn advised. Sindre stood there with his hands on his hips. Sylve kissed me on the cheek before patting her brother on the shoulder on her way toward the house.

"I've never seen him so worried," Sindre whispered.

"I had no idea they sent out an announcement. I would've written if I knew that." He walked over and put an arm around me, pulling me in to walk beside him.

"I'm glad you're okay. We were all worried." I wrapped my arm around his waist and took a couple of steadying breaths. I wasn't prepared for this reaction upon my arrival. *I should have thought about them and what they might be thinking.* Of course, there would be an announcement. The fucking castle was breached. Why didn't I even consider that? *I should have written anyway, as they were worried for other reasons before I left.* I was so wrapped up with Erikka in all my spare time it didn't even cross my mind. *Gods, what is wrong with me?*

Sindre cleared his throat and stepped in front of me to open the door. I didn't even realize I had just been staring at it. We walked in, and I plopped on the couch, laying my head back for a second. Sylve sat next to me while Sindre opted to lean on the hearth. Bryn came in a few minutes later after setting Arvak up in her stall. I shot my eyes towards the stairs and then back at Sylve. She offered me a reassuring smile.

"We moved them to Frith a few days ago. All clear."

"Is everything ready for tonight?" I asked the room, but no one jumped to answer, which was odd.

"When was the last time you slept?" Bryn asked plainly.

"Uhm...Yesterday?" I answered, rolling my neck around.

"We rescheduled the raid for tomorrow night in anticipation that you would need rest." Sindre chimed in.

"You didn't need to do that. I've participated in raids with less rest." I offered, looking to Bryn to confirm that I could be reliable despite being sleep deprived. Instead, he just shook his head at me.

"We needed to make sure you were alive. The rest part is more for all of us." Sylve added, placing a hand on my leg.

"I'm sorry for not writing. I would've if-" Bryn raised his hand to interject.

"We need to know the extent of this breach."

"It was just me and the King during the initial attack. Then Erikka and I were there when the man appeared." Sindre shifted his stance, more attentive.

"Why were you two alone?" Bryn asked, his face darkening.

"We were meeting to discuss my injuries." I shifted to sit on my crossed legs, and Brax jumped up to sit next to Sylve. Then, out of the corner of my eye, I caught her looking away from me.

"What does that mean?" Sindre asked, crossing his arms over his chest. *Here we go, initiate damage control.*

"He was questioning what caused my injuries to be so intense, but we had only gotten a few minutes into the meeting when the breach happened. His consensus was that I needed to wear a face covering the remainder of my shift."

"Ridiculous!" Sindre emphasized with a wave of his hand. "Said injuries seem to have all but vanished. Why would you need a covering?"

"Well, I have Erikka and Astrid to thank for that. The healing pastes they concoct are magical." I contended, internally thanking the Gods that they, in fact, did work like magic and have since completely healed most signs of injury.

"A *coincidence* that the Royal Family has access to such materials." Sindre countered, his voice dripping with sarcasm as he tilted his head forward to lock eyes with me.

"I'm not following," Sylve cut in, looking between the two of us.

"To have available at the castle some magical healing paste that completely heals wounds in what, two days? With access to something like that, we would never know if you acquired any injury during your time at the castle. *Would we?*" He was analyzing me, waiting for me to give him something. *I'm so tired of this stupid fucking game.*

"The only injuries I acquired from my time at the castle were from the breach." I reiterated.

"I trust her word, Sindre. Things could have turned out a lot worse." Bryn chimed in. "The castle breach may have been your saving grace," he added before stepping into the kitchen. He returned with a bowl of warm food and a mug of freshly brewed chamomile tea. *Mmmmm.*

I finished retelling the events as requested, hoping this would be the last, and placed my empty tea mug down on the small table.

"We can talk more tomorrow, but we will head home now and let you rest." Sylve said as she stood and motioned for Sindre to follow.

I stood, hugged them goodnight, and walked them to the door. Once they had gone, I turned back to find Bryn standing at the base of the stairs, motioning at me with his head to go to bed. I paused at the first step, turned to him, and threw my arms around his waist. He wrapped his arms around me and returned a hug that could melt the ice caps on the Sylph Mountains in the dead of winter.

"I'm sorry I didn't write. I'm sorry I worried you," I whispered.

"Even if you did nothing to cause worry, I would still worry, dear," he reasoned under his breath. He gently kissed the top of my head and then gave me one last squeeze. "I just want you to know I love you."

"I know. I love you, too." I smiled and turned to head up the stairs.

"I would have burned that castle to the ground, Veronica. No hesitation, if he-" his voice trailed off, but his concerned eyes met mine, and he shook his head, unable to finish his sentence.

"I know," I reassured him, placing my hand atop his that rested on the handrail. "Goodnight, Afi."

He offered me a half smile. Half happy. The other half...I'm still determining. His eyes seemed heartbroken all over again. "Goodnight, girl."

Seventeen

I t takes about two hours to sail from the small port in Lykke to arrive at the mouth of the Reaching River, then another quarter-hour to drift down to our access point in Stillridge. So far, this town has been the easiest to raid since it remains secluded due to a delta break in the river further inland. Bryn draws the line at venturing past the split because of what happened with my mother, so we have no idea where the river eventually leads.

We travel in two smaller longships that were retired to the city of Lykke upon its establishment. Two groups of eight Ravens are split into two vessels, six to power and navigate and two staffed on either end as lookouts. Bryn has long since painted the golden dragonheads black and somehow engineered the masts on the ships so they can collapse and fold in on themselves, increasing our stealth abilities when needed. Unfortunately, his age caught up to his body a few years ago, so his participation in the raids is now off the table. However, he keeps himself busy with engineering and planning. We had just passed the Royal Sol ships stationed outside of Port Sisu and were working on raising the mast when Sylve cleared her throat. I looked over my shoulder as she finished lighting the lantern at the front of the ship and armed herself with her bow, pulling an arrow out of the quiver stored against the side of the boat.

"I want an update on Erikka."

I released the rope that raised the mast to its full extension and tied it off. I wiped the built-up sweat from my forehead with the back of my sleeve, then marveled at the painting that donned the white canvas. A giant black raven, one on each boat's sail, signifies a bright future for those we are blessed to save and death for those who stand in our way. I turned and sat on a chest behind an open ore and leaned the front of my body against it, suspending it above the waves.

"What are you referring to?"

"Ummm, where do I start? The post-sex glow? Yeah! Let's start there."

"Gods, Sylve! Could you say that any louder?" I tried my best to hush her, but it was too late. The other Ravens had stopped their conversations and now had their full attention on me. I let out a nervous laugh. "First of all...That's not a thing."

"Oh, it's *definitely* a thing," a feminine voice chimed in. I felt a hand push down on my shoulder before they popped their head around so I could see them. "And you *definitely* have it." Siv laughed, her short red hair falling in front of her eyes. She kept half of her head shaved close to her scalp, and the other half was curly and longer in the front, falling just past her cheek. Another person commented at my expense.

"You had sex with the princess? Do share *all* of the details." A rough voice cut through the sound of the waves. Tormod sat down next to Sindre, forcing him to scoot away to make room for his equally large body. He leaned forward with his elbows on his knees and offered a smile only a needy, sex-deprived man could conjure up. A tooth was missing along his otherwise straight set of teeth, and his black beard was long and braided into two, his head completely bald, allowing his tanned skin to shine in the moonlight.

"I will absolutely *not* be sharing any details while you are around, Tormod," I declared, physically cringing at his imagination.

"So, it finally happened?" Sylve turned the conversation back to her, eyes wide.

"Uh-I-wait, that's also not what I said." I stammered, overwhelmed with all the eyes and questions directed at me.

"Okay, Veronica's got game!" Siv joked and shook me by the shoulders. "Good on ya!"

"That's enough!" Sindre roared, coming to his feet and silencing all on the ship immediately. "All of you go back to your own conversations! And mind them!" He ordered. Tormod and Siv returned to their posts at the opposite end of the vessel. Only when they took their seats and started small talk did Sindre sit again.

"Thanks," I muttered, embarrassed.

"Don't mention it," he answered plainly, turning his attention away from me and fixing it somewhere in the black abyss ahead of us. Sylve crouched in closer to me, taking a few steps away from her post for a moment.

"So? What happened?"

"Uh-h-h. Well, you guessed it. We kind of jumped over a few of the more *traditional* ways of discovering stronger feelings between people and...went for it." I insinuated with my tongue, and two fingers spread apart. Her jaw dropped. I reached out to close it, but she swatted it away.

"Don't you touch me with those dirty hands," she joked.

"Gods!" I rolled my eyes. "Can I tell you something?"

"Absolutely! Just don't touch me," she smirked but leaned in closer.

"She told me she loved me...and I think I feel the same. Actually, I knew that I loved her after we kissed the first time. It was as if I rubbed my eyes, and all the fog disappeared."

"That's amazing, Veronica! I'm so happy for you." She placed a hand on my knee. "But did you say *the first time*? As in, there were multiple times?" I laughed at her and shoved her hand off me.

"We did have an argument though," I added.

"A lover's quarrel already?" Sindre muttered from his side of the aisle. I shot him a look he didn't see and turned my attention back to Sylve.

"She mentioned that she had her own suspicions about what I partake in that causes my injuries."

"What the *fuck* does that mean?" Sindre cut in again, this time turning completely to insert himself into the conversation.

"I don't know, exactly." I raised my hand towards him to try to halt his growing annoyance. "When I questioned her about breaking her vow of silence to tell me what she and her father spoke about in their debriefing, she told me that since she doesn't push me on my lack of reasoning for my injuries, I needed to drop it."

"I don't like that," he declared, turning away.

"I have to agree with him," Sylve confessed.

"I don't disagree! Trust me. I was fuming. But since I wasn't planning to disclose more information that might lead her to the Ravens, I dropped it. I'm planning on being more careful in the future anyway. So, I shouldn't have to worry about coming up with any more piss-poor excuses."

"Yeah, right." Sindre scoffed and shook his head.

"Is there a problem?" I asked, turning to face him head-on.

"Yes, actually. I do have one," he retorted, turning and locking eyes with me.

"Feel free to share."

"The fact that Erikka has suspicions about your activity, and you still thought it was a good idea to pursue sleeping with her, bothers me."

"Sindre, she and Erikka have a deeper relationship history than just 'pursuing to sleep with her,' and you *know* that," Sylve interjected.

"I only just found out. It's not like I knew about her suspicions." I added.

"It's a fine line to walk, Veronica." Sindre cautioned.

"How so?" I questioned.

"If you continue complicating your relationship with her, she could change her mind about keeping her thoughts to herself. Those suspicions can manifest into a genuine concern for the safety of a significant other. What if she sends someone to follow you? Find out what type of danger you willingly put yourself in when she isn't around?" I attempted to respond, but my thoughts refused to form into words. I looked over to Sylve for some sort of backup, but her sad eyes let me know it wasn't coming.

"I didn't think about that." I cast my eyes downwards as more thoughts crashed into the carefully placed doubt.

"I don't expect you to. Live in the moment! Enjoy what you have every chance you get. I just ask that you *hear* us when we need to advise you of the risks." Sindre insisted, putting a hand on mine. "The same goes for us, too. *All* of us," he motioned to everyone on the ship. "If you see risks in our personal lives, we must *hear* those too."

"I hear you," I reassured him.

"Still, congratulations on reaching a new step in this relationship," Sylve noted. "I'm so excited and happy for you. The post-sex glow looks fabulous on you," she laughed and took her post back at the prow.

"Yeah, congratulations." Sindre offered half-heartedly, turning back to the darkness beyond us.

I sat looking out at nothing, letting the conversation sink in, before turning my attention towards Sylve. "How have YOU been? Anything interesting to share?"

"Oh yeah...I've got something I need to tell yo-" A drawn-out whistle sounded from the ship ahead of us, and we all sprang into action instantly. "Looks like it will have to wait until later." She laughed and blew out the lantern next to her.

I turned around and hurried to untie the rope I secured earlier before throwing the end of it to Sindre, who then tossed the excess to Sylve. Together, we swiftly raised the sail and locked it in place so the remaining Ravens could collapse the mast. We crouched low next to the side of the boat and got ready at the ores. Sylve stood in line with the prow and blended in with the dragonhead she stood under, her bow and arrow notched and ready to go.

The six Ravens at the ores maneuvered us directly behind the first ship. Luckily, the moon was full, so you could see the shoreline a few meters ahead, which was also the mouth of the river and barely south of the direction we were heading. Sindre sent out a set of three quick whistles so the Ravens on the boat ahead understood his order. He slightly turned to the rest of us and whispered.

"Masks and hoods up!"

The Ravens' outfits consisted of all dark attire, leggings, and deep dark brown leather armor, with all black tunics, armguards, boots, and a head scarf used to completely keep our hair obscured. Another scarf wrapped tight around our neck was used as a face covering to keep our lower face hidden. We wore long winter cloaks year-round to conceal the weapons we chose to arm ourselves with, although the color changed depending on the time of year. In the winter, our cloaks are white; in the summer and fall, black; and in the spring, dark green. Additionally, black war paint is applied thickly from temple to temple in the shape of a raven. *You can't forget the war paint.*

I pulled my mask and hood up, letting it hang just past the brim of my forehead, and let my eyes scan the shadowed scenery as we entered the mouth of the river into Skirrian territory. Sylve raised her bow above her waist as she stood a bit taller, scanning the bank ahead. I feel sorry for anyone who might've felt a midnight swim was a good idea tonight, as she doesn't ask questions, and she doesn't miss.

Everything went smoothly as we neared our entry point. We kept our eyes on Sylve as she signaled us to steer left, right, and left again, then raise the ores and brace. I anchored my body weight down on the ore to keep it raised and staggered my feet as we absorbed the impact of the longship sliding onto the sandy bank. Sylve motioned for us to hold our positions as the archers scanned the tree line. We stayed here for a few minutes longer while the four archers exited the vessels and scouted ahead past the trees before they all returned and held their bows with one arm above their heads, the signal for '*all clear: advance.*'

The remaining Ravens exited the longships and quietly made their way to the tree line. Once there, we executed a weapons check before continuing. All my favorites, my sister knives on both thighs and my small ankle knife, were in place and secure. Additionally, for raids, I prefer to use a battle axe secured around my waist and then my prized Valkyrie axe, gifted by Brynjar, is strapped across my back.

Once everyone cleared their weapons, we spread out and formed a line, leaving at least six feet between each of us, and combed our way through the approximate acre of woods until we saw the warm glow of light from the small village. Stillridge is mainly a farming-run town. It consists of only a handful of houses scattered across acres of farmland. This infuriates me because they shove at least a hundred thralls under insignificant wooden roofs they consider "a house."

We remain in the tree line awaiting the signal for safe passage across the acre or two that separated us from the thralls' quarters. A single man, a prisoner of Skirra, has worked with the Ravens for the past six years, surrendering his opportunity to escape to someone in greater need than him. He has, instead, asked if he could facilitate our operation. So, we have established he will flicker the oil lamps on the back of the thralls' home to signal clear passage, along with having our next group of Skirrian thrall ready to go as soon as we arrive. This system has remained the most successful since he was incorporated.

The light extinguished and re-lit three times before remaining off, our signal to make our way to the house. Six Ravens will stay back in the woods, ushering the future Frithians to the longships in wait. The rest of us and the four archers crept into the open field and made our way to the shelter.

We got about halfway across when the light turned back on, and we all dropped flat to the ground instantly. It was uneasily quiet besides the occasional gust of wind and the crickets orchestrating their song of the night. My breathing sounded significantly amplified, so I held it for a few seconds, checking to see if I could hear anyone else breathing. *No, just me.* The light turned off again, and we were up, stealthily maneuvering towards our destination. There was a bale of hay at our halfway point, and Sylve took her post here, notching an arrow in her bow and peering around the side of her acquired blind on watch. As we drew closer to the back of the house, a Raven would fall off and maintain their position, crouched, anticipating the stream of people I would lead past them in a few minutes. Another archer fell off and found a lookout position crouched behind an abandoned cart with a quarter of the way to go. By the time we reached the back of the house, our final two archers had taken a position on either corner of the house, with arrows pointed at the neighboring homes, which left Sindre, Siv, and myself to aid the thralls in crossing the open field.

Sindre very lightly knocked three times on the back door. A few minutes passed, and a gangly older man opened it slightly, whispering through the opening. "They are ready when you are."

"Thank you for your continued sacrifice, Nightbane. We could never repay you for your service." Sindre whispered, holding a closed fist across his chest and offering a Slight bow. Siv and I repeated Sindre's gesture. The man nodded in response and returned inside to ready our group.

"Is he sure he doesn't want to come this time?" I asked under my breath while I kept a watchful eye on our surroundings.

"I will ask him again after the last person has crossed the plain," he responded under his breath. "Are you ready to go?"

"Yes. Let's get them the fuck out of here."

The door completely swung open, exposing faces filled with terror and small glimpses of hope. Nightbane handed me a toddler who donned shredded scraps as clothing, and I braced him on my hip opposite the axe. His mother, I'm assuming, stood first in line, clutching an older child's wrist in her hand, her eyes screaming to be saved, yet caution and fear were still visibly battling for control. Sindre was reiterating the importance of moving quickly but quietly before he looked at me for confirmation. I nodded my head.

"From here on out. Do. Not. Speak. Until your feet touch the soil at our destination, you *must* remain silent. It is imperative for the success of this freedom raid. Do you understand?" he questioned quietly. The group of people nodded their heads. I turned to the woman behind me.

"Are you ready?" I asked calmly. She stared between me and her son, who had a death grip on my leather armor but seemed to enjoy the additional warmth under my cloak. I offered her my free hand, leaving it suspended in the air. "The fear doesn't outweigh the reward." I nodded toward her children. Her entire frame trembled, but she straightened herself and forced a brave face.

"I'm ready." She placed her freezing hand in mine, and I gave Sindre a final nod before turning and starting the expedition back to the longships.

I looked back to check on our progress as we passed each Raven in wait, those who would rejoin us to escort the group progressively as we passed. Sindre and Siv will wait until this group completely enters the woods with the archers, except Sylve, who returns to the tree line before crossing the plain to meet us at the boats.

I led the front of the group through the first checkpoint at the trees. I squeezed the woman's hand to reassure her that we were making progress, and she let out a breath she had been holding. Tormod was waiting for us when we passed him, and he took the lead, stepping in front of me to follow the path of least resistance through the woods they had scouted while we were gathering the group. It only took a few minutes in the woods until we stepped on the sandy bank again. I helped the woman at the front of the line into the longship and handed her son to her over the vessel's side.

"Take a seat on the floor at the back and remain silent; we are not in the clear yet." She nodded. "The rest of you find an open spot along the sides of the boat and remain silent," I instructed, waiting to fill the first ship with half of the group before leading the rest to the second.

A woman stumbled out of the woods near the back of the line and looked around as if she was lost. She finally locked eyes with me and staggered over, hyperventilating with tears streaming down her face, but she didn't dare speak.

"What's wrong, what's going on?" I questioned quietly. She looked at me wide-eyed, terrified to even open her mouth. "It's okay; speak very quietly. What is going on?"

"My-my daughter-they..." She looked back to where we came from, and she spoke as quietly as she could through her distraught tears, her uneven breathing prolonging her explanation. "They took her tonight to...to discipline her. They...chained her outside." She covered her mouth with her hands and groaned in anguish at the reality of what she had to say.

"Shhhh. Shhhhh. Breathe." I instructed as calmly as I could. "I will go get her. Where is she?"

"Two-two houses down from ours. They have her chained outside, behind the house...please, Gods, please. I can't leave her here." She begged, dropping to her knees and grabbing onto the edge of my cloak. Her tanned hands were riddled with open sores and dotted with scars. Tormod walked over and carefully supported the woman by the elbows.

"I need you to take point. They have her daughter two houses down chained up outside. I'm going to go get her." I explained to Tormod, who nodded and started ushering the frantic woman towards the boat.

"Alert archer one on your way there," he added over his shoulder.

"She-she can't speak!" The woman cried out. "They got angry that she wouldn't answer their questions, bu-but she can't speak. I-I mean she *can communicate*, but only with her hands." Her tears continued to stream down her face as Tormod guided her away.

I took off again through the woods and reached the tree line as fast as possible. I needed to pull this off as quickly and efficiently as I could to avoid jeopardizing the raid. Archers two, three, and four were in the tree line waiting for Sindre and Siv's return since they had yet to begin their trek back. I tapped Archer Four's shoulder.

"Detour for a missing child. I'm alerting archer one and taking her attention to my location. I'll need you to cover the position she will be giving up." I explained plainly. They nodded and adjusted their aim to where Sylve currently had hers pointed.

I started walking along the inside of the tree line, aligning myself with the targeted house before I turned and released a sharp whistle to get Sylve's attention. I watched as she turned her bow abruptly and scanned the tree line until she faced my direction, and I stepped out into view. With clear, exaggerated movements, I placed a hand on my chest, held up two fingers, and then pointed at the house across the open field. She adjusted her aim accordingly. Then, with her aim on the house, I threw caution to the wind and sprinted across the field towards another hay bale adjacent to the one Sylve was positioned at.

I took a second to catch my breath before peering around my cover. Then, I turned to Sylve and crossed my arms above my head to form an 'X,' asking if it was clear. She took a second to respond but raised her arm straight in the air and motioned towards my destination. *Good thing I trust her with my life because there is no way in hel I would do this on anyone else's watch.*

I turned and sprinted towards the house without scouting my path. I don't have time to be overly cautious. I need to find this child and get her unchained, a task that could be time-consuming. As I drew nearer to the house, I slowed my sprint to a brisk but stealthy walk, scanning the side and back of the house for any signs of danger.

I heard a scraping noise and dropped flat to the floor, watching the direction of its origin. A small head poked out from behind a wooden beam that protruded from the house. She looked to be about six or seven. However, she was so thin and barely clothed that she could be older. I got on my feet and crept closer to get a better idea of what I had to work with. The child's wrists and ankles were chained and secured to the post next to her. Her entire frame was trembling, and her lips were blue. Although winter has turned, early spring nights can still drastically drop in temperature, and tonight seemed as cold as any winter day. My anger gauge was quickly rising, which was a terrible time for that to happen. So, I focused on breathing as I inched closer.

The child's eyes bulged, and she shook her head violently. I pulled down my face covering so she could see my face and hopefully gain her trust. "It's okay. I'm here to help you." I whispered ever so lightly. I moved toward her, but she shook her head frantically again. I checked my surroundings quickly and turned my head in confusion. She carefully pushed the inside of her wrists together so as to not rattle the chains and curled her fingers into claws before bringing them together to interlock them. I shook my head, but she continued repeating this movement. *I don't have time for this.*

I took two more steps and heard a metal clank and a violent snap. My hand slapped over my mouth, cutting off the guttural scream I had let out as I crumpled to the floor. I dug the nails of my free hand into my calf to try and disperse the excruciating pain radiating throughout my ankle. I kept my hand over my mouth as I pushed hard breaths into my palm, looking at the girl who had now covered her eyes. *Now that fucking makes sense.*

A lamp flickered on in a room on the second floor of the house where I was now trapped. I turned and looked toward Sylve's direction, only to see her sprinting across the fields and almost to me. I clenched my teeth and removed my hand from my mouth to slip my battle axe out of its sheath. I braved a look at where my leg was caught in the trap, and sure enough, a set of heavy steel teeth was currently crushing my bones. Blood was flowing out of either side of my ankle, which now formed a very unnatural angle. *Fuck.*

I shimmied the head of the axe between the set of teeth and turned it to face me before pushing on it in an attempt to pry it open, alleviating only a mere ounce of pressure. Sylve reached me just as I had lost the strength to keep pushing the teeth apart, and they re-clamped on my leg, extracting another audible groan from me.

"Stop. Stop!" she whispered to me. "Hold on." Her hands hovered above my injured leg and studied the gory scene. "There should be a release pin somewhere." She continued to look around the contraption until she located her target and carefully pulled a pin. The trap released, and she used my axe as a lever to open the trap enough for me to lift my leg out of the center. I scooted away as I held my leg in the air. I looked at the damage and back at Sylve, who shook her head.

"You have to." I urged.

"Shhhhh," she stood and swept over to the opposite corner of the house. She looked at the girl, who stared at her in awe, shushing her with an index finger placed vertically on her lips, as she flattened herself against the wall. I heard the soft sounds of footsteps a second later, but Sylve was already on it. She took half a step from the wall and rammed her elbow into an unsuspecting man as he turned the corner. He stumbled back, and by the time he gathered himself to curse at Sylve, she had turned a circle and sent a foot into the man's jaw, sending him flying away from the house and into the grass unconscious.

I heard heavy footsteps and panting coming from the opposite direction. Sindre and Siv had run over and were analyzing the expanding crime scene. Sindre's eyes connected with mine. I looked at my mangled leg and then back at him, shaking my head in defeat.

"What was the initial plan here?" he asked quietly.

"A woman told me her daughter was taken earlier today and chained outside this house as punishment. I told her I would get her." I took another deep, calming breath, anything to keep my mind off the pain. "It was going fine until this." I gestured at my leg that I still couldn't set on the ground quite yet. Sindre looked over at the young girl.

"Are you okay?" he asked sincerely. She nodded as Siv knelt next to her to start gently manipulating the chains around her ankles. Sylve returned to my side, unsure what to do next.

"You should just..."

"Don't even, Veronica," Sindre warned under his breath.

"There is no other choice. Carrying me back is not an option; we all know what that would do." I pushed.

"Shut. The. Fuck up," he emphasized with his fist pounding on the ground. "Sylve...do you think you're ready?" He looked up at his sister, weighing what few options we had.

"I'm not sure. I've never actually tried it on someone else." Sylve responded apprehensively.

"What are you guys talking about?" I cut in.

"You are going to have to *try*," he advised, ignoring my question.

"I don't kno-"

"NOW!" he demanded. "Siv, come here." He motioned for her and stood up as she came to stand across from him. "We need to completely close them in under our cloaks. Create a makeshift tent, if you will."

Sylve moved to sit on her knees next to my ankle, and the other two stood above us, interlocking their arms to drape their cloaks over and around us.

"What are you going to do?" I asked nervously in the pitch black of our resourced cave.

"I need you to trust me." She attempted to assure me, but her voice cracked.

"Do *you* trust you?"

"Not really."

I felt the blood drain from my face and my stomach tighten with uneasiness. All went still and silent for a few minutes, and I was wondering if I should check to make sure I didn't pass on to the next life. That's when a delicate ball of light appeared under her palms for just a second before dying out.

"Sylve?" I whimpered under my breath.

"You got this, Syl," Sindre stated from above me. A few seconds later, the ball of light reappeared and consistently grew until it was the size of her palm. The white light was radiating from her. *Is this magic?* She moved her hands to either side of my injury and hesitated, looking up at me.

"I have no idea what this is going to feel like," she offered shyly. I nodded at her to continue.

"I trust you. *Whatever* you're doing...You can do it." She inched her hands closer to my leg until the light embraced my skin. I gasped at the sensation, and Sylve's eyes shot up to mine.

"I'm fine! It doesn't hurt. It just surprised me." I assured her quietly. The light was growing and spreading around the entirety of my ankle, totally encompassing it to where I couldn't see past the light any further. The sensation was difficult for my brain to figure out. It's warm but not in temperature. It almost feels like her hugs, familiar and inviting. But it also feels like...love?

The light began to peel back from my skin until it danced in her palms again. Her eyes smiled as she looked at me.

"Well?" She asked curiously. I glanced at my leg and was stunned. It didn't look broken anymore. I risked moving it. I rotated my ankle in a circle, and there was no pain. I hesitated for a moment before bearing some of my weight on it as I set it on the ground. *She fixed it.* I looked up at her with the same awe as the little girl had.

"You healed it...ho-how? Is this what you were going to tell me about?"

"Yes," she laughed, stood up, and offered me her hand. I cautiously put weight on it at first before jumping and running in place to get a feel for its capabilities, realizing how much time we'd wasted.

"Just like new." I placed an arm on Sylve's. "Thank you." Her eyes smiled in response before she moved to reset her bow.

Sindre walked over to the girl and looked at the chains. He unfastened his axe from his back and twisted it in his hand for a moment, contemplating what he would do with it. He then swung it over his shoulder and down on the portion of the chain that kept it secured around the wooden post, and it shattered. He bent down and picked the girl up, chains still attached to her extremities, and handed her to Siv. "Hurry her back to the ship now. You can work on getting those off once there. Order the first crew to sail back. Give us fifteen minutes to clean this up and return. If we aren't there, *leave*. We can trek through the Nott Forest if we take longer than that."

Siv looked at him incredulously. "We are not leaving you all here!"

"You will! That's an *official* order. Mind the mission, warrior!" he reiterated. She looked between all of us, then conceded.

"Yes, sir." She tucked the girl into her cloak and wrapped the excess chains around her hands to quiet them before running across the field toward the safety of the trees. Sylve headed toward the front of the house.

"I'm going to scout the front and linger a few minutes to ensure that the only activity came from this house." She pulled her bow over her head and slipped out of view. Sindre looked past me towards the thralls' quarters.

"I need to update Nightbane and tie off plans for the next raid. You got this?" He motioned his head back toward where the man should be. I nodded in response, and he touched my shoulder as he passed. "I'll meet you two at the boat in ten."

"See you then. Watch where you step," I warned. He chuckled quietly, and we went our separate ways. I crept around the back corner of the house, expecting to see the man still lying on the ground, but he was gone. I lowered myself and focused on analyzing every sound I heard. I scanned the ground for any tracks and noticed faint indentations in the grass. *That was where his body landed.* I followed the trail for a few feet. *Maybe he rolled over.* There is another foot. He was walking, and the faint tracks turned and now showed he was headed where I came from. *Behind me?* I whipped around in time to barely dodge the swing of an axe.

"There you are, you sneaky bastard." I taunted.

"What do you think you're doing around here?" he questioned, twirling his axe in his hand. I didn't respond. Instead, I circled him, positioning my back to the woods to keep an eye on the house in case more activity picked up. He glanced at where the girl had been and then whipped his head back to me. "So, you're responsible for my thrall missing?" *Look at that; the man figured it out and became a loose end.*

He stomped over to me, raising his axe in the air. I squatted to the ground and picked up a handful of loose dirt, throwing it into the man's face as I dodged his clumsy strike. He groaned in pain and stumbled around, wiping his eyes. I can tell he had no formal combat training, especially by how loosely he held his weapon. I attacked a weak point and kicked his forearm, sending his axe flying a few feet away.

He glared at me as he turned around, then noticed the steel trap that lay abandoned between us, half open with my axe still lying in its center, surrounded with a pool of blood. The man analyzed me with confusion, looking between me and the sprung trap. Just as I thought I had evaded any suspicion, a sudden gust of wind swept my cloak aside, exposing my ankle. I felt the breeze on my skin, so I knew my trousers had torn halfway up my calf.

"What are you? Some kind of magic wielder?" he questioned. I shrugged in response, and he didn't appreciate that. He charged at me, swinging his meaty fists furiously. It was relatively easy to dodge with the speed at which he was moving. Dodge, sidestep, dodge, sidestep. *Hey, this is kind of like training day.*

The man was growling at his lack of productivity. I waited for the right moment to dodge his attack before sending my shoulder under his ribs and ramming him backward until he tripped on the disarmed trap and fell to the ground. This gave me enough time to turn around to grab the axe he had dropped. When I got back to him, he was attempting to get up, so I sent my boot up into his nose, causing him to whine in pain as he landed on his back.

The man pushed himself up by his elbow and tried to kick at me, but I shoved his leg out of the way before bringing my foot down onto his knee, extracting a deep yell from him. I crouched and sent the back of my hand across his face to shut him up within the exact second. The look he shot me was murderous, but I felt nothing. I don't feel anything when we dispose of people like him, not joy, not sadness.

"You think you will get away with this?" he sneered between his bloodied teeth. I cocked my head in confusion, then turned sideways, looking away from him for a moment, and readjusted my grip on his axe, taking a second to feel the weight of it in my hand. I tossed it into the air and caught it, taunting him, before turning towards him to bring the axe down onto his face.

As the axe I held reached peak height, I felt a sharp blow to my side, causing my axe to fly off course. I gasped sharply and staggered a few steps from the force of the blow. I stayed frozen in place, shocked and unsure of what to do next. *I underestimated my opponent, and it might cost me my life.* My eyes met his, and they now donned a triumphant glimmer, but only for a moment. I looked down at my side to find my own axe jammed under my ribs, and blood was slowly seeping out around the blade. *I assumed he wouldn't have thought of using any nearby utensils to help himself…but my own weapon. Fuck.*

My eyes interlocked with the man's who had fallen back onto his elbows after snatching my weapon and slamming it into my side. Suddenly, the man's face drained of all color, and he gaped, almost as if he had come to a deadly realization. He started to fumble his words, which I couldn't make sense of.

"W-wait-you…" He rubbed his hand down his eyes and blinked a few times more. "You're the–" his words were cut off abruptly, and a gurgling noise came from his throat. An arrow now protruded from his mouth. His body fell still, and everything quieted once again, returning to the calm the spring nights offered. My eyes flicked towards the direction the arrow came from to find Sylve lowering her bow just past the corner of the house.

I took as deep a breath as I could without causing myself too much pain and looked around to see if we were leaving anything behind. She rushed over to me, and her eyes widened at what she saw.

"This area is clear...besides...that." I nodded at the man's body. I staggered past her, making my way toward the tree line across the field.

"You...Veronica!" she called after me, rushing to the side I kept my hand pressed against. "If you were unaware, you have an axe in your side." I shooed her hands away from me and focused on breathing and closing the distance between me and the longships. "Stop, let me try to heal you," she pleaded, attempting to put her hands on me again. I turned to her and grabbed her wrist with my free hand.

"We...don't have time...Help me get to the boat...tha-" I tried my best to keep the axe lodged where it currently was. I'm sure I would lose blood faster if I tried removing it. Regrettably, I bent over too far, sending a tearing sensation through my core. I pulled in a sharp breath between my clenched teeth. "Let's get out of here." I pleaded with her.

She nodded and moved around my un–axed side and supported me by pulling my arm over her neck, looping her arm under me and securing her grip just below my armpit. We walked as quickly as we could to the tree line before we slowed under the safety of cover. Navigating the woods was difficult, but eventually, we came to the bank where Sindre and the remaining Ravens were eyeing the trees intently as they awaited our arrival. We both tripped while exiting the woods and stumbled out into the open, where I let out a loud groan of discomfort. Sindre ran over and took over for Sylve, who hurried to place her bow in the boat.

"What happened?" Sindre asked calmly. I can always count on him to stay level-headed in an emergency. Once we are in the clear, though, that's when he'll let me have it.

"I don't want...to talk about it." I pushed out the words between each labored breath I took. We neared the edge of the longship, and the thought of trying to climb into it was daunting.

"Throw a chest down here," Sindre ordered the Ravens stationed on the vessel. Within seconds, a chest flew over the side and landed in the sand next to the boat. Sindre and Sylve helped me step up onto the chest, and Siv and Tormod lifted me over the side by grabbing onto my biceps. Sindre heaved the chest for Tormod to place back on the boat. "Get down there to help push the boat out," he ordered Tormod and Siv as he swiftly hauled himself over the boat's edge to assist me. He opened the chest I was going to sit at and pulled out a thick wool blanket.

"Oh no, you don't. To the prow." He ushered me away from my station and sat me on the floor just under the dragonhead. He placed the blanket over me and tucked it behind my shoulders before he jumped back over the side and helped push the boat off the shore and into the river.

Once they all hoisted themselves back into the ship, everyone took their position at their ores, navigating as fast as they could up the river—all except for Sylve, who detoured and came to me, reaching for my side. I moved my arm to stop her.

"Get us…out of here first. Once we are clear…of Skirrian waters…" I grunted under my breath. She reluctantly shook her head, stepped back to where I should be, and navigated in my place.

Sleepiness was catching up to me with my sudden lack of movement. My eyes rolled heavily around in my head until I noticed the woman with the wounds on her hands, holding her daughter in her arms under a wool blanket. A smile forced its way to my lips, and a deep feeling of relief settled over me. Her eyes met mine, and guilt washed over her facial features. She mouthed the words, "I'm sorry." I shook my head loosely.

"Even if...I knew what the outcome...would be..." I slurred deliriously between increasingly strained breaths. "I would...do it again...without...hesi...ta..." I was tired, *too* tired to continue speaking. I closed my eyes for just a second and heard Sindre yell for me from a faraway place. But I was so exhausted that I couldn't open my eyes to find him. I allowed sleep's comforting embrace to take me far from my throes of agony.

Eighteen

*T*he sky was on fire. I spun in circles, trying to find my friends. What the hel happened here? The earth split in the distance, and a massive root unfurled itself out of the ground, opening a portal to Helheim. Undead warrior-like creatures that I could only assume were Draugr ran from its opening towards me. I reached for weapons I didn't have and braced for a fight as they neared...but they passed me. I turned to watch the Draugr collide with more Draugr? No. Spirits? Warriors of light were fighting the creatures from Hel. Why is this happening? How did I get here?

As if something willed my body to move, I began to run. An axe appeared in my hand, and as I entered the battle, I swung and ran it through a light warrior, who dissipated into dust. I continued pushing through the line, swinging my axe through any warrior who dared attempt to stop me. Finally, the final light spirit turned to dust and dispersed with the next breeze. I turned around to scope the battlefield, and everything disappeared—everything except for a shadowed figure silhouetted by the flaming sky and smoldering ground.

An uneasy feeling settled deep within my stomach. As I walked towards it, I noticed a body sprawled on the floor, then another one, then another. I stopped at the first body, and my heart sank. Familiar golden locs splayed out on the floor, peppered with blood.

I crumpled to the ground and felt a sob jolt through my chest as I turned over Sindre's body to find the cause of his death - a knife through his chest.

I thought I was screaming, not a sound escaped my throat. Instead, my tear-filled eyes shot over to the next body. Golden hair. I scrambled over to her, hoping I could still save her, but her neck rested at an uncomfortable angle. Bile crept up my throat, and I turned to expel the eternal heartbreak that had consumed me.

I gathered the courage to look over at the next body lying in a pool of blood. Silent tears streamed down my cheeks as I crawled through crimson puddles to reach Jerrik and cradle his head in my lap. I sent a blood-curdling scream out into the fervent heavens above.

Rage's icy hands clenched my mutilated heart and shielded it in an impenetrable darkness. Even if Light's promise of protection scoured the Ninth Level of Hel, it would fail to find it. I will never be hurt again, and I will find vengeance. So, I stood, my axe in hand, as I marched relentlessly toward the figure that stood there and mocked me.

The closer I got to the figure, the haziness cleared, and it took human form. It was a man, but I still couldn't tell who it was from the shadow that fell upon him. I was ten meters from him when I stopped dead in my tracks. Somehow, I felt a beastly nail run down the icy fortress that had formed in my chest, sending me straight to my knees.

I gasped at the sensation of such an assault. I have no idea how such an attack is possible. My hands clutched at my chest as I made myself look at the man who kept his distance. Ice ran through my veins, freezing me to the ground where I knelt.

These eyes were blazing silver, illuminating his face enough for me to watch a ravenous smile spread across his wide mouth. Every sane brain cell screamed at me to run, but I didn't move. I couldn't.

The man's body began to shift and morph, slowly buckling over onto all fours. The sound of bones cracking and skin tearing flipped my stomach, threatening to force bile up my throat, when silence took over abruptly. The figure somehow stepped out of his own shadow, no longer a man. Instead, a blonde dire wolf with silver eyes slowly stalked towards me, teeth bared and growling.

It stopped only a few feet from me and lowered itself back on its haunches, ready to pounce. Dread encompassed the final moments of life I held on to. I screamed deep inside my chest as the wolf launched itself at me.

I gasped, and my hand flew to my throat as my eyes shot open. I was in the safety of a darkened room. The only light was from the other side of a door slightly ajar. *It was just a dream.* I exhaled a breath of relief as I ran my shaking hand down my face. My other arm was trapped underneath Brax, who was whining softly, so I folded my arms around him. I looked over and saw Sylve stirring in her sleep next to me, with her hand wrapped around mine that was stuck under Brax. Gods, I had completely forgotten about the incident - I felt *normal.* I squeezed her hand and stretched over to hug her.

"Wha-Is everything okay?" she asked, still half asleep.

"Yes. Everything is great." I whispered into her ear before placing a kiss on her cheek. "Thank you. Thank you so much." She patted my arm and stilled again, falling back into slumber.

I threw the blanket off my legs, only to find Brynjar slumped over the side of the bed, asleep. I can't imagine how worried he must have been with me showing up in the state I was in. I'm sure his stress took a few years off his life. I slipped out of my blanket prison and crouched down next to him, placing a hand on his back.

"Afi," I whispered, lightly shaking him. It took a second for him to stir, but then he shot up, and his bleary eyes focused on me.

"Gods." He spoke under his breath. "You're okay." Neither a statement nor a question.

"I'm more than okay." Since I don't know how I arrived or if Bryn knows about Sylve's abilities, I kept my responses short. "Come lay down now." I pulled his arm to coax him to stand, and he complied sleepily. I guided him over to the couch that had been moved from the common room, knowing he would be too stubborn to use it. I guided him to sit down, but he turned to me, grabbed my face with both hands and kissed my forehead before suffocating me with a bear hug.

"I'm proud of you, and I love you... but don't ever do that to me again," his voice was groggy but stern. He released me, and I helped him lay down to sleep again.

"Sleep, Bryn." I pulled a blanket over him and laid my hand over his before slipping through the door and gently pulling it shut.

I was heading for the kitchen but noticed Sindre had fallen asleep on the chair near the hearth, where the embers from the final log were slowly fading. I walked over to a small dresser near the front door and pulled out a blanket, unfolding it as I crept back to place it over him, stopping myself when I noticed what he held in his hand. It was the corset that I had worn the previous night.

I draped the blanket over the small table in front of him and reached over to take the corset when he swiftly grabbed my wrist and pulled me down closer to him, holding a knife under my chin. I was shocked by his speed, but also...*where did the knife come from?* His sunken eyes opened wearily before staring me down intensely, an eyebrow raised in amusement.

"I–Uh...didn't see the knife." I offered embarrassingly. His burning gaze made my chest tighten. I was expecting a witty comeback, but it never came. He released my arm and slipped his knife into its holster on his ankle while I stood straight and hugged myself around the waist. Sindre stood and pulled me into him, wrapping his arms over my shoulders, my corset still clutched in his hand. I allowed my arms to relax and carefully held onto his tunic at the waist, falling into another hug I would never again take for granted.

"I really thought that might've been it." His words rustled softly into my hair. "You stopped responding. We had to wait until we were clear...before we could help you." I felt him shake his head before he nuzzled further into my neck. I wrapped my arms tighter around him. It was the only thing I could do to console him; I had no words that could diminish his fear. "To sit and watch the life fade from your body was agonizing and terrifying."

"I'm sorry you had to go through that. I shouldn't have underestimated him."

"No. There is no need for an apology. Things happen all the time that we don't expect, and that isn't anyone's fault." He released me and contemplated the corset in his hands, running his thumb over where the axe had broken through the leather; my blood had stained the material a darker hue of brown. "I just needed you to know that we would have done as you asked. We would have gotten those people to safety first before helping you." He held out my corset, and I took it, examining the raven myself. A wing was mutilated from the attack, but it still flew proud and strong.

"Thank you for that." I smiled softly, knowing my passion for our work would have been honored in the event of an untimely death. As morbid as that seems, it brought me peace.

"How do you feel?" Sindre interrupted my reflection.

"Normal. Honestly, I woke up and forgot that it had happened." He laughed silently and shook his head at me in amazement. I glanced behind me toward the stairs before asking, "What does Bryn know...about Sylve? What about those that might've witnessed it?"

"The soon-to-be-Frithians were sworn to secrecy while we were still on the ship. They fully understand their lives would be what they barter for loose lips." He crossed his arms over his chest, just as he always does when he puts on his serious face. I stifled a laugh before clearing my throat.

"Bryn?"

"He doesn't know yet, but I'm sure we will have to explain things to him soon. We couldn't exactly change your bloodied clothes once we got here. When I carried you in after all of the Frithians were settled, he looked as if he would have MY head for the state you were in."

"Oh. Wha-But how do you expect him to react about Sylve?" I rubbed the back of my neck before motioning toward the kitchen with my head.

"Honestly?" he questioned. I stopped once I reached the counter and turned back to him, confused.

"No, lie to me. Please." I bent over and searched through the few ice chests that lined the wall.

"I think he is going to be furious. He will most likely try to ban her from using those abilities again."

"Try?" I questioned with a raised eyebrow and a half smile. "It's unlike you to be rebellious, Sindre. Am I finally rubbing off on you?"

He didn't smile in response; he was as serious as he gets. "Why should she?"

"Are we role-playing? Am I supposed to answer as Bryn?" I realized I wasn't even looking in the right place for a mug and shook the grogginess from my head before reaching into a cabinet to grab one.

"I'm serious, Veronica. Why would she stop practicing and honing that ability? Without it, you would have died. Imagine what she could be capable of if she kept learning." His eyes lit up with a fiery passion, the same passion that always seems to get me in trouble.

My heart grew heavy from the weight of needing to bring a passion killer to the table. It's not my thing. "Sindre, have you considered how dangerous this path is? It far surpasses any of *my* impulsive paths." I walked over to the water barrel on the other side of the room and filled my cup, taking a sip.

"We don't even know the bounds of this ability. What if Sylve learns to create things? Homes? Clothes?" His hands were flying in every direction from the excitement building within him.

I contemplated the possibilities and how it would take so much off the entire organization's plate. "Does Sylve share these feelings?"

He froze and reined in his crazed passion, leveling himself out again. "Not quite."

"Don't you think it's the most important thing to consider out of all of this?" He dropped his head in defeat, knowing I was right. "Magic has been banned in this Kingdom, and if she ever got caught..."

"I know." Sindre muttered resentfully.

"It's not fair to put such a heavy burden on her shoulders. It's a sacrifice only *she* can decide to make *without* anyone's influence." I finished my water, washed the mug in the sink, and placed it back in the cabinet. "We will have more time to talk in Frith," I offered, walking over to him and placing a hand on his arm. He nodded and followed me back into the family room. He sighed as he reached for the chair cushions, tossing them on the ground.

"Do you want one or two blankets?" He asked.

"Just one is fine," I answered while grabbing a single log from the stack next to the hearth and tossing it in to feed the fire. "Do you have any idea how long until sunup?"

"Mmmmm." He craned his neck to try and see if he could catch a glimpse of light through the crack in the door. "Not sure. It should be soon. Everyone had just settled and dozed off about an hour ago." He handed me a blanket and took his spot on the floor before the fire, fluffing his pillow before laying on it. I wrapped my shoulders with the fabric and sat beside him with my legs crossed. "Are you not planning on getting more sleep? We've got a busy day of packing ahead of us."

"Maybe not. I'm a bit nervous about sleeping. I had an awful nightmare that woke me." My gaze caught in the flickering dance of the flames. They were slow and methodical: hypnotizing. I felt my body relax, my mind cleared, and I felt an urge to move closer to them, as if they were calling me, dancing for me. I rolled over to get closer to the show, but Sindre's hand pulled at the back of my tunic, snapping me out of my trance.

"Hey, I'm sure you are not nearly rested enough. We can try what we used to do as kids when we had nightmares?" he offered, as a kid-like smile spread across his face. I laughed at the thought of us crafting a blanket fort and cradling each other so we could feel safe enough to sleep again.

"I don't think we would fit underneath a blanket castle anymore."

"Says who?" he retorted, a sly smile on his face.

"You're right. Let's try it."

We both stood and started moving the furniture as quietly as we could. We only had two chairs and a small table to work with. I began scooting a chair to the other side of the hearth, but it made a loud scratching noise along the floor, causing Sindre to turn around and shush me before laughing to himself. I held mine in, but for some reason, between the two of us attempting to stifle our laughs, the situation grew funnier, and breathing became difficult between the wheezing sounds our lungs produced.

Sindre placed the table on its side where our heads would go, and I threw one of our blankets over the two chairs as he draped the edge over his makeshift wall. I snorted at the sight of it. It *might* cover Sindre's shoulders, maybe.

"This is the most pathetic castle we have ever made," I stated, placing my hands on my hips to judge our work.

"I think it is pretty damn good for us being out of practice for so long," he added, lowering himself to the ground and crawling underneath. I laughed into my hand at the sight of it. "Well, are you coming?"

"Gods." I conceded and dropped to my knees, crawling under to join him. Sindre's large frame took up most of the space as he lay on his side, propped up on his elbow.

"Welcome to 'No Nightmares Allowed' Kingdom." He addressed me in a formal greeting.

"Are we really doing this right now?" I questioned with a smile.

"You need actual sleep. I'm sure near-death sleep is not as rejuvenating as regular sleep." He held out his arm to make room for me. A flashback raced across the forefront of my mind, the two of us hiding under our blanket castles as children during a bad storm. He had told me he was gifted the power to ward off scary dreams that night, and as long as I slept in his arms, I would be safe. That was the first night we fought off nightmares together. I smiled at the fond memory and laid down, settling on his muscular arm. The warmth of him was relaxing; the smell of the sea and woods still lingered on his skin and hair. "Sleep well, V."

Nineteen

I was a few doors down, helping a neighbor transfer her vegetables to her wooden cart for their transport to Exris. It was almost midday, the sun was out in full force, the sky was clear, and it was a beautiful day to prepare the rescued thralls for tomorrow's journey.

I heard a familiar horn sound off, deep and long. My eyes darted down the street to the crest of the hill, and I spotted the top of the royal banner peek above it. I dropped everything and sprinted back to the Inn. *Shit!* I forgot to tell Bryn about this supposed visit. *Why today of all days?* Two young Frithians were playing out in the front yard, and as I got to them, I scooped up the youngest and placed him on my hip then grabbed his sister's hand and hurried them inside.

I slammed the door shut with my foot and found Sylve and the children's mother sitting in the common room. The mother's face paled at the sight of mine, and she immediately came over to take her son.

"Please, go up to your room and close the curtains. Stay silent until we come to explain what is happening." She nodded and pushed her daughter up the stairs.

"What is going on?" Sylve asked, moving to pull a weapon from her belt.

"The King is here. I need you to tell everyone upstairs to close their curtains, lock their doors, and stay silent. Our lives may depend on it." I ordered, peeping out the front window to see how fast they were traveling.

"Got it." Sylve nodded.

"Where is Bryn? Sindre?" I asked, my voice cracking from the surging panic that operated my limbs.

"Barn!" She yelled down the stairs as she pounded on the first door.

I ran out the back of the house and found both Bryn and Sindre, each carrying a barrel of water. Sindre had one on each shoulder and was carrying them towards the awaiting cart.

"Calder's here!" I yelled out to them. Brynjar immediately put his barrel down and turned, passing by me to head into the house.

"Where?" As soon as he asked the question, the horn sounded again, seemingly a house away now. "Sindre, put those two on the cart and cover it. Get inside for crowd control when you're done." He nodded and disappeared into the barn.

"Bryn, I'm sorry. I forgot to tell you they had mentioned a visit to Lykke in one of their meetings," I explained, following him in through the back door.

"What is the status of the Frithians?" He called out in the house.

"Secure and understanding the severity of the situation. Where do you want me?" Sylve responded from over the railing. The back door opened and closed. Brax ran to me, tensing and lowering to the ground, growling at the door. The horn went off once more from the outside. They were in front of the Inn now. *We are out of time.*

"Veronica, put Brax in my room. Sylve, stay stationed at the end of the hallway and out of sight. Sindre and Veronica will greet them with me." Bryn ordered, and we were in motion. No questions asked.

After I closed Bryn's bedroom door, I turned and found the young girl I had saved leaving the small private bathroom, deep bruises on her wrists and ankles. *Gods, no.* She looked around, confused. Sindre and Bryn both turned to say something to me and noticed her, their eyes widening in fear. I picked up the young girl and pushed past them just as someone knocked on the door. We didn't have time to make it up the stairs, so we hurried into the small library and rushed to the back left corner. I hid her behind a bookshelf.

"I need you to be silent. All of our lives now depend on our guests not finding any of you. Do you understand?" I whispered gently, brushing her hair away from her face. She nodded and curled herself into a ball. I patted her head and stood but bumped into Sindre, who had followed us into the room.

"You need to be out there with Bryn. I can stay here with her," he said under his breath.

"There is no time." We stood at the back of the room, holding our breaths, listening. The front door creaked open, and Brynjar welcomed our visitors.

"Welcome to Lykke, Your Majesty!" He exclaimed with excitement. It sounded as if he yelled out toward the King. His tone changed drastically as he addressed the person at the door, "Ulrik."

"Your Highness requests your presence for a debriefing. The Lykke war room is the preferred location. Is it in good condition?" Ulrik questioned, sounding bored.

"Pristine! Let me grab my cloak, and I will lead the way."

"Where is Miss Leif?" His question sent a pang of adrenaline through my chest. My eyes darted over to the girl who was curled into a ball, peeking at me over her arms that hid her face. I brought my finger to my lips, signaling her to stay quiet.

"Uhm, you know. I think I last saw Veronica heading into the library. Right through there. Veronica, we've got company!" My eyes widened, and I lightly pushed Sindre closer to the child as my brain whirled with a thousand possible explanations.

"*I'll* get her. Thanks." Ulrik boasted. His thick boots sounded on the wood floor of the common room, closing in on my location. I shot over to the doorway and attempted to leave the library but bumped into Ulrik, who was a step too close to entering the room.

"Miss Leif." He grumbled under his breath, dusting off his shoulder.

"Ulrik," I said plainly, glancing past him to find Bryn. "To what do I owe the pleasure?"

"Why were you not waiting to welcome the King?" he asked suspiciously.

"I–Um–I was distracted. My sincerest apology."

"What is so distracting in there that you would disrespect the Royal Family in such a way?" He taunted, attempting to take a step past me. I slid before him, throwing my hand up against the opening.

"Nothing."

His eyebrows rose with interest. "I think you will let me find out for myself." He threatened under his breath.

I yielded and let my arm drop to my side, allowing him to enter the room. I turned and watched nervously, but he didn't get far before Sindre stepped out from behind the bookshelf...shirtless, his large chest and carved abdomen on full display. My jaw dropped.

"My apologies, Ulrik. We only heard the horn when you arrived outside the house. We had to prioritize being decent *before* welcoming the King." He implied, pulling at his waistband to tighten it slightly. The temperature in the room increased dramatically. Ulrik nodded and turned to face me; his face reddened in embarrassment.

"Getting around, are we?" He hissed, bumping into my shoulder as he passed.

"Oh, Ulrik! I'm a no-strings kind of gal." I offered a shoulder shrug, but he found no amusement in the situation.

"I see that." He paused, turning back and retracing his steps to level with me before leaning closer. "If you think the Princess won't find out about this, that would be foolish." He warned me so quietly that only I could hear. I felt a towering presence appear at my side, and when Ulrik stepped back, Sindre stood over him, the façade of a playful lover long gone.

"Is there a problem?" His tone turned grave. I watched Ulrik falter for half a second. Just half a second, but that is all I needed to feel confident that we still controlled the room. Ulrik cleared his throat.

"Not at all. If you must know, I was informing Miss Leif that the Princess sent her personal guard to discuss a matter with her. He will be waiting outside the house for you to..." He eyed us both up and down. "Freshen up. Don't keep him waiting. The meeting shouldn't be long." He nodded and turned on his heel, leaving us in the room.

Bryn was waiting at the door for Ulrik. Once he exited the building, Bryn nodded with a silly smile and closed the door behind him. I slowly turned to look at Sindre, who still stared at the front door with his jaw clenched.

"I don't know if I should punch you or kiss you. That was genius!"

"I don't like him." He responded plainly, completely ignoring my praises.

"Yeah, me neither." I rolled my eyes at the thought of Ulrik and walked over to the girl who was still hiding. Sindre's tunic was covering her. "It's safe for now," I whispered, throwing Sindre's shirt back to him. "He will take you to your room, but you will all still need to remain silent and out of sight until we come back and tell you they have gone. Okay?"

She nodded and stood beside me. Sindre slid his tunic back on and offered a hand to the little girl, who took it shyly.

"Are you going to be okay? Do I need to come with you?" He asked me.

"No, I will be fine. I'm positive it's Mazen: non-hostile." I winked at him as I made my way to the front door. I waited for Sindre to reach the top of the stairs and pass the girl to Sylve before reaching for the handle.

"You sure?" He asked again.

"I have never been *more* sure," I emphasized and stepped outside. Mazen's back was to me, his brown hair showing red streaks in the sunlight I had never noticed before. He turned his head slightly, then faced forward again, offering only his arm to me.

"So *formal*, thank you." I joked, taking his arm and letting him lead me down the street in the direction the King had come from. We passed by a few warriors stationed outside the Inn, donning the Kingdom's insignia on their chests and holding the royal banners. Only two were in all-black fighting attire without designs, wearing the same steel masks as the strange guard had worn during my debriefing. They stared specifically at me, watching me as we walked by them, sending a shiver down my spine. Are *these* the 'advanced warriors' they mentioned? Mazen kept quiet the whole time. We had passed three houses when I finally decided to break the silence.

"Did you just want to walk me around town? Or do you have something to tell me? Our dearest friend, Ulrik, mentioned the latter." His lips thinned into a hard line as he looked off into the trees lining one side of the road. I was about to ask another question when he quickly looked behind us and slipped his hand into mine, pulling me into a stretch of thick woods.

"What the hel are you doing?" I asked, annoyed, focusing on not getting whacked in the face by branches. He didn't answer and kept pulling me through the woods until we reached a small clearing. The ocean was only a few yards ahead of us, with a steep drop-off keeping the waves at bay. Mazen kept pulling me towards it. "Mazen!" I yelled, yanking my hand from his and drawing my swords from their place on my thighs. He came to a slow stop before turning around with his hands raised slightly. "Are you going to try to kill me?!" I yelled incredulously.

"No, Veronica. I needed to make sure we were away from as many ears as possible, " he offered, lowering his arms.

"When were you going to stop then? When you threw me off the side of the cliff?" I questioned, pointing at the edge with the tip of my blade.

"I would've stopped. It's harder to hear with the added sound of the waves," he explained. "Will you please come sit with me closer to the ledge? I swear on my life. I won't try and push you off." He motioned his finger in an 'X' shape over his heart.

"Mazen, I swear to whatever Gods that are listening, if you kill me, I will torture you for all of eternity in the afterlife." He laughed. He *actually* laughed at me as he nodded towards the edge. I followed hesitantly, sheathing my swords. He sat only a few feet from the edge, and I mirrored him. I had to sit closer to him than I wanted because it was significantly louder the closer we were to the water.

"What's the big secret?"

"I looked more into the magic thing," he confessed. "But what I found...is a bit *alarming*." My ears perked up at this news. I leaned in a bit closer, hugging my knees to my chest. He turned, his back facing the ocean, and sat parallel to me so he could speak while keeping an eye out for any eavesdroppers.

"What is it?"

"Seidr-wielding *humans* cannot perform an ability like you described."

"Which ability?"

"Disappearing into thin air..."

"Oh, right. So, are we talking trolls? Light elves? Dark elves? Dwarves?" He shook his head and stared at me briefly, opening and closing his mouth a few times, debating on how to continue. "Come on! Out with it!"

"I found a book; an ancient text, that mentioned an ability similar to what you described." I waved at him, hurrying him along. "Deities."

I stared at him, waiting for the jest, but he said nothing. He raised his eyebrows in confusion. A laugh burst out of my mouth, sending me rolling onto my back.

I perched on my elbows, looking at Mazen curiously. "Deities? Like Gods?" I laughed.

"Yes."

"Stop fucking around, Mazen. Did you even find anything? Or is this another attempt at a joke?"

His face fell with annoyance.

"You're serious?"

"Yes."

"Wait..." I sat up straighter. "You're fucking serious?!" Unease settled over me. He nodded, staring off into the distance. "Wha-no, maybe we saw wrong then. Maybe the leaves released a hallucinogenic. Maybe the man didn't even exist in the first place."

"I spoke with the archers. They confirmed seeing the man." He reassured me.

"What-What does this mean?"

He rubbed his temple and said, "The man *could* have been a Deity? I'm not a hundred percent confident. My head can't quite wrap around this possibility. I have clarity on magic wielders and found two different kinds of magic usage. The magic-wielding *human's* practice is called Seidr, while the type of magic *Deities* use is Aesir, which can also couple with other elemental abilities if it's magic. There wasn't enough information to imply it's a good thing to have a Deity hiding in Sol."

It was only then I noticed the dark circles under his eyes. "When did you discover this?"

"Yesterday."

"Have you slept?"

"Would you be able to sleep after making this discovery?" He huffed and laid back on the grass.

"Does the King know?" I asked cautiously.

"Gods, *no!* Are you going to tell him?" He shot up, concern in his eyes.

"No! Why would I do that?"

"I don't know if telling him would do any good. I'm sure he wouldn't believe us anyway." He sighed again.

"Does Erikka know?" I questioned quietly.

"No. I was going to tell her, but I have been off-duty since the new personal guard was pla-"

"What *new guard*?" I cut in sharply. "I hadn't been informed there was even a potential personal guard in training. Where did they come from?" I demanded.

"She showed up around the same time as those new advanced warriors did." He explained.

"The people with those stupid masks? Those are the advanced warriors?" I made a face that earned a laugh from him.

"Yes, yes, they are. Unfortunately, no one I have talked to knows anything about them, who they are, or where they came from."

"Or why they are wearing masks?" I inserted.

"Or that." He laughed.

"Does the new guard wear a mask?" I asked.

"No, she is the only one who doesn't."

"And Calder just *trusts* this random person with Erikka alone?" I pushed, annoyance building in my tone. The realization that almost every personal guard I know who has worked closely with Erikka, or the King, is in Lykke. A day's travel away from the castle…and Calder has left her in some *random person's* care? "What the fuck is going on? We had to train for *years* before we received the honor of that position. Who is this person?"

"I haven't spoken to her yet," he cut in. I gave him a look and scoffed. "Sorry, let me rephrase. I haven't gotten any information about her yet, but she and Erikka seem to get on fine." I looked out at the water. My chest tightened, so I stood and walked towards the tree line.

"Is that all? We need to head back soon," I stated, preoccupied with what could possibly be happening at the castle.

"Yes, that's all I have for now." He stood brushing the wrinkles from his pants.

"Is it too much to ask to keep all this between us? I don't trust Erikka to keep it to herself. She won't understand its implications on us if she goes to her father with it." He nodded and began to walk through the trees, leading us through the woods. "What do we do now?" I asked as we came up to the road.

"I'm not sure. I want to keep looking into it before we come to any conclusion. Let's consider this an assumption until then?" He asked, looking at me for my opinion. I nodded, as this seemed to be our only safe option.

Once the Inn was in sight, he offered me his arm again, and I took it. We walked in silence back to the house. Sindre was waiting outside with Brax, who was holding a 'down' position at his feet.

"Komdu!" I spoke to Brax, and he got up and bounded over to me. Sindre side-eyed me for taking him out of his position, but I wanted to introduce him to Mazen. I got down on one knee and opened my arms for Brax to jump into, and his tongue planted kisses all across my face. I laughed and wiped them off. "Mazen, this is Brax. My best buddy!" I smiled and motioned with both of my hands to show him off.

Mazen crouched to Brax's level and held out his hand, which Brax completely ignored, and leaped into his lap, knocking him on his bottom. Brax took this opportunity to take up the space between his legs and roll over onto his back, asking for belly scratches. Mazen happily obliged. "It's nice to meet you, Brax," he laughed.

"And this is Sindre, one of my closest friends. He has a twin sister, Sylve, who is around town somewhere." I motioned to Sindre, who came forward and bowed slightly, as Mazen was preoccupied.

"So, you are one of the famed Nyhus twins? It's an honor." He placed a hand over his heart and attempted to reciprocate Sindre's greeting but was met with a wiggling dog who demanded more attention.

"What? You know of them?" I questioned, impressed.

"I know many things. But most warriors in the Kingdom know about them. Are you ever going to participate in the trials for any royal positions?" He asked Sindre, who raised an intrigued eyebrow.

"Being bound by castle walls isn't really my thing." He shrugged and turned his head in the other direction. I followed his eye and saw the petite escort leading the King, Ulrik, and Brynjar towards us. Brax started to grumble, and Sindre whistled quick and short.

"Med Mer!" He ordered, and Brax was next to him in an instant, waiting for his next command. "I'm going to put him up. I'll be right back." He explained before disappearing into the house.

I turned to help Mazen onto his feet, and we both moved to the front of the building, standing at attention and awaiting the arrival of His Highness. Sindre slipped in line next to me just as they came to a stop.

Brynjar came to stand before Mazen, who bowed and stepped around him to mount his horse. I snuck a look at Bryn, but he turned away from me, his eyes distant.

"I trust you will do the right thing." Calder boomed at us. Confused, I looked at Bryn, who nodded and bowed deeply. Sindre and I mirrored him.

"Yes, Your Highness."

Calder nodded and then looked at me. "We won't need your services next week. Resume your regular shift the week after."

"Yes, Your Majesty." I bowed again. He waved at the warriors in front of the escort, signaling for them to move onward.

"Safe travels." Bryn responded monotonously as they moved onward.

They were two houses away when I spoke to Bryn without turning. "What was *that* about?"

"Wait," was all he said as we continued watching our guests disappear down the hill. "Inside," Bryn ordered. Sindre went in first, and I followed. Bryn slammed the door shut, causing Sindre and me to spin around and look at him, stunned by his aggressive behavior. Sylve slid down the railing and landed beside Bryn, placing a worried hand on his shoulder.

"What's wrong?" She asked.

He stared at the floor, took a deep breath, and exhaled heavily before looking between us. I couldn't tell if he was sad, angry, or going to puke. He sighed, rubbing the back of his neck before stepping away from Sylve to look at all three of us simultaneously.

"He is going to merge with Skirra."

Twenty

"WHAT!?" All three of us spoke in unison.

"He told me that he has been in contact with the Skirrian King, and they have agreed to merge the two Kingdoms." He explained, mindlessly walking over to the chair to sit.

"Wha-He has been in contact with them? For how long?" Sylve questioned, slowly approaching Bryn, who did not raise his eyes to meet hers.

"A few months." He answered. Sylve turned to look at Sindre and me, tears in her eyes. *This can't be happening.* Maybe this is all just another nightmare. I pinched my forearm to double-check.

"What does *merging* mean?" Sindre questioned quietly.

"He is inviting Skirrian warriors to move into the Kingdom to give orders to Sols' warriors. Adopting Skirrian ideologies..." Bryn's voice trailed off. We all know what that meant. Enslave the people of Sol.

"Why?" I asked, walking over and dropping to my knees before him. I took his hands in mine, waiting for his answer.

"Because Sol is non-prosperous. His concern lies in the sustainability and longevity of the Kingdom's lifestyle." He shook his head before letting it fall once more.

"You mean his lifestyle?" Sindre added, and Bryn nodded in agreement.

"Sol was established and expected to be self-sustaining. If he wanted the Kingdom to be more prosperous, there are other measures to do that instead of letting Skirra take over the entire territory." Sylve declared, frustration building in her words. "Incorporating new taxes on goods, land, or travel would have been a good starting point. The citizens here would be more than willing to deal with that rather than falling under Skirrian rule again." Bryn just nodded in agreement but said nothing more. I looked up at Sylve and then Sindre, whose faces were long and concerned.

"It has all been for nothing," Bryn sighed brokenly. My head whipped back to him, my mouth gaping at what he said. "Halle *sacrificed* herself for nothing." Tears streamed down his face now, and defeat encompassed his entire being. I shook my head.

"No! No, this isn't it. We can't just accept that." I stood in defiance, looking between everyone in the room. I was met with saddened eyes, unsure of what we could possibly do to stop this. *I lost my mother to this cause.* The Frithians have split their families up, hoping to be reunited one day, just to be free from Skirra. All of the sacrifices from generations of Ravens can't be for nothing. Hel, the sacrifices made by the Elders who fought in the war can't be in vain. "We have to do something," I said stubbornly, throwing my hands up, hoping an idea would magically land in them.

Sylve and Sindre looked at me and shared a look between them before glancing over at Bryn, who remained hunched over, lost in his thoughts. Sylve walked over and placed a supportive hand on his back.

"I need some air," I announced before walking out the front door.

I looked up at the sky, still clear and the same bright blue as this morning before we learned our lives were on the brink of falling apart. It goes to show that the world will continue despite the evil that threatens to destroy it. It will sit back and change seasons, year after year, while its inhabitants die without a sign of discontent. My anger was at its boiling point. *This isn't fair.* I needed to scream.

I looked around for something, anything, that I could punch or release my frustration on. My eyes scanned past the dock and the rocky shoreline that hid the longships out of view. I was about to turn toward the barn when I saw them. Scarlet red leaves were blowing along the shore and into the ocean. I didn't hesitate and hurried towards them, running up to my shins in the water to grab a leaf with my hand. I contemplated it, turning it over and running my fingers against its soft texture.

I gazed down the shoreline and found the scarlet tree rooted into the ground before our longships. I marched over to it and paused to look around. Into the woods. Out into the ocean. For any sign that the magic wielder would be nearby. I saw no one.

"WHERE ARE YOU?!" I called out. No answer. My breathing increased, and I spun around in another circle, looking for the man. "WHY ARE YOU HERE?!" My breathing continued to quicken, causing my chest to feel as if it was shrinking, offering less and less space for me to fill my lungs with air. Tears stung my eyes, threatening to escape. "WHAT DO YOU WANT FROM ME!?"

I swung my fist into the tree trunk, and just as I was about to make contact, a cluster of leaves formed, absorbing the impact. I aimed for a different spot, and another group of leaves formed. I relentlessly used the tree as a punching dummy until fatigue clasped onto my muscles and the tears stopped falling. I fell to my knees and let my head drop.

"What am I supposed to do?" I sobbed into my hands.

The sound of tree bark twisting and cracking stretched behind me. I wiped the tears from my eyes and turned to find one of the roots had stretched over to our longships and crept into the vessel. I followed the branches' growth up towards the sky, where it had caught onto the corner of the sail. The Ravens' symbol rose into the air and lazily danced with the breeze from the ocean. A different emotion replaced the anger and sadness that had consumed me moments ago. Undeniable pride swarmed my chest, and brought me to my feet.

I searched the area once more for the possibility of spotting the man or Deity that had controlled the scarlet tree before. *Maybe there are multiple magic wielders.* I shook the thought from my head and walked down the shoreline towards the Inn. Before I trudged up the small hill to the road, I turned and glanced back at the tree; it had disappeared, leaving only a few branches to hold up the sail. I found comfort in this anomaly and let the remnants of its effect guide me to the house.

I pushed through the front door, and Sylve was still trying to console Bryn while Sindre leaned against the stairs. They all looked at me, waiting for me to speak. I stood a bit straighter, ready to believe the reality of the words I was about to say.

"We have to start a revolution," I revealed. Sindre and Sylve were the only two who looked at me now. Bryn kept his eyes lowered. I walked over and crouched before him, placing my hands on either side of his face. "We don't have time to sit here and comb through every reason why it's not a good idea or how complex this process will be. I just know we don't have a choice."

I stepped back to the center of the room and placed my clenched fist over my heart. "I hold my heritage and ancestors sacred and vow to defend my people and my family to the death. I will sacrifice so others may live free. I have sworn to uphold the Raven banner, to follow the ways of the North, to always act with honor and bravery, and to be ever true. By the Gods, I have so sworn. By my honor, I have so sworn." I recited the oath we took when becoming Ravens years ago. The same oath the older generations of Ravens had sworn before us. The same oath Brynjar had created and sworn himself, the one that gave my mother her fulfilling life.

Bryn looked up at me through glazed eyes, a pained look on his face. I kept his gaze, adamant in my newfound purpose. He rose from his seat and came to stand in front of me, raising his fist to his heart.

"By the Gods, I have so sworn. By my honor, I have so sworn." He recited. In turn, Sindre and Sylve also mirrored our stance and recited the oath in unison. A tear of rage fell from my eye, and Brynjar caught it with his thumb.

"Harness this anger, my dear, and release your power on those who seek to destroy all that is good and free." I swallowed my emotions and hugged Bryn tightly.

"I'm so sorry this is happening again. We won't let them take this. I won't let them." He pulled me in tighter.

"Thank you. For being the light. You are a warrior." He released me and turned to face the twins. "We need to have a discussion before we go any further into the plans for Sol. Veronica, can you speak with the Frithians and release them from their temporary confinement?"

"Of course. Call for me when you're finished." He nodded. I turned and walked over to Sylve for a warrior's embrace, then Sindre, who nodded with pride as I stepped away.

Twenty-One

The moon had long replaced the sun when Sylve and I finished packing the carts for tomorrow's travel. Jerrik had come to assist on our journey to Frith, and Bryn was updating him now with Kingdom news. Sindre was explaining tomorrow's plans to the families upstairs. First, we must escort this group safely to Frith. Then, we plan for wherever this rebellion takes us.

The back door flung open, creaking from the speed it moved, and Jerrik stormed out of the house, heading right for me with his eyebrows furrowed. I ran to the other side of the cart to keep my distance between us, unsure why I was in trouble this time.

"What did I do now?" I asked. He stopped across from me and put his fists on his hips.

"You almost died?!" He choked out, clearing his throat a little.

"Oh. *That.*" I walked over to him, and his arms went limp at his sides, his face fell, and fear filled his eyes.

"I was saving a youn-" His bear-like arms scooped me up, squeezing me tight before I could finish explaining myself.

"I know it's your job...but please, *please* stop scaring me. Twice in one week has passed my limit of heartache. Okay?" He begged as he placed me back on the ground.

"I'm sorry. I will try my best." I offered, turning back to the cart to finish tightening the ropes and securing Jerrik's supplies to our cart.

"Also," he added, "you promised you would return to the Tavern with Elias and Rune. So, you can't die until all of your promises are fulfilled. I don't make the rules."

"Wow, Jerrik." I turned to him, "I'll let the Gods know that I can't die until all of my promises to you are seen to. I'm sure they will make an exception." I laughed.

"I don't foresee any issues. It is me we are talking about." He responded with a shrug.

Sylve returned from checking all the stationary carts covered sporadically between the neighboring houses. "Everything is cleared and ready to go in the morning."

Jerrik held his arm out towards her, and she walked over and fit herself under it, wrapping her arms around him. "You are a God, Sylve."

She looked up at him, confused.

"How you managed to save her life...you never cease to amaze me, woman." He said, amazed by the situation.

She smiled brightly and laughed to herself. "Oh, it wasn't *too* difficult. Saving any of you would be the easiest decision of my life." He squeezed her shoulder before letting her stand straight again. "Do you mind going to get Sindre for me?" She asked, her hands clasped together over her chest, eyelashes batting persuasion through the air.

"Anything for you, dear. I've got to talk to Brynjar more in preparation for tomorrow anyway. " He bowed deeply, then pointed a stern finger toward me before walking inside. "Keep it together."

I shook my head and laughed as I came to stand before Sylve. "Does he know? How did you save me?"

"I'm not sure. I'll double-check with Bryn." She contemplated, her gaze following Jerrik as he walked towards the Inn.

"What did Bryn say about that? Did you guys end up having to tell him?" I questioned, hopping up to sit on top of a barrel.

"It's complicated...We did tell him, but with the recent turn of events, Brynjar doesn't feel as confident in the laws as he would have before."

"Wait, what does that mean?"

"He explained it like this: the laws they established with the creation of Sol were a collaborative effort before they crowned the first King. Originally, they were going to allow structured study and practice of magic. However, Calder was adamant about banning it. If I skip the history lesson, Bryn is now even questioning the creation of that law in the first place and Calder's intentions behind choking it out of the Kingdom completely." I nodded, thinking of possible reasons myself. His ego is the most delicate thing I've seen, so I'm sure it stems from the fear of a power struggle.

"So…going forward?" I asked quietly.

"We still need to keep my abilities under the radar. Do as I have been doing. Don't tell anyone, and never use them in public, ever."

"Even from the rest of the Ravens?"

"I didn't specifically ask, but I probably should. I'll get that answer and let you know in the morning." I nodded in understanding.

"I can't thank you enough, Sylve," I started. She tried to stop me from continuing, but I hopped down and walked over to her, jumping onto her and wrapping my arms and legs around her. "You changed my fate, and I will forever be in your debt." She conceded and wrapped her arms around me, accepting my thanks.

"You're welcome, Veronica. Thank you for believing in me."

"I never doubted you for a second." I winked and released my grip, placing my feet back on the ground. Sindre had walked out and paused, looking between the two of us. "What?"

He smiled but was interrupted by Jerrik pushing out of the house behind him, looking between Sindre and me. "You guys got caught by the King's escort?" he asked enthusiastically.

"What do you mean?" Sindre questioned, stepping to the side to make room for him.

"Brynjar just told me that you two were sharing an intimate moment when the King arrived and got caught by the Chieftain."

Sindre looked at me with a cheeky grin, and Sylve covered her mouth with her hand, leaving me to address Jerrik's gullibility. "Uh…We-"

"How long has this been going on? Why did no one tell me? I feel like this is something I should be involved in. I've been asking you for yea-" We all burst out laughing simultaneously. "What? What is it?" He looked around at us, confused, and Bryn stuck his head out the door.

"Hey guys, I need everyone to start heading to bed now. We'll wake in a few hours, and all of you need to be focused when we travel."

"You got it!" Sylve laughed, grabbing her satchel from next to the cart. Bryn gave me a knowing smile and chuckled to himself as he went inside and closed the door. I should've known he would leave that story hanging. I shook my head. Sylve, with her hand outstretched towards me, said, "You and Jerrik can sleep at our place. We will double up and at least sleep comfortably before tomorrow." I nodded and intertwined my fingers with hers.

"Wait, is anyone going to tell me what's happening between you?" He complained, picking up my bag and his own from the back of his cart. Sindre walked up behind him and patted him on the back.

"I'll tell you all about it tonight for our bedtime story." He joked, walking with him back to their house.

We said goodnight to the boys and were getting ready for bed when I found myself contemplating my reflection in a small hand mirror. My black hair still looked like a bird's nest, even after brushing through it. My face was free from bruising, but the scar remained. I wonder. I lifted the end of my slip under my breasts, exposing my undergarments, and there it was. A faint white line, the length of the head of my axe, spread just under my ribcage. I ran the tips of my fingers up the curve of my hip until they met the edge of my newest battle prize. I brushed over the healed skin and was startled by a faint vibrating sensation, causing my hand to pull away.

"I'm sorry about the scar," Sylve said regretfully as she walked toward the private bathtub, wrapped in her towel. She sighed thoughtfully, looking as if she was replaying each step of the raid back in her mind. "You have been the only person I have tried using magic on besides myself. So, I'm still very unsure about how it all works, " she explained shyly.

"Don't worry about me. I'll take a scar over death any day." I winked, letting my slip fall over me again. "Can I ask you a question?"

"Of course."

"How did you discover your ability?" I asked, leaning against the wall as she stepped into her awaiting bath.

"Well, it was an accident. I wasn't going out of my way to learn or practice it, I swear."

"I believe you," I reassured.

"Sindre and I were training late one evening. Luckily, the rest of the Lykke guards had finished their training and were gone because it happened in the middle of the training arena."

"Wait, when was this?" I interjected.

"A few days after the winter solstice." I nodded, allowing the information to sink in. "Anyway, we were training, and I was trying to teach Sindre how to use my rope dart, and we were practicing with a straw dummy." She shook her head and laughed to herself. "He missed the target and moved to reset himself but let the rope slip way too far from his hand, AND he took like FOUR steps back towards me, so it sliced me." She patted the top of her shoulder next to her neck, insinuating where she sustained the injury. "There was a lot of blood. More than I had expected. Especially since it felt like it barely got me, but when it wouldn't stop, I started to worry. Sindre kept trying to get me to Brynjar, but I didn't want to go. Something was telling me I didn't need to. I don't know how to explain it without sounding crazy. It was just a weird subconscious thing."

"I think I understand what you felt."

She waved her hand airily, moving on to the rest of her explanation. "I held my shoulder and kept thinking, 'If it would stop bleeding, I can sew it shut myself. Just stop bleeding. Stop bleeding.' And I swear, I only thought, 'Stop bleeding,' and the light formed, and it stopped just enough so I could tend to the wound. It was the craziest thing." She trailed off and fell into deep thought. I walked over to her, moved her hair back, and held it up so she could dip into the water and rest her head on the back ledge. "Sindre and I just sat there, for only Odin knows how long, just trying to process what I did and what it could mean going forward. After that, I tried my best to read up on magic to get a good idea of what to expect, but access to those kinds of texts is limited. And I don't want to draw attention to myself by traveling to Kron's castle to look in the royal library."

"Well, that makes sense. Maybe during my next shift, I can look for you. See if I can get my hands on anything." I offered sincerely, knowing I wouldn't necessarily have to do that since Mazen had already read most of the information at the castle.

"No, Veronica." I looked at her, confused. "Not with what is going on. Especially since we know how Calder..." she lowered her voice to barely a whisper, "how he can be...That is too risky."

"I want to help you however I can. I have access to the texts. Why would I walk by when I can pop in and take some time to read?"

"Please, Veronica. Brynjar has promised that once we get these Frithians settled and the situation explained to the Elders, he will ask them what they know or remember about magic. Then, we can go from there." She turned to me with a pleading look. Her giant brown eyes reached out, begging for my compliance with her request. I looked away and nodded before she could persuade me to do anything else. "Thank you." Sylve whispered.

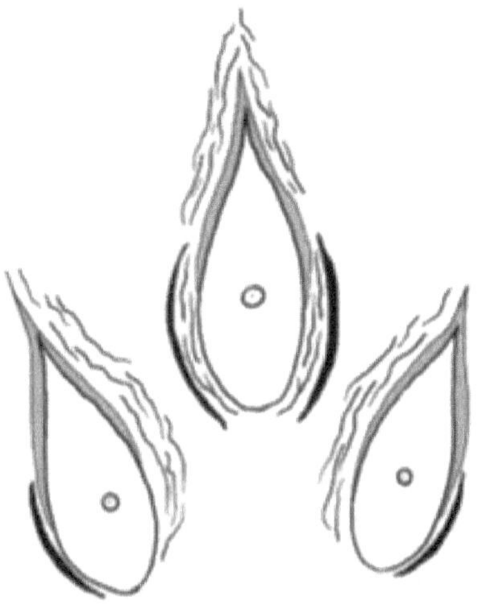

Twenty-Two

"Everyone is accounted for!" Jerrik announced as he walked back towards Bryn and me at the rear of the line of carts.

"Horses are strapped in and ready to go!" Sindre called from in front of the cart closest to us, most likely finishing attaching Alsvid to it.

"We passed out all the blankets to the Frithians and hopefully have them seated as comfortably as possible between the supplies. I think we are ready to go," Sylve added, lifting the back of the cart and latching it upright.

"Alright, let's mount up and start moving," Bryn ordered, looking up into the night sky. "We need to be gone before the sun comes up." We all nodded, and Sindre whistled a smooth, long melody before pulling himself onto the seat at the front of the cart and grabbing the reins. Sylve climbed up next to him, arming herself with her bow. Jerrik armed himself with his bow and climbed up on the cart in front of Sindre and Sylve, sitting next to Siv.

Bryn walked over and mounted his all-black gelding, Grani, the largest of all our horses, before turning to me. "I haven't been to Frith in some time. It will be nice to see what has been done."

I mounted Arvak and turned towards him. "The Elders always ask when you are going to visit them. How long will you be staying?" Just before it began moving, another whistle sounded from the front of the line. Bryn and I remained at the rear.

"Just through tonight. I don't want to leave the Inn too long if a Royal Guard comes looking for me. They have been sending messages to Lykke far more frequently lately."

"Well, the Frithians will be happy to see you." I offered, urging Arvak forward in unison with Bryn and Grani.

One by one, the lookouts stationed on each cart lit a small lantern as we crossed the open acres of farmland toward The Willingman Woods. Once we broke the tree line, another whistle sounded, quick and short, in four spurts. Then, one by one, each cart broke off in opposite directions. In case of being followed or seen, the tracks left by the carts will likely be less prominent with the differing routes we take each time we travel. We will all meet at the foot of the incline and realign before starting our ascent to the hidden village.

Bryn waved towards me as he broke off to trail behind Siv and Jerrik, leaving me to Sindre and Sylve. We drew the short stick this week and were positioned the furthest inside the woods. The rest of the carts will stagger closer to the outer perimeter. We ensured all the children were on the carts farthest away from the dangers lingering in the woods, leaving us with a group of parents who volunteered to ride in our carts.

Sylve turned to the side and motioned with her head, so I urged Arvak to the side of the cart to hear her better. "Have you met Kalyani yet?"

"Yes, last week. She has the two boys."

"Oh, my goodness, those two are the sweetest boys I've ever met."

"Really? I haven't had the honor of spending time with them, just Kalyani."

"You will be surprised by her," she remarked proudly. I smiled but noticed Arvak stiffen and look off to the east. Sylve's smile waned as she aimed her bow, noticing the shift in the air as Sindre slowed Alsvid to a halt, listening.

I scanned the trees above that seemed to stretch high into the night sky, which was barely beginning to show signs of morning. I could hardly see anything past the soft glow of the lantern that offered light around our cart. Leaves rustled behind us, and I turned Arvak to face it.

"How long has it been since there was an incident?" I asked quietly.

"Four weeks," Sylve responded.

"So, it's about time for another, isn't it?"

"Seems like it." Sindre agreed. He turned to the group of Frithians who were sitting in the cart. "We might be experiencing one of the disturbances I mentioned last night. Do you remember what is expected of you?" The group nodded and lowered themselves to be level with the supplies, grabbing onto anything they could to brace themselves.

Another quick rustle spooked Alsvid this time, hurrying Sindre to calm her. I forced my eyes to focus between the trees and saw a figure appear, then another, then a third, darting from one tree to the next, closing the distance between us. But, as they closed in, they remained shadowed, faceless.

"Dark Elves!" I yelled out to Sindre and Sylve, who ushered Alsvid to full speed. I pushed Arvak to follow closely behind the cart, keeping my eyes moving between the Frithians and the creatures that had begun their hunt.

"We have at least five miles until we meet with the others! There is no way the horses will last that long like this!" Sindre shouted over the sound of pounding hooves and screeching wheels. *Think, Veronica! What can we do?* An arrow whizzed past my head, and my eyes shot up to find Sylve notching another one and drawing it. I looked behind me to see an obscured figure rolling into the shadows from Sylve's blow. However, the others didn't break stride and only seemed to run faster toward us. One was reaching for Arvak's hind quarters. I swerved her off to the side just as Sylve's second arrow flew past and hit its target.

"Hey! There should be a clearing about a mile off course to the east!" I yelled up to Sindre, who turned his head slightly to try to hear me. "Do you know where I'm talking about?!"

He shrugged and shook his head before pulling the reins sideways, breaking off from the path to avoid a fallen tree. Unfortunately, I had to pull Arvak to the other side, splitting us from the group and enveloping us in the darkness under the canopy.

I couldn't risk stopping. Especially since I couldn't take even a second to look behind us while navigating through the trees. I heard an ear-piercing scream from directly beside us, and when I turned to look, something heavy slammed into my chest, throwing me off Arvak and sending me rolling in the dirt.

I coughed a few times before standing up cautiously, pulling out my sister swords while I whistled for Arvak to return. There is no telling how far she got from me in that short time, and I wasn't even sure I knew what direction we were going. Then, a force hit me in the center of my back, sending me to my knees. I scrambled to my feet, swinging my swords in a circle, trying to make contact with the shadowy creatures that thrive in the dark. Then, a predatory laugh bounced off the trees surrounding me, sending a shiver down my arms. *I need to get out into the daylight quickly, the one place they cannot go.*

A familiar dim light formed on the ground in front of me. It was the same luminescent snake that led me through the forest after the fight. It started to slither away from me, and I didn't hesitate this time to follow, but something pounced on my back, pulling me to the ground. I rolled over quickly, throwing the elf off me. I had lost both swords from my impact with the ground, but I didn't have time to look for them before the creature jumped on me again. I could barely make out its outline when I raised my hand to catch its arm, stopping it from sweeping its shadowy claw at me. It lifted its other arm, readying another attack, but I grabbed ahold of that as well, putting all my strength behind holding the creature away from me as it leaned all its surprisingly heavy weight onto me. The Dark Elf moved its head closer to mine and revealed its face that had rough pasty skin with rock-like texture. On it were three sickly green, beady eyes and a too-large mouth that spread open to show rows of backward facing teeth, similar to those of a snake. It inched its mouth closer to my face despite my effort to hold it back.

"I will receive a pretty penny for your head." It hissed.

My eyes widened as the creature unhinged its jaw, opening its mouth wider than anything I've ever seen, and reached out over my head. "NO!" I screamed with all the air left in me and thrashed against its weight.

A blur of green light flashed past, and the shadowy creature was flung off me. The snake had latched onto the elf's throat, illuminating the creature's outline. I rolled over and felt around on the ground until I found one of my swords.

Then, I turned back to the now furious elf who was currently holding its throat, thrashing and screaming in agony. I jumped on it and twisted my sword through the back of its neck until the gurgling sound stopped.

I removed my weapon and wiped the blood, or whatever the liquid might be, onto the sleeve of my tunic and returned it to my thigh. The smell of its bodily fluid was nauseating and the consistency was much thicker than my own blood. I turned, watching as the snake illuminated again, and continued down a path I couldn't see, passing by my other blade. I bent down to pick it up and sheathed it. Running after the snake, I let it lead me through the woods once more.

The eerie feeling had disappeared, and I had been lightly jogging on the path for a few minutes. Just as I heard hooves in the distance, it suddenly veered off and dimmed until I could no longer see it. I stepped behind a tree and whistled, hoping it wasn't some creature bound and determined to kill me.

A whistle sounded off in response, and relief fell over me. I would recognize Sindre's whistle anywhere. I stepped out of my hiding spot just as he came into view with Arvak, who wasn't slowing down as they neared. I could barely make out Sindre's outstretched arm as my eyes tried to adjust to his outline coming closer. *Shit.* I lowered myself slightly, bending my knees and taking a few steps towards him, grabbing onto Sindre's forearm and jumping into the air, letting his momentum swing me up and onto the back of Arvak in one swift motion. He pulled the reins and turned us around, hurrying her into a sprint back in the direction they came from.

"Are you okay?" he asked over his shoulder.

"All good back here, thanks!" I answered, pulling myself closer to him for comfort.

A few moments of silence passed when I noticed the trees begin to thin in front of us, allowing the morning light to pass through freely until we entered the clearing in the middle of the woods. *Thank the Gods, I was right.* I'm usually terrible with directions. The cart, along with the Frithians and Sylve, was waiting in the center of the open field. Deep scratches had been made on the sides of the cart, along with a scratch on Alsvid's hind leg—*poor thing.*

"Is everyone alright?" I asked Sindre as we neared the group.

"Some of us have a few scratches, but we are all intact." He answered, pulling Arvak to a stop. I dismounted, and he followed suit, guiding Arvak to the back of the cart. "Are you okay? We heard screaming." He repeated, taking my arm in his hand, examining my bloodied tunic, and then eyeing my chest. "Gods, what did that?"

I looked down at my chest, and there was a slash from one side to the other through my tunic, exposing the irritated skin underneath. "I have no idea. I might have run into a tree if I'm being honest. I couldn't see anything and was trying my best to navigate Arvak in the dark."

"Well, I'm glad you're alright." Sylve cut in while tying off a bandage on her forearm. "We need to get to the meeting point quickly before we throw things off course and they send a group out to find us." She ordered, picking up her bow that was leaning up against the side of the cart and turning away to reassure the group of people waiting for her direction. I went to grab the reins for Arvak, but Sindre stepped in front of me.

"I'll take the rear position." He announced plainly.

"I'm fine. I can't use the bow anyways."

"You can navigate the cart. Sylve will remain on lookout."

My face twisted in annoyance. "I have only moved that cart once. I'm staying at the rear. What's the problem?" I tried sidestepping him again, but he blocked my path.

"I think you could use a break."

"I don't give a fuck what you think." I pushed his arm out of my way, but he grabbed my shoulder and walked me around the cart toward the front of it. I ducked out from under his grip and sent my elbow flying toward his face, making contact with his jaw. He stumbled back in surprise, and I sent my boot into his chest, sending him to the ground. He looked up at me with an astonished grin. A grin I had to stop myself from wiping from his face completely. "Do your job, Sindre. And don't try to stop me from doing mine again. I said I'm fine. I'd tell you otherwise."

"Would you?" He retorted, pushing himself onto his feet.

"If you would wait and give me the chance to, yes," I stated, mounting onto Arvak and urging her forward.

We rode for about an hour when we finally met up with the rest of the group. Bryn waved them up the beginning of the steady incline once he saw us and realigned with me as we passed him.

"Experience a hiccup?" he asked jokingly.

"Dark Elves," I answered, his face turning solemn instantly.

"How many?"

"I saw three initially. But Sylve shot two, and then we were separated, and only one bothered me."

"Two were on the cart." Sylve cut in from ahead of us. Bryn nodded toward her in acknowledgment. He looked me over quickly, noticing my torn shirt.

"Did the elf do that?"

"I'm pretty sure a tree might've done this," I smirked.

He laughed at my expense.

Twenty-Three

As the aspen trees began to thin and the sun secured its place in the sky, we passed a marker that was cleverly hidden among them, reassuring us we were on the correct path towards Frith. Random cuts had been slashed into what seemed like arbitrarily located trees, staggered over a short distance, but when you were level with them, the cuts aligned, creating the image of a raven. I breathed a sigh of relief, which caught Bryn's attention.

"Tired of riding already? It's been a pretty smooth trip, I think." He remarked with a sideways glance. I rolled my head towards him and stared blankly once my eyes found his cheeky smile.

"Now that I think about it, it has been a pretty easy travel day, hasn't it?" I stacked my hands on my saddle horn, giving the most lifeless smile I could conjure.

"That's the spirit!" He laughed and slapped his heavy hand on my shoulder before taking off to the head of the escort. Sindre looked over his shoulder and laughed, earning an elbow to the back from Sylve.

"What?" I yelled up to him. "What's so funny?"

"You gotta love Brynjar." He responded back. Sylve rolled her eyes and returned her unused arrow to her quiver, snaking herself through the bowstring.

"Can I hit him again?" I asked Sylve, who snorted at Sindre's quick turn of the head and expression of feigned offense.

"You don't need my permission." She laughed before jumping off her seat and continuing to close the distance while enjoying a walk next to the cart.

"I think you might need mine, though!" Sindre offered. I shrugged off his suggestion and followed him as we reached a plateau in our ascent that would open to the city of Frith.

Some of the Ravens' homes were built along the perimeter of the city, placed throughout the thinning woods, the first line of defense if anyone happened to journey too close. This is why the Elders traveled well past Willingman Woods while searching for a place to establish this safe haven, hoping the danger it poses alone would deter any adventurous folk. We rode up to a small clearing that led us to a rock formation and a stockade stretching from one side of the sole opening to the other. Two Ravens were stationed on either side of the gate that was only wide enough for the carts to barely squeeze through. Six Ravens stay on patrol at the entrance to the city, so the other four are most likely hidden within the trees.

As the front of our entourage reached the two guards, Bryn dismounted from Grani, opening his arms wide for one of the two men to walk over and embrace him. The other man waved to the guard at the top of the gate and a long whistle sounded from somewhere above us. The sound of creaking wood and iron bounced off the trees as the gateway sluggishly opened, allowing us to pass. Bryn took Grani by the reins and led us through the tight passageway, where we met with another group of Ravens who welcomed all the travelers with smiles and warm embraces. We offered them a chance to stand, stretch their limbs, and reunite with their kin for the final stint of their journey. An Elder Raven named Askel climbed onto the cart and whistled to get the small crowd's attention.

"On behalf of the Ravens and the current occupants of the city, we want to welcome you to Frith. Well, not just welcome you...We want to congratulate you as well. Your bravery and courage to take a chance on freedom, for a better life, a life you deserve, any living human being deserves, does not go unnoticed." He cleared the emotion from his throat before continuing. "Congratulations! You have all just become Frithians! Welcome home!"

The Ravens erupted with cheers, whistles, and applause for the travelers, who seemed shocked at their new reality. Smiles, *genuine* smiles spread across their faces, and tears began to fall. They embraced each other, the Ravens, then one another again. Tears formed in my eyes as I dismounted from Arvak and walked over to Sylve and Sindre, wrapping my arms around their necks and pulling them down to me for an embrace. When I finally let them go and turned around, the mother and daughter duo stood there; the daughter was smiling, but the mother had rivers cascading down her cheeks. I opened my arms and walked over to them, enveloping both in a warm embrace, letting the emotion flow freely from my own eyes. She pulled herself away from me, attempting to wipe the wetness from her face.

"Thank you..." She sobbed, looking behind me at the twins. "Thank all of you...Thank you." She continued to repeat her thanks as she walked over to Sindre and fell into his arms, unable to hold back the years of raw emotion that finally had a safe place to be felt.

All the Ravens who had just traveled left the carts and allowed the new group of warriors to replace us. I whistled for Brax, who jumped out from his place on the front cart and made his way over to us, stopping to give kisses to some of the children he had traveled with. He is a great protector and has always loved being around the young ones. So, it is only natural that he became their personal guard dog and travel buddy on our journeys to Frith. Brax doesn't mind being away from me when he has younger humans to protect. Plus, it makes me feel like he is safer on the inside route instead of something possibly happening to him on the outer perimeter. *What if he had been with us today during the ambush?* I shook the thought from my head and opened my arms up for him to jump onto me, squeezing him tight.

We waved to Jerrik as the escort headed towards town to bring the Frithians to their new homes and distribute the supplies he brought. The rest of those we traveled with slowly dispersed after lingering and congratulating each other on a job well done. Bryn joined us where we stood, a content smile on his face.

"Great job, everyone." He offered his arm to Sindre, who embraced it, then Sylve, before throwing an arm over my shoulder. "You all never cease to impress me. Not even the founding Ravens were this efficient and caring." I leaned my head into him, and Sindre put a hand over his own heart.

"Thank you, Brynjar. That means everything." Sylve beamed.

"We have had the best person to learn from," I added, slapping his belly before ducking out from under his grasp. I grabbed Arvak and Grani to lead them towards the large house and barn that stands guard at the forefront of Frith.

The main house is twice the size of Brynjar's Inn and can house all the Ravens, Elders, and visitors.

The barn off to the right of the house has thirty or so stalls and a few acres of fenced-in pasture behind it for their supply of horses and highland cattle. Frith was just beyond the few acres on the backside of the house used for growing crops. The city was close-knit and cozy. The homes were mostly made from stone with a blend of thatch and wooden roofing. The miles of land that Frith inhabits are surrounded by towering birch trees on all sides. The yellow and green hues of the leaves brightened from the spring rains and melting ice from the northeast mountain, referred to as Mount Eir by the founders.

Once I finished putting up the horses and began to head back to the house, I noticed Sindre sitting on the fence. I walked over to him and leaned on the wood railing beside him.

"How can anyone not appreciate this?" He questioned over his shoulder. The sun was setting next to the mountain, painting the wispy clouds with stunning shades of pink and oranges, emphasizing the golden canvas behind them. The Seven Sisters Falls on the south end of the mountain sprayed mist that caught the color of the sky. There was a subtle hum of activity coming from the city. Lanterns that hung outside of doors were being lit. Children were getting called inside to ready themselves for bed as the livestock moved back into their covers for the night. Peace and safety blanketed Frith, unaffected by the evils that threatened our livelihood. For now, that is.

"I think everyone here appreciates this." I offered.

"It's beautiful," he remarked breathlessly.

"The most beautiful thing we will ever see." I reiterated.

"Almost." He offered softly, looking down at me with a warm smile, his golden hair glinting in the sun as he turned to face me. I caught his eyes, and my face flushed pink immediately at his insinuation.

"Hey! Only *I'm* allowed to ogle over *your* beauty." I contested, slapping my hands over my face after elbowing him in his side. He leaned back with a laugh, nearly tipping himself off the edge of the fence.

"It's worth fighting for." He added. "When shit gets rough during the upcoming weeks...this is what will keep me going. This moment right here is worth dying for. If that's what it takes." I pushed myself off the railing and walked behind him, running my hand along his back.

"Whatever it takes." I echoed, offering my hand for him to join me on my way back to the house. He nodded and gracefully lifted himself up and off the fence, taking my hand in stride. As we walked up to the main house, you could hear loud, booming voices and laughter. Sindre opened the door for me, and I entered to find all the Elders sitting at a long oak dining table with Brynjar, Sylve, and a few other Ravens. They all stopped talking and looked at us, and I paused in anticipation of the usual uproar.

"VERONICA! SINDRE!" The group sang in unison, all standing to embrace Sindre and me. The ones closest to us were Torsten and Dagna Balke, brother and sister whose parents were a part of the original Ravens' raids but have since passed. They work at the orphanage in Frith, where they help raise the children whose families had chosen to sacrifice their freedom in hopes that they would be reunited one day. Torsten's burly arms swallowed me as I felt something scratching at my leg. I looked down to find a long-bodied herding dog jumping up for her hello.

"Frannigan! Hey girl!" I laughed as Dagna came over, scooped her up, and slipped under my arm for a hug. Her strawberry-blonde hair smelled of fresh wildflowers, which tickled my nose. She moved over to hug Sindre, who gave her a sweet smile, causing her to blush.

All the Elders were here catching up with Bryn. Askel, Liv, Bergunn, and Thora piled on top of Sindre and me. There were so many arms, and I wasn't sure who I was embracing. Ragnhild took his time getting up from his seat to make his way over to us. His beard had significantly grown since I'd last seen him, long enough now to lay on his chest, and he had shaved his head. Where a cloud of gray hair once sat was only smooth brown skin. He stood taller than Bryn, but the two were identical in body size.

"Ragnhild! I love the new look." I stated, practically jumping into his arms.

"I figured it was time to let go of the dream of my youth." He laughed deeply.

"I think it makes you look younger," I added, moving to see Ylva gliding over with grace; her tattooed arms opened wide. After losing her lower right leg during the war, she struggled for years to adapt but has since recovered and mastered fighting and riding horses better than before. Her silver hair was pulled off to the side in a bundle of thick braids, and her tunic was loose around her chest, letting her bronzed skin underneath shine through. She has three tattooed lines that flow from her bottom lip to her chin and singular lines straight out from the corner of her intense brown eyes, which grabbed my attention. I couldn't help but smile brightly at her presence. "Ylva."

"Veronica, how have you been, dear?" She asked, wrapping her arms around me and stroking the back of my head with a soft hand.

"I've been good. I'm sorry I haven't prioritized coming to visit. First, the King requested my presence at the castle and raids...then life. I explained. She made a face when I mentioned the King and waved her hand at my reasoning.

"No worries. I know you all have been busy taking over responsibilities we can no longer do." She shrugged and squeezed my shoulders before stepping around me to greet Sindre.

"How are you, Sindre?"

"I'm good, but...things could be better." He replied, sneaking a furtive glance at Bryn returning his attention to her. It was quick but it was enough for Ylva to notice.

She turned and looked between Bryn and Sindre, whose eyes were downcast to avoid hers. "What's going on?" She questioned, concern filling her voice. She looked at me, but I pursed my lips, waiting for Bryn to steer the conversation. The room fell silent, and Bryn cleared his throat.

"Torsten and Dagna, do you mind giving us privacy to discuss a few things? We will be holding a town meeting tomorrow morning outside of the orphanage, and I would appreciate it if you could grab a few other Ravens and let the Frithians know." They both nodded and said their goodbyes. Once they left, Bryn motioned for all the Elders to take their seats at the table. Askel sat between Bergunn and Ylva on one side of the table while Liv and Thora sat on the other. Ragnhild sat at the opposite end of the table from Bryn while Sylve, Sindre, and I came to stand behind him.

A few moments of silence passed through the room, but seeing Brynjar struggle to find the right words to say made my throat tighten. Reality had found us again. We respected the time he needed to prepare himself. He opened and closed his fists on the table a few times before shaking his head and letting it hang. Sindre stepped forward and placed a hand on his shoulder, earning a nod from him. Bryn let out a big breath before speaking.

"About fifty years ago, we decided enough was enough. We knew that we and our loved ones were treated with unfairness and injustice. We deserved happiness and the freedom to choose how we lived our lives, so we decided to fight for that right." The Elder Ravens got antsy in their seats; Ragnhild Hall seemed the most unsettled, leaning forward, bracing his elbows on his knees, listening intently. Bryn continued.

"We have all lost people we cared about for the existence of Sol and the freedom she offers. But it is worth it in the end...because we made it here. Their death was not in vain. Their death is honored with Sol's continued independence." He shook his head and braced his hands on the table, taking a second to breathe in another calming breath. "Since the founding of Sol, we have dedicated our lives to helping people who remained trapped in Skirra with no way of creating a fulfilling life for themselves. With no way of leaving or getting out...even if they tried, death would find them one way or another. The Ravens have been the only glimmer of hope for those still in Skirra, but we continue to answer that call for help. Over the years, this organization has grown tremendously. Three generations of Ravens, all fighting for those who need us simultaneously, is something I hold proudly in my heart." He looked over at me, and his eyes began to redden as he prepared to break the news, forcing my gaze to the floor.

The women and men he fought next to in the war, his sisters and brothers in arms, his family...everyone in this room holds a special place in Bryn's heart, which I could feel breaking from the weight of his words. He will hold an immense amount of misplaced guilt upon himself. Ylva slid her hand over to Bryn's, held it as if she could feel the emotional storm brewing within, and offered hers as an outlet. He squeezed her fingers, and their eyes met. Bryn cleared his throat once more.

"We continue to lose lives to this cause, but we also continue to risk them for it. The lives lost have had the most impact on our success, yet they do not get to delight in the prosperity we do. They have not seen the fruits of their labor, but we can only hope they know their sacrifices have not been in vain. Will *not* be in vain. All of the sacrifices that everyone in this room has made will not be futile." He stood up straight, letting go of Ylva's hand.

"Calder came to Lykke to meet with me about the future of Sol. He has been in communication with the King of Skirra, and they have agreed on merging the two Kingdoms." An immediate uproar from the Elders ensued. All of them stood and began hurling curses and questions one above the other, all except Ylva and Ragnhild. Ylva sat back in her seat, letting her hands fall limply in her lap, while Ragnhild remained still and stoic, staring at Bryn, the two of them communicating through whatever bond they shared. Finally, Ragnhild stood, and the Elders quieted, looking over to him before retaking their seats.

"How long do we have?"

"He didn't specify."

"Do you have any ideas yet of what we can do?" Bryn shook his head before looking at me.

"Veronica has one." They all looked at me, and I clenched my jaw, hoping the uneasiness I felt would dissipate so I could speak clearly. I looked at Ragnhild, and he nodded his head.

"We have to start a revolution," I stated confidently.

"Another revolution?" Thora scoffed and ran her hand through her auburn curls, revealing the thick scars that ran down one side of her face and snaked up her hands. "We have significantly fewer warriors to even attempt a fight against, *just* the warriors they keep at Sol's castle." She downed the last bit of mead in her mug and then stood to refill it from the barrel along the wall behind her. "Not to mention, if the Kingdoms merge soon, we would be completely fucked." Bergunn added, stroking his red braided beard that rested on his chest. Bryn smiled at me, urging me on.

"The citizens of Sol don't know about this, and I am almost positive neither do any of the Royal Guards or Warriors at the palace. If we tell them, they will fight. The whole Kingdom would fight to keep the freedoms they've earned."

"You are *almost* positive?" Askel questioned, craning his tattooed neck back to look at me as he did. He had his coppery hair braided down the middle of his head so it laid down his back, his hair shaved on both sides to reveal tanned skin, and a look on his square face that could cause the sturdiest of trees to tremble.

"I can't confirm. But some warriors have been promoted to *Advanced* Warrior, and no one knows who they are. They wear steel masks and aren't allowed to speak when working. If Calder keeps that a secret, I'm almost positive he hasn't made the announcement yet." The Elders looked at each other with disgust. Meanwhile, my palms began to sweat.

"They wear masks?" Thora asked, a confused look on her face. I nodded in response. Liv cleared her throat, and my eyes found hers.

"I have another option to throw on the table. One that might not eliminate everything we have worked our entire lives for." She ran her hand with a few missing digits up the back of her completely shaved head and down the side of her face that housed a dragon tattoo. "We could evacuate to Frith and bring the remaining families of the Ravens who have chosen to stay in the Kingdom here."

"You want us to run and hide? What about all of the people who fought in the war?" Sylve broke in, surprise in her voice.

"What about them?" Liv responded with confidence.

"Their sacrifices matter just as much as the Ravens do. You're okay with leaving them to succumb to whatever fate would await the Kingdom?" Sylve countered, waving her hand across the room.

"If it means avoiding another war...a war we have no hope of winning? Yes." Liv answered.

"Sacrifices will have to be made, regardless of the course of action we decide to take." Askel chimed in. "It is important to remind everyone before this continues that we cannot save everyone. From this moment on, you need to accept the fact that people will die, no matter what we do." He turned and addressed the three of us directly.

"I promise you, Askel, they understand the gravity of what this means. They have even more to lose than we do." Bryn interjected. "So please refrain from addressing them differently than you would address one of us."

"They have never fought in a war, Brynjar. I'm just passing along knowledge." He retorted.

"They might not have seen war, but they are well-versed in conflict. To doubt them and their credibility is an insult. I'm just passing along my knowledge and understanding of them since I have spent the most time with this group of Ravens." Bryn reiterated, sitting back in his chair.

"My apologies if I offended anyone." Askel nodded toward us before turning back to the Elders. "Keeping Frith a secret is imperative. If we evacuate people to this city, it *must* be done in one trip. We can't go back a second time. We might not be able to go back at all. A disappearance of that magnitude will raise concerns and make its way back to the royal pain-in-our-ass swiftly. The risk of a return would most likely lead to Frith being discovered."

"Anyone we would plan on bringing here would have to make an instantaneous decision, as well. We can't risk giving them a window to decide. They could flee. The day after we inform them, people we didn't talk to would know, and that circle of knowledge will grow each day we wait," Bergunn added.

"Now, I know this will be unpopular, but I am just throwing it out there...We can eliminate the risk of exposure by not evacuating anyone." Thora advised. The Elders nodded in thought while I looked between Sindre and Sylve, who both shook their heads. I can't listen to them talk about hiding. These are not the same people I've watched come home from raids in the dead of night, bloodied, carrying children and the elderly into my home to offer them a warm bed and compassion. *Where are those people?* Bryn scooted his chair back and stood, placing his hands on the table and leaning towards the Elders as he spoke.

"Fighting for our freedom is not off the table. I understand the risks of it, and the outcome doesn't seem like it would favor us this time, but it is an option." He looked at us and smiled. "And with this group, convincing them not to fight would be the bigger obstacle."

Ragnhild stood and walked around the table to Bryn, taking his arm in an embrace. "We will consider all of our options, brother. If we fight, it might have to be only in Sol. Frith is not our home to risk." Bryn nodded his head, and Ragnhild turned to us. "We will make the announcement to the Frithians in the morning." He glanced at the Elders, "Then we will spend the remainder of the day, and most likely the rest of the week, taking questions and suggestions from them." They all nodded. "We can reconvene after that and discuss it further, with a better consensus of how the Frithians feel and what they are willing to risk for a problem that is not theirs." The twins and I nodded in understanding, but when he turned around, I placed my fist over my heart, and the twins mirrored me.

"By the Gods, I have so sworn. By my honor, I have so sworn." We recited in unison. This froze Ragnhild mid-step, and he turned back to face us, admiration glimmering in his eye. He placed his fist over his heart and bowed deeply.

"By the Gods, I have so sworn. By my honor, I have so sworn." He echoed. "We have an unexpectedly busy day ahead of us. We all need to keep thinking of solutions and be prepared for tomorrow's meeting. The Ravens don't need to attend. Brynjar, if you wouldn't mind informing them for me tomorrow? I know you said you won't be visiting long, so don't let tomorrow's chaos keep you." Bryn nodded. "The rest of you, I would advise you to get some rest." With that, the Elders cleaned off their areas, saying good nights to everyone.

"Thora, either you should stop drinking or drink six more mugs so you can get some sleep!" Bergunn shouted as he headed toward the stairs, earning a laugh from the others. He stood shorter than everyone else, around four feet in height, which aided him in avoiding the fist thrown his way as he passed Thora.

"I know where you sleep, Bergunn!" She spat back before downing another mug of mead. I noticed Ylva was still sitting at the table and hadn't said anything. Bryn realized seconds after me and headed over to her, bending down to say something I couldn't hear. She shook her head and stood, pushing herself away from the table before rushing out the back door with Bryn at her heels.

"Do you think she is okay?" Sindre asked, coming to stand beside me.

"I'm sure she is hurting. She lost her family to Skirra and her husband to the war." I answered. "She and Bryn take on that guilt in the same way. I'm just grateful they have each other."

"It's a shame they won't marry. The love they have for one another is obvious." Sylve remarked. I smiled at the thought of them marrying, allowing themselves to love like that again.

"You know, I used to joke with him about it, but he said, 'Maybe in another life, we were once soul mates...the heartache in this one would be too much to bear.' Once I was old enough to understand that, I stopped bringing it up and just let them enjoy their moments together." I explained softly.

"Well, that is absolutely heartbreaking and heartwarming at the same time," Sylve announced as she headed toward the stairs. "I am heading to wash up and head to bed. Goodnight, everyone."

"Goodnight!" We responded in unison. I turned to ask Sindre a question, but a tear in his sleeve distracted me.

"What is that?" I questioned, reaching out to inspect the fabric on his bicep. I spread the cloth apart to reveal a dirt and blood-crusted slash on his arm. He looked down to see what I was looking at.

"Oh, would you look at that."

"*Oh, would you look at that.*" I mimicked and stared at him through narrowed eyes. "All of that bullshit about ME getting a scratch on my chest, and you are completely oblivious to the fact that you have an open gash on your arm?" I mocked while walking over to the kitchen sink, grabbing and wetting a rag.

"Well...you see..."

"I see nothing but bullshit right now. Come here." I ordered, taking his wound and trying to clean the gash through the cut in his shirt.

"Oh, stop; let me make this easier." He snorted and took his shirt off, folding it over his knee. I stared for a moment, caught off guard every time by his God-like physique. He moved his thumb over to the side of my mouth, wiping something off it. "Wha-What was it?" I asked, wiping my face after him.

"I think it was a little bit of drool." He joked as he offered me his massive arm again.

A laugh erupted from me, but I muffled it quickly with my hand, keeping it to myself. "Thank you, kind sir." I laughed. "I do appreciate that." His soft chuckle mirrored mine. "And I do appreciate your kind act of charity." He turned to me, confused, and I smiled. "Allowing those less fortunate to behold your beauty." He smiled and shook his head, holding back another laugh. I snorted and tried my best to avert my eyes from analyzing all the tribal lines that created the wolf tattooed across the expanse of his chest.

I cleaned his wound and gave him a pat on the knee to signify I was done. I stood, took the dirtied rag to the kitchen, and cleaned it in the sink. Looking out the window, I could see Bryn and Ylva outside through a gap in the shutters. She had her forehead resting on the center of his chest while he slowly and methodically rubbed the back of her arms she had wrapped around herself. Every few seconds, her shoulders would rise and fall as if she had just finished sobbing. Bryn moved from resting his head on hers to place a gentle kiss on it before wrapping his arms around her.

I wrung out the wet washcloth and stepped out of the back door slowly, subtly making my presence known as I walked over to the clothing line that hung a few feet from the house. When I turned back to head inside, both had separated and were waiting for me to approach them.

"I'm so sorry." I offered Ylva, who shook her head.

"This is not your fault, dear." She held out an arm and pulled me in for a hug. "By the Gods, I have so sworn…By my honor, I have so sworn." She whispered into my ear. And, as if it were a switch, tears pooled in my eyes, but I batted them away quickly.

"Thank you," I smiled. Relief passed through me knowing that we have her support with our proposed revolution.

"I am going to try to get some sleep now. Goodnight, Veronica." I nodded as she turned to Bryn and touched his chest. He moved his hand to cover hers, and they stared into each other's eyes for a moment before she turned away and headed inside. In that brief moment, they shared countless thoughts and so many unspoken words, and the idea saddened me.

"Do not mourn, child." Bryn jested, pulling me under one of his arms and kissing the top of my head.

"I can't help it!" I whined. "You two *kill* me sometimes." I wrapped my arm around him, and we waited, looking out at the dimly lit village pathways just beyond the homestead.

"You did well today. I know the Elders can be difficult to speak to. Under these circumstances, things will only continue to get more frustrating. Show patience and understanding, and they will do that for you too." He advised.

"I can't leave the people of Sol knowing what we do…what Skirra will bring here. I can't." I straightened myself.

"I know. No one expects you to." He assured. "But, as Ragnhild said, you will have to consider all of the parts in play here. He made a good point; Frith is not ours to gamble or to use as a pawn. We may need to part ways with them to fight this." I contemplated his words because I hadn't considered that. I feel that Frith is just as much of a home as I do Sol, but they are not the same. Only one is in immediate danger, and it will come down to how we execute our plans going forward, whether Frith remains out of the crossfire. I felt Bryn's thick hand grab the top of my head and playfully ruffle my hair.

"Try to bite that tongue in the next few meetings. They will be testing your ability to lead a revolution whether they know it or not."

"Odin, help me," I muttered under my breath, which earned me a chuckle from him.

"I'm headed in. Get some rest." He stepped closer to kiss my forehead before heading to the door.

"Love you, old man."

"Love ya, kid."

Twenty-Four

A week of vigorous training had passed quickly while the Elders spent most days speaking with the Frithians. Last night had been a particularly long night with Brax. He had gotten into something that upset his stomach, and between his constant whining to be let out once an hour to shit and the atrocious farts, I didn't get much rest.

My back was to the door when the quiet creak of its opening pulled me from the light sleep I had just fallen into an hour ago. I fingered the blade under my pillow, opening my ears to listen to the soft footsteps approaching until I felt a presence take up the space behind me.

I swung my blade blindly and barely missed my target when the person quickly moved out of the way. However, Brax was on the floor behind them and yelped as the figure stumbled over him, holding a bridge-like position to avoid landing on Brax, who then swiftly jumped on the bed. I could have stopped there, but not only was I annoyed that someone woke me up, but now I'm incensed that Brax could have been badly hurt.

I leaped from the bed and jumped onto the person's back, pushing them down to the floor, and holding the tip of my knife to their back. That's when I came out of my sleep-deprived fugue and realized it was Sindre.

"A little jumpy, are we?" He asked, a slight smile in his voice.

"What are you doing?" I questioned, annoyed.

"Coming to wake you for training?"

"Gods..." I breathed out a sigh of exhaustion. "I need a break. Brax was sick all night." I explained, lazily twirling the knife's point in the center of his back.

"A break sounds great, but no. Look how alert you are. That means what we are doing is working. I'll watch Brax tonight, though, so you can get some sleep." he offered, turning his head to try to look at me. "Time for you to get up and head down to eat."

"I don't think you're in a position to make those kinds of demands," I stated, wiggling my knife in my hand, smiling slyly. Faster than I could counter, Sindre pushed his torso off the ground, bucking me off him. I landed on my bottom on the floor behind him, with my legs now on the outside of his. "Hey!" I grumbled. But he wasn't finished. He interlocked his knees with mine and twisted, flipping me onto my stomach while he turned himself upright behind me. His hips were pressed to the back of mine, and my heart skipped a beat at the swiftness with which he got me here. I went to swipe my knife at him, but he grabbed my wrist and secured it to the ground, mirroring it with my other hand before I could push myself up. I heard him chuckle as he leaned into me, lowering himself to speak into my ear. I became very aware of every inch of him against my bottom as he did.

"I don't think *you're* in a position to *disobey* my demands." He growled quietly. Someone stepped into the room, and we both snapped our heads to find Sylve standing there. Only then did I realize the tunic I had slept in had crept up above my waist, leaving my undergarments exposed. Sylve's mouth was open, and her eyes widened as her face reddened. Sindre cleared his throat, and she snapped out of her state of horrific shock.

"Oh, *Gods!*" She covered her eyes with her hand. "I think I'm going to puke. Oh! I'm sorry!" She blurted out, turning to walk out of the room and quickly closing the door. My face felt a hundred degrees hotter, so I laid my forehead on the floor, too ashamed to look at Sindre, who laughed as he released me and stood up.

"I'll go do damage control." He joked, taking the end of my tunic and returning it down the back of my legs. "So, I'll see you in a few minutes for training, yes?"

"Yup," I mumbled onto the floor, waving a hand at him to leave me to my embarrassment. I lazily threw on leggings and wrapped my Raven's corset around my waist. I went downstairs to find my boots, and Ylva intercepted me with a plate of food.

"Eat, girl. You have been working hard all week. You need to replenish your body." She insisted, placing a hand behind my back and guiding me to the table.

"Thanks, Ylva, but I'm not hungry this morning," I mentioned and noticed Sylve and Sindre sitting at the table with their plates.

"Pish Posh! Sit down and eat, or I'll tell Askel you requested to spar with him today." I took the plate from her and hurried to the table, sitting across from Sylve with Sindre at the end between us. "Good. I'll see you all later tonight. And don't leave until all that food is gone!" she demanded as she walked out the front door.

I looked between Sindre and Sylve; she looked between Sindre and me, and Sindre remained utterly oblivious, eating his food. I looked down at my plate and pushed around the contents.

"Are you going to eat that?" Sindre questioned after a few moments of painfully awkward silence. I looked up at him slowly and shook my head, sliding my plate over to him as he slid his empty plate over. I peeked at Sylve, who had finished her meal already but kept her gaze toward the front door.

"*Please* say *something*." I conceded, laying my hands on the table in defeat. She shook her head and said nothing. "Come on, Sylve! This is terrible. I can't even think about training until this is addressed." I pleaded.

"I don't know what the deal is here," Sindre interjected, putting down his utensils and wiping his face. "I already explained what happened, and *you* know what happened." He nodded his head at me.

"It's *his* fault!" I yelled across the table, pointing a finger at Sindre.

"What! Mine? You are the one who jumped on me as soon as I came in!" He scoffed, waving an accusatory hand at me.

"Well, you are the one who continued asserting *dominance* after I had already finished!" I retorted, crossing my arms over my chest.

"Oh, so you expect me to let you finish without me finishing?" He quizzed, placing his forearm on the table and his hand on his chest in mock surprise.

"Yes!"

"That is so selfish of you. How do you think that makes me feel?"

"Wha-What are you talking about?!" I asked, my mouth dropping open in surprise.

"You just use me for a quick fix, and then that's it?"

"Would you guys SHUT UP!" Sylve broke in, slamming her hand on the table. Sindre and I sat up straight at the sudden outburst, giving each other a sly smile and a fist tap under the table. "I get it! It looked worse than what was happening, okay?" She wiped her hands down her face. "But that doesn't mean I don't have the memory of my best friend and brother, like that, burned into the back of my mind forever."

"Did we look good, at least?" Sindre added, getting punched in the arm by both Sylve and me at the same time.

"I am going to head to the training arena without the two of you so I can continue scrubbing the scene from my head without being teased about it." She announced as she stood, put her plate in the sink, and walked out the door without another word.

"That was great. 'Finishing'? Perfect word to throw in there." Sindre praised, patting my shoulder.

"I almost lost it when you kept on with that. OH, that was terrible!" I laughed, taking Sindre's second plate after I finished washing his first one.

We ran from the house to the training arena near the middle of the town. When we arrived, Sylve was already at the archery field with someone. I walked over to them, trying to catch my breath, and observed for a moment. Whoever she was training wore a head scarf loosely wrapped around their head and draped over their shoulder. They hit every target Sylve had instructed them to. She even told them to add specific footwork while they moved around the archery field, and they still hit every mark. They weren't consistently hitting the center, but they were close enough. Sylve held her hand up, and the archer lowered their weapon. Sylve waved me over and the archer turned to see who Sylve was motioning at, and their face lit up immediately.

"Kalyani!?" I beamed, jogging over.

"Veronica." She was mid-bow when Sylve held her arm out, stopping her, and shook her head. "Oh, sorry. I'm trying to get used to not being treated like our jarls treated us in Skirra. That we are equals here." She straightened herself and held her arm out for an embrace, and I took it in mine enthusiastically.

"You will adjust in time. And by the way, you are fantastic! Wha–How? When did this happen?" I questioned, looking between her, the targets, and back to her again. She blushed at the attention.

"She approached me shortly after she arrived in Frith and expressed her interest in learning how to fight in some form or another. So, we started with some physical training, and when we got to the weapons tests, she took to the bow very naturally." Sylve explained proudly. I shook my head in amazement, looking to Kalyani for a more elaborate explanation.

"I thought about what you said. I decided I want to be able to protect my family and myself if need be," she explained, casting her eyes down. Sylve lightly elbowed her, and Kalyani straightened, holding my gaze.

"You aren't afraid?" I asked.

"The fear doesn't outweigh the reward." She smiled, and I pulled her in for a hug, catching her off guard.

"I am so happy for you! You should be so proud of yourself." I commended.

"Can I introduce you to my boys?" she asked as a smile spread across her face.

"It would be an honor," I assured, placing a hand over my heart. She turned and jogged over to a small makeshift shelter where people could sit and watch the training if they wanted, and bent down to talk to her boys, whom I hadn't even noticed sitting over there. She led them back to us. The eldest saw me, and his face brightened. He ran over to throw his arms around my waist. I looked up at Kalyani in shock as she reached us. The boy looked up at me while maintaining a tight grip.

"You are the horse lady!" he said confidently. I looked up for assistance.

"Yes, she is the horse lady who did fun tricks on the horse." Kalyani laughed.

"Oooh! Yes. Yes, I am the horse lady." I smiled. "My name is Veronica. What is yours?" I lowered myself to the ground to speak to him on his level.

"My name is Raoul! I'm eight!" He announced confidently, his golden eyes gleaming with pride. I looked at the younger boy, who stood shyly behind his mother's leg. Raoul approached him and placed a hand on his brother's shoulder. "This is Hemming. He doesn't talk much, but he is four!" He showed me his brother's age with his fingers and patted his brother's curly hair before walking back to me.

"It's nice to meet you both." I barely added before being cut off.

"Your face is all better!" Raoul pointed out.

"You remember me that well?" I questioned, putting my hands on my hips. "I'm impressed."

"Yes! My mom always tells me I have a great memory." He emphasized by tapping his index finger to his head.

"Ah! Well, that holds true. Aren't you proud of your mom? It's pretty amazing that she is discovering these hidden talents, huh?"

"I think it is so awesome that mom could be a Raven someday! I want to be a Raven someday, too! So maybe I can go back and save my friends, and we can all be Ravens!" My heart dropped, but I put on a brave face. I looked up at Kalyani, and she was smiling proudly at her eldest while letting her youngest take his time to acclimate to his new surroundings. I jumped at Raoul's sudden squeak of excitement. "Sindre!" He yelled before running past me. Hemming's eyes lit up too, and a small smile crinkled his nose, emphasizing the freckles that danced along his brown skin. He released his mom's hand and slowly walked past me before running over to meet his friend.

"Boys! Good morning!" Sindre boomed, picking up Raoul in one swoop and tossing him over a shoulder before lowering himself for Hemming to latch onto his side as they walked back to us. Seeing him being so gentle and playful with the kids warmed my heart. The hysterical giggling that escaped the two boys forced a smile from me.

"They make you look even more like a giant, Sindre," I noted as he made it over, placing Raoul and Hemming gently on the ground.

"He is a giant! But sometimes I'm taller than him! Only when he throws me, though." Raoul asserted, putting his hands on his hips.

"Do you mean...like THIS?" Sindre asked, picking up Raoul suddenly and launching him in the air. The boy's two long auburn braids flew up as he lingered in the air before Sindre caught him, charging up his strength before tossing him in the air again. Hemming was pulling at Sindre's pants, demanding that he get his turn next. I turned to Kalyani, who was laughing to herself.

"It makes me so happy they feel comfortable with him," I noted.

"It's such a relief." She breathed. "They haven't been treated well by the Skirrian men we have had to work for...Seeing them only take a few days to warm up to him..." Emotion caught in her throat, and she cleared it quickly. "I tried my best to protect them. Maybe it means my efforts weren't a complete waste." She admitted, tears forming in her eyes.

"You did what you could," Sylve reassured, placing a hand on her shoulder. "And you are here now, doing even more than you thought you'd EVER be able to do. You are an amazing mother." She smiled.

"Thank you." Kalyani said, covering Sylve's with hers.

"Alright, boys! It is time for me to go train with horse lady." Sindre announced, placing Hemming down next to his mom.

"Are you going to teach him cool tricks like you did your horse?" Raoul asked me excitedly. I snorted at the question, and Sindre dropped his head in defeat.

"No, no, no. It's his turn to teach me something new today." I laughed. Raoul hugged me once more, grabbing my hand to keep my attention.

"I didn't get to tell you thank you like I did the others when we got here. So, thank you!" Raoul asserted; his eyes were the same golden color as his younger brother's and glimmered the same way.

"It is my honor, Raoul." I dropped to one knee and placed a closed fist over my heart, offering him a half bow. Sindre and Sylve did the same thing while standing, and Raoul lit up proudly. He ran over to his brother to take his hand and pull him away.

"Come on, Hemming! We can play Ravens!" He yelled, running back to the covered sitting area.

I stood from my crouched form and turned to Kalyani. "You have amazing children. Raoul seems so fun." I beamed, utterly amazed at the resilience the boys have shown.

"They admire the Ravens. You all have given them a new outlook on life, and I can't thank you enough." She thanked us once more before Sylve took her back to practice so Sindre and I could head over to the sparring field.

We were passing a few dummies when I attempted to stop at one of them for a warmup, but Sindre shook his head and nudged me forward with his hand on my back.

"Are we not running through the usual routine today?" I questioned, letting him push me forward until we stood in the center of the sparring circle.

"No." He answered plainly.

"Are we..." I looked around the area, searching for any equipment that he may have already laid out, but found nothing. "Are we running a circuit?"

"No."

"Okay, I give up." He was fastening his boots and looked at me with an evil glimmer in his eye.

"We are sparring today." He announced confidently. I looked at him with a grimace on my face.

"You...and me?"

"Yes. Are you ready?"

"Um, no? Is this a joke?" I asked, looking around for some hint of a facade.

"No. You seem to enjoy fighting opponents that are two or even three times your size. So, you have officially graduated from whatever pathetic weight class you were in for sparring and have upgraded to me." He explained, throwing his hands on his hips.

"There is no way Bryn approved this." I countered, mirroring his posture.

"Oh, indeed he did. He suggested it. If you can efficiently and consistently spar with Sylve and me, he will allow you to start fighting again. It's as simple as that."

"At the beginning of the training week, I would have been more excited to spar with you. But this week has been exhausting. How about next time?" I turned to walk out of the sparring circle as Sindre stepped into the inner ring, awaiting my advance.

"So, you're scared?" He teased.

I howled with laughter and waved back at him. "Yeah, right! I'm more scared of Sylve than I am of you." I responded casually, heading back toward the dummies.

"Ahh...I see Erikka is rubbing off on you." He stated.

I froze mid-stride, turning slightly to look at him. "What?"

"Hmm?"

"What was that? I don't think I heard you clearly." I emphasized, turning to face him head-on.

"It seems Erikka is rubbing off on you." He teased, shrugging his shoulders nonchalantly.

"Do you care to elaborate?"

"Well, this lazy, entitled *attitude* has to come from somewhere, and it sure as hel isn't from us." He quipped through a half-smile, swinging his arms towards himself and Sylve. "And before you contest..." he held out his hand to stop me from defending myself, "Expecting to be allowed to fight *without* putting in the work to earn that right." He inhaled sharply between clenched teeth before pursing his lips tightly, shaking his head. "That is Princess behavior." He sounded disgusted without having to admit it aloud.

"I'm not expecting anything. But that's beside the point." My face twisted with annoyance. "What do you know about Erikka? You have only met her *once*, in passing, might I add." I contested, glowering at him, daring him to say more.

"First impressions say more than any other interaction you will have with a person. Once is all I needed."

"All you needed to what? Pass such a ridiculous judgment on her?" He shrugged and kept that infuriatingly smug look on his face. As if what he believes is the truth, and I was a child arguing the legitimacy of Odin bringing gifts to the children for the winter solstice. *How dare he make such a ridiculous statement.* He has no idea what she has been through, what we have been through together, what we *still* endure at the hands of the King, her father, and the unreachable expectations he sets for her. I could feel the anger in my face, in my limbs. I noticed my hands shaking, so I tightened them into fists.

"Yes. Maybe the next time we cross paths, I can give her a taste of reality." He lowered himself into a fighting stance, already knowing what he said would set me off, but I held on for a second longer.

"Is that a *threat*?" I asked coldly, calmly walking toward him.

"It's a *promise*." He spat. He cracked his neck, and I saw nothing but red as I ran at him full speed, dropping to the ground to slide underneath him, hitting him with a fist in the groin. He fell to one knee and groaned. "Cheap shot." He hissed through clenched teeth.

He turned to face me, half slumped from the blow, and barely blocked the spinning kick I had aimed towards his head to send me circling back in the other direction. I secured my fighting stance and blocked the barrage of blows he attempted on me. I grabbed his arm, stopping a high attack, and held it above me while I punched him repeatedly in the ribs, aiming higher and higher until I was about to aim for his throat. Instead, he pulled his arm down, twisting it to grab my wrist, and spun me around so my back was to him before putting me in a headlock. "Is this what it takes to get you to fight effectively?" He questioned in my ear. "It seems a little *backward*, don't you think."

I punched his nose, knocking him off balance and loosening his grip. I reached up to lock onto the back of his head and heaved my legs into the air, whipping them back down to create enough momentum to flip Sindre over me and onto his back. I attempted to send my fists to his face, but he rolled out from under me. He swiped his hand, grabbed my arm, and pulled me over the top of him as he rolled another time, bracing me at my ribs to send me to the ground across from him. I choked on the impact, unable to breathe, giving him time to scramble to his feet. I snuck in a breath and played on a fake injury as he stood over me, assuming victory.

"You'll need more sparring practice." He remarked, breathing heavily.

"Do I?" I questioned quietly. I had pushed myself onto my hands and knees while he stared down at me with a false sense of victory. This was the perfect moment to strike. I leaned to one side and sent my foot up and into his stomach, causing him to stumble back in surprise, giving me the time to stand. I ran at him again and faked an attempt to tackle him, wrapping one arm over his shoulder and the other under his arm. As he had the strength to hold me, I swung my legs past him, up into the air, and back down behind me, using the momentum to send us both to the ground. I heard the sound of his breath being knocked out of him as he landed on his back, and I landed on my knee. He scrambled on all fours, wheezing, an audible to fill his lungs, but I was past the point of caring. I delivered a spinning kick up and over him to land between his shoulder blades, just below his neck, dispatching him to the ground again, and this time he stayed there. I stepped over to him and pushed a knee into the center of his back, slipping my knife from my boot and pressing it into the side of his neck.

"I think I'm pretty damn efficient." I sneered at him. He nodded, and I stood, releasing him from my hold. I wiped the sweat from my forehead and slipped my knife back into its place, walking away from him as he stood.

"Veronica!" He croaked from the effort it took to upright himself. I ignored him and kept walking. "Veronica!" I heard him quickly running over to me, reaching out for me, but I countered by grabbing his fingers and bending them at an unnatural angle, twisting his arm to add to the pain of the hold.

"Try to touch me again, and I'll break them," I seethed, applying more pressure.

"Okay! Okay, okay! Hey!" He put up his other hand as an offering of submission, and I yielded, releasing my grip on him.

"What?" I snapped.

"I didn't mean what I said. I was just trying to get you riled up as a test to see where you draw your strength from. That's all." He explained softly, reaching his hands out to hold my elbows. I swatted his hands away and swiped his knife from his belt, holding it between us to create space. His hands flew up again.

"Whether you meant to attack Erikka to entice me to fight or not, it's obvious that you believe what you said."

"I swear, Veronica-"

"Don't!" I extended the knife further, forcing him to step back again. "*Don't* lie to me," I growled, waiting for him to finish, but he didn't. Instead, his hands fell to his sides and he clenched his jaw shut. "I don't care about yours or anyone else's opinion on Erikka. No one, NO ONE, will know her as I do. But if you EVER threaten her again..." I raised his knife and threw it into the ground between his feet. "I will not hesitate to do my job."

"I-I'm sorry. I didn't mean it." He replied regretfully, his sweet honey-filled voice reaching out to me as he slumped his shoulders in regret.

"I don't care," I said callously. I turned to walk away from him but stopped, turning my head so he could hear me. "She is *not* the enemy. Remember that." I resumed my course to the Elders' home, but Sindre called after me.

"Are you coming back for Sylve's portion?"

"I'll see you both in the morning."

Twenty-Five

I had just finished packing my things and threw my travel bag towards the door when someone knocked lightly on it. "Come in," I responded, turning back to my bed to change the linen.

"Hey..." Sylve's voice whispered as the door creaked open. I glanced back at her and motioned for her to come in. "Sindre told me about yesterday." She started hesitantly.

"Don't worry about it. I overreacted anyway." I cut in, throwing the blankets on the floor.

"No, you didn't. He shouldn't have said what he did."

"I know." I chuckled under my breath and shook my head. I paused what I was doing to face her. "But why are *you* apologizing? You didn't say those things. What do you want to tell me?" I questioned, narrowing my eyes on her.

"Look...we spoke with Brynjar about your fighting capabilities." She fiddled with her hands anxiously as she spoke. "And why they seem, sometimes, to be a bit inconsistent." I raised my eyebrows at her but kept my pride in check. Besides, it's not like she wasn't stating the truth. She cleared her throat. "Anyways,

Brynjar suggested we run some trials on potential triggers during upcoming training sessions. We were planning on doing-"

"I understand wanting to help me improve, but going as far as intentionally hurting me just to see how well I might fight from one offense to another without telling me first doesn't sit well with me." I broke in, turning back to finish putting the fresh linen over the bed.

"We were supposed to talk to you about it!" She pushed, walking over to the opposite side of the bed so she was facing me again. "I don't know why he decided to do what he did. We agreed to tell you about our plans first. I was going to explain all this to you before, I swear." Her bright, round eyes were honest and pleading. I heaved a sigh and looked at her. "I let him have it! That was *not* okay, and I'm sorry." She reiterated quietly.

"I'm not upset at the reasoning. I just..." I finished folding the top blanket over the bed and sat on the edge. "I don't expect everyone to get along. I-I," I sighed again in defeat. "I have known her for as long as memories could form. She means a lot to me. So, I know I might have overreacted, but he still threatened her, whether he meant it or not. Work mode just kicked in after that, and my emotions definitely fueled my strength. Had I known the reasoning behind his words, I might not have taken it so hard." I tried my best to justify my reaction because I still felt bad about cutting off Sylve's training time when she had done nothing to upset me.

"Trust me. I respect you and Erikka both. Your relationship is also no one's business, and you should not have to defend yourself in such a manner. Sindre should feel even worse after the words I threw at him," she added, placing a supportive hand on my leg.

"Thank you, Sylve."

"You're welcome, and again, I'm sorry!" She repeated with a squeeze. I looked around the room to make sure I remembered everything when she quickly stood.

"What are you doing?" I questioned, furrowing my brows. She hurried over to the door and pushed it shut, snatching a pillow off the bed as she passed. She threw the pillow on the floor to cover the small opening at the bottom of the door, instantly darkening the room. When she turned back to me, her face was full of excitement. I watched her curiously as she skipped over and plopped before me on the bed.

"Look." She ordered softly. She held her hand out in the space between us, palm up, and closed her eyes. I looked between her offered hand and her face before reaching out my own and taking hers. Her eyes flew open, and she swatted me away. "No!" She laughed. "Just watch." She resumed her position, and I waited anxiously for whatever it was she wanted me to witness. A few silent moments passed when a bright white light flickered in the center of her palm. My eyes centered on where her magic was growing. It had started small, as if she had plucked a star from the sky and held it in her hand. Then, it began to grow steadily until it became a small ball of light that hovered comfortably in her palm, lying lazily up against the perimeter of her fingers. My mouth dropped open in awe.

"Sylve..." I whispered breathlessly. Her eyes fluttered open, looking at me just above the magic she held in her hands. I felt as if I had stopped breathing. While her hair was pulled back into its usual ponytail with two twists, one black and the other gold, kept down to frame her glowing face. I hadn't noticed when she used her magic the last time. But now she was illuminated slightly from the inside; a hint of the same magical light she was summoning swirled underneath her russet skin, enhancing its warm tone. Yet, something seemed different about her. Not her personality, physical abilities, or frame, but...her aura. It's as if she was radiating something powerful, but I couldn't pinpoint it.

"It's beautiful, isn't it?" she asked, rolling the magic ball in her hand.

"*You* are beautiful," I answered in admiration. I'm sure I was still gawking at her, which caused her to laugh.

"I wanted to show you what I figured out. Don't ask me how, but I need you to trust me anyway."

"No worries there," I stated confidently, standing as she stood. She backed up a few steps to put space in between us. She slowly moved her hand into the air and angled her hand toward the ground. The magic steadily left her palm to fill the space before her, forming a wall. She didn't have to bend towards the floor to move it there, as it must have been automatically filling the space she was mentally asking it to. The light left her hand completely, and she stood straight, proudly crossing her arms over her chest. What had formed before us was a wall of transparent white light, just tall enough and wide enough to cover Sylve's frame.

"Get your knife out." She instructed with a mischievous grin. I became weary but complied, slowly lowering to the ground to take it from my ankle and standing foolishly with it in my hand. "Now throw it at me."

"What?" My face twisted with concern and confusion.

"Throw it at me." She repeated. I went to toss my knife at her, but she held a hand out. "Don't you dare! Throw it at me, Veronica! As you would an enemy!"

"I can't! Are you nuts?!" I yelled.

"Just DO IT!"

"No! I am not going to throw a KNIFE at you!"

"Veronica! Do it now!"

"No!"

"Gods, you're a coward! Do it!"

"FINE!" I screamed as I flipped my knife in my hand to grab it by the blade, cocked back, and released, aiming straight for her chest, praying it wouldn't get there. A moment or two of silence had passed when Sylve cleared her throat, making me realize that I had squeezed my eyes shut. When I opened them, I was, once again, astonished. The blade of my knife had caught in her wall-no, her shield of light. She had created a shield. I walked over to study it, stepping to the side of the shield to see that just the tip of my knife was poking out on the other side. I looked up at her, my mouth agape. She reached her finger out to press the tip of the blade, which sent it clattering to the floor. "H-How? That is amazing!"

"I was just practicing by myself, trying to see what else my mind could guide this magic to do." She shook her head in her own amazement.

"How big of a shield can you make?" I questioned eagerly.

"That's as big as I've ever gotten it." She answered, running her fingers along her creation.

"Can I?" I asked, nodding towards it. She shrugged, and I reached out my fingers to caress the shield. As thin and transparent as it looked, it was as solid as any tree. The tips of my fingers began to burn the longer I kept in contact with it, and then a jolt of energy whizzed through my arm and down my spine, bringing me to my knees.

"Veronica!" Sylve gasped and dropped down next to me, her magic dissipating in the air as she did. The door to my bedroom flung open in the same instant, catching on the pillow as Sindre tried to barge in, the look of concern riddling his features as he fought the door to open it completely.

"What are you *doing*?" He demanded, closing the door behind him.

"I was showing Veronica my newest development. Relax." Sylve retorted sourly. Refocusing on me, she bent over to peer into my eyes.

"What happened?" He asked.

"I-I'm not sure." She answered quietly. "Are you okay?" I hadn't been able to catch my breath since the shock of whatever had happened kept my muscles uncomfortably contracted. A pressure was building between my shoulder blades, making me keep my eyes shut and jaw clenched.

"Sylve, do something," Sindre urged, dropping to a knee in front of me. She adjusted herself to stand behind me and placed her hands on my back, and within a few seconds, they relaxed enough for me to pull a breath in. I wiped the sweat that had beaded at my temple with the back of my hand.

"Thanks," I uttered through a tight jaw.

"I felt something was up, Sylve. I guess I was right..." He scanned the room. "We agreed to only practice when we are in complete isolation. It's too risky." He warned.

"We *were* isolated. I made sure of it." She pushed back, helping me to my feet.

"I wasn't here to help." He snapped, glancing over at me. "Did you hurt her?"

"I..." She trailed off, but I finally felt I could speak, so I added my two cents.

"I'm fine," I took in another shaky breath. "I touched it myself, and now I know not to do that again."

"Wha-Why would you touch it? In what world does some magical ball of light scream 'touch me'?"

"We are all learning, Sindre!" I sneered. "If I saw Sylve touching it, why would I think it would hurt me?" I asked, standing up straighter, stretching out my spine.

"Sindre, I can handle myself, and Veronica is a curious creature." Sylve gave me a sideways smile. "But thanks to her, we learned a valuable lesson. One we might have taken significantly longer to find out." She smiled and elbowed me gently.

"Odin, help me." He sighed, wiped his hands down his face, and turned to the door. "Are you two almost ready to go then?" Sylve and I shared a look between each other, then smiled at him sweetly.

"Of course," Sylve answered.

"Ready when you are," I added.

Twenty-Six

The journey back to Lykke was slow and uneventful. Sylve, Sindre, Tormod, Siv, and I made up the last Ravens to travel with the two carts needing to get back so we could regroup for the raid in a few days. We mobilized and traveled along the outermost path through Willingman Woods, ensuring we utilized the quickest route. Jerrik left two days before us to return to his shop.

The second group of Ravens veered onto their own course to take them to their residences when we reached the outer acres of farmland surrounding our home village. As we passed the road to Sindre and Sylve's house, they broke off, promising to head to the Inn once they parked the cart and put away the lingering supplies. I called Brax to me, and he leaped out of the back of the carriage and fell into a lazy walk next to Arvak. As I rode toward the Inn, I noticed a person and their horse standing in front. I hurried Arvak along. As we got closer, I could finally recognize who was waiting there.

"Mazen?" I called from down the street. This drew his attention to me, and he started to move in my direction. We met at the edge of the property, and I dismounted, leading Arvak toward the barn in the back, Mazen following silently. "I'm surprised to see you here. To what do I owe the pleasure?" I asked. Brax ran over to him excitedly, sitting before him, asking for some pets.

"Where have you been?" He asked me earnestly, bending over to honor Brax's request. I waited to respond and untacked Arvak, ushered her into her stall, filled her water bucket, and then turned back to Mazen cautiously.

"What do you mean?"

"I've been here since yesterday and couldn't find anyone." He explained, irritation dancing between his words.

"Wha-Bryn didn't answer the door?" My face twisted in confusion as I glanced past him toward the house.

"No. No one has answered. I was just about to leave when you showed up." He nodded back toward the front of the Inn and turned to head that way.

"I'll be up there in a second," I stated. I placed the water bucket in Arvak's stall and gave her some reassuring scratches along the top of her neck. "I'll give you a good bath when he leaves," I whispered as I slipped an apple out of my travel bag and handed it to her. I called Brax away from the barn and shoved him inside the house through the back door. When I got to Mazen, he was leaning against a post with his arms crossed.

"Soooo?" I leaned over to get his attention. "Why the random visit? And where is-"

"The new guard is on Erikka duty. The King sent me here to make an announcement to all of Lykke's residents." My ears perked up. "But I want to know what you were doing first." My shoulders slumped, and I sighed in annoyance.

"We were running training exercises," I answered nonchalantly with a wave.

"What training exercises keep you from home for a full day and night?" He questioned, heaving himself off the post to stand before me. I racked my brain for a good explanation and stretched my arms and legs to buy some time.

"Oh, you know...Well, maybe you don't know. We run a survival training exercise once a month. It is more like a-a test of how well we can use all our combined skills in real-time. Then, we get an evaluation of what we need to work on individually. It's really boring stuff. Anyways! Tell me why you're here." I pushed. He looked at me through narrowed eyes but ultimately shook his head and cleared his throat.

"The King has called a Kingdom meeting two days from now. At least one representative from each household is required to attend, and all Kingdom warriors are required to be in attendance." He returned to his horse and reached into his travel pack, pulling out a rolled-up piece of parchment with a scarlet ribbon tied around it. I watched him curiously as he strode over and handed it to me. "An official summons from the King."

"F-For me?" I pulled the ribbon loose and read over the message inside. It's signed with the King's official dragon-stamped seal. I shook my head.

"Yes..." He looked up at me with his usual serious expression. "He wanted me to reiterate that if you do not attend, you will be tried for treason." My mouth gaped open.

"That seems a bit *excessive*, don't you think?" I protested, glaring in annoyance as I unraveled the parchment.

"Yes, I do." He stated plainly. I looked at him, not necessarily surprised by the lack of emotion in his words. He was looking at the ground, seeming lost in a long train of thought. I cleared my throat to get his attention. "Sorry. Things have been off lately."

"Do you know what this meeting is about?" I asked, earning a sarcastic look from him. I nodded in acknowledgment, realizing how ridiculous it is to assume that Calder might have shared his plans with anyone, let alone a random Royal Guard. "What do you mean about things being off?"

He shook his head and mounted his horse. "I have to head back. Otherwise, it might raise suspicions about why I have been away so long. When are you going to head to the castle?" He avoided my question entirely as if he hadn't heard it.

"I'll make the trip tomorrow."

He nodded and tapped his ear twice. I nodded, realizing that he was worried about being overheard. Something I usually motion towards Erikka when we are at the castle, and I worry our conversation could potentially escape us. "I'll see you then." He responded, waving back at me as he rode off down the street, leaving me alone. I studied the words on the scroll a second time, annoyance and confusion building inside my chest at the absurdity of such a thing- threatening me with treason. I scoffed. I hadn't even gotten the chance yet. I shook my head and looked towards the Inn, snapping my thoughts back to Bryn. *Why hadn't he answered? For an entire day at that.*

I walked over to open the front door, but it was already slightly ajar. I shot a look down the street toward Mazen's direction. *Did Mazen go into the house?* I stepped inside and closed the door behind me.

"Bryn, I'm home!" I called out. The hearth was empty of firewood, and the house was quiet. "Bryn?" I walked over to his room, but it was empty, although his bed seemed to have been recently slept in, so *where was he?*

I decided to leave the Inn and head down the road to Arlan's home, whistling for Brax to join me on my walk. Bryn sometimes visits him and some of the other retired men in town for game nights. Arm wrestling is a crowd favorite, with chess and Nine Men's Morris a close second. Dusk was settling over the homes as I traveled past the tree line that blocked the view of the ocean. Crickets started to warm up their strings to perform their nightly tunes while the wind blew through the trees, telling tales of another time.

As I walked up to Arlan's home, I noticed it was too quiet for any gathering or event to be going on, and my stomach sank. My confidence wavered as I raised my fist to knock on the wooden door. The door opened, and Arlan's bright smile greeted me, the wrinkles around his eyes creasing pleasantly.

"Hello dear. What do I owe ya?" He asked sweetly.

"You don't happen to have Brynjar hiding in there, do you?" I nodded toward the inside of his home, and he peered over his shoulder, turning back to look at me with confusion.

"I'm sorry to say that I don't. I actually haven't seen Brynjar at all today," he responded. Now, it looked like even *he* was concerned, making my heart pound much faster in my chest. I plastered on a reassuring smile and waved my hands at him to calm him down. *Or to calm me down.*

"No worries! I just wanted to see if he was still in town. He might have gone ahead early." I reassured. Arlan nodded.

"I guess we will see him tomorrow then, huh?"

"Yes. Tomorrow doesn't sound too bad. Have a good night! Sorry to be a bother," I said as I began to turn to walk back down the road, whistling for Brax to follow.

"Have a good night, dear!" He called out before closing the door.

After I reached the Inn, I grabbed firewood on my way inside and finished packing away the small satchel of supplies I had brought back from Frith. Even after having bathed and packed for my unexpected trip to Sol's Town, Bryn still hadn't shown up. *Did he actually go to Kron's castle without me? No note or anything?* I was walking toward the kitchen in one of Bryn's tunics to grab a drink when there was a knock at the door. I ran to open it, pulling my damp hair over my shoulder.

"Oh, hey." Disappointment reflected in my greeting, which earned me an offended look from the twins who stood in front of me.

"I know we have been together all week, but really? You are *that* enthusiastic to see us?" Sylve questioned, crossing her arms over her chest.

"I'm sorry! No, I was hoping it would have been Bryn," I explained, stepping to the side to let them enter. Brax came running from the bedroom and gave them the greeting they deserved.

"He hasn't been home?" Sindre followed, looking around the room himself, confused.

"No."

"Hmm. That's strange." He echoed.

"What's this?" Sylve chimed in. She noticed the summons I left out on the small table in front of the fire. "A Royal Summons?" She picked up the parchment to read it. Sindre turned to me, asking a hundred questions without saying a word. I shrugged in response.

"When did you receive this?" she asked, her demeanor changing from curious to concerned.

" Mazen delivered it right when I rode up," I explained, stepping into the kitchen to get a drink. "Do any of you want one?" I called out.

"Yes!" They answered in unison.

"We had a summons as well, posted on the door," Sylve stated from the other room. I walked back in with three horns of wine in my arms, offering one to each of them.

"That's interesting. Do we think the King will announce his plans to the entire Kingdom?" I asked, taking a seat on the floor by the growing fire, allowing the heat to aid my hair's drying process.

"What?" They both questioned at the same time.

"Oh, Mazen said there is a Kingdom-wide attendance requirement for this assembly. One person from each household has to go." I explained, taking in a long drink and relishing the liquid's warmth in my chest.

"Oh, we didn't know that. " Sylve admitted, glancing at Sindre, who was staring into his mug.

"Did Mazen ask where we were?" Sindre questioned, eyes still fixated on his drink.

"Yes, I told him we run a survival training exercise once a month, and that's why I wasn't home the day before." Sindre nodded approvingly.

"The day before? How long had he been here?" Sylve asked.

"Apparently, he had been waiting around since yesterday."

"And Brynjar didn't answer?" Sindre questioned, looking up at me. I shook my head in response before a big yawn overtook me. "Maybe he was summoned earlier than us." He suggested coolly, finishing his drink.

"That's possible. I'll look for him when I get there tomorrow evening." I looked over to Sylve, who had curled up under a blanket on the couch. "Are you guys leaving in the morning as well?"

"Yeah, we have our bags packed already. We were going to leave from here with you, maybe get drinks at The Dark Sun on the way in." She raised her eyebrows playfully a few times, and I laughed.

"No drinks for me tomorrow." I smiled. "If Bryn is at the castle already, I want to try to see him before the meeting."

"Don't forget Erikkaaaaa." Sylve drawled out her name and continued wiggling her eyebrows up and down like a maniac, forcing me to laugh again.

"Yes, I have so much to do in such little time," I added with a yawn. "Well, I'm off to bed," I announced, finishing the final sip of my wine and pushing myself from the floor with an accompanying groan from the effort. "I will see you two bright and early." I offered to take their empty horns to the kitchen, and they handed them to me. Sylve kissed my cheek goodnight, then headed upstairs as I left the room.

"Hey, can we talk about the other day," Sindre asked, slipping into the kitchen behind me. I started to wash out each horn and put them away.

"About what?"

"Our training."

"There is nothing more to say about it, Sindre." I finished with the horns and turned to face him, leaning against the counter behind me. "Sylve explained the intent behind it. I understand. And you already apologized. I just needed some space to cool off." He stood there awkwardly, looking for more words to say. "See, I told you. There is nothing more to be said about it." I smiled softly and went to walk past him, but he stepped in my way, placing a hand on the counter.

"I should have listened to Sylve." He admitted, looking into my eyes apologetically.

"Yes, you should have." I chuckled quietly.

"I'm serious. I'm sorry." His eyebrows pinched, and I placed a hand on his broad chest while guiding him backward so I could pass him.

"You don't need to apologize. We should be able to call each other out on our bullshit, right?" I winked at him as I walked out.

Twenty-Seven

Upon arriving at the castle, I walked the entire grounds looking for Bryn, but I had no luck finding him. The only thing that gave me a sense of direction was when I bumped into Mazen as he left the library. He told me Calder was currently holding a meeting, which was where Bryn could be, especially if he had been summoned earlier in the week.

I was now headed to find Erikka. The only thing I knew about her whereabouts was that she wasn't invited to the meeting with Calder. I decided to start my search at her personal quarters and go from there. As I walked through the vast stone halls of the castle, I noticed how eerily quiet it was, especially for such an event tomorrow. The sound of my boots clicking along the floor was one of the few sounds bouncing off the walls. I rounded the corner and heard her soft voice coming from ahead. I quickened my pace so that I didn't lose her.

"Your Highness," I called out calmly. Her head snapped, and she looked at me with an expression I couldn't quite read. She cleared her throat, and it was gone, her usual Princess grace returning once again. A woman, who must be the new guard Mazen had mentioned, turned to face me, looking me over sternly. She sported the same updo I had, with her honey-blonde hair pulled back into a braided bun required of us when working at the castle. As I walked closer to them, I noticed her stout frame. Despite having a similar thickness in her thighs and rounded hips as I do, she is shorter than both Erikka and I, maybe even Mazen. She looked strong and sure of herself as she analyzed me, causing waves of irritation to ripple through me. "Could I request a private meeting with you?" I asked Erikka, who nodded and turned to open her door.

I stepped to pass the new guard but was met with a solid hand on my shoulder. I swiftly grabbed her wrist and seized her arm just above her elbow with my free hand, pulling her toward me and twisting her arm behind her back in the same movement. I released her bicep, swiped a knife from her belt, and pushed it against her throat while pulling her back against me.

"Don't get familiar," I threatened in her ear, pulling up on her arm slightly, forcing her to bend to relieve the tension I created in her shoulder.

"I'm doing my job!" She pushed through clenched teeth.

"No," I stated plainly. "You are doing my job. And not very well."

"Enough!" Erikka demanded from behind us. I released the new guard, and she whipped around to look at me, her face red with anger. I offered her her knife back, and she snatched it, sheathing it back in her belt to ensure it was securely fastened.

I raised an eyebrow in amusement. "Veronica, this is Eire. Eire, Veronica." Erikka's clipped tone revealed her impatience. I nodded, and she mirrored me. "Eire, do you mind staying out here?"

Does she mind? Since when did she start asking people for their opinions on her orders?

"A little." Her auburn eyes shot a nasty glance my way. "I'll be here when you need me," she said begrudgingly, walking over to take her place outside the door. I rolled my eyes and walked in after Erikka, locking it behind me.

"So that's the new guard I've heard so much about," I prodded, coming to a standstill in the center of the sitting room.

"What all have you heard?" She questioned as she opened the double glass doors to her balcony, letting the breeze fill the room. The outside air was crisp and cool, while more clouds began to drag across the sky. A storm must be coming in.

"Well, that you two get along well." I raised an eyebrow, but she hadn't turned to face me yet. "Nothing in particular about her capabilities, but I've seen what I needed."

She turned to me with her eyebrows pinched in annoyance. "You caught her off guard. She is as capable and talented as any other guard here. I've watched her trial myself."

"Mazen would not have been disarmed that easily." I countered, crossing my arms. "And I have been distracted plenty of times with you but had no issue putting Ulrik on his back when needed," I reiterated.

She shook her head and seemed to move on from the conversation. "It's unimportant."

"I think it's plenty important. Considering there is still some magical madman in the Kingdom attacking the Royal Family. How am I supposed to trust you are safe if Mazen is in Lykke with me, telling me *that's* who has been left here to protect you?" I questioned, motioning at the door towards Eire.

"Veronica, drop it," She ordered. Her jaw was clenched tight, and her eyes colder than I had ever seen them before, so I dropped it.

"Fine. Has anything developed about that man anyway since I left?" I asked, relaxing my shoulders slightly.

"No. Nothing has come up. My father hasn't spoken about it with anyone or asked any further questions since right after the attack."

"Is he unconcerned with the threat? Maybe he found the guy?"

"He acts as if it never happened, actually."

"What? He was at the center of it. Why-" I trailed off from what I was saying because my attention was drawn to something else. Erikka looked up at me when she noticed the silence and followed my gaze toward the balcony.

A large raven had landed on the railing just beyond the opened doors and seemed to be watching us. It turned its head around to reveal one milky white eye, while the other was black. I could feel my heart begin to pound harder in my chest. Unsure of why I was reacting this way, I slowly walked over to the doorway. Even as I closed the distance between the raven and myself, it did not fly away.

Then, suddenly, my view changed, and I was staring at myself. Erikka stood a few feet behind me, slowly tying off the dress she had changed into. I analyzed myself as if it seemed I had been frozen in place, staring at...myself? The Raven? It took me a moment to realize I was seeing through the Raven's eyes. Erikka cautiously walked over to my body and placed a tentative hand on my shoulder, peering around to look at my face. That's when I noticed my eyes. They had gone completely black, as if liquid smoke had glazed over them, making my eyes akin to onyx stones. Erikka's eyes widened with shock before she stepped in front of me, shaking my shoulders hard. I blinked, and suddenly, was back in my body. My hands flew to my chest, patting down my sides and arms, checking that I was myself and not a bird. I looked over Erikka's shoulder, and the raven spread out its midnight purple wings and sent a shrieking caw out into the sky. Erikka and I had to cover our ears to diminish the piercing cry before it flew off into the distance and out of sight. I could still hear it as Erikka dragged me back into the room by my arm and closed the doors, drawing the curtains closed.

"What the hel was that?" She turned to ask me suspiciously.

"I don't know..." I retorted sourly.

"What happened to you? Your eyes..." She trailed off, her eyes full of distrust.

"I blacked out for a second," I lied. "What happened?" I feigned ignorance, hoping to take what I had just experienced to my grave.

"You just...I'm not sure. You froze, and then your eyes...disappeared. I got scared." She lied, too, maybe to avoid scaring me. That has to be why, but she seems off from her usual self. Besides having just witnessed what she did, I have yet to speak with the Erikka I knew. She is still very much in Princess mode, forcing me to keep my guard up.

"Are *you* okay?" I asked sincerely. She looked at me as if I was crazy to worry.

"I'm fine. Why are you asking?"

"I've only been gone for a week, and you already forgot who you are speaking with?" I laughed, moving closer to her to place my hands on her shoulders. "I know something is up. You don't have to talk about it if you don't want to, but I feel like I need to remind you that I'm here for you." I smiled, and she loosened her posture slightly. She hung her head, and her crown slipped out of place. I lifted it from her head and placed it on a small side table.

"I'm sorry." She whispered, taking a step closer to me to rest her head on my shoulder. I wrapped my arms around her and took a deep breath, hoping she would mirror me. The crisp scent of wildflowers in her hair tickled my nose.

"Are you okay?" I asked again under my breath, letting my hands slide down the backs of her arms as she returned space between us.

"Yes. Things have been weird here...stressful, but in a 'not talked about' kind of way." She shook her head and ran her hands up the back of my arms, taking a step back. I nodded in understanding. She couldn't talk about it, so prying was pointless.

"Do you know if Bryn has been here?" I asked. "I haven't seen him for a few days, and I'm worried. Something doesn't feel right." She stiffened and looked away for a moment as if she was searching for something, then snapped her eyes back to mine.

"Yes, actually. He has been in meetings with my father the last few days." I sighed a breath of relief.

"Oh good," I stated. "I couldn't find him anywhere and was starting to feel desperate." Erikka pulled me in for a sudden hug. When she released me, she placed her hands on either side of my face.

"I have a meeting in a few minutes I must get to." She pulled me in and laid a gentle kiss on my mouth. One so soft and slow it caused me to blush at the surprise of its intimacy. She pulled away from me, her eyes lingering on mine before she turned to grab her crown and placed it on her head.

"Okay," I announced dazedly while my thoughts lingered at the fleeting sensation of her lips on mine.

She took my hand in both of hers. "I love you," She whispered with a smile that didn't quite make it to her eyes. She wanted to say more but stopped herself and, after a quick pause, pulled me along as she exited her room, dropping my hand as we passed through the door's threshold. Eire resumed her position just behind Erikka as she walked away from me without another word, leaving me in the center of the hallway, floating in a cloud of confusion.

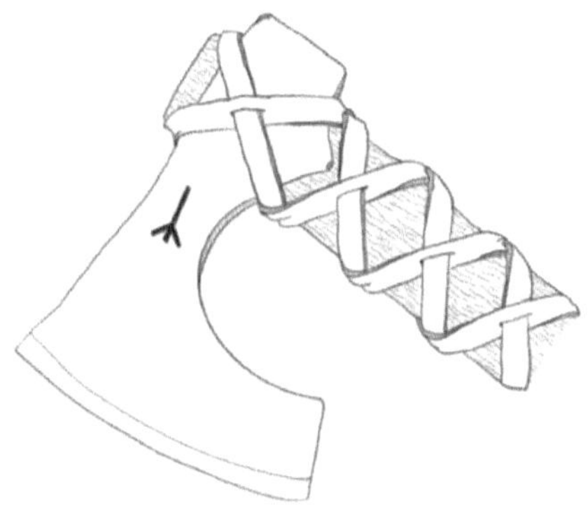

Twenty-Eight

I dozed off before Bryn had finished his meeting with the King, and when I went to check the room I was told was his this morning, he had already gone. I would have to catch up on everything that has kept him busy after the assembly ends. So, instead of moping around, I decided to stop by the twin's room. I let any lingering thoughts on the odd event last night leave the forefront of my mind as I knocked incessantly on their door until Sindre flung it open with his mouth tight and eyes flexed. I smiled brightly in the presence of his annoyance.

"Of course! Good morning, *Veronica*." He scoffed loud enough for Sylve to hear.

"Veronica! Get your ass in here!" I heard her say from behind the door. I complied and walked in past Sindre, who had half bowed sarcastically, allowing me in the room. When I saw Sylve, she was fumbling with the strings on the back of the Kingdom's corset she was required to wear. "Can you help with this mess? Sindre is useless." I laughed and looked at Sindre, who shrugged his shoulders and continued securing his weapons in place.

I took over and tightened the strings to hold the corset over the same floor-length black dress I wore. Like me, Sylve's hair was in the same braided bun, and the cloak over her shoulders was secured by the same brooch. Clean, pristine, and uniform, just as Calder expects everyone to be.

"Odin, help me make it through the day." She took a deep breath as I pulled on the last row of string and finished tying it in a bow, I tucked the excess up the back. "Thank you, dear. I prefer the front ties over the back for this exact reason."

"Did you get to speak with Brynjar?" Sindre asked, rolling his sleeves to his elbows as he turned to face me. I shook my head.

"Is he even here?" Sylve questioned, pulling up her dress so she could fasten her knife to her ankle.

"Erikka said he has been in meetings all week with Calder." I cleared my throat, catching myself on my casualness. "The King," I corrected.

"Maybe he made some ground with pull-" I quickly stepped over to Sindre and clamped my hand over his mouth. I looked into his eyes sternly and shook my head, motioning toward the opened door behind us with my eyes. He nodded as he began to understand what I was insinuating. I dropped my hand and patted his chest, walking to the door to check if anyone was in the hallway before shutting it.

"Sorry," I offered with an embarrassed look. "You've got to *always* be on your toes when you're here."

"It's okay. I haven't been here in months, so I'm definitely way more relaxed than I should be." He stated, rubbing the back of his neck. Horns sounded from outside, informing everyone in the immediate area that the meeting was being called into motion. The sky had darkened from the mass of storm clouds brewing around us. *I hope this is over before it starts pouring.*

Sylve, Sindre, and I walked from the castle to the training arena together. We used the warrior's entrance to get to the floor level as the citizens of Sol entered through the main entry, accessing the upper-level seats for viewing. This arena was probably five times the size of the one in Frith. Its circular floor usually housed different training areas like combat, archery, and training dummies, but it was cleared to accommodate the crowd. It also had about two dozen rows of seating that encircled the entire arena, closing it in completely.

From where we entered, I noticed Mazen standing at attention with the other Royal Warriors along the left side of the arena while the warriors from Exris and Lykke filed in on the right side. I felt someone grab ahold of my arm, and when

I turned to shake them off and reach for my sword, they yanked me into their chest, their hand catching mine as it grabbed the hilt.

"Let's play nice now." The familiar voice purred into my ear. I looked up into the silver eyes of the masked man from my debriefing. *Vali was his name?* I tried to shake his grip, but it didn't falter. Sindre and Sylve were beside me immediately.

"I would let go before you cause a scene," Sindre warned, his hand resting on the hilt of his own sword. Sylve stalked around the man, coming to a standstill behind him, almost breathing down his neck. People were still filing into the arena, passing us with curious glances as we were in the middle of the walkway. Vali chuckled to himself but loosened his grip enough for me to pull my arm back to my side.

"I'm here to show you to your designated positions." He explained, glancing back at Sylve, who wore her brightest smile.

"Shall we follow you then?" she asked, her voice like a bell. He nodded and walked ahead of us, Sylve following close behind him with Sindre and me in her wake. He stopped walking and motioned to us. "Front row. We feel so *special.* Thank you." She beamed at him, graciously bowing as she took her place. I couldn't tell if she was sarcastic or seriously genuine as she addressed him. I didn't even bother to acknowledge Vali again as I passed him and took my place next to Sylve. He held his hand out to stop Sindre from standing next to me and instead guided him behind me. We had been placed directly at the front of our section, bordering the walkway to the entrance we came in from.

"Who was that?" Sindre asked in my ear. I shook my head and turned slightly to speak toward him.

"An annoyance. I know nothing more than that." He nodded in acknowledgment and returned to stand at attention as Sylve and I did. Vali passed by again, staring me down while escorting three more people to stand beside Sylve and Sindre - Bergunn, Thora, and Ragnhild. *What was Ragnhild doing here? What were they all doing here?*

They each greeted us as they passed and took their places. I didn't dare look back at the three Elders. Vali's eyes felt like coals on my skin as he took his place at the center of the arena. While awaiting Calder's arrival, a chill crept down my spine. *Something doesn't feel right.* I glanced at Sylve, who nodded as her eyes darted around the arena. *She must feel the same way I do.*

The influx of people slowed to a trickle. The horns sounded once more for the citizens of Sol to stand and greet their King. The warriors all turned to face the entrance we had come in from, executing bows that were precise and formal; I did the same. We did not straighten until they had passed and were heading to the makeshift dais at the heart of the arena. Both Calder and Erikka wore red clothing, the ultimate showcase of their status. I rolled my eyes. Calder's tunic was bright red, the silken material revealing the strength he still harnessed. In contrast, a black cloak sat atop his broad shoulders and draped over his back gracefully. The brooches on either of his shoulders were jade dragons, another status symbol.

Erikka looked as stunning as ever, but I had never seen this dress before. Every detail was more intricate than the next. The red silk flowed down her frame and danced along her body as she walked, making it look as if she was floating. The silk clung tightly around her chest, where her phoenix peony pendant was secured. An intricate pattern of detailed lace sprouted from her waistline, like vines reaching up from the ground, and hugged her collarbones and shoulders, falling into loose sleeves down either arm. The dress also included a hooded cape made of matching red lace. Her snowy blonde hair was pulled up into a curled ponytail, further accentuating the intricacy of the lace pattern. The horns rang out again, and the citizens took their seats as the warriors remained standing, tearing me from my moment of adoration.

"It is no surprise that the Kingdom of Sol has fallen into difficult times. Trades are few and far between while crop growth has slowed tremendously, yet we continue to grow!" Calder declared to the crowd. One could hear a pin drop as everyone fell deathly silent to listen to the King's announcement. "As your King, I am dedicated to finding the solutions we need as a people to prosper into plentitude once again!" He paused, pacing along the dais as he spoke. "It has come to my attention..." He crossed his hands behind his back. "That there may be a group of people who disagree with our wish to be a prosperous Kingdom." He paused again; a murmur passed over the crowd. My back stiffened, and I clenched my jaw. I felt the others do the same but did not dare risk a glance toward them.

Calder motioned toward the entrance, and the crowd turned to see why. All the warriors shifted positions to follow the attention of The King , and I immediately felt the blood drain from my face.

He was covered in filth, and his clothes were tattered and bloody as if he had been fighting...beaten. Deep cuts donned his eyebrow, his bottom lip, and his cheeks. The state of him sent bile creeping up my throat. His brown eyes darkened as they found mine, an unspoken apology emanating from them. Brynjar stood between two masked warriors with his arms bound behind him and looked forward at Calder, who motioned them over to him. The men pushed him forward as they came to stand just before the dais. My breathing became uneven as I watched them shove him again onto his knees before the King.

"I have been made aware that *this* man had planned to rebel against the Kingdom of Sol. Against YOUR path to prosperity! Against YOUR happiness!" He stared down at Bryn with a wicked look on his face. I wanted to gouge out his eyes for looking at him with such disrespect. *How dare he twist this. How dare he pin this on Bryn.* Calder began pacing again as he spoke. "If the people of Sol, TRULY, want to be a prosperous land...then the people of Sol must understand that a rebellion will only push you further from your dream. The dream to live in a time of peace! The dream to raise your families and work your land without the fear of famine or blight! I want nothing more than to protect our people from these things! HOWEVER, a rebellion?" Calder scoffed.

My eyes bore into the back of Bryn's head, wishing now more than ever that I had been blessed with the gift of communicating between minds. *What the hel is happening, Bryn? Why aren't you fighting this? Why are you letting this happen?* The wind had picked up, and the scent of rain came along with it.

"We cannot afford to lose any more time in our fight to fix what has been broken in this Kingdom! The system my father had implemented is NOT working! This Kingdom was not created with longevity in mind. I am determined to right these wrongs against all of you! I am determined to see your dreams fulfilled!" He was pandering to the citizens of Sol, and as I looked around, it was clear they were buying into it. *How do they believe what this man is saying? Don't they know Brynjar?*

"What type of a King would I be if I let this threat against the Kingdom go unpunished?" My brow furrowed as Calder came to a halt in the center of his platform. "Let this stand as a warning to anyone who may have been conspiring to rebel against the Kingdom. Brynjar Leif! You are hereby charged with high treason!" A masked woman handed Calder the staff of judgment, a long steel cane designed to look like the body of a dragon, with its head and mouth curled at the top. "And sentenced to death!" He pounded the staff onto the wooden floor once. A second time. A third. The echo of its sound blocked all other noise from passing through my ears.

I began to move, but Sylve gripped my arm and held me back. I immediately felt as if roots had grown from the soles of my feet, anchoring me in place. Calder motioned with his arm to the side, and a man brought forth a wooden block as the two masked warriors forced Brynjar to his feet and marched him over to it.

Bryn looked at me, willing me to understand as he shook his head slightly. *Don't act.* My throat tightened to the point it felt as if it had closed completely, halting my urge to call out to stop what was unraveling before me.

Calder nodded, and my attention flew to the entrance from which the citizens had entered. An executioner stepped into the arena, clad in the executioner's blackened hood with slits for eyes, and holding an axe with a blade as long as a man's forearm, enforced with steel along its sharpest edge.

My eyes darted to Erikka, pleading, screaming at her to do something, *anything* to stop this. I looked back to the executioner as he neared Bryn, who was being forced to his knees, then back to Erikka. She wasn't looking at me. She was watching this happen with an icy expression, emotionless at best. I could feel my foundation cracking. My eyes flew around and found Bryn's again. He mouthed the words *I love you* just before they forced him to bend over with his neck on the block.

My eyes widened in horror as I watched the executioner bring his axe high into the air. It happened so fast. Sindre cupped his hand over my mouth and pulled me into his chest, spinning me away from the scene before the blade made contact with its target.

The arena fell silent.

The only sound was the rumbling of the sky in the distance.

Sindre leaned into my ear and spoke under his breath, trying his best to control the emotion in his voice. "Do. Not. React." He wiped away the trail of a single tear on my face that had slid onto his fingers before letting me go and returning to face forward. I remained where I stood. A cold numbness swept out from the remnants of my shattered heart and encompassed my entire being.

I swear I could feel a mare lying on my chest. Surely, any moment now, I would wake up, and relief would wash over me just as it does after I come out of a vicious nightmare…But something was different this time…*I can't wake up.*

I looked up in disbelief at who I was standing in front of and was met with glowering violet eyes filled with rage and sorrow. Ragnhild stood before me, his chest heaving unsteady breaths and his fists clenched. His gaze softened as I looked at him but quickly snapped back to neutrality as he returned his eyes to the dais. There was a ringing in my ears that continued to intensify, with the thoughts violently circulating throughout my brain. The words being said by the King were muddled and distant in comparison to the screaming that was taking place inside my head.

Why didn't you speak up?!

You killed him! You let this happen!

They all let this happen!

Everyone is against you!

Your fault!

You killed him!

He is DEAD because of you!

You stupid bitch! How could you have trusted her?!

She killed him! She let him die!

She watched him die!

She never cared!

She said he was okay…

She lied!

You let him die!

You should die!

You should've died to save him!

You are worthless!

You betrayed him!

How could you!

Stupid!

Selfish!

Coward!

My thoughts were interrupted by the blood-curdling sound of Calder's voice in my ear. He had been exiting the arena but stopped as he came to stand next to me.

"I expect all rebellious efforts to be disbanded." He leaned in closer and spoke so softly only I could hear his threats. "Otherwise, your *friends* will be next." My eyes snapped up, and I looked ahead with a numb stare, refusing to acknowledge the fear he had planted inside me.

Calder nodded toward his entourage, and they continued forward, leaving the stench of death in their path. My eyes shot over to the back of Erikka's head as she left. Not a look, glance, or gesture in my direction. I would have taken her pity if she had offered it…but she gave me nothing.

Within half an hour, the majority of the crowd had exited the arena, while I remained paralyzed in the exact spot, as did the twins and the Elders. Jerrik had come down from where he sat with the general population and stood beside me, holding my hand in his. Once we were the only people left, Ragnhild placed a hand on my shoulder and nodded solemnly. I let go of Jerrik's hand and turned slowly to face what hel my reality would be from this moment forward. The rain had begun to trickle in, the rumbling nearing. My eyes found Bryn's lifeless body strewn across the wooden block, blood still seeping slowly from his neck. My lips quivered, and I pinched my mouth shut as I averted my eyes, only to arrive at his head, which had tumbled a few feet away. As I approached his body, each step I took became heavier, as if the motion itself was draining my life from me. Once I stood before his head, I crumpled to my knees. Tears blurred my vision as I reached down to hold and cradle him in my lap.

His eyes were closed, but I found he had more bruising on his face that I hadn't noticed past the gashes. *They tortured him.* Tears of sorrow turned to tears of rage as I looked over to his body and noticed similar bruising along his arms, and what I thought was just dirt on his clothing were, in fact, tears. Gashes ran underneath each opening—torturously long gashes caked in dried blood. I pushed a laborious breath from between my teeth. I felt every muscle in my body vibrating. Tears stung my eyes as I bent over and kissed his forehead.

"I'm so sorry," I whispered. My tears began to fall then, one after the other, and ran down the sides of my face and Bryn's. "I… am…so sorry."

The shakiness in my breathing intensified, but I stopped and took a few deep breaths. I couldn't break down here. *It's not safe.* Sylve knelt next to me, covering Bryn's head with her cloak. She laid her arm over my shoulder and leaned her head onto mine. Sindre dropped to a knee and put his arm over me as well, with Jerrik following suit. Then, the elders placed a hand on my back in solidarity. The rain was starting to intensify as Bergunn came to stand in front of me.

"We will escort him to Lykke, my dear. We should all get going. The storm does not look like it will ease up tonight." He offered earnestly. I looked up at him and met his eyes level with mine, his face pained. I nodded, and he reached across me to retrieve Bryn. "We will take good care of him," he reassured, wrapping Bryn's head gently within Sylve's cloak. Sindre had draped his cloak over Bryn's body as he, Ragnhild, and Thora worked to remove him from the block and lay him down in the cart the executioner left at the edge of the arena.

While everyone else had begun to help ready Bryn for travel, I remained on my knees in front of the wooden block, blood staining my hands and dress. The rain was already washing away the blood that had spilled onto the floor, dissolving it into nothing, as if the world was ready to wash away his existence and move on. *I'll be damned.*

I clenched my fists and pushed myself to my feet. I began walking out of the arena from the way we entered. Sindre ran over and cut in front of me, bringing his hands up to caress the backs of my arms.

"Slow down there, warrior...Where are you headed?" He asked softly but loud enough so I could hear him above the increasing rainfall.

"I need to get my shit out of my room. Change clothes. Get Arvak from the barn." He nodded and scrunched down to catch my eyes.

"Don't do anything stupid, V." He warned, pulling me into his chest. "Seriously...Don't do anything rash. We can regroup in Frith." He spoke gently into my ear before kissing the top of my head.

"I'm fine." I said numbly, batting the rain from my eyes. "Don't wait on me. I'll see you guys in Lykke." I stepped around him but stopped, turning back again. "Take care of him. *Please*," I begged, tears resurfacing to sting my eyes once more.

"Of course," he said, placing his closed fist across his chest. I nodded and turned away, wiping the tears from my face.

Twenty-Nine

I got to my room and closed the door quietly, locking it behind me. My dress had been soaked through twice and clung to my skin, adding to the feeling of being suffocated with every breath I took. I wrung out the wetness in my hair onto the floor without a second thought and looked around the space I had called mine. Everything is different now. *I want to set the room on fire.* I went to my travel pack and pulled out a pair of leggings and a black tunic, throwing my weapons belt to the floor while struggling to rid myself of the Kingdom's attire that was burning my skin.

I grunted in frustration and flipped the end of my dress onto my leg, pulling the dagger at my ankle. I grabbed the fabric closest to my neck and pushed the blade through, splitting it down the middle until my knife caught on the corset. I reached behind me and struggled to cut the strings on the corset, finally getting through and letting it fall to the floor. I returned to the front and continued slicing the dress in half until it was loose enough to peel off. Then I threw the torn garment on the bed and changed into a dry set of clothes, re-strapping my weapons belt around my waist.

I dug through my travel pack, looking for anything I might want to take with me, but ended up throwing it against the wall across the room. My breathing was erratic, and my thoughts were attacking the silence.

You killed him.

He would've died for you.

Coward!

Selfish!

I looked around the room for something that would disrupt my thoughts, anything. I eyed the corset with the Kingdom's emblem across its center. I picked it up and grabbed a royal axe from the floor. Since I planned to leave it here anyway, I held the corset on the wall with one hand and swung the axe over my head into the center of the emblem with the other, securing it there.

Coward!

Die!

You don't deserve to-. I muffled my screams with my hands and ran them through my hair, tugging at it to try to get the tormenting thoughts to stop.

I glanced over at the bed—the bed where Erikka and I shared such tender moments. My stomach flipped, and I had to look away to ease the bile creeping up my throat. I walked over to the chair where I left the rope I gathered from the barn and threw it over my shoulder. I shoved the shutter open and felt the stormy wind swirl into the room. Arvak whinnied at me. I had tethered her just outside before coming in, and luckily, I was only on the second floor, so climbing down the stone wall wouldn't be a huge feat.

I snatched my cloak and flung it over my shoulders, pulling the hood over my head. I turned and grabbed the oil lamp from the wall, contemplating momentarily before making up my mind. *I must create a distraction.* I needed the extra time to get into Erikka's room. *Fire leads to a lockdown, giving me time to lead Arvak underneath Erikka's balcony, scale the side of the building, secure the rope along the railing for a swift getaway, and wait for her arrival.* I threw the oil lamp onto the mattress and climbed out the window.

I guided Arvak around the outskirts of the castle, heading west with my hood up and head down. I only passed a few people since the warriors' quarters were facing the northeast, with only the rise separating the inner city from the Nott Forest. As I turned to take the path to the courtyard, I heard someone call out, "Fire! Fire!" The guards that stood watch along the path under Erikka's room ran past me toward the cries for help. I feigned a worried look as they passed by before turning and stopping just under her balcony while keeping Arvak calm and letting her graze in the flowering bushes. I checked again that the rope was still secure under my cloak and that the guards would remain preoccupied for a few moments. As the calls for help intensified, I waited patiently while tending to Arvak until I noticed the archers run along the top of the wall above me toward the east wall and out of sight. *It's now or never.*

I turned and began to scale the latticed wall that led me to the bottom of the balcony. Once I had my hand locked around the stone railing, I let my feet fall, swaying a bit as I worked to limit my body's momentum and hoist myself up. Finally, I got a foot up onto the balcony and quietly pulled myself over the top. *Flawless.* I undid my cloak to remove the rope around my chest before re-securing it around my shoulders. After I knotted the rope around the railing, I laid it straight along the balcony floor, throwing it into a neat pile near the opening of the door.

I sat in a chair behind the door to Erikka's private quarters and waited. A few minutes went by when the sound of hurried footsteps came from the other side of the door, followed by the click of the lock. A shadow fell over me as the door opened, and Erikka walked through. I stood swiftly, grabbing the back of Eire's tunic and turning her so I could run my elbow through the side of her face, knocking her out completely. I caught her body and stepped in a circle to throw her out the door and into the other guard, Mazen, who was a part of her lockdown escort, sending him to the floor with Eire in his arms. His eyes widened as he recognized me. I stared down at him briefly, numbness painted on my face, before slamming the door shut and locking it, shoving the chair I sat in under the door handle.

I lingered where I stood, unsure how to react when I faced her. My heart was pounding in my chest and throat. I turned around slowly, removing my hood. She was standing behind the chaise, her face paler than I'd ever seen it, sickly contrasting against the same red dress from earlier. Bryn's lifeless body flashed to the front of my mind, the color of Erikka's dress reminding me of his blood still running warm from where his head had been severed. I laughed manically to myself and shook my head. She was in no hurry to rid herself of the outfit because she didn't care what it represented or what part she played in his murder.

"Veronica..." Errika whispered, her lip trembling slightly.

"Don't. Speak. My name." I ordered quietly. I began to stalk toward her patiently, calculating every move her eyes made, every inch she backed away from me.

"Veron-" I held up a knife and pointed it at her.

"Ah ah ah." I shook my head, and she continued to back away toward the balcony. I left the doors open for my use, but it seemed she wanted to do the same. I threw my knife at the ground, catching the excess of her dress and trapping it to the floor, keeping her from moving any closer to the opening. Mazen was pounding on the door frantically, and every now and then, he would ram his shoulder into it, but it didn't budge.

"Don't do this!" His calls for inaction were muffled through the door. "Stop it now!" I ignored his pleas and remained zoned in on Erikka.

She let him die!

Liar!

She lied to your face!

She told you he had been in meetings!

She knew what they were doing to him!

Liar!

Murderer!

She killed him!

She shook her head as I neared and lunged for her dresser just within her reach, grabbing a knife from a leftover plate of food. As she turned back to me with it in her hand, I struck the space between my forefinger and thumb into the inside of her wrist while slamming my other hand down onto the top of her hand, sending the knife flying across the room. Fear and surprise flashed over Erikka's face as I pulled her wrist across my waist, using my free hand to send a backhanded strike into the side of her neck, continuing with another strike, now from my other hand, to grab her throat. I then hooked my leg around one of hers, pulled it towards me, and pushed forward onto her throat, slamming her onto the floor and knocking the breath out of her.

Her hands flew up to pull at mine, which were putting pressure on her neck. I threw my legs over her waist, straddling her as the pounding on the door stopped, catching me off guard. I paused and listened. Suddenly, the wood cracked as the tip of an axe broke through the door. It made contact again, slightly widening the split in the wood. I turned, ripped my knife out of the ground, and held the blade to her throat just above where my hand was restricting her ability to breathe. Tears welled in the corners of her eyes as her mouth gaped open and closed, hoping to get air in her lungs. My jaw clenched, and my lips curled in disgust at the tears she shed out of fear for her own life.

Selfish!

Murderer!

Liar!

The door cracked loudly as the split Mazen created was now large enough for him to look at me from the other side.

"HEY! HEY!" He called, and I looked up at him. "Don't do this! I know you're hurting, but don't do this!" He pleaded. I cocked my head to the side. He knows I'm hurting, does he?

TRAITOR! LIARS!

I shook my head and increased the pressure on Erikka's neck. Her thrashing became more violent. She began clawing my arms. He banged his fist on the door. "Ve-" He turned to look down the hallway before looking back at me, lowering his voice. "They're coming! Don't do this!" He pleaded again. His words drew my attention to him again. "Not now...Get out of here," he said under his breath. "NOW! Please..." He continued to beg, banging his fist on the door again. I realized he was avoiding calling out my name as the other warriors came to help.

I looked back at the door, and he had stepped back out of view. I pulled my hood over my head and sheathed my knife, releasing my grip on Erikka's throat. She gasped in a labored breath as I stood over her. The door crashed open from two massive, masked warriors barreling into it, but I had already run for the balcony. As I made my exit, I bent over and picked up the rope, launching myself off the railing and into the air. The rope caught, and I swung back toward the building. I braced my momentum with my foot on the stone and pushed myself back off again, whistling for Arvak and landing on her back.

Someone yelled from above, and when I looked up, an archer was waving to his comrades, taking aim in my direction. I turned Arvak around and pushed her into a sprint, narrowly dodging a small barrage of arrows that flew in our direction. When we ran out from the tunnel's cover to break the perimeter, archers were waiting on the rise, ready to fire again. I pulled Arvak to the right, then the left, weaving in and out of the stands in the inner city, using them as cover. I thought I was in the clear until I felt the sting of an arrow grazing my arm, ripping my skin. I inhaled sharply, hissing between my teeth, but continued to urge Arvak forward.

"Faster! Let's go!" I yelled through the wall of rain.

As I neared the gated bridge, a horn sounded off, an order to raise it. I didn't hesitate. Instead, I pushed Arvak harder and faster toward the drawbridge, and she ran forward without fear, up the inclined runway, and leaped off the end, landing gracefully on the other side of the bank. Rain poured hard, and I rubbed her neck as I hurried her onward away from the castle, past the longhouses, and into the trees, heading toward home…or what was left of it.

Spotify Playlist

The Bargain with Fate Series (By: Becca Anne)

"Everybody Wants To Rule The World" from *The Hunger Games: Catching Fire*
By: **Lorde**
"Snakes" from the series *Arcane League of Legends* By: **Imagine Dragons**
"Kingdom Dance" By: **Alan Menken**
"Darkness of Light" By: **Secession Studios**
"New Emotion" By: **The Aces**
"Stay" By: **The Aces**
"By the Sword" By: **iamjakehill**
"Chaos In The Confines" By: **Ruvlo, AFTERMYFALL**
"Out of Time" By: **Hidden Citizens, Erin McCarley**
"Wolf River" By: **Reignwolf**
"Nothing Is As It Seems" By: **Hidden Citizens, Ruelle**
"Everybody's Fool" By: **Evanescence**
"Towards The Sun" from the *Home* soundtrack By: **Rihanna**

Acknowledgements

Wow, it's finally here…I really don't know what to say. This has been a life-defining journey over the past two years and might have been one of the most challenging things I have ever done. To have published the first book in a series is an accomplishment I am so extremely proud of but shocked by. So much so, that it still doesn't feel real.

I want to thank my husband, Tristan, for always believing in me and my ability to form stories and compel people's emotions. Without your constant reminders and genuine reactions towards my writing ability with each new chapter or paragraph I would force you to read as soon as I wrote it, I would never have had the confidence to keep going. That, and the fact that you were always willing and ready to help me choreograph all the fight scenes. Being able to throw you around really helped make all the fight sequences make sense, ya know?

I also want to thank Sandra for being an OG beta reader too, right alongside Tristan, and putting up with my constant need for instant feedback during the writing process, and then turning around and demanding the next chapter every few hours. It really kept me writing for that first year!

I want to thank my sister, Micayla, for letting me bounce ideas off her head when I was deep in the trenches of world and character building, and my mom for reading a beta copy despite not being a reader, and genuinely loving the experience of TBWF. I could not have asked for a better reaction, and it helped my confidence grow so much during the build up towards the publishing process.

I want to thank my first editor, Leanne, for how much support she showed me early on. I was very unsure if I could solely trust my family's word on if what I had created was ACTUALLY good or not, and you became such a huge fan so quickly that you made me feel as if I was taking another step in the right direction. Thank you so much for the constant support for this world and for Veronica! She would love you just as much as you love her!

I want to thank all my Beta readers: Rebecca, Keith, Amber, Kristen, Paula, Sandra, Tristan, and Anne, for all your amazing feedback during the early development of TBWF. All of you helped mold this story into what it is today. I also want to thank my sensitivity readers: Neisha, Sruthi, Amarie, and Neeks, for being so super helpful and holding me accountable to my goal in keeping TBWF a safe space for everyone!

I want to thank ALL my wonderful ARC readers for giving me a chance and being so helpful with hyping up my debut novel! I'm thankful for all the new relationships that have sprouted from this experience. I want to especially thank Chelsey for helping me gather this ARC team and being more than willing to help make posts all over social media for me.

I want to give a special thanks and a massive imaginary hug to Amarie for being the amazing human being that she is. I can't even begin to express how much your support has meant to me. Your constant little reminders that these characters have a story to be told and push to get them out into the world, came during a time when I really needed it the most. Our working relationship is one I cherish so greatly, and your help with suggestions and guiding the character and world building near the end is so appreciated. I seriously can't thank you enough for really helping me pull Erikka together as well as other lagging pieces of the story. I am so lucky to now be able to call you a friend, and I genuinely mean this when I say it, Sindre would love your heart and your mind so much. You are such an amazing human, and don't you EVER forget it.

I want to thank Shiloh for her assistance in getting me self-published! This has been a giant scary monster that I wanted to avoid all together, but you really came in and made it seem significantly less daunting. I most definitely still would be unpublished if I hadn't been connected to you, and honestly, I don't know if I would have ever figured it out on my own.

I want to thank Ivy (@Ivy_gwendolline on Instagram) for helping bring my characters to life with her incredible artistry skills! As well as Jake (@_artjake_ on Instagram) for creating my dream movie poster of the entire TBWF cast to life in a magical way!

I want to thank my cover artist, Jaqueline (@jaquelinekropmanns.coverdes ign on Instagram) for being so so so talented and creating the PERFECT covers on the first try. You literally made it seem so easy, and they are stunning!

Finally, I want to thank you, the reader, for trusting me with your time and energy. I can only hope that you enjoyed TBWF experience. If I could ask for one favor now that you've met me at the end of the road, if you could leave a review, it would be incredibly helpful! Reviews drive the success of books and in the Indie space, it is detrimental to the success of a story. Thank you so much for your support!

Glossary

- **Aesir:** The group of Gods of the principal pantheon of Old Norse religion.

- **Aesir (Magic):** The ability to use elemental powers to enhance their physical abilities and weaponry.

- **Askel:** Name means 'cauldron of the gods, protected by god'.

- **Bergunn:** Name means 'from the fortified hill or castle and unn means love'.

- **Brynjar:** Name means 'warrior in armor'.

- **Calder:** Name means 'cold and harsh waters'.

- **Dark Elves:** Thought to be the same as dwarves and burn if exposed to the sun. Can cause human disease or heal it.

- **Draugr:** The undead army of Norse mythology. Resembling zombies more than vampires, possess superhuman strength and are able to grow in size.

- **Dunga:** a useless company or fellow.

- **Dwarves:** Small misshapen creatures that live underground. Said to have crafted the finest weapons and jewelry, including Mjolnir.

- **Eir:** Norse goddess/valkyrie associated with medical skill.

- **Erikka:** Name means 'feminized word for ruler'.

- **Exris:** The kingdom of Sol's trades town.

- **Fenrir:** Child of Loki. The father of Skoll and Hati. Is foretold to kill the god Odin during the events of Ragnarok.

- **Fossegrimen:** A water spirit and creature who plays the fiddle with incredible talent and can be coaxed to teach the skill. Found in water-falls/moving water.

- **Frith:** A hidden city where the ravens take the freed Skirrian thrall to live and establish their new lives.

- **Gudmund:** Name means 'god is protecting'.

- **Gungnir:** The spear of the god Odin.

- **Halle:** Name means 'heroine; derivative of Hallr means rock'.

- **Hel:** Child of Loki. Goddess who rules the underworld and presents as being cruel, harsh and indifferent to the concerns of the dead and living.

- **Hemming:** Name means 'changing shapes'.

- **Huldra:** Wardens of the forest that were beautiful and seductive. Had cow tails and bark along their backs. Will lure men into the forest and keep them as slaves or lovers.

- **Jerrik:** Name means 'king forever'.

- **Jormungandr:** Child of Loki. A giant sea serpent whose body was so long it wrapped around the entirety of Midgard and bit its own tail.

- **Jotnar:** Giants of Norse mythology that have powers that rival the gods and embody chaos. Enemies of the gods despite being descendants of them.

- **Kalyani:** Name means 'Auspicious, Excellent, Fortunate'.

- **Kraken:** An aquatic monster that is said to dwell near the shores of Norway and Greenland. Depicted as a gigantic octopi or squid.

- **Kron:** Name means 'crown'.

- **Kynda:** Name means 'kindle'.

- **Lagom:** Name loosely translates to 'not too much and not too little, just right'.

- **Light Elves:** Much like the gods of Aesir and Vanir, and could cause human disease or heal it.

- **Leif:** Name means 'descendant'.

- **Liv:** Name means 'protector of life'.

- **Loki:** The god of mischief: Sigyn's husband.

- **Lykke:** Name means 'happiness'.

- **Mare:** A monster that gave people bad dreams at night by sitting on them in their sleep.

- **Mazen:** Name means 'to make' OR the Arabic version means 'rain cloud'.

- **Midgard:** The human realm. (Earth)

- **(The) Nine Realms:** Niflheim, Muspelheim, Asgard, Midgard, Jotunheim, Vanaheim, Alfheim, Svartalfheim, Helheim. The nine worlds in Norse mythology are held in the branches and roots of the world tree Yggdrasil.

- **Nokken:** An ancient water spirit who shape-shifts into a beautiful man to lure women into the water and drown them.

- **(The) Norns:** Deities in Norse mythology responsible for shaping the course of human destinies. They are powerful maiden giantesses (Jotuns) who had the important task to help Yggdrasil stay green and healthy.

- **Nott:** Goddess of night.

- **Nyhus:** Name means 'new house'.

- **Odin's Ravens** : Secret viking group that raids Skirra to save the enslaved thrall and offer them a life of freedom, without the Sol government knowing.

- **Osera:** The continent that Sol and Skirra are found on.

- **Ragnhild:** Name means 'advising in battle'.

- **Ragnarök:** The final destruction of the world in the conflict between the Aesir and the powers of Hel led by Loki.

- **Raoul:** Name means 'as wise as a wolf'.

- **Ran:** Goddess of the sea.

- **Reisa:** Name means 'raise'.

- **Rune:** Name means 'secret'.

- **Seidr:** Actions ranging from shamanic magic (spirit journeys, magical healing, magical psychiatric treatment), to prophecy.

- **Sigyn:** The goddess of victory and fidelity and Loki's wife.

- **Sindre:** Name means 'one who is small and trivial; also means the sparkling one'.

- **Sisu:** Name means 'arctic nature has given us guts'.

- **Skadi:** Goddess of winter.

- **Skirra:** The "enemy" kingdom that the inhabitants of Sol fought a war against to earn their freedom : Name means 'scare'.

- **Skuld:** The fate of the future.

- **Sol:** The home kingdom of our main characters.

- **Sol:** Goddess of the sun.

- **Stillridge:** A city in Skirra that the Ravens target on their raids to rescue the thrall.

- **Sylve:** Name means 'she who holds the strength of the sun.

- **Sylph:** Air spirit.

- **Thora:** Name means 'fem variation of Thor'.

- **Thrall:** Slave.

- **Tormod:** Name 'derived from thor and *mod* means mind, wrath, courage'.

- **Troll:** There are two types of trolls : large ugly trolls that dwell in forests and mountains, and small gnome-like trolls that live underground.

- **Trond:** Name means 'to thrive and grow'.

- **Trygg:** Name means 'trustworthy or faithful'.

- **Urd:** The fate of the past.

- **Valerian:** Veronica's fighting personality.

- **Vali:** God of revenge who was created solely to enact revenge upon Loki after he killed Baldur.

- **Valknut:** Old Norse symbol composed of three interlocking triangles.

- **Vanir:** The second pantheon in Old Norse Religion, who value nature, mysticism, wealth, and harmony.

- **Verdandi:** The fate of the present.

- **Veronica:** Name means 'victorious woman'.

- **Veslingr:** a coward or annoying person.

- **Volva:** A seeress who was honored and sought as a wise woman, healer, prophet, oracle, and priestess.

- **Yggdrasil:** The world tree that connects the nine realms.

- **Ylva:** Name means 'wolf'.

About the Author

Born with a creative fire that never wavered, Becca Anne emerges as a first-time author passionate about reshaping ancient tales into vibrant narratives. At her Hill Country home, she shares her life with a devoted husband and a charming menagerie of animals, all cared for under the umbrella of her animal rescue. This sanctuary not only speaks to her love for animals but also symbolizes her dedication to positively impact the world.

Beyond the realm of fiction, Becca radiates empathy and compassion. A member and staunch advocate of the LGBTQ+, mental health awareness, and supporter of BIPOC communities, she uses her literary prowess to prioritize diversity and inclusivity. Her commitment to fostering understanding and acceptance reflects her deep-seated belief in the power of unity and love.

With each word she pens and every life she touches, Becca weaves a narrative of compassion, acceptance, and hope. Her artistic and altruistic endeavors merge seamlessly, painting a portrait of a soul whose light shines brightly, within her community and beyond.

Sneak Peek

Here is a sneak peek at book two in *The Bargain with Fate* series.

The Awakening of Fate

**The following text is not final and is subject to change.*

As we walked through the gathered crowd, my skin burned from the heat of the collective gazes. Each step felt heavier and heavier as I noticed the sound of stifled sobs. *You did this.* I looked up and was met with many red, teary, and swollen eyes. The energy became suffocating as we passed through the sea of emotion. Jerrik squeezed my hand and coaxed me forward. *Coward!*

Sindre, Sylve, Ragnhild, and the other two elders stood patiently at the edge of the pier, waiting to start the ceremony. Ragnhild stepped forward and hugged me tightly.

"Stay strong, child." He urged softly. I nodded and moved over to greet Bergunn and Thora. I noticed they had tethered two smaller boats to Bryn's that had already been filled to the brim with parting gifts. Keepsakes. Memories. I looked back at the grieving landscape and saw the expanse of Bryn's impact; all the lives he touched. My breath caught in my throat, and my eyes stung. I can't do this. I turned back to Ragnhild and shook my head, clenching my jaw tight as ragged breaths pulled their way past my teeth, making my chest hitch rapidly as I attempted to stifle a sob. He put a supportive hand on my shoulder.

"There were more people in attendance than we had anticipated," he smiled softly. "I hope you don't mind, but we went ahead and let people say their goodbyes and place their offerings in the boats prior to this." I shook my head.

"I don't mind at all. It's best they had their time without me here anyway." Ragnhild cocked his head thoughtfully but didn't comment as I continued. "Who all is left?"

"Just our group...but I will make an announcement one more time just in case someone hasn't had a chance to place their offerings." He explained quietly.

"Okay, you all can go first. I can wait." I offered, stepping out of their way. *Delaying your goodbyes won't change the fact that he is dead because of you.* He nodded and ushered the others to form a line in front of him. One by one, they stepped away after their farewells, and within what felt like a few minutes, I was back to standing in front of him. Brynjar was placed on his back on a bed of straw, a woolen blanket folded over him. All that was visible was his bruised face.

Tears stung my eyes as they escaped and streaked down my face. I brushed them away quickly and pulled out my knife, leaning over the edge of the wooden carved boat to be closer to him. I laid the blade in my palm and closed my fist around it, pulling it free from my grasp. I felt the warmth of my blood pool in my fist as I sheathed the knife and pushed the blanket out of the way that kept his hands hidden. I brought my closed fist over his folded hands just below his chest and allowed my blood to drip onto them.

"In hopes of being reunited in the next life." My voice was wobbly, so I cleared my throat and quietly recited the Raven's oath. I put my bloodied fist over my heart. "By the Gods, I have so sworn. By my honor, I have so sworn." I stood and stepped back in line with the others, letting my still trembling hand fall to my side, blood steadily running down my fingers and onto the wood beneath my feet.

Ragnhild turned to the mourning crowd. "Before we bring the ceremony to a close, if you missed the opportunity to bid your final goodbyes and offer your parting gifts, feel free to spend the next few minutes doing so." Movement rippled through the mass of people as families met with Bryn to bestow their gifts. It seemed as if every other family was taking the time to stop and share their condolences and tell me stories of their experiences with him…

…I looked down at the ground where I stood, in front of the overwhelming crowd, and closed my eyes to recenter myself.

Am I really here right now? Is this really happening?

It could have been avoided had you stopped them from killing him.

But you let this happen!

You should be the one in that ship!

What use are you to these people?

What have you done for them?

Nothing!

I opened my eyes with the intent on keeping my mind far from the scene in front of me. Maybe this way I could maintain a strong facade, fool everyone into thinking that I am able to fill Bryn's role as a solid base for our people to build upon. Be someone they could rely on and look to when things got difficult…To save them all from a fate they have no idea looms in the future…but the edge of a silken black dress flowed to a stop before me and broke all delusion of composure. My eyes snapped up in fury, assuming it was Erikka from the silk but was met by a stranger.

A woman, a few inches shy of Sindre and Sylve's height, with scarlet red curls draped over her chest from under the hood of a muddy green cloak. Her eyes seemed a familiar bright green that looked even more luminous under the shadow of her hood, but I couldn't figure out where I had seen her before. She looked at me plainly, almost as if she was utterly uninterested in being here, but she was breathtaking.

We both stood there momentarily contemplating each other until Sindre cleared his throat and nodded toward the line that had formed behind this woman. She didn't acknowledge anyone else besides me as she reached out to grab my hands, pressing a cold ovular object into my palm as she held onto me. I looked down at our hands and noticed she had scars on top of hers. Raised and whitened, the runic shapes seemed almost as if they were branded into her skin. When she pulled her hands away, I noticed that the scars were also on her palms. My eyes shot up to her, confused, but she was already walking away without a word.

I looked down to find a golden amulet in my hands the size of my palm. One made of two snakes, intertwining with each other to form an 'S' shape. As I flipped it around, a delicate golden chain unfolded and fell through my fingers. I gasped at the delicacy of what I was holding. I can only imagine what it's worth. I quickly scanned the crowd, but she had disappeared. Something deep in my gut was pulling me back towards Bryn. I slowly turned around and, as if in a trance, passed the line of people who had stopped to speak with the twins and Ragnhild in place of me. As I came to the side of the boat and knelt down, I could have sworn the emblem started vibrating: almost like a purring cat.

Although the woman had given me no instruction, I knew what I was intended to do with it. I pulled back the blanket from Bryn's hands once more and placed the golden amulet in them, wrapping the golden chain around his wrists and placing the blanket back over his chest. It hit me then, as Ragnhild ushered people from the pier so we could prepare to send him off, that this would be the last time I would ever see him. I looked at his face, forcing each softened feature to burn itself into my memory. Despite the bruises, he seemed at peace.

I can only hope.